Nichole Severn writes explosive romantic suspense with strong heroines, heroes who dare challenge them and a hell of a lot of guns. She resides with her very supportive and patient husband, as well as her demon spawn, in Utah. When she's not writing, she's constantly injuring herself running, rock climbing, practising yoga and snowboarding. She loves hearing from readers through her website, nicholesevern.com, and on Facebook, @nicholesevern

New York Times and *USA TODAY* bestselling author **Cindy Dees** is the author of more than fifty novels. She draws upon her experience as a US Air Force pilot to write romantic suspense. She's a two-time winner of the prestigious *RITA*® Award for romance fiction, a two-time winner of the RT Reviewers' Choice Best Book Award for Romantic Suspense and an *RT Book Reviews* Career Achievement Award nominee. She loves to hear from readers at cindydees.com

000000 3146423

Discover more at millsandboon.co.uk

PRESUMED DEAD

NICHOLE SEVERN

HIS CHRISTMAS GUARDIAN

CINDY DEES

MILLS & BOON

All rights reserved including the right of reproduction in whole or in part in any form. This edition is published by arrangement with Harlequin Enterprises ULC.

This is a work of fiction. Names, characters, places, locations and incidents are purely fictional and bear no relationship to any real life individuals, living or dead, or to any actual places, business establishments, locations, events or incidents. Any resemblance is entirely coincidental.

This book is sold subject to the condition that it shall not, by way of trade or otherwise, be lent, resold, hired out or otherwise circulated without the prior consent of the publisher in any form of binding or cover other than that in which it is published and without a similar condition including this condition being imposed on the subsequent purchaser.

® and ™ are trademarks owned and used by the trademark owner and/or its licensee. Trademarks marked with ® are registered with the United Kingdom Patent Office and/or the Office for Harmonisation in the Internal Market and in other countries.

First Published in Great Britain 2022
by Mills & Boon, an imprint of HarperCollins*Publishers* Ltd
1 London Bridge Street, London, SE1 9GF

www.harpercollins.co.uk

HarperCollins*Publishers*
1st Floor, Watermarque Building,
Ringsend Road, Dublin 4, Ireland

Presumed Dead © 2022 Natascha Jaffa
His Christmas Guardian © 2022 Cynthia Dees

ISBN: 978-0-263-30363-6

DUDLEY LIBRARIES	
000003146423	
Askews & Holts	13-Oct-2022
AF ROM	£6.99
2DU	

PRESUMED DEAD

NICHOLE SEVERN

For the Mills & Boon authors: you inspire me
on a daily basis. Keep writing.

Chapter One

Battle Mountain had lost its innocence.

Because of him.

Reserve Officer Kendric Hudson climbed the built-in ramp leading up to the cabin's front door. Trees of every size and age—along with the surrounding snow-covered mountains—seemed to suffocate the bare acreage around them. Wouldn't have taken much for the kidnapper to get in and out without being seen.

No one would've even heard Sabrina Bryon scream.

He scanned the small living room for signs of a struggle, coming up empty. There wasn't much to the place. Dated. Neglected. Just like the rest of the town. A simple kitchen with the brightest blue countertops he'd ever seen stood off to the right, an old-school wood-burning stove, the kind pioneers would've used a hundred years ago, to the left. According to the 911 call from the husband, the abduction had taken place in the early morning hours. The victim would've been in bed, asleep.

His boots reverberated off worn hardwood as he slipped a pair of latex gloves over his hands. Despite the majestic views, bone-chilling silence and the fact he could escape on a property like this for hours, he was standing in the middle of a crime scene. He couldn't make any mistakes.

Rounding into the back half of the house, Kendric took in the first bedroom decorated in pink wallpaper, a fuzzy rug and a glittery mobile hanging above an empty crib. Sunlight pierced through the open blinds, and his gut twisted harder than he'd expected. He kept moving. This wasn't his first rodeo, but he never could get comfortable with crimes involving kids. Not like the agents he'd worked with in the ATF. Detached. Single-minded. Job oriented. To them, it wasn't about the victims affected by the psychopaths they set out to dismantle. It was about solving the case, about reassembling the crime and catching the culprit. For a while, he'd convinced himself he'd been one of them.

Then Battle Mountain had gone up in flames.

A place he'd never been before in his life, one he hadn't intended on getting to know. Now he'd do whatever it took to make up for the pain the people of this sleepy old mining town had suffered.

"Gregson." He moved into the controlled chaos of the master bedroom, targeting the former Larimer County bomb expert turned reserve officer. A flash popped from the camera in Gregson's hands. As Battle Mountain's few protectors, the officers here had a responsibility to cover every base. Evidence collection, scene photography, witness statements, securing perimeters and the thousand other tasks required to uncover the truth. Without federal or state resources. That lack of support was what had driven Kendric to leave everything—and everyone—he'd known behind and start something new. It was the least he could do after Battle

Mountain's entire Main Street had been under the siege of a bomber. "Any word from the kidnapper?"

A stretch of fresh burn scars added to the intelligence and experience in Cree Gregson's expression, the very air around the town's newest officer thick with control. His own scars tingled with remembered pain as he took in the scene through his dominant eye. The one not impacted by scar tissue hanging from his eyebrow. For the two of them, fire had changed their lives in a single event. And nearly taken them. If Gregson hadn't pulled that hero crap on an assignment gone bad that had left the former tech with a stretch of mangled skin down his back, Kendric wouldn't be here at all.

"Not yet." Gregson maneuvered around the end of the queen-size bed. "Alma's with the husband at the hospital. He's touch and go. Nothing he's saying is making sense right now. The EMTs had to sedate him. They're not sure he's going to make it. From what I can tell, perp walked right in the front door, came straight back here to the bedrooms. Husband wakes up, tries to fight back here in the hallway. The struggle moves into the bedroom. Kidnapper puts two rounds into him for making trouble, leaving a pool of blood on this side of the bed and takes our vic. Sabrina Bryon. Twenty-eight-year-old female. Married to Elliot Bryon, going on two years."

"The kidnapper knew the layout of the house. He's done his homework, got access." Or he'd been in the house before. But why not make the ransom demand? Why go through all the trouble—and an attempted murder charge—without getting something out of this in the end? Kendric hiked a thumb over his shoulder. "And the baby? I passed a nursery on the way in."

"Sabrina Bryon's pregnant. About eight months, according to the ultrasound taped on the fridge," Gregson said. "A girl."

Damn. "You're thinking this is a two-for-one deal. Take mother and child, ransom them both, but put in half the work. Is the husband talking?"

"Not with a bullet in his chest," an all-too-familiar voice said from behind. "His lung was on the verge of collapse in the ambulance on the way to Grand Junction. Unfortunately for us, Elliot Bryon won't be saying anything for a while."

Ice clawed through Kendric's veins. He turned to face the blonde investigator capable of castrating a man with a single glare of those cerulean blue eyes. The form-fitting pantsuit did nothing to hide a lean, feminine frame Kendric had tried to forget. Waves of silk hair cascaded over her shoulders and down her back, and his fingers curled in memory of what they'd felt like in his hands.

Campbell Dwyer scanned the room as though he didn't even exist. Then again, he'd made it perfectly clear when he'd left Loveland, that he couldn't. Not in her life. She'd had her sights on transferring out of her small-time investigative duties for Larimer's sheriff's department, and as a bomb tech barely hanging on to his own skin, he hadn't fit into that plan. He'd done what he'd thought was best. For both of them. "Detective Dwyer. I wasn't aware Colorado's Bureau of Investigations had an interest in small-town abductions. Isn't that a little beneath your pay grade?"

"Isn't playing cop in a town nobody's heard of beneath yours?" She moved into the room, giving him a wide berth, every inch the intense, defensive woman he remembered. Always knew exactly where to strike, too.

His new life with the ATF after surviving a bombing had ended the moment one of his colleagues had tried to burn Battle Mountain to the ground with a series of explosives to cover up a murder. Rescue crews, the town's entire Main Street, and Gregson and his partner, Alma Majors, were all still trying to recover. Kendric studied the exposed skin of Campbell's wrists, her bare fingernails—cut too short—and the elaborate but subtle detail of her makeup. Still the epitome of opposites. Even after all this time.

He forced his attention to Gregson. To prove she didn't still have a hold on him. "I take it the state's powers that be want one of their own involved in this investigation to keep an eye on things. Make sure the small-town folk are doing their jobs right."

"You certainly haven't lost your deduction skills since making your career change, have you?" Armed with a set of her own latex gloves, Campbell extracted an evidence bag from her blazer and crouched. She targeted the broken wristwatch on the floor beside the bed. "May I?"

"I've got everything I need," Gregson said.

"Battle Mountain has seen two spree killers, a serial killer and a rogue ATF agent try to rip this town apart in less than a year. Even you can understand that raises some red flags, Agent…" She squinted, turning toward Kendric, the watch still in hand. "I'm sorry, what are you now?"

His jaw ached under the pressure of his back teeth. She knew very well what he was. Just as he'd followed her career after a bomb had failed to rip off his face, she would've done her homework on him before taking this assignment. "Officer."

"Right. Officer." Her gaze skimmed down the length of his chest, the corners of her mouth softening. "You always were eager to side with the underdogs, Kendric. This place suits you."

"Dwyer." Gregson extended his hand in greeting, and Kendric realized he'd created an alternate universe in which only he and Campbell had existed. "It's been a while."

Right. The crime scene. A missing young mother. A husband in the hospital. And a whole lot of unanswered questions. "You remember Cree Gregson."

"Of course. Good to see there's someone here keeping Kendric out of trouble. I've read your report concerning your last case. Your partner's, too. Impressive work. The both of you." The undertone in Campbell's voice conveyed her confusion over why his friend had given up a promising career in explosive ordinance to play cop in a town this small. Like Kendric had. Her eyes tracked to his, and her point drove home.

Suspicion lodged in his gut. As much as he hated to admit he'd missed their own personal brand of banter, it wouldn't change the fact she wasn't supposed to be here. "Cut to the chase, Campbell. What does CBI want with a simple abduction case? Our department is more than capable of running point for Sabrina Bryon's safe return. Unless you were invited by Chief Ford himself, you don't have jurisdiction here."

"Actually, I do." Campbell lowered the wristwatch she'd collected from the floor into an evidence bag, then pulled a folded piece of paper from the inside of her blazer. She handed it off, and every cell in his body burned in warning. "Take a look for yourself."

Gregson stepped behind him to look at the directive

over his shoulder. Kendric read through the brief signed by none other than the CBI director himself. What the hell? "This says—"

"That's right." She sealed the evidence bag. "It says this case falls under the jurisdiction of the Colorado Bureau of Investigation in the name of public safety, and that through a series of fortunate events, they sent their lead missing persons case agent to take point and negotiate the ransom for Sabrina Bryon on their behalf. In case you're having a hard time processing that little tidbit, that would be me."

How was this possible? Campbell didn't have this kind of pull on her own. She would've had to convince someone high up to put her here. What kind of favors had she called in to get herself assigned to his case and why?

The low *thunk* of her heels ticked off in rhythm to the headache pulsing at the base of his skull. Handing over the watch to Kendric, Campbell penetrated his personal space. "Look on the bright side, Kendric. Looks like you and I get to be partners again."

HER HANDS SHOOK as she peeled her gloves free and stepped outside.

Campbell Dwyer had been waiting for this moment. Rehearsed conversations, practiced reactions under the stress of seeing him again. Detachment. None of it had worked. At least not for her. Kendric, on the other hand... He'd barely registered any kind of emotion when she'd stepped into the room. How was that for closure after all these years?

She walked the perimeter of the small cabin surrounded by walls of intimidating nature. Kendric had been a city boy through and through. What could've possibly urged him to leave his life, his extended family, his friends and his career to relocate to the middle of nowhere? Dirt skimmed over the toes of her heels as she studied the scene.

Sabrina Bryon, twenty-eight years old, married to Elliot Bryon a little less than six years. No living relatives. No record of domestic disputes. Good credit history. Nothing to suggest she was in financial or physical danger. The victim worked as an online English teacher. Not the kind of profession targeted for a large payday, but the Bryons weren't clawing out of poverty, either. The calendar pinned near the front door of the cabin had listed two recent appointments. Both for the ob-gyn Campbell intended to interview as soon as she was done here. Her heart squeezed behind her rib cage until her lungs spasmed for another breath of air. Battle Mountain had become a hunting ground for the worst kinds of criminals, and their missing victim had just been the latest in a long line of reasons why she'd been assigned to take a look. But without contact from the kidnappers, they had nothing to propel this case forward.

"How did you get to the house without waking them up?" Campbell mused out loud.

If Sabrina's abductor had used the main road, there should've been tire tracks, something to tell them how the UNSUB—the unknown subject—had arrived and escaped. Rounding to the front of the cabin, she targeted a deep set of impressions that matched others in the dirt driveway. The victim's car? If the abductor had taken it to escape with his target, where was the vehicle he'd arrived in?

At the back of the structure, Campbell caught sight

of a series of boot prints. One set in. One set out. She unpocketed her phone and took a photo of the design. Size ten, maybe eleven. Ridged, like a hiking boot. Patches of grass made it difficult to ascertain whether anyone else had come this way. Whoever had surprised the Bryons had been prepared for the terrain. "You had to be strong enough to carry Sabrina out on your own."

In her experience, women tended to gain between twenty to fifty pounds during pregnancy. It wouldn't have been easy to manage on his own. Unless the victim hadn't fought back.

"Talking to yourself again?" Kendric's deep tone resonated through her. It triggered a chain reaction starting with a gut clench and ending with heat flaring up her neck. No matter how many times she'd tried to protect herself against his effects, he'd always had the effortless ability to let her know she could wind up as his next meal.

And she'd liked being his chew toy while it had lasted.

"The voices in my head get cranky if I don't answer." Straightening, Campbell turned to face him. The air between them seemed to shift with tension and resentment, and tightened the muscles down her spine. His intelligent, piercing green eyes intensified her discomfort in stepping into his investigation, but from where she was standing, neither of them really had a choice. They'd been trained to follow orders. Even in his new position as one of this town's first line of defense, that hadn't changed. "That was a joke."

"I see you haven't lost your terrible sense of humor." Kendric leaned against the side of the house, arms crossed over a broad chest. Styled, dark hair matched the thin beard growth he'd let get out of hand. There was a reason for it, a self-consciousness he obviously still couldn't escape, but the scars that had contorted the skin along one side of his face had never bothered her. He'd just used them as an excuse to push everyone away.

"You used to laugh at my cheesy jokes." She'd tried so hard to let go of the past, to banish it, but it was always there just under the surface. Waiting to stab her in the heart all over again. "I've got a set of boot prints. One set in and out, heading for those trees over there. I haven't followed them yet, but they look to belong to the same UNSUB. Are you equipped to take impressions?"

"We're not as backward out here as you might think, Detective. I'll get the kit from my vehicle." He disappeared around the same corner where he'd ambushed her.

Detective. The title grated against her nerves. If he was going through anything like she was at seeing him again, he'd hidden it behind a very thick layer of rock-hard annoyance. Or maybe her hopes of finding him as miserable as she was since their breakup five years ago had been nothing but a fantasy. "Get yourself together, Dwyer."

Footsteps registered from behind, and she realized Kendric was making an effort to announce his arrival this time. He settled the kit into the dirt beside her and popped the lid. Without so much as a glance in her direction, he handed off a photo evidence ruler and pulled an aerosol can of dust and dirt hardener. She positioned the ruler beside the boot print and took another photo right before he handed off the hardener. He mixed the casting material and solution into a small mixing bowl with a spatula and reached over her to pour it into the mold.

They moved as though they'd done this a thousand times. In a way, they had. Dozens of cases she and Kendric had partnered on with the sheriff's department reeled through her mind. Him as a bomb technician. Her as a detective. They'd met and fallen head over heels doing this very kind of work. Evidence collection, crime scene searches, following leads. She wouldn't have been able to close any of them without his ordinance expertise, and he hadn't been able to put the pieces together without her investigative skills.

They'd made one hell of a team.

And created something amazing in the process.

Until the bombing that had nearly killed him.

"I was surprised to hear you'd taken a job out here as a reserve officer." She watched as each centimeter of casting solution hardened, one section after the other. The longer they took to process the scene, the higher risk they'd lose evidence. They didn't have time to wait for the cast to dry before following the trail into the trees, but she couldn't seem to break this moment, either. Not yet. "Can't imagine what could've pulled you away from the ATF. I thought becoming one of their instructors was what you'd wanted."

"It was." Kendric shifted his weight between both heels, still so unwilling to give up that legendary control. It was aggravating, really. Because the man testing the edges of the footprint cast beside her wasn't the man she'd known at all. "Until one of my colleagues set this town on fire to cover up a murder."

"Agent Freehan." Campbell still couldn't get comfortable with the fact a federal agent had taken her extensive knowledge in explosives and used it against the very people she'd been sworn to protect. "I reviewed the reports on my way down. She used a series of explosions to cover up the murder of her sister, even started a forest fire in the process."

Kendric pried the cast from the footprint. The rubber bent and flexed at his direction but kept its perfect shape of the treads left behind. They'd compare it to the homeowner's shoes to eliminate the potential for error. He secured the cast into an evidence bag from the kit and sealed it inside. "Guess it was only a matter of time."

"What does that mean?" she asked.

"Doesn't matter." Shoving to his feet, he headed toward the trees. "We need to see where these tracks end. The kidnapper might've been strong enough to carry Sabrina Bryon from the house, but he wouldn't last in this wilderness without transportation."

Another layer of distance wedged between them. Right when she thought she'd gotten a hand on his determination to keep her at arm's length, he changed the game. Mud clung to her heels and threatened to suction them off her feet as she followed along the tracks. Their kidnapper had been prepared for this terrain. She wasn't.

Kendric disappeared into the trees, every ounce a predator she hadn't expected. He was comfortable here, aware, knowledgeable. He liked it here, and a sour taste spread over her tongue. He wasn't a small-town cop. He'd investigated terrorist attacks, served his country and saved lives on a large scale. This wasn't him. "Over here."

Her legs and feet cramped as she struggled across

the uneven ground. Frost clung to shrubs and bushes and melted against her skin the deeper into the trees she dared. Warning iced through her as sunlight failed to breach through the thick canopy above. Silence crystallized around her. Her breath fogged in front of her mouth. "Kendric?"

No movement. No sign of him ahead. The trail of boot prints had vanished in the undergrowth of foliage, rocks and broken twigs. They'd never be able to search this entire plot of land. Not with the limited amount of resources Battle Mountain PD held. She hunkered into her thin blazer. Her ankles threatened to buckle as the cold sank past her clothing and into muscle and tendons.

A hand latched around her arm.

Campbell reached for her sidearm a split second before recognition flared. Kendric. Her lungs collapsed as she released the breath she'd been holding. "What are you doing? I could've shot you."

"Bet that wasn't even the first time you thought about it." Offering his hand, he helped her cut through a particularly thick bush. Calluses scraped along the inside of her palm as Kendric led her to a fallen tree that had been carved out over decades by insect, wild animal and erosion activity. He nodded at one end and released her hand. "Take a look."

Campbell circled to meet him. And froze. "Is that…?"

Auburn hair splayed over the edges of weathered wood. Leaves wove through the tangled mess and clung to pale skin. Nausea churned in her stomach as she took in crusted blood, torn clothing, waxy discoloration and obvious similarities to their missing woman. Darkness encased the body from the shoulders down. Whoever had stuffed the victim inside hadn't wanted her found. Not until they were ready.

"It's not Sabrina Bryon." Kendric pulled a flashlight from his coat and highlighted the woman staring up at them. Same hair color, similar frame. The resemblance was uncanny to someone who hadn't studied photos of their missing woman all morning. Only this woman wasn't pregnant. "But someone went through a hell of a lot of trouble to make us think she is."

Chapter Two

They didn't have an identification.

The woman he and Campbell had recovered seemed to fit the same basic criteria to describe their missing victim, but he noted distinct differences between them now that the coroner had removed the body from the tree to begin her on-site examination. Her teeth, for one, were far too uneven to match the recent photos taken of Sabrina Bryon. Wrong color, too. According to the town's dentist—Dr. Corsey—the missing mother had taken great care of her teeth and had gone through years of braces and whitening to show for it. This woman had never met an orthodontist in her life.

Then there was the fact she wasn't pregnant.

"Do you have any idea who she is?" Campbell folded her arms across her chest, her expression carefully set. She'd investigated plenty of homicides with the sheriff's department, had learned to remove emotion from the equation to get a better understanding of evidence. Why had he expected this one to be any different?

"No." He watched as Dr. Chloe Pascale pierced through the woman's side with a liver thermometer. He didn't know much about medical exams and autopsies, and he was sure as hell going to keep it that way.

"I sent a photo to Chief Ford to see if he or Macie recognized her. They have no idea who she is. He's got his brother Easton and Officer Majors headed to the properties around here to get a possible ID. See if someone recognizes her. Hard to believe she wasn't involved in what went down this morning, given her proximity to the scene."

"She was pretending to be pregnant." She nodded to the round pillow with straps Cree Gregson was pulling from the other end of the tree. "Men sometimes strap them around their stomachs to experience the feeling of pregnancy. Whoever she was, I think you're right. She had to be involved in Sabrina Bryon's abduction."

He couldn't argue. It wasn't a coincidence they'd followed the only set of footprints from the primary scene right where a body had been dumped. Jane Doe hadn't walked herself out here to be stuffed in a tree. But the connection between their victim and the Bryons was still out of reach. "That's an odd piece of trivia to know. You have much experience with pregnancy pillows?"

He regretted the question the moment it escaped his mouth. In reality, he had no right to ask about her life. He'd walked out of it because he hadn't been able to stand the thought of her committing herself to a lost cause. Losing feeling in one side of his face had only been the beginning. He'd just saved her from going down with the ship. "Sorry. None of my business."

"I asked you why you relocated to Battle Mountain. Guess it's only fair for you to ask personal questions, too." Campbell didn't elaborate as she circled around the sanitary sheet the coroner had placed under the body. "That looks like a small-caliber entrance wound in her back. Not a whole lot of blood. Thin smudge ring, little contusion. I'd say from a .22. Do we know what kind of weapon the husband was shot with yet?"

Admiration filtered through his tunneled focus on the victim. As much as he hated to accept Campbell's help in this case, she had a better handle on homicide investigations than he did. Give him a scene in which a bomber had gutted an entire town with a single device planted in the Battle Mountain police station, and he could tell investigators the experience level of the bomber, pull DNA from the components and reassemble the thing blind. This was a whole new ball field in which he was playing an entirely different game. But that still didn't explain why CBI had sent her.

"No word from Grand Junction just yet, but I'll be sure to follow up with them to run a comparison." Dr. Chloe Pascale bagged both of the victim's hands to protect any evidence under the fingernails and preserve prints. With any luck, she'd be able to match dental, DNA or fingerprints to give their victim a name. "From what I can see, the deceased was shot from a distance. The bullet was small enough to pass through the back of the rib cage and nick the right atrium of the heart. There isn't any sign of an exit wound from my preliminary exam, but I'll know more once I get her back to the funeral home."

"The funeral home?" Campbell's gaze cut to him a split second before her laugh died on her lips. "You're joking, right?"

"Thank you, Dr. Pascale. We'll be in touch." Kendric hiked his way through the density of underbrush as Gregson and the coroner searched what was left of their scene. Every second Sabrina Bryon was missing was another second she might not make it home alive. They had to keep moving.

Campbell caught up with him, slightly out of breath, and he couldn't help but enjoy watching her squirm out here in the great outdoors. Out of the two of them, she'd always been the one least acquainted with adapting. "She wasn't joking, was she? Battle Mountain has to perform their autopsies in the back of a funeral home. Do you even have a forensic lab to process evidence?"

He pulled up short, facing her. "What are you really doing here, Campbell? Why did you take this case?"

"You read the letter." Defensiveness ticked the small muscles in her jaw. "Given the drastic rise in crime here, the CBI wants to keep a close eye on this one. I'm the lead missing persons case agent. It made sense for me to be the one assigned."

"That's bullshit, and you know it. You never take a case without doing your homework first. You knew I'd left the ATF after my last investigation for them. You followed me here. Why?" His gut warned him to back down, to let it go, but he'd never been one to follow his instincts. Not when it came to her.

Color drained from her face, her mouth parting slightly. "You've got some nerve. Because from where I'm standing, I'm the one with experience here. Your department is unequipped and undertrained to bring Sabrina Bryon home. What you should be saying, Kendric, is thank you. So let's cut the pleasantries, shall we? My assignment here has nothing to do with you. Despite what your ego might be telling you, I've moved on. And in case you've forgotten, I don't let my personal life compromise my cases." Campbell tucked her hands into her blazer pockets. "Now, are you going to help me bring Sabrina home, or do I need to partner with Gregson on this one? Think about it."

She didn't wait for a response, balancing on those ridiculous heels as she headed back toward the Bryon cabin. Hell, the clock had already started ticking for their victim, and he'd wasted precious time suspecting Campbell had an ulterior motive. She was right. They had a job to do. Even if it meant working with the one person he'd told himself he couldn't ever see again.

"Damn it." He scrubbed a hand down his face, then rushed to keep up with her escape. Following her across the wraparound porch, Kendric blocked her entrance back into the cabin. "Fine. You were right. You're more qualified to recover Sabrina Bryon than I am, but that doesn't mean you're taking the lead. I know this town. I've gotten to know the people here, and the last thing they need is a CBI investigator making their lives harder than they already are. So we do this my way. Understand?"

"Understood." Campbell straightened.

"Good. In that case you should know, yes, Dr. Pascale was serious about doing her examinations in the back of a funeral home. And no, we don't have a forensic lab to analyze trace evidence. Everything we've pulled from the body and this scene will be sent to Unified Forensics in Denver." He didn't know what else she wanted from him, but the urge to settle the dust between them struck hard. "Whatever else you need to find Sabrina Bryon, it's yours."

Tension drained from her shoulders. "I don't think this was a kidnapping for ransom. Elliot Bryon is the only one who would've paid, but the kidnapper took him out of the equation the second he was given the chance."

She was right. Why shoot the only person who could meet the ransom demands? It was Kidnapping 101. "Abduction gone wrong, then?"

"I don't think so." The defensiveness left her expression, leaving behind soft eyes filled with compassion and urgency. "Whoever shot Elliot Bryon brought the gun for a reason. It's possible getting him and Jane Doe out of the way was the plan all along, in which case our missing vic is in more danger than we believed. Either way, once we identify the woman in those woods, we'll have a better chance of connecting her to who's behind this."

"Then this is strictly about Sabrina Bryon." Admiration sucker punched him in the gut all over again as though he'd been physically hit. The way her mind worked effortlessly to connect the pieces was something he'd never been able to ignore. It was what made her a great investigator. This was what she was good at, what she was trained for. "The kidnapper wanted her for a reason."

"Or her baby." Her gaze snapped to his, and his insides went cold. "Most kidnappings throughout the country fall under parental, and from there a female relative is the most likely suspect. Sometimes they believe the child is in danger and the abduction is out of a sense of protection. Other times it's because of jealousy or financial gain, but this… I don't think a woman is behind this."

"What makes you so sure?" he asked.

She slipped her hands into her slacks. "Women tend to internalize their problems. They don't manifest frustrations or emotional injuries aggressively. Instead, they'll become self-destructive. Drug or alcohol use, suicide attempts, punishing themselves. Very few women actually have the capability of putting two bullets in an innocent man. Add that to the fact Sabrina Bryon was carried out of here, we're likely looking for a male UNSUB."

"Hell, sounds like you don't have much use for me." His laugh took him by surprise.

"Yeah, well, when you've worked as many of these cases as I have, you tend to pick up a few things." Her mouth lost its curl. "And you miss others."

The weight of that statement—combined with the drop in her voice—said it had happened one too many times, and his heart rate ticked up a notch. "I'll have Gregson and Majors start the canvass. Maybe one of the neighbors heard or saw something."

"We should also get in touch with her ob-gyn. They've most likely drawn blood from both parents throughout Sabrina's pregnancy to run genetic testing." Campbell tugged her phone from her slacks. "They'd be the ones to compare Elliot's DNA to the fetus."

Did all women know this much about pregnancy and babies? "You're thinking the baby might not be his. There was no evidence of another woman in the house or in the vehicle here."

Campbell nodded, her attention scrolling across the porch. "That's the thing about secrets. Three people can keep one, if two of them are dead."

THE CANVASS HADN'T turned up anything solid.

Then again, with more than a few acres between each home out here in the middle of nowhere, she hadn't expected much. Still, no recollections of gunshots. No sounds of screams or a car engine. The only 911 call had come from within the Bryon home itself, after Sabrina had been taken. Apparently gunshots weren't rare in a town that lived for hunting season and the Second Amendment.

Campbell paged through a collection of personnel records between bites of something she could only describe as the best thing she'd ever eaten. Considering she hadn't slowed down long enough for a meal in the past twenty-four hours, that wasn't saying much. Greta's on Main was small but mighty. The scent of smoke still clung to the walls of the original town diner and blackened old mining recruiting signs screwed into the tiled wall. This place had been lucky to escape the bombing that had occurred a few doors down two months ago. Not many other establishments on Main Street could say the same.

She flipped open the cover of the next file, her heart jumping in her chest at the official photo paper-clipped on the first page. Kendric. Before an explosion disfigured one side of his face. Postured in official dress blues, he stared straight at the camera as though daring her to look away.

He'd always been handsome. Charming, warm. But an ecoterrorist attack during one of Loveland's annual conferences had changed everything. For him, for them. She traced the photo with the edge of her thumb. She hated the hot and cold vibe she'd gotten from him at the scene this morning when she knew what lay under all that resentment and bitterness. He had every right to be angry with the damage he'd sustained from the bombing, but it hadn't stopped him from being the strongest man she'd ever known.

Time and space should've dulled her emotional response to him, but faced with the likelihood of working this abduction case together, she found it only stronger. A reminder of how much power he'd wielded over her from the beginning. She'd compartmentalized the hurt of their breakup, but that obviously wasn't working anymore. She'd missed their connection, his smile, the way he always made her feel safe and protected. Now there was nothing but a hardened shell beneath the scars.

"Wasn't expecting you here." His voice held a hint of detachment as he moved into her peripheral vision, and Campbell closed the file she'd been reading.

Tucking the stack onto the pleather booth beside her, she secured her hands around her near-empty coffee cup as he took a seat across from her. "I didn't realize we were having lunch together today."

"Jane Doe is on her way to the funeral home with the promise Dr. Pascale will call as soon as she has a match to fingerprints, DNA or dental scans. And the forensic evidence we collected is headed to Denver. I also took the liberty of comparing the cast of the footprints outside to the homeowner's shoes. No match." He interlaced his fingers, then splayed them wide as though not sure of how he used to act around her. "Until we get the analysis of the blood and gunpowder from the scene, there's not a whole lot we can do."

The burn of guilt slid up her throat as she repositioned her coat over the personnel files. There was a reason she'd been assigned this case, and it had nothing to do with a missing woman. She had to be more careful around him. One mistake was all it would take to destroy her future with CBI. "Right."

The seconds ticked by in silence as one of the waitresses set a cup down in front of him and filled it before moving on to refill Campbell's. She didn't know what else to say, what to think. Her brain tried to convince her the man sitting across from her was nothing but a stranger, but her heart knew better. "It's nice to see the locals still come here after everything that happened."

"Is that why you showed up in the middle of my investigation? To talk about a diner that's seen better days?" Kendric took a slow pull of his coffee, the steam twisting and arching over scars that demanded attention.

"Would you rather talk about how I came off shift one night to find your side of the bed empty, your half of the closet cleaned out and a stack of cash on the kitchen table with a note that said 'I'm sorry'?" She hadn't meant to let the past infiltrate the present, but hiding the anger didn't mean it had gone away. It had just gotten more volatile.

"What do you want me to say, Campbell? We both know why I left like I did," he said.

The hell she did.

"You know, I'm a pretty good investigator, but even after all these years, I have no clue what I did to push you over the edge." Heat flared into her face. Her heart raced at the potential of confrontation, and there wasn't anything she could do to stop the escape of resentment she'd held on to all these years. "This is hard for me, too, you know. You think I wanted to be here? Do you think I wanted to step into your case or have to see you?"

"I saw what you thought of me after I came home from the hospital, Campbell. I saw the pity in your eyes." He pressed one finger into the table to enunciate the caged emotion he'd held back at the scene. "Every time you looked at me, your voice changed like I was some kind of wounded animal. You were there for me in the hospital and after I was discharged out of obligation, but you didn't want to be. You wanted out of our relationship just as much as I did. Only I was the one who had the courage to do something about it."

"I didn't…" Ice blistered through her veins and stole her intention to see this through. That… That wasn't what happened at all. "You wanted out?"

"You'd been pulling away before the bombing that turned me into…this, Campbell." The fight seemed to leave him just as it had left her. As quickly and as painfully as it had arrived. "You were obviously miserable. What was I supposed to do?"

The urge to reach for him, to explain, outweighed her own self-control, and she set her free hand over his. Calloused tendons tightened beneath her touch. "The bombing had nothing to do with—"

"Dispatch to Hudson, the chief is in a mood." His radio staticked from its position over his left shoulder. The female voice—smooth as whiskey and full of personality—countered the battle-ready hardness in Kendric's neck and shoulders, and Campbell pulled back. She hadn't seen it before, but she couldn't unsee it now. Despite her claim to have moved on, he'd actually succeeded. Plain and simple. "Something about that CBI agent taking jurisdiction on our missing persons case like the cockroach she is."

A flash of that crooked smile threatened to melt any woman in the vicinity with a pulse. Kendric pinched the radio between his thumb and index finger, craning his head toward his shoulder. The effect intensified the strength running along his neck and arms and stopped her heart cold. "I'll give him a call, Mace. By the way, the cockroach says hi."

Mace. Short for Macie Barclay, Battle Mountain's one and only dispatcher. The nickname shouldn't have bothered her, but Campbell felt as though her emotions were on a roller coaster. Out of control and making her nauseous. So what if he had a nickname for someone he worked with closely these past couple of months? That was Kendric. Once upon a time, he'd had a nickname for everyone he knew, including her. Besides, it wasn't as though she had any say in his life now. He'd most likely dated since their breakup five years ago. It made sense, and she had no reason to be uncomfortable with that fact.

Still, it hurt to actually hear the change in his voice when he'd spoken to Macie. Softer around the edges, lighter. He used to talk to her like that. Not to mention Macie Barclay was so different from her. The bohemian redhead lived in a tree house, for crying out loud. If Kendric had set out to scrub Campbell from his life, he'd done a damn fine job.

Campbell collected her coat, hiding the files she'd been reviewing beneath it. Choosing the diner as home base hadn't been the best idea, but she couldn't pass up the enriched promise of coffee and chili cheese fries. "Seems you're a hot commodity."

Damn it. Why did her voice have to shake?

"Comes with the territory. The chief and Dr. Pascale just had a baby, his brother Easton is busy running the veteran rehab facility up the mountain, and Cree and Alma just ended a double shift." Kendric tugged his wallet from his back pocket, molding his uniform across his chest, and tossed a twenty on the table between them. "Someone's got to have a level head around here."

"You like it here." She didn't know where the thought had come from or why she'd felt the need to say the words out loud, but she couldn't deny them, either. So many things had changed since the last time they'd been face-to-face, to the point she wasn't sure she knew him at all. "I can tell."

"It's quieter out here." He scanned the diner and the faces he would've gotten to know since quitting his instructor position with the ATF. "Simpler. I feel like I can actually breathe for the first time since…"

Since the bombing.

She understood that. Because, in a weird turn of events, she felt the same way. Campbell slid from the booth and threaded both arms into her coat, careful not to drop the files. "Well, this cockroach needs to check in with her own CO. Thanks for the coffee."

"I'll walk you out." Kendric stepped into line behind her and followed her out into the wet, cold street. He tucked deeper into his own coat, nodding to her. "Full caseload?"

"Something like that." She gripped the files closer. "Let me know when Dr. Pascale gets back to you about Jane Doe's autopsy. I'd like to be there for the exam if possible." The devastating consequences of one bomber's choices sucker punched her in the gut as she took in the destruction along Main Street, but it was nothing compared to the pure heat of Kendric's attention. Right then, she couldn't help but liken the rebuilding of this small town to the reconstruction going on inside him, and it was then the theory of why he'd been drawn here in the first place surfaced. They were both broken. But not beyond repair. "I can drop you off at the station if you need."

"That would be hard considering it was blown up two months ago." He nodded toward the end of the street where backhoes and construction workers tried to sift through the blackened rubble. "Two devices. Gregson managed to decommission the first one. Missed the second. We're working out of the Whispering Pines Ranch outside of town for the time being."

"Sounds cozy." She turned to face the rental she'd picked up in Boulder.

And froze.

Confusion rippled through her as she studied the beautiful glass snow globe positioned on the hood of her SUV.

"I knew you had a thing for snow globes," he said. "Didn't think you'd have one mounted on the hood of your car."

"I didn't. It's a rental." Her throat dried. The gingerbread wonderland captured inside had come fully alive, as though someone had shaken the globe at the right moment, then simply walked away. Her gaze scanned the street, but she couldn't make sense of any distinct features. "I… I packed it in my luggage I left at the motel down the street."

She crammed her hand into her jacket, wedging her files into her rib cage. Faster than she meant to, she snapped a latex glove over her hand and reached for the globe.

A note fell at her feet, tucked underneath the ornament.

Kendric collected it and unfolded the creases. It was then she understood. He turned the note to face her, and the slanted handwriting came into focus. "Looks like Sabrina Bryon isn't the only one our kidnapper is interested in."

Chapter Three

Stop looking for her.

Those four words echoed on an endless loop in his head until he couldn't differentiate between his own thoughts and those of the bastard out to scare Campbell.

Kendric twisted the dead bolt of the front door and crossed the threshold. The alarm panel signaled warning, and he punched in the code to disarm it, all the while unable to shake the feeling of being watched. "Whoever took Sabrina Bryon knows you're investigating her disappearance. They've done their homework, they know your background and they're obviously not afraid to make a point. You'll be safe here."

Campbell hauled her overnight bag she'd collected from Cindy's Motel over one shoulder as she stepped inside. She stomped the snow from her heels and shook so much from her blazer it created a ring at her feet. The pink in her cheeks and at the end of her nose added a bite to flawless skin he'd barely held himself back from touching in the diner. The back of his hand still burned with the sensation of her skin pressed against his as though she'd branded him. In a way, she had, but allowing himself to give in would only put them right back where they'd ended. Closed off. Distant. Emotionally starved. "Be honest. Babysitting duty wasn't exactly your plan tonight."

No, it wasn't, but the last time he'd disobeyed a direct order from his commanding officer, he'd ended up flat on his back with a wall of fire breathing down on him.

"It's just temporary." Everything was. He'd learned that lesson the hard way. "Guest bedroom is down the hall to the left. The bathroom is across the hall from that. You're welcome to clean up and get settled before we figure out our next move."

She set her overnight bag at the door, that brilliant gaze taking everything in. Hands on narrow hips he could grip in both hands, Campbell studied every inch of the cabin as though strategizing a defense. His gut told him she wouldn't miss a single detail. It was what made her such a good detective, but having her in this place... He wanted to make a good first impression. He didn't know why. She hadn't been part of his life going on five years now, and he sure as hell didn't care what anyone thought of his lifestyle or choices. Decorative and otherwise. "Wow. This seems a little too nice for a safe house. You guys like to live large down here."

"It's mine." Kendric tossed his keys on the small table. The open two-story log living room demanded attention. He hadn't done much decorating in the short amount of time he'd relegated himself to staying in Battle Mountain, but the structure did what it was supposed to.

"This isn't a safe house?" Her gaze snapped to his, and a hint of the fire he'd once admired graveled her voice. "Kendric, what the hell are you thinking? Someone broke into my motel room and went through my personal effects to send a message, and your first thought was to bring me home?"

"Believe me, if I'd had any other choice, you wouldn't be here." At all. He left that last thought to settle between them, not in the mood to drive the invisible knife carving through him deeper. "You might be used to state and federal resources, but down here we're on our own. No safe houses. No forensic lab. No crime scene, homicide or missing persons units. It's me, a sleep-deprived chief of police, a part-time veteran rehab founder, a washed-out bomb squad tech and a rookie who barely survived her first case." He spread his arms wide to make a point. "Welcome to Battle Mountain, Detective. You're going to love it."

He headed for the kitchen and wrenched open the refrigerator. Every nerve in his body had been stripped raw from the moment he'd seen her in the middle of his crime scene. He needed a distraction. Prying the cap from a bottle of beer with his thumb, he swallowed a mouthful to take the edge off. Just for a little while.

Her knuckles threatened to break through the thin skin along the backs of her hands as she slid onto a barstool on the other side of the peninsula between them. "I can't imagine how difficult it must've been for your fellow officers to have to deal with those past cases on their own. Two spree killers, a serial killer. That ATF agent you knew. They're lucky to have you."

The sincerity in her expression stole the fight right out of him, and Kendric reached back into the fridge for an identical bottle. Her eyes widened at the offer, and he was rewarded with a thin smile and a nod of thanks. They weren't partners. Hell, they weren't even friends, but as long as they were assigned to work this case together, a small token of understanding was better than anything else he had to offer. The list of differences between them was just too damn long. Her ability to emotionally detach, fully commit and take a step back to get the larger picture had outgunned him from the beginning. It had just taken third-degree burns over ten percent of his body to show him the truth. Neither of them would change for the other.

He took another pull from his beer and settled back against the cold granite, watching her. "I'm just sorry I wasn't able to stop this place from going up in flames before it was too late."

"Does it get tiring?" she asked.

Confusion rippled through him. "What?"

"Taking on the weight of the world. Always assuming the responsibility of trying to fix everyone else's mistakes." She tipped the neck of her beer toward him and took a drink for herself. Sliding off her barstool, Campbell rounded the end of the counter, leaving her bottle behind. His pulse rocketed into his throat as she closed the distance between them. "You've been in law enforcement long enough to understand Agent Freehan's motive. She killed her sister out of jealousy. She set devices all over this town to hide the evidence and to make sure no one could identify her victim. She would've killed everyone if it had helped her get away with what she'd done. So why are you trying to convince yourself you're the one who triggered the explosives?"

Because in a way he had. Kendric finished the last of his beer, her intelligent, assessing gaze studying his every move. His heart slammed against his ribs as the truth clawed free from the box he'd tried to bury it in. "I taught her how to set those charges."

"You were an ATF instructor." Her shoulders hiked a bit higher as though that was enough to excuse what he'd done. "That was literally your job."

"No." He shook his head. "Christine—Agent Free-han—was with the agency for nearly fifteen years before I transferred from the sheriff's department. I taught her how to set the charges she used to kill her sister, to try to kill Officer Majors, the ones that nearly demolished this town."

"I don't… I don't understand." Campbell took a step back, and the part of him that had missed her, that wondered if he'd made the right choice, raged. "She'd spent years studying explosives. She would've known—"

"No. She came to me about a month before her sister was found in the bottom of a gulch not too far from here. Said she was working a case." His hands shook as a meaningless conversation between colleagues that had turned deadly played through his head. But it was more than that. He just hadn't wanted to admit his part. "A homicide victim who'd been killed with a small device but thoroughly enough that police hadn't been able to put the victim's body back together for an identification. She asked me what the device might look like, how much C-4 would be required to contain the blast, where the killer might've placed the explosive on the body. I hadn't heard of an open investigation with those specs, but it was my job to prepare the agents who came through my seminars for any possible scenario. I thought I was helping with an active case."

"Instead she was using you and your specs to design her own explosive." Not a question. Campbell folded her arms across her midsection. A habit she still hadn't broken after all these years, one she'd used a lot leading up to when he'd ended things. Like she was protecting herself against him, and he hated that. Hated that she couldn't be herself around him, that she had to lie to him, that she had to guard herself against him. But had he honestly given her any other choice? "I'm sorry. I didn't know. None of that... None of that was in the official reports."

"I didn't know until it was too late." He wanted another beer, but drinking himself into false security wasn't going to do either of them any good. And it wouldn't bring Sabrina Bryon home or find Jane Doe's killer. Whether Kendric liked it or not, he and Campbell were the only ones equipped and trained to handle this caliber of a case.

"But because of you, Agent Freehan was apprehended." Campbell notched her chin a bit higher, countering her earlier escape. "You were the one Battle Mountain PD turned to when they got stuck in their investigation. You were the one they called in to handle transporting her into federal custody. You saved a lot of lives here. Shouldn't that count for something?"

"I'm not sure that's enough." He wasn't sure anything he did would be enough. Because it wasn't just about that conversation. It wasn't just about the havoc a colleague had caused here.

"Why wouldn't it be?" she asked. "Kendric, I understand why you might feel responsible, but Agent Freehan would've killed her sister one way or another. You cannot tell me you are responsible for what happened to this town. Why are you doing this to yourself? What's keeping you here?"

"It doesn't matter." He couldn't get into this. Not with her. It wouldn't end the way she thought it would. Heading for the hallway leading to the bedroom wing of the cabin, he tried to shut down the shame, the guilt, the embarrassment from tearing through him all over again. It wasn't any use. Campbell had always known how to hit his buttons. Years of distance hadn't changed that.

"Yes, it does." She followed after him. "You came here for a reason, Kendric. You gave up an entire career with the sheriff's department in favor of your dream job with the ATF. I understand why what happened with Agent Freehan shook your confidence, but you left your family, your friends, everything you knew to play a small-town reserve officer with no experience with serial killers or homicide investigations. For what? Because of some distorted responsibility to a town you've never seen?"

"To protect them from me!" Kendric turned on her. She flinched under the severity of his tone, and he instantly regretted losing his temper. The outburst echoed off the two-story opening of the living room and shook him straight to his core. Then again, hostility was always what he'd done best. It was the only way to make sure no other emotions could escape, but the truth wouldn't die. No matter how many times he'd tried to suffocate it.

The bitterness, the anger that came with having his entire world ripped out from beneath him in an instant simmered just below the surface, but he was better than this. He was better trained than this. Repression had become an old friend these past few years, and he called on it now. Only it wasn't enough. The wound had been opened, and there was no turning back. Not from Campbell. The last of his air reserves escaped his lungs. "Because they deserved to be free of the obligation to help a defective has-been who couldn't even see a threat when it was right in front of him. And so do you."

EVERY MINUTE SABRINA BRYON was missing increased the search area, but none of that mattered as she considered Kendric's words.

He'd left to free her from caring about him. To free everyone who'd loved him.

The narrow hallway closed in around her. It had been different before, listening to him talk to the Battle Mountain PD dispatcher. Her own insecurities had taken a public conversation and inflamed the hurt she'd carried all these years. Because it hadn't been tangible. This… This was different. This was real. She could see his pain. Feel it. Hear the strain in his voice, and she hated every second it squeezed her lungs until there was nothing left.

The explosion that had ripped apart his life and his body hadn't been a one-time event.

He was still living those horrifying seconds. Every single day while the rest of the world moved on. Campbell took a step toward him. "Listen to me, because I'm only going to say this once, Kendric Hudson. You're not defective. You're not a has-been. The voices in your head telling you otherwise have been lying to you, isolating you from the people who can help. They've been forcing you to relive the same nightmare all these years, and they're very good at it, but you're stronger than them. You just can't see it yet."

He didn't answer, didn't even seem to breathe. The small muscles along his jaw flexed under pressure. He'd heard her loud and clear, but in the end, he'd have to be the one to do something about it. Because she wasn't part of his life anymore.

They had a case, a missing young mother, and a Jane Doe taking up space in a funeral home. Compartmentalize. Detach. She'd gotten so good at it over the years. What was one more time? Campbell cleared her throat. "You know, I think I'm going to take you up on freshening up before we come up with an investigative plan. There's still mud in my heels, and I don't want to risk spreading it through your house. Excuse me."

She maneuvered past him—to escape, to hide. Because there was no way in hell she'd let him see what came next. He'd been the love of her life. He'd been her greatest supporter for a time, but she couldn't force him to see the truth. No matter how much she wanted to fight this battle for him, she had two investigations to unravel.

"I never stopped thinking about you," he said.

She swiped at her face before turning to face him, mere feet from the guest bedroom that promised a space to get herself under control. She couldn't work like this. She couldn't investigate a homicide and a kidnapping and carry out CBI's orders while the past kept puncturing through the present. She couldn't go back to Denver empty-handed, and staying here, working with Kendric—losing herself in him all over again—wasn't a risk she was willing to take. Not anymore. "We all have choices we regret."

"I don't regret a single minute of you." The use of his nickname for her triggered a chain reaction of familiarity and comfort she hadn't felt in years. One word. That was all it had taken to stop her in her tracks. Kendric slid his hands into his uniform slacks. "When I left, I tried to forget you. I did everything I could to get you out from beneath my skin. I transferred to the ATF. I found a new apartment you hadn't stepped foot inside. I dated anyone who didn't look like you, but none of it worked."

Campbell reached for the practiced distance she'd coached herself through before getting into her rental and putting herself back in this position. "I'm not sure what you expect me to say to that."

"I couldn't scrub you from my life. No matter how many times I tried. You were always there." His throat convulsed with an exaggerated swallow. "With them… it wasn't like it was with you. I couldn't be myself with anyone. I thought I knew what was best, but I wasn't happy. Not like I was with you, and I have been kicking myself every minute of every day since I walked out that door."

Her heart jerked in her chest. The urge to reach out again—to test the limits of their partnership, to test herself—exploded through her. But what scared her the most was how much she wanted to touch him. She'd spent the past few years numbing herself to rejection and pain and loss, but for the first time since he'd left, she actually felt that physical weight he'd put on his shoulders. Heavy, suffocating, crushing. It was an impossible expectation for one person to suffer on their own. How had he done it all these months?

Kendric took a step forward, then another. For every foot of distance closed between them, her chest tightened, and before she understood his intentions, he'd wrapped his arms around her waist.

The combination of woodsmoke and dirt dived into her lungs and filled the farthest recesses of her senses.

The muscles down her spine only hardened in defense while the hollowness she'd tried to ignore waned. She closed her eyes despite the storm of anger at herself for letting him get close, and her hands splayed across his back. Peaks and valleys of muscle and scar tissue rippled under her palms, and her guard slipped a little more.

"I'm glad you're here." His rushed exhalation tickled the underside of her chin a split second before she surrendered. Securing his hands at her back, he held on to her as though she were the only thing anchoring him to the earth. In that instant, he wasn't the annoyed reserve officer she'd met in the middle of a crime scene this morning. He was Kendric, the one who'd committed to making her smile every day, who'd laughed along with her at life's absurdities and pushed her to climb the investigative ladder outside of the sheriff's department. His inhalations matched her own as the minutes ticked by, and after so many years of wondering what she'd done wrong or if she'd been able to help him get through the aftermath of the bombing, she found herself not wanting this to end.

"Do you know what I was thinking about the other day? That house in Loveland." She could picture it now, so clearly. The dirt front yard, the broken chain-link fence. The hole in the roof after a bomber had made a mistake building his device and killed himself in the process. It was their first case together. "The lime-green one with red brick."

Kendric pried himself from her but kept his hands secured on her waist. One corner of his mouth hiked higher, giving the impression of a smile, but he'd obviously been out of practice for too long. "You mean the crime scene where you asked me out."

"Took some convincing. Especially since you were trying to clear everyone out of the house before it collapsed in on itself." Her laugh escaped easier than it had in years. Lighter, freeing. "But I didn't give up. Because I knew we were going to make a good team."

"We did." The familiarity between them drained from his expression, and sooner than she wanted, he stepped free from her personal space. "For a while, at least."

Her gut twisted at the physical and emotional distance he'd weaponized so quickly. The uncertainty she'd become all too comfortable with returned, and Campbell scrambled to pull herself back together. They'd gotten through the first hurdle, but the hurt wouldn't be placated so easily. "Yeah. For a while."

"I'm going to find us something to eat while you clean up." He turned as he backed away. "Should only be a few minutes."

Was this how it would always be between them? One of them trying to leave while the other tried to get them to stay? Were things so bad between them it had really come to this eternal tug-of-war they couldn't escape? "Back in the diner, you said I was pulling away before the bombing, that I was miserable."

"We've got a case, Campbell." Kendric pulled a box of pasta from the pantry, followed up by an array of mushrooms, tomatoes and spinach from the fridge. "We're not going to solve everything between us tonight."

"You were right. I was miserable, but not because it had anything to do with you. I wanted to be there for you. I did, especially after the bombing. You needed me, but I didn't know how to... I didn't want to add to your stress while you were recovering," she said. "I didn't think you could handle it, and by the time I was ready to tell you the truth, you were gone. You wouldn't answer any of my calls, you'd blocked my emails and messages. I even tried to reach you through your parents, but you never answered back."

"What are you talking about?" Dark eyebrows drew together as he turned to face her.

"I was pregnant." The truth ground the last bit of fight from her bones, leaving nothing but emptiness and exhaustion. "Around eight weeks. I'd found out a week before the bombing. I had this whole surprise party planned for you for when you got home, but then your CO called to tell me what had happened."

"You were pregnant." The words barely registered between them in that too-narrow kitchen. Kendric scrubbed a hand through his hair as shock slapped the color from his face. "So when you recognized that pillow found by Jane Doe's body, it's because you...you have personal experience." Green eyes snapped to hers as his voice hardened. "We've been together all day, and you're just telling me this now?"

"I wanted to wait until the right moment." She shook her head as though the action could rewind the past few minutes, but there was no running from it this time. She'd started this. She had to see it through. "You revealed a personal secret. I figured it was my turn."

Kendric stumbled back as if she'd physically struck him. His Adam's apple dipped and rose on a strong swallow as the silence closed in. "We have a baby?"

"She's not a baby anymore. She just turned four. Her

name is Penny. She stays with my parents when I'm on assignment. I can show you a picture." Campbell unpocketed her badge, careful to bend her credentials beneath the leather, and exposed the smiling blonde beauty behind the clear plastic window on the other side. The one who looked just like her dad but had been blessed with her mom's blond hair and blue eyes. "The pregnancy was hard. Especially at the beginning."

His hand shook as he took the picture from her. "She's beautiful."

"She's also very intense." Campbell took a step forward. "Do you understand now? I tried to hold it together for you, Kendric. I tried to be what you needed me to be. I really did, but learning about the bombing and the baby and dealing with the physical problems that came with her… I couldn't. I understand why you felt I wasn't there for you when you needed me the most. Because I wasn't. You leaving… it nearly broke me, but I was willing to hold on to us." Her heart threatened to beat straight out of her chest. "Why weren't you?"

"Dispatch to Hudson." Macie Barclay's incoming interruption from the radio at his shoulder destroyed his chance to answer. "Please respond."

Kendric locked that unreadable gaze on the photo as reality broke through the walls they'd built around them. He handed back her badge and answered. "This is Hudson. Go ahead."

"The chief found Sabrina Bryon's vehicle out on the Alpine Loop. You're going to want to get there as soon as you can." The channel fractured over broken radio waves. "Oh, and please be advised it's on fire."

Chapter Four

Flames had blackened the cliff face containing the fire to the road.

The Alpine Loop's circular route navigated through the high elevation of Cinnamon Pass and Engineer Pass in the San Juan Mountains, connecting Silverton, Ouray and Battle Mountain. Sharp peaks, withered tree growth and deep valleys demanded attention from every angle. Kendric hadn't ever seen anything like it. With snow already working its way down the surrounding mountains, the isolated one-lane dirt road had been the perfect location to destroy evidence. No tourists taking advantage of the views this time of year. Slowed cargo shipping. No witnesses.

Campbell rounded the hood of the SUV and approached ahead of him.

Mud squished under his boots as Kendric caught sight of Battle Mountain's chief of police, Weston Ford.

The sleepy town of less than a thousand residents hadn't had much in the way of a police department. At least, not until Chief Ford had scrounged together a solid team over the past year. He and his brother Easton, the town's second reserve officer, had brought down not one but two serial killers in a span of months in addition to taking on Kendric's former colleague from the ATF. Together, they'd protected Battle Mountain with a fraction of the resources he'd relied on during his career and given this town a reason to believe in heroes. The chief craned his head over his shoulder, backlit by the smoldering remains of what was left of Sabrina Bryon's sedan.

A few days' worth of beard growth intensified the sharp angles of the man's oval face, accentuated by the shade thrown by his ten-gallon hat. Dirt and ash clung to the new father's dark T-shirt hugging an athletic frame and washed the color from the chief's jeans. Despite the lower temperatures at this elevation, sweat trickled from Weston's short dark hair as he sidestepped to give Kendric and Campbell a view of the vehicle. "Just in time. Fire and rescue just gave us the all clear to take a look."

"Did you find any remains?" Campbell snapped a pair of gloves over her hands and approached the steaming blackened frame of the vehicle. Instantly focused on the task at hand.

Kendric circled around the front of the car toward the driver's side.

"No, but considering how long the wreckage was burning before it was spotted and the amount of accelerant we can smell from here, my guess is if there was, there won't be any evidence of them now." Chief Ford extended a work-gloved hand. "You must be the investigator from the CBI. Weston Ford."

"Campbell Dwyer. Who spotted the fire?" Campbell didn't even seem to acknowledge the chief as anything more than a potential resource, her entire being consumed with finding answers.

"A private passenger plane flying over radioed in." The chief lowered his hand, settling a suspicious gaze on Kendric as Campbell got closer to the vehicle's remains. "They ended up circling until fire and rescue arrived on scene to keep an eye on it and make sure the blaze didn't spread. The last thing this town needs is another round of evacuations. Lucky for us, most of the trees up here have given up the ghost for winter."

"I don't see any other vehicle tracks leading away from the scene. No gas cans, either." Campbell straightened, moving slowly along the length of the cremated car. "Whoever set the fire most likely used the gasoline from the vehicle itself to start it. This doesn't look premeditated. The kidnapper improvised to make a clean getaway." She pointed to the ground, trailing her finger along the flattened grass lining the edge of an open cliff on the other side of the road. "Whoever it was used the grass to hide their shoe impressions."

Hell, she'd read all that in under a minute. Admiration simmered under his skin as Kendric caught the slight narrowing of her gaze. A bomb could've gone off right then, and Campbell still wouldn't have shifted her focus. Even on his best days, Kendric and his team would've taken hours of surveying a scene before coming up with any kind of conclusions. She was good at this, and Sabrina Bryon was lucky as hell to have Campbell on her trail.

"Fire and rescue said the same thing, but that's not all. Your perp has definitely done their homework, maybe even trained in forensics. I found pieces of a duffel bag in the back seat. Torched but intact enough for us to prove there were two sets of clothes as well as some toiletries and a pair of boots inside." The chief headed for a blue tarp spread out along the ground high-lighting different scraps of evidence. "Looks like the kidnapper had Sabrina Bryon change into clean clothes before destroying the rest." Weston unpocketed a pen and gathered up a stained scrap of fabric.

This was all starting to feel too familiar.

"You're thinking this might be another law enforcement officer." Kendric's gut clenched. He hadn't wanted to voice the theory, but after what these townspeople and this department had already been through, they couldn't discount the possibility. Agent Freehan had swept into this town on the back of surviving two serial killers, and taken every last ounce of safety from Battle Mountain. He couldn't let it happen again. "Knowledge of forensics and protocols?"

"I'm not sure yet." The chief nodded, his expression more grave than a moment before. "Chloe's going to try to run DNA from what's left of these clothes. See if we can get a match. But as of right now we've got a missing woman, a gunshot victim who looks a hell of a lot like her pretending to be pregnant and a frantic husband who might not make it out of surgery. What the hell is going on here?"

Pops and hisses of dying embers broke through the low whistle of wind whipping through the valley. Heat flared along Kendric's neck as he took in the damage. "An affair gone wrong?"

"Elliot Bryon sought a lover who looked identical to his wife and asked her to role-play a pregnancy?" Campbell asked. "In my experience, when a man is stepping out on his pregnant wife, finding someone who looks like her isn't his highest priority."

"Or our Jane Doe's significant other discovered her

secret. Figured he could get back at the man sleeping with his wife by taking Sabrina." Kendric reviewed the list of friends and family associated with the Bryon family. It would take days to interview them all with his limited amount of manpower on this case. Hell. Twelve hours into this investigation, there were still too many unanswered questions, and without Jane Doe's identity, he didn't know if they'd make any headway in finding answers. "Either way, we won't get anywhere until we can talk to the husband."

"I'll check in with the hospital." The chief pulled his cell from his back pocket. "You two stay on this. The kidnapper destroyed this car because they knew it could lead us back to them. I want it all pulled apart and searched." Weston headed back toward his vehicle down the road, leaving Campbell and Kendric alone.

"Gasoline burns at fifteen hundred degrees. Any DNA the kidnapper or Sabrina left behind wouldn't have survived." Kendric rounded to the back of the vehicle. Twisted metal steamed as the sun dipped behind the cliff face. They didn't have but a couple more hours before evening hit. Whatever they needed to do, they needed to do it now.

Campbell didn't answer, didn't even seem to breathe, as she stared at the charcoaled remains. "This is the victim's car."

"According to Macie, the VIN number matches to the registration from the DMV. Same make and model, too," he said. "Why does that matter?"

"We never found another set of vehicle tracks leading to the Bryon home apart from the victims' vehicles. This one and Elliot Bryon's pickup, which you'd already searched. At first, I thought the kidnapper and Jane Doe had come from the tree line. Maybe with an ATV or a dirt bike, but Gregson and Majors haven't found anything that supports that theory."

Hell, she was right. And he hadn't seen it before now. The smoke from burned leather and metal drove into his lungs, singeing the back of his throat. "All right. So how did the abductor get to the Bryon home?"

"Let's assume you were right before. Jane Doe and Elliot Bryon are having an affair. He brings her to the cabin for a rendezvous while his wife is out of the house, but surprise, Sabrina Bryon comes home early and catches him in the act." A humorless laugh escaped full pink lips and broke the connection between the hardened investigator and the woman he hadn't been able to sanitize from his life.

"Okay. She's upset. They're expecting a baby, so emotions are already running high, and she's just learned her husband is having another woman role-play a pregnancy. A woman who looks frighteningly just like her." He followed the curve of the burned-out vehicle until he and Campbell stood on the same side, and something deep inside aligned with her. "Something goes wrong. They argue. Sabrina's either brought a gun with her or she knows where Elliot stores his. Jane Doe is shot in the process."

"Jane Doe escapes. Sabrina can't keep up with her because of the pregnancy, so she shoots her husband's mistress from a distance, hitting Jane Doe in the back. Then focuses on her husband. She shoots him, and Sabrina flees with the murder weapon, a change of clothes and toiletries and her vehicle." Campbell had somehow masterfully fit the pieces together, but it was only the beginning. Raising her gaze to his, she seemed to snap out of her own internal study. "What background information have we pulled on Sabrina Bryon?"

"The basics. Financials, employment history, driving records, cell phone data." Anything included in the standard protocol when someone went missing. "From what we can tell, she doesn't have any living relatives. No debt. She moved here a few years ago, married Elliot Bryon within a year. Macie said it was in all the papers. Kind of like a Cinderella story. Elliot Bryon comes from money. Something to do with a family-owned business. Sabrina had been struggling finding work. They met, and it was happily-ever-after since. All that was about two years ago."

"Where did she move from?" The slight octave change in Campbell's voice said the story didn't line up for her. "Did she go to school? Was she married previously?"

"I'll have to dig deeper when I get back to the temporary headquarters at the ranch." Kendric caught himself comparing the photo she'd showed him of their daughter to the missing persons agent in front of him. Same shade of blue in their eyes, same texture of hair. Beautiful. She met his gaze head-on, and a different kind of heat altogether burned through him. He did know one thing for certain. Campbell wasn't going anywhere. Whether he liked it or not, they were in this together. "Why? What are you thinking?"

"Whoever shot Elliot Bryon put two in his chest center mass. That's nearly impossible if you've never handled a weapon before. And whoever burned this vehicle did so to destroy DNA and any chance of forensics recovery. Civilians, especially those who are scared and on the run, don't stop to think about things like that."

She pointed to the car. "I'm thinking Sabrina Bryon isn't who she convinced everyone she is."

Shock nearly knocked Kendric back a step. "Then who the hell is she?"

THE SCENT OF fire and gasoline clung to her coat as she stripped it from her shoulders. Night had fallen, shutting down any chance of searching Sabrina Bryon's vehicle further without the support of floodlights. There hadn't been much left, as Kendric had theorized. The gasoline had all but eviscerated any evidence that would've helped their case. With Easton Ford securing the scene overnight, they'd have to wait until morning to pick up where they'd left off.

How did a town like Battle Mountain manage to solve any kind of investigation with the limited manpower and resources they had? Well, that was why she was really here, wasn't it? To unearth the source of the evil closing in around this town over the past year.

Campbell peeled mud-crusted heels from her aching feet and tossed them onto the floor. The room Kendric had lent her since her motel room had been raided was simple. Just like him. Little decor, neutral colors, clean aesthetic. No personal photos or signs he'd made this a home, but the way he talked about this town said he never intended to go back to Denver. Maybe not even for his daughter. She wasn't sure how she felt about that. She and Penny had been fine on their own all these years, but now that Kendric knew of their child's existence, she'd expected…more. Curiosity. Maybe even desire to meet Penny.

The queen-size bed called her on a deep, exhaustion-heavy level, and Campbell stripped free from the rest of her clothing to keep odor transfer to a minimum. She needed a shower. A hot meal. Twenty hours of sleep. To hear Penny's voice.

She tugged her credentials from her blazer pocket and pulled the photo of her daughter free. After setting it upright against the nightstand lamp, she donned her sleepwear—an oversize shirt and a pair of sweats—and headed for the kitchen. Her stomach growled as though sensing sustenance nearby.

"I can hear your stomach coming from a mile away." A low laugh permeated through the dim lighting above the kitchen table. Kendric raised his gaze from the shuffled paperwork in front of him. "I take it you're hungry."

"Sorry for interrupting. Apparently cheese fries aren't very filling." She pointed to the refrigerator. "You mind?"

He nodded permission. "No apology needed. I stopped being able to see the reports an hour ago." Scrubbing his face, he looked as tired as she felt in that moment, but it was nothing compared to the last look she'd had of him in Denver. "At this point, I couldn't even tell you what time that clock over the stove says."

"Thanks." A cool burst of air slammed against her overheated face and neck as she searched the fridge. Bare. Just like the rest of the house, but a block of cheddar cheese in one of the drawers promised to ease her craving for comfort food. "Sounds like you could use one of my famous grilled cheese sandwiches."

Kendric sat back in his chair at the kitchen table. "I'd give up my right arm for one of them right about now."

"You got it." It was hard to fight the smile hooking her mouth at both corners. She'd almost forgotten how charming he could be at times. She set to work and moved through the kitchen as though she owned the place, the pressure of his gaze sliding between her shoulder blades. If she was being honest with herself, she'd missed the easiness they could fall into. She'd missed him.

"Whose name is on Penny's birth certificate?" he asked.

Tension replaced the smile lingering on her mouth. She forced the butcher knife down through the block of cheese, trying not to slice her fingers off. They hadn't been given the time to slow down since discovering Sabrina Bryon had gone missing, but she owed him answers. "Yours."

"Gotta say, that's not the answer I was expecting." His voice dipped, barely rising above a whisper.

Campbell set down the knife and turned to face him. "I was never trying to keep her from you, Kendric. I wanted to make it as easy as possible for you if you decided you wanted to be part of our lives. You're the one who refused to have any kind of contact with me."

"I know." He swiped his empty mug off the table and shoved back in his chair. Pulling open one of the overhead cabinets in the small U-shaped layout, he brushed against her hip as he pulled a loaf of bread free. Electricity shot through her side, fighting the tightness in her muscles as he set the bag on the counter and filled his coffee cup. "I just meant… I figured you would've wanted someone else. Gotten married, had him adopt her and take his last name. Made yourself a family."

Her mouth dried as the waves of warmth spread through her. One touch. That was all it had taken to ratchet her nerves into overdrive, and Campbell squeezed her hand firmly around the knife to finish what she'd started. She sliced through a few more pieces of cheese and unpacked four pieces of bread, arranging it all. "Families come in all shapes and sizes. What Penny and I have is all I need."

"Yeah." Kendric shifted his weight between both feet, taking a sip of dark roast with just a hint of cinnamon in the air. "Tell me about her. Our...daughter."

"That word isn't typically used as a swear word, but sure. Um, well her pediatrician is worried about my mental health." A lightness penetrated through the violence and uncertainty that had fisted in her gut throughout the day. "She refuses to eat meat and loves broccoli. Anything green, actually."

"Broccoli?" His face twisted into hard lines just as Penny's did when she wouldn't accept no for an answer, and Campbell couldn't help but laugh. "Are you sure she's mine? What kid actually likes broccoli?"

"This one." She assembled the sandwiches, smearing butter with a good helping of garlic powder from one of the drawers on the outsides. "She loves imaginary play. She can make any two items talk to each other. The other day she'd found two straws in the car. Before I knew it, one was accusing the other of sneaking a cookie from the pantry and had gotten sent to time-out."

His deep laugh resonated through her, creeping under the wall she'd built over the past few years to protect herself from him. "She sounds amazing."

"She is." Campbell set the sandwiches in the pan, and the scent of cheese filled the small space between them. "Her confidence is off the charts. I keep telling my mom she's either going to be a CEO or a serial killer."

"Why not both?" he asked.

"You have a point." She turned to grab for a spatula across the counter, stopping short.

Kendric held one out, and in that moment, he seemed so much…bigger. More real. More…attainable. The bitterness he'd become all too comfortable with had melted from his voice and released the anger from his expression. Right then, he resembled the man she'd fallen in love with all those years ago. Her partner.

His gaze dipped to her lips a split second before he closed the distance between them.

His mouth crushed to hers.

He speared one hand into her hairline. Desperate to keep her from backing away? Her breath mixed with his as she savored the bite of black coffee and man. Lean muscle backed her against the refrigerator and held her upright. Instinctively, she opened her mouth to give him better access, and he deepened the kiss as though trying to prove something to both of them. His heart pounded against her chest, unsteady but strong. Every sweep of his tongue worked to undo the guard she'd built between them until Campbell wasn't sure where he started and she ended.

Then pain seared down her front.

"Oh my gosh! Hot, hot, hot!" Stepping back, she fanned her shirt with both hands. The thin, vintage-feel fabric burned her midsection and thighs as coffee slid down her body.

"Oh, crap. Here. Let me." He set the mug on the counter and reached for a dish towel in the same move. Crouching, Kendric moved to get as much of the coffee from her legs and feet before the burns set in.

"That's… That's okay. I can do it." Campbell ducked to take the towel from him but failed to dodge his skull as he straightened. Pain exploded across her face, and she fell back against the refrigerator. Lightning flashed across her vision, her eyes watering from impact.

Kendric gripped the back of his head. "Hell, woman. You could've just said no. You didn't have to beat me to make a point."

"At least you're not the one bleeding." She tipped her head back to contain the blood flow from her nose. "Could you get me a paper towel?"

"Damn it." Kendric ripped a clean towel from the stand, soaked one corner in cold water and faced her. "Let me see."

"I think you've done enough damage for one night." Mentally and physically. Campbell shook her head, unable to hold back the absurdity of the past couple of minutes. It was just like them to turn a heated, passionate moment into chaos. "It'll stop in a minute."

"And until then, I can make sure nothing is broken." He set his free hand along the side of her neck, tipping her head back gently with his thumb.

Her pulse thudded hard as she followed directions, and the gravity of this moment—of them being in the same room after all these years—set in. She wasn't sure if she'd ever see him again, and now they'd been assigned to work a missing persons case with more questions than answers.

"I'm sorry," he said.

She stared up into the canned lights as he pressed the wet towel beneath her nose. "It was an accident, Officer Hudson. I won't be pressing charges."

"Not about the bloody nose." He dabbed at her nose and mouth. "Well, yes, about the bloody nose, but also about before. That you felt you couldn't tell me you were pregnant because you didn't think I could handle it on top of everything else. Funny thing is, you were probably right."

An apology. Her heart squeezed harder than it should have. "To be fair, you had a lot on your mind at the time."

"More than what was left on my face." His attempt at sarcasm fell flat, and the reality of their situation solidified. He'd walked out on her without warning. There was no argument or excuse. He'd hurt her and deprived Penny of a father's influence. "I wish I could go back. Change things. If I'd just done the job I was hired to do—"

"Stop." Campbell set her hand over his, taking the paper towel. She tipped her head forward and swiped the last of the blood from her face. "You almost died, Kendric. If Cree Gregson hadn't tackled you to the floor when that second bomb had gone off, you wouldn't even be here. I know it doesn't feel like it, but I'm grateful. You're alive. That's more than what a lot of ordinance techs can say. You still have a choice about how you want to live your life. Is it going to be here, where you're haunted by the devastation wreaked by your colleague, or in Denver, where your friends and family are waiting for you to come home? Where your daughter is waiting to meet her dad?"

He didn't answer, didn't even seem to breathe, and it was then she knew. For him, there was no choice. The man he'd been didn't exist anymore. The life he'd had didn't exist anymore. He'd cut himself off from anything and everyone that connected him to that time. Including her. Only in the end, he'd be the one to suffer, and her heart broke a little more.

"You were so angry about the bombing that you wouldn't talk to anyone. Not even the people in your unit. Not to me." She raised her hand to frame the side of his face, and he flinched. From her. Her gut clenched at the loss of the passionate, uncontained man he'd been a moment ago. The one who'd helped her forget the world with a single kiss. "You're still angry about it. I can hear it in your voice."

Kendric backed into the opposite counter, trapped in his own kitchen. Nowhere to run. Nowhere to hide. It was just the two of them and a long list of mistakes they'd made together over the years.

Cold worked through her as the coffee cooled. There wasn't a single brain cell in her head capable of processing what had happened between them the past few minutes. Sensory overload and exhaustion had already started forcing her body to shut down. "We were always better at managing our careers than our personal lives, weren't we?" She pointed to the smoking pan a few feet away. "You're going to want to flip the sandwiches before they burn."

She didn't wait for an answer this time as she headed back toward her room, losing her appetite. In truth, considering why she'd really come to Battle Mountain, she couldn't afford to hear one.

Chapter Five

He'd made a mistake.

Kissing Campbell. Wishing things had turned out differently for both of them. Eating both of their grilled cheese sandwiches. Obsessing about his and Campbell's conversation last night hadn't helped one bit. Kendric tried to hold in a yawn, failing miserably, as he shuffled into the kitchen. She'd wanted an answer. She'd wanted him to tell her he planned to head back to Denver, to pick up where they left off and be part of his daughter's life.

But he couldn't.

That little girl—vegetarian or not—deserved better than him for a father. Campbell deserved better than a broken ghost of himself. What she wanted, what their daughter needed…he couldn't give. Maybe not ever.

Movement registered from the living room.

"Didn't realize you were already up." He scrounged for a clean mug and poured himself a fresh cup of coffee.

"I'm on the there's-a-child-in-my-bed-at-five-a.m.-watching-cartoons schedule. Hard to kick." She swiped her fingers expertly over the laptop trackpad balanced in the middle of her crossed legs. She'd changed since he'd dumped nearly an entire cup of hot coffee on her chest, but the outfit was made up of the same pieces. T-shirt and sweatpants. And damn if having her so relaxed in the middle of his living room wasn't the sexiest thing he'd ever seen.

Kendric cleared the morning dryness from his throat. "Campbell, about last night—"

"I've composed a list of Sabrina Bryon's closest friends in town based off her phone records. There hasn't been any activity since she disappeared and the phone is turned off to keep us from triangulating a signal, but if she's on the run, she'll go somewhere familiar for help. I think I've narrowed it down to the most likely person based off her call history. The number is registered to a Chelsea Ingar." She set the laptop on an old wood end table he'd taken off Gregson's hands when the reserve officer had moved in with his partner, Alma. "Give me about thirty minutes to shower and dress, and I'll be ready to go."

The detachment was back in her voice, and Kendric mentally kicked himself for screwing this up. "Wait. Please."

"It's fine, Kendric. I didn't come here to try to bring you back to Denver, and to be honest, I shouldn't have said anything in the first place." She moved to push past him, but he held his ground. Swiping her hand under her slightly bruised nose, she pulled up short. She stretched a hand toward him, enunciating her next words. "You don't owe me answers. Really, you don't owe me anything, and it was out of line for me to expect you to explain yourself. Besides, we have a case. We're good. I promise."

"No, we're not. We're not even close to being good."

He fisted one hand as the past threatened to consume the present. Images of fire and pain and death wouldn't recede, but keeping them bottled up all these years hadn't helped, either. "You don't know what it was like. Lying in that hospital bed, being able to see, hear and feel everything but not having the ability to do anything about it. My throat was so burned from the explosion, I couldn't even scream when the nurses changed my bandages. I couldn't move. I couldn't be touched."

Campbell dropped her gaze to the floor, crossing her arms over her lean frame. "I'm sorry. That sounds... miserable and terrifying."

"Gregson got it worse, but he can hide the scars. I can't." The dead nerves along the right side of his face tingled with phantom sensation. "I can still feel my skin slipping when I let myself stop long enough to think about what happened. I can still hear Gregson's screams in my nightmares, knowing there was nothing I could do to help either of us. I was the team leader on that assignment, Campbell. I disobeyed an order to evacuate because I thought I could get to the device before it went off. I was supposed to protect my team, and I failed. And you...you're telling me I have the choice about how I live the rest of my life, that I can just go back to Denver to be with my friends and family. To be with my daughter. But the truth is, I don't. Because any life they would have with me isn't a life worth living."

Shock snapped her gaze to his, and Campbell stepped forward. "That's not true. You—"

"I can't give you what you want, Campbell. What's more is I can't be the father that little girl deserves. Not with this face and with all the stuff that comes with it. So I'm not coming back." He motioned to the waves of scar tissue contorting his face. Kendric countered her approach, but voicing the deepest fears he'd kept to himself all this time was freeing in a way. Acceptance was the first step. Wasn't that what they said? He retreated for the hallway. "Ever."

"You're wrong, you know. You're not broken, Kendric. You're not defective or any less lovable because of what you've been through, and I feel sorry that you've accepted that's the only path for you. Because you have so much to offer. More than you can possibly understand." Her voice softened. "I only hope you realize it before it's too late."

His grip tightened around his mug. "I don't need your pity, Campbell. Just your experience with missing victims to solve this case."

"Then I guess we better get moving. According to GPS, Chelsea Ingar is home right now. The victim's phone records put them in contact several times a day over the past few years. She might be able to give us more insight into Sabrina's life while we wait to hear from the ob-gyn." The floorboards creaked in protest as she made her way down the hall in front of him before she disappeared behind the solid wood door of the guest bedroom.

Kendric retreated to his own room and went about his normal routine. The hot water ran out halfway through scrubbing the scent of burnt rubber and dirt from his skin and beard. Just as well. Every second he and Campbell wasted on trying to hash out the differences between them was another second Sabrina Bryon wasn't on her way home, and he couldn't allow his personal life to obstruct this investigation. Neither of them could. He dressed in full uniform, securing his weapon in the holster on his hip, and stepped out into the hallway.

The sound of water hitting tile reached his ears. Campbell hadn't finished in the guest bathroom, but he couldn't imagine her shower was any warmer than his. He had every intention of stalking past her bedroom without so much as a glance inside to honor her privacy, but a small rectangle set upright on the nightstand caught his attention.

The photo Campbell had showed him last night. Penny.

His shoes scuffed against the hardwood as though the smiling four-year-old had some invisible rope tied around his waist to pull him closer. Before he realized what he was doing, Kendric picked up the photo for a closer look. A waterfall of blond hair cascaded around a heart-shaped face, soft and shiny and a little bit frizzed. Big blue eyes stared straight ahead as Penny charged toward the camera with two giant fistfuls of multicolored leaves. She was poised to attack, ready to take on everyone and anything that got in her way. The photo had probably been taken a couple months ago—a mere glimpse into a life he'd never have—but Kendric felt as though she were right there. With him.

"She has your smile," she said.

His nerves flinched at the sound of Campbell's voice behind him. He hadn't heard her leave the bathroom, and he quickly replaced the photo where she'd positioned it on the nightstand. "I didn't mean to invade your privacy. I just…" He didn't know the end to that sentence. "Hell, I don't know what I was doing. Sorry."

"Once I had four nurses, an ob-gyn and a medical student witness a baby come out of my vagina, I lost any need for privacy." Campbell dumped her pajamas and toiletries onto the bed beside her unzipped duffel bag, whose bottom was lined by a stack of manila folders. The same files she'd tried to hide from him at the diner. She quickly repacked her bag. "On top of that, Penny thinks breasts are the greatest thing on the planet, and she tries to get to mine every chance she can. Even in public."

"To be fair, she's not wrong." He caught himself envisioning the exact image she'd described and wanted to kick his own ass for his hypocrisy. He'd made it clear he couldn't be part of her and Penny's lives, but his imagination had yet to get the message. "I'll, uh, let you finish getting ready and meet you at the car."

"No need." Securing her sidearm at her hip, Campbell flared her blazer—this one a deep gray—and buttoned up. Tendrils of wet blond hair slipped free from her shoulders, and he wanted nothing more than to thread his hand into the strands all over again. "We can go."

"Lead the way." Within minutes, he was behind the wheel with Campbell in the passenger seat, heading south.

Chelsea Ingar's home was located in the heart of town with a front-door view of the devastation left behind by a psychotic ATF agent now serving the remainder of her life behind bars. The sight was a hard reminder of why Battle Mountain had become his new home but failed to drive the photo of his daughter from his mind.

They walked up the cracked sidewalk to a rambler-style home that had seen better days. Bare trees and dying shrubs lined the rectangular yard fenced in with a dilapidated picket fence that all combined to contrast with the Christmas-red front door.

"Probably better if I do the talking. People around here, they're starting to get suspicious of outsiders." Kendric pounded the side of his fist against the door, welcomed by the echo of footsteps on the other side. The door opened inward and revealed a short blonde woman yelling over her shoulder to the three kids rampaging through the house.

"Can I help you?" Blue eyes ping-ponged between Kendric and Campbell, then back again.

"Mrs. Ingar, we're sorry to disturb you. I'm Officer Hudson, Battle Mountain Police, and this is Detective Dwyer. I'm sure you've heard about what happened up the mountain at the Bryon place. We just have a few questions for you, if you're agreeable," he said.

"Not sure how much help I can be." Chelsea glanced over her shoulder, exposing a pattern of dry, angry acne scars down the side of her face. Nervous? "We don't live anywhere near there. We wouldn't have seen or heard anything."

"But you do know Sabrina Bryon, the woman who's gone missing," Campbell said.

Chelsea folded her arms across her midsection. "Only what I've read in the papers. I might've seen her a few times in town. That's all."

Suspicion exploded through him. "Mrs. Ingar, according to phone records, you and Sabrina have exchanged messages every day for the past two years. I'd say that's more than a passing acquaintance."

"I'm sorry, Officer. You're mistaken." Chelsea Ingar stepped back into her house and started to close the door. "I've never met the woman in my life."

"SHE'S HIDING SOMETHING." Campbell could feel it. She replayed the interview through her head. Over and over until every word had been scratched into the surface of her brain. Every syllable. The landscape passed in rushed layers of white snow, melted slurry and thick mud along the street. Gray clouds stitched together in a blanket of darkness and cold and had her wishing for the comfort of the bed she'd woken up in this morning. The one that smelled of Kendric, even though she'd been an entire room away.

The trip to Grand Junction would take most of the day, keeping them from exploring more immediate leads, but given their only witness was finally awake and talking, they couldn't afford to miss this opportunity. Elliot Bryon had been in the house when his wife had gone missing. He was the way to solving this case. "Chelsea Ingar knows where Sabrina Bryon is. She lied to us."

"We don't know that. I told you, the people of this town are on edge. You have no idea what they've been through the past year." Kendric stared straight through the windshield, green eyes more gray. It was an optical illusion. A minor shift in perspective. One she was frequently reminded of in Penny's eyes when the blue gave way to the same hint of gray on cloudy days. "First a guy burying women in refrigerators, come to find out he was sent here by someone else, then the Contractor, and then Agent Freehan. They're afraid they're next, that one day they'll wake up and BMPD will be on their doorstep telling them someone they love is gone. These people can barely stay afloat during the off season since the mining companies jumped ship. Now we've got a Jane Doe with the coroner, Elliot Bryon has been shot and his wife is missing. Don't tell me Chelsea Ingar doesn't have a right to want to stay away from it all."

"Why Battle Mountain?" She hadn't meant to ask the question that had been nagging her since before she'd taken this case, but it was too late to take it back. Campbell ripped her gaze from the haunting, empty terrain between Battle Mountain and Grand Junction and settled on him. "What do you think it is about this place that draws killers here?"

He didn't answer right away, and her own law enforcement experience immediately tried to fill in the blanks. Corruption, lies, secrets. Every town—every department and officer—she'd investigated had them, but Campbell couldn't imagine the man sitting beside her getting involved. Not knowingly. "I think it attracts people in need more than killers. I think this town offers something not a whole lot of other places do. Apart from location and access to back roads, it's quiet. Isolated. The people here are friendlier than in the big cities. They've grown up with one another, they're raising their kids together and they like to make an effort to know your name. They're genuine. No tricks. No manipulations. It's simple living at its finest, and they're happy. How many other places can say the same?"

A wistfulness bled from his voice as though he'd experienced all that firsthand. "Is that what attracted you here? The quiet? The community?"

"It wasn't Denver, which was good enough for me." He pressed broad shoulders back into his seat, accentuating fine muscle and tight tendons down the length of his neck. He was handsome. Now more than ever, but weathered and lost. His past had beaten him down, and he hadn't yet found the strength to stand back up.

"After everything went down with Agent Freehan, I took one look at the damage she'd caused and knew Battle Mountain was where I could make a difference. I don't know how to explain it other than that when I got here, something just felt…right. Like I was supposed to be here."

She didn't know what to say to that, what to think. She'd felt that sense of rightness, too. With him. But given how he'd already made his decision concerning building a relationship with her and their daughter, Campbell couldn't see any way to get that back. Not yet. Maybe not ever. She directed her attention back out the window, to the miles of pristine, snow-covered farmland laid out in perfect white sheets. The clouds had descended, spreading out in dark layers and blocking the view of the mountains.

They passed the rest of the trip to Grand Junction in silence. Within the hour, Kendric maneuvered the SUV into the parking lot of St. Mary's Medical Center. Layer upon layer of varying shades of red rock protected the city and allowed the limited afternoon sun to reflect off the one-way glass windows of the towering hospital. Kendric had been right before. It was nothing compared to the beauty and peace she'd felt in Battle Mountain. They moved as one through the building's double glass doors and checked in at the security desk.

Elliot Bryon had been released from the intensive care unit, but considering the circumstances of his need for medical care, visitors were limited to law enforcement and approved family members. Of which he hadn't seen any. Two bullet wounds to the chest created a need for added security measures.

Bright white tile, blinding fluorescent lighting and

the scent of bleach in the air were enough to trigger violent memories of her last visit to a hospital like this as she followed Kendric down the hallway.

"Everything okay?" he asked.

Awareness sucker punched her. "Why wouldn't it be?"

"Your breathing changed, and you look like you're about to throw up," he said.

He saw all that? The weight of his attention settled her nerves, somehow talking her down and grounding her at the same time she wanted to jump out of her own skin. Campbell kept her gaze straight ahead and not on the individuals inside the rooms they passed. She tucked her hair behind one ear, hoping for a distraction, but it wasn't enough. "I'm just not a fan of places like this."

Kendric slowed. "Any reason in particular?"

"It doesn't matter." She shook her head, determined to get to Elliot Bryon's room. "I'm good. Promise. My personal feelings about hospitals won't get in the way of what we're doing here."

He reached out to grip one arm, and a shot of heat exploded through her. The effect drowned the hard thump of her pulse behind her ears to the point all she saw, felt and heard was him. "It matters to me."

Her inhalation sawed along her throat. "Penny, uh, stopped breathing during the delivery. She got stuck in the birth canal, and the ob-gyn told me she wasn't going to make it, that there was nothing they could do without risking my life. They were choosing me over her." Campbell slid her hands into her slacks, not ready to meet his gaze. "You can imagine how terrifying that was to someone who hadn't been allowed to eat during twenty-six hours of labor and had no energy to push anymore. I started panicking. I was alone. I didn't know what to do. All these nurses were staring at me with pity and tears in their eyes, and I just... I couldn't take it. I carried her for nine months. It's such a short time, but she was part of me. I didn't want to let her go."

Her eyes burned at the memory.

Kendric drifted his hand higher, sliding his thumb across her cheek. His jaw had released the tension it had been holding, and easier than she thought possible, she leaned into the strength he offered. "But she survived."

A humorless laugh escaped her control. "I fired the doctor and all those nurses on the spot and demanded another team. The ob-gyn who took over saved her life. Saved both of our lives, but coming here... I'm not a fan."

"I'm sorry you had to go through that alone, that I wasn't there." He motioned to the right side of his face and to the scar tissue that had changed his life, and she was once again reminded of how handsome he was. "Would it help if I told you I'm not a fan, either? This place gives me the heebie-jeebies."

"The heebie-jeebies? Is that a medical term? I've never heard of it until now." Her smile melted at the realization he was still touching her. The heat he'd curated along her arm had transformed into a blister down the length of her jaw and neck. Controlled chaos circled around them, but right then, it was as though they'd created a bubble between them and the outside world. Just the two of them. The hunt for Sabrina Bryon, the investigation into Elliot Bryon's shooting, the identification of Jane Doe—none of it existed inside this moment. For the first time in years, she felt like she wasn't destined to get through this life alone.

The interruption from the PA system above ripped her back into the moment, and Kendric dropped his hand from her face. "We better get in there. Visiting hours are almost over."

"Yeah." She hung back as Kendric headed for the witness's room. She had to get a hold of herself. He'd made himself perfectly clear on the drive up. He wasn't coming back. He didn't want to be part of her life now as much as the day he'd walked out. And he didn't want a relationship with his daughter. Campbell took a deep breath. Then again, her nerves weren't on high alert anymore. Because of him.

They stepped into the single-bed recovery room. Elliot Bryon lay under the bedding, his face turned away from them. Short dark hair, shorn almost down to the scalp, didn't conceal the receding hairline around a sharp widow's peak. Wide-set eyes turned toward them with a struggle of someone who'd taken two bullets to the chest from close range.

"Mr. Bryon, I'm Officer Hudson from Battle Mountain. This is Detective Dwyer. We'd like to ask you about what happened at your home yesterday morning." Kendric tugged a chair from against the wall beside the bed, then followed up with another. "I understand it may be difficult for you to speak, so please, take your time."

"Did you…find her?" Elliot struggled to form his question despite the help of the oxygen tube. "I already talked to the detectives here. Do you have news?"

"Your wife, Sabrina?" Campbell took her seat closest to the man in the hospital bed. Close enough to count the spouts of gray in his carefully maintained facial hair. A nose that had been broken one too many times angled across a set face, and instantly triggered an ache across her face from last night's antics. She saw no hint of fear, of pain, of nervousness on Elliot's countenance. A blank canvas. "We're doing everything we can. Can you tell us what you remember from the incident? Do you know who shot you and the young woman we found near your home?"

Elliot Bryon nodded. "Sabrina. She tried to kill me."

Chapter Six

"You're saying your wife is the one who shot you and the woman we found dead near your home?" They'd had this all wrong—at least, he had. Campbell had floated this theory, and hell if she hadn't been right. This wasn't a missing persons investigation. This was a manhunt, and Kendric had wasted nearly thirty hours working off the wrong intel. Sabrina Bryon could be anywhere by now. Could have a whole new identity. "You're sure?"

"She found out about me." Elliot Bryon succumbed to a lung-crushing episode of coughs that tensed his shoulders and neck and, Kendric imagined, had landed the man in excruciating pain. He knew the feeling. Their witness relaxed back against the pillows propped behind him, reaching for the glass of water on the side table with shaky hands. "The woman you found... She was a friend."

"You mean you were having an affair." Campbell helped pass off the water.

"Yes." Taking a drink, Elliot Bryon cleared his throat with a lot more color in his face. "I'm not proud of it, but after Sabrina told me she was pregnant, she changed. It was like she was an entirely different person. She wasn't the woman I married."

"What do you mean?" Kendric asked.

"She lost her temper over the smallest things. She just seemed…angry all the time. Distant. She wasn't keeping to her usual schedule and stopped exercising. It didn't matter what I did or if I tried to help, it wasn't good enough. I'm not even sure if she was sleeping," Elliot said. "I'd never seen anything like it. Not with her."

"Pregnancy can affect every woman differently." Campbell's gaze flickered to Kendric, and he was reminded of an entire nine months she'd carried their daughter without his help. And how he never wanted her to go through that again. "Can you think of any reason for her sudden behavioral changes apart from the baby? Were you two planning on starting a family?"

"No." Elliot shook his head. "She made it clear from the beginning, she never wanted kids. Something about her family history. I don't know. I've never met her side. Sabrina was adamant they weren't part of her life, but once she saw that pregnancy test, she was excited. She turned our second bedroom into a nursery the week she found out, not even bothering to wait for the doctor to tell us if we were having a boy or a girl."

"And how did you take the news?" Kendric asked.

"Me?" Elliot's gaze narrowed slightly. His grip tightened on the glass of water in his hand as he moved to set it back on the side table. As though buying himself time to answer. "I come from a big family. I've always wanted a few kids of my own." His expression softened. "If you find Sabrina, if she goes to jail, what's going to happen to the baby? She's due in less than a month. That's my baby. I don't want anything to happen to her."

"Mr. Bryon, we're getting ahead of ourselves. Right now, we just want to bring Sabrina home safely. Any custody issues can be sorted out then." A wrenching twist in his gut reminded Kendric he had his own child to worry about. While Campbell hadn't asked for anything in the way of support for Penny, he had his own obligation to make sure their daughter was taken care of. And he would follow through, even if he couldn't be part of her life. "Can you tell us what happened yesterday morning?"

Elliot Bryon tried to shift his weight in the bed, obvious pain flaring in his face. "Sabrina was supposed to be in town with a friend. They were going to be shopping for the baby all morning, but she came home early. I don't know. Maybe she'd suspected something was going on and lied about where she was going, to see what would happen. All I know is she found me and Rachel together."

"Rachel? The woman you were sleeping with?" Campbell unpocketed a notebook from her blazer, along with a pen, to take notes. "Does Rachel have a last name?"

"Stephenson. Rachel Stephenson." Elliot stared toward the bottom of his bed, a distraction Kendric had become all too familiar with in his own hospital bed for all those months. "We met at work. I run the auto parts store in town. She's one of the parts managers. I mean she...was." He fisted both hands in the hem of his sheets. "She was sweet. She smiled at me. Before I knew it, we were taking our lunch breaks together, telling each other about our lives. I never meant for anything to happen between us. Yesterday... That was the first time we got together. She was so nice, and it just... happened. I can't believe she's dead. Sabrina never gave her a chance. She just started shooting."

"Do you own a handgun, Mr. Bryon?" Kendric asked.

"Yes. I got it at a gun expo last year." Elliot ran one hand across his chest as though the simple act of talking about the gun that had shot him aggravated the two holes in his sternum. He'd been lucky. One inch to the left, and none of them would be sitting here having this conversation. "Sabrina had just found out about the baby, and she wanted some extra protection. Never thought she'd use the damn thing against me. I thought we were happy."

Obviously not, considering the man had been caught with his pants around his ankles. Kendric caught sight of his partner making another set of notes, her pen nearly going through the notebook. "We didn't recover a weapon at the scene."

"Sabrina must've taken off with it," Elliot said. "I guess I was a little preoccupied with not dying to notice."

"In that case, did Sabrina already have the gun when she came home, or did she go for it during your argument about the affair?" Campbell poised her pen above her notepad.

"I don't… I don't remember." Elliot shook his head, still not meeting their gaze. "Everything happened so fast. I heard her car pull up. I was trying to get Rachel out the back door. Sabrina caught us. She must've already had the gun. She shot Rachel in the back as she was trying to leave. Then she turned the gun on me. I don't remember much after that."

"You don't remember calling 911?" Kendric had listened to that call. Elliot Bryon hadn't said anything about his wife being the shooter, nothing about another victim. Just that he needed medical attention. Kendric had disregarded the lack of information due to extreme panic and the pressure of bleeding out. But his own experience of facing death had him recalling every minute—every second—he'd been trapped in that building after the bomb had gone off.

"No." Another headshake. "Not at all."

"Just a couple more questions, Mr. Bryon, and we'll leave you to rest. You said Sabrina shot you and Rachel by the back door." Campbell tapped her pen against her notebook, and it was then Kendric saw it. The detective on the trail of a possible lead. Her gaze locked onto their witness and refused to let up. Mouth parted, she studied Elliot Bryon with her full attention, and Kendric couldn't help but fear for the man or any other she targeted. "How was it your watch ended up broken in the bedroom?"

Kendric clenched the arm of his chair tighter. The watch she'd collected as evidence from the scene. She was right. Elliot's version of events didn't line up.

"Mr. Bryon?" Campbell asked.

"I remember crawling into the bedroom to hide. That's where the EMTs found me. That's where I must've made the call to 911. I guess it broke then. It's all such a blur." Their witness checked his wrist as though expecting to find the timepiece in place, then rubbed the lighter, watch-shaped skin. "I'm starting to get a little bit light-headed here. Maybe we could cut this short." Elliot Bryon hit the call button for the nurse. "Please. Whatever happens, please don't hurt Sabrina. This is my fault. I did this to us. She's not herself, and I couldn't stand the thought of something happening to her or the baby."

"We'll do our best, sir." Kendric rose to stand. "For

now, just focus on getting your rest." He motioned Campbell over the threshold as he closed the door behind them, out of earshot of their witness. "That son of a bitch is lying," he said.

Campbell replaced her notebook in her blazer, turning to face him. Even in this horrible, unnatural lighting, she was a thing of beauty and grace he'd gone too long without appreciating. Strong, independent, capable of upturning his entire world in a twenty-four-hour span. "What gave you that idea? The fact he couldn't make eye contact or that his hand hasn't stopped shaking since we walked into the room?"

"You knew." And he hadn't seen it until a few minutes ago.

"It's my job to spot the signs." Campbell headed down the hallway, not bothering to check if he'd followed after her. "Everything he told us is a lie. If he broke his watch by trying to hide from his wife, who unclasped the band and left it on the floor beside the spot the EMTs found him? Not to mention he went pretty heavy with his wife's behavioral changes due to the pregnancy. Even if we learn Sabrina Bryon is suffering from prenatal depression or is going through some kind of breakdown, it's unlikely she'd turn murderous from hormone changes. Apart from that, it would be extremely difficult for Sabrina to drag the mistress's body into those woods. Something else is going on here."

Kendric strove to keep up with her as they rounded into the corridor leading to the elevators. He hit the descending call button.

"You don't believe me?" she asked.

"The problem is I do." Questioning their only surviving witness was supposed to supply answers into this investigation, but it had done nothing but create new loose ends. "Something he said. That he didn't remember making the 911 call. I listened to that call, same as you, but it doesn't add up. If your wife is the one who shot you, wouldn't that be something you'd mention to police off the bat? Wouldn't you tell them there's another victim?"

Campbell straightened her shoulders. "I guess it depends on the circumstances. I've listened to calls in which someone beaten within an inch of their life remained calm in order to get police all the details they could before they passed out. Others are so out of their minds they can't even hear what the dispatcher is saying. They just want help."

"Exactly, and Elliot Bryon was neither of those things." The elevator signaled its arrival, but Kendric didn't move to step on. Closing the distance between them, he lowered his voice. "I remember every second after that bomb went off, Campbell, and there is not a single day that goes by that I couldn't tell you exactly where I was, where the members of my team were, what time it was, how many seconds were left on the device when I found it, or the last thing I said to you that morning. All of it. Elliot Bryon?" Kendric pointed down the hall. "He can't remember making a call that saved his life? I don't buy it. Because when you're in that position, and your life is on the line, all you can think about is what you've got to lose if you don't make it."

"What are you saying?" Blue eyes scanned him from forehead to chin, and a wake of warmth trailed down his face as though she'd physically touched him.

Kendric couldn't prove it, but he had no doubt in his mind. "I'm saying I think Elliot Bryon made that 911 call before he was shot."

WAS IT POSSIBLE?

Had the surviving witness in their missing persons case been playing his own game from the beginning? Campbell couldn't wrap her head around an answer as she memorized the rise and fall of the mountains out her window. Or as she considered Kendric's words. *When your life is on the line, all you can think about is what you've got to lose if you don't make it.* He'd remembered the last thing he'd said to her that morning. When it had mattered most, one of his last thoughts as he fought for his life had been about her. She'd blocked so much of that time from her mind—to protect herself against the hurt, the confusion, the emotion that came with so much fear when she'd gotten the call—she couldn't remember any of it. "What was it you said to me that morning?"

Kendric adjusted his grip along the steering wheel. "I said I was going to pick up something for dinner on my way home so you didn't have to cook. You'd been especially tired that week. I was trying to be a hero by taking dinner off your shoulders."

"I would've been around eight weeks pregnant at the time. Tired doesn't even begin to describe it." A smile played across her mouth. "She asks about you, you know. Penny. Where her daddy is. Why he's not there. She's already planning her wedding and wondering who's going to walk her down the aisle. I think she's trying to convince me to give her a brother so he can do it."

"What have you told her about me?" His voice caught

in his throat. Just enough for her to notice before he cleared the blockage.

"That you're out saving people's lives." She wedged her palm beneath her chin as she visually followed the designs along his face. The slightly puckered, shiny skin hadn't changed much over the years. They were still part of him. Made Kendric who he was despite his hatred for the scars. "That you can't come home until you've saved the entire world. I wasn't too far off, was I?"

"What are you doing, Campbell?" he asked. "Why are you pushing this?"

"Because whether you want to accept it or not, you have a life back in Denver. You have people waiting for you to come home." Couldn't he see that? The man she'd known then wasn't completely gone. There were still pieces of him staring back at her from his eyes when he let down his guard. The Kendric Hudson she'd loved was still in there. "I'm not saying something is going to happen between us again. Maybe there is. Maybe there isn't, but pretending there wasn't anything between us at all—that we don't have a child together—isn't going to make it so."

"I'm not pretending, damn it." The tops of his thighs hardened under the thick layer of jeans. "I know what I gave up. I know the world and all the people in it are moving on without me, and that there's not a damn thing I could do to stop it."

"So why fight?" she asked. "Because you're punishing yourself?"

He didn't answer, didn't even seem to breathe.

"What happened at that conference wasn't your fault, Kendric. What happened to Battle Mountain wasn't your fault, and these scars are as much a part of you as that thick skull on your shoulders. They don't make you any less of a man or a father to that little girl." Campbell set her hand over his face, against his scars. There was nowhere for him to run. Nowhere to hide here in this small cab of the SUV. "Are you really willing to give up a shot at a family, at being happy, because you refuse to see yourself the way everyone else does?"

"What if she's scared of me?" His words barely registered over the white noise of slushy water and pavement, but they'd struck right through to her heart. His gaze found hers. "What if she won't love me because I look like this?"

A pair of headlights switched to high beams behind them, filling the vehicle and the mirrors with blinding light. It highlighted Kendric's jawline and cast shadows under his eyes.

Campbell removed her hand from his heated face, not really sure how to answer.

His gaze locked on the rearview mirror. He lifted his foot off the accelerator, and the SUV's momentum nudged her forward in her seat. But the pickup refused to go around. Kendric's eyes volleyed between the road ahead and the mirror.

"What are you doing?" she asked.

"This guy won't get off my tail." His knuckles whitened under his grip around the steering wheel.

She spun in her seat, but the brightness of the high beams kept her from seeing through the vehicle's windshield to the driver. Her heart rate picked up. The truck was too close for her to catch the front license plate through the back window. "You think we're being targeted?"

"There's only one way to find out. Tighten your seat

belt." Kendric slowed even further, pulling off the side of the road. The belt cut into her shoulder and across her chest as the lights from behind skidded through the cabin of the SUV. The pickup had slammed on the brakes to avoid running into the back of them a split second before Kendric accelerated away from the hood of the second vehicle. Any other driver would've passed by now. Why weren't they?

"I've got a license plate. ADL 211. Colorado. Registration current." The license plate disappeared beneath the bottom edge of the back window. Right before the pickup truck tapped their fender. The jerk thrust Campbell forward, and she gripped the front dash. She grabbed for the radio velcroed to the middle console and hit the push-to-talk-button. "Battle Mountain PD, this is Detective Dwyer, CBI. Officer in need of assistance. Interstate 550. We've got a pickup truck trying to run us off the road. Repeat. Officer in need of assistance. License plate number—"

"Hang on!" Kendric secured an arm across her midsection.

The pickup rammed them a second time.

The radio fell from her hand as the back of their vehicle fishtailed. Kendric tried to keep control of the slide, but freezing temperatures had turned the shoulders of the interstate into an ice rink. Her fingers ached as she braced for impact. "Kendric!"

The back tire caught on something along the road.

Before she had a chance to scream, the fender ripped free of the shoulder and took flight. The hood of their SUV dipped toward the road. Glass shattered from impact and cut across her oversensitive skin. Pain lanced through her temple and across her forehead, but she couldn't distinguish the source. The ground rolled up and over through the windshield as gusts of blistering wind filled the cabin. Metal screeched—too loud—in her ears.

Until there was nothing but silence.

Tendrils of black encroached around the edges of her vision. The lights from the dashboard flickered in and out. Or was that her head playing tricks on her? The high-pitched whine of pavement water and tires filtered through the hard pulse of her heartbeat behind her ears. A vehicle slowing down to help?

Gravity increased its hold on her, the seat belt doing its job keeping her in place, as she realized they'd landed upside down. Snow mixed with broken glass along the ceiling like sparkling diamonds just within reach. That was a weird thought. Searing pain pinched along her forehead, and she managed to bring her hand to the source. Blood crevassed inside of her fingerprints and highlighted the unique loops and whorls. She'd hit her head. She must've sustained a concussion. She had to get out of here. They both did. Blinking to clear the encroaching haze, Campbell stretched her bloodied hand to the driver's side of the vehicle. "Kendric."

No answer.

His face turned away from her, Kendric wasn't moving, and a deep-seated panic took hold. No. No, no, no, no. Her hand shook as she pressed two fingers to the base of his throat. A pulse. He had a pulse. It was unsteady, but it was there. He was still alive. Her lungs released the breath she hadn't realized she'd been holding. "Come on. Wake up. We have to move."

Someone had run them off the road. Targeted them.

They couldn't sit here waiting for whoever it had been to finish the job.

Campbell hit the release for her seat belt. Collapsing against the ceiling of the SUV, she moaned as broken glass embedded into the palms of her hands and left shoulder. It didn't matter. She couldn't think about the pain right now.

Footsteps penetrated through the rough exhalations burning up her throat. Movement registered through the back driver's-side window. A pair of boots. Campbell stilled. A Good Samaritan would already be on the phone calling for emergency help. Whoever was on the other side of the vehicle stood stock-still, as though waiting for her and Kendric to make a run for it. Her breath shuddered past her lips as she reached for her sidearm still holstered at her hip.

Cold metal warmed in her hand. One second. Two. She visually followed the boots back toward the other vehicle. A deep growl from the truck's engine vibrated through the frame of the SUV. Relief crashed through her, and Campbell closed her eyes. The driver was leaving.

Setting her weapon against the asphalt now exposed from the broken windshield, she braced one arm against Kendric's shoulder and hit the release for his seat belt. A groan escaped his lacerated throat and mouth.

"I'm going to get you out of here. Okay? Hang on. Help is already on the way." Every muscle in her body protested as she fisted both hands into his jacket and pulled him toward her passenger-side door. There was no telling how much damage he'd sustained until the ambulance and backup arrived, but she would keep him alive. Whatever it took. Her shoulder socket threatened to dislocate as she cleared his body from the vehicle, her instincts on fire. "Why did you have to put on so much…muscle? Why couldn't you consider how it would be for me to drag you across the snow?"

A pinch burned at the base of her neck.

Campbell dropped her hold on Kendric and turned to confront whoever had sneaked up behind her. Too slow. A solid strike across the face thrust her hands first into a foot of snow.

The same pair of boots she'd noted through the SUV's back window penetrated the edge of her vision. "Hello, Detective Dwyer. I think it's time we talked."

She moved to sit back on her heels to get a better look at her attacker, but the world went black.

Chapter Seven

Dying wasn't supposed to be this hard.

Sirens chirped from somewhere off to his right and triggered a splitting headache unlike anything he'd felt before. Kendric forced his eyes open, staring up into a seamless blanket of gray. White flakes drifted from above and melted against his face. What the hell… "Son of a bitch."

Pain lanced through his chest where the seat belt had bruised his sternum and shoulder. Another ache made itself known across his hips as he tried to haul himself up to sit. The red and blue lights blurring at a distance were too bright. Most likely a sign of a concussion or some other kind of head wound. Nothing he hadn't survived before. This time an entire building wasn't threatening to come crashing down at the slightest nudge. Just his pride. "Campbell, you okay?"

He scrubbed both eyes with one hand. No answer. Snow soaked through his jeans and jacket as he fought to stand. The slam of two car doors triggered a low ringing in his ears. An endless ocean of white stretched out in front of him.

"Kendric?" a familiar voice asked. "What the hell happened?"

He turned, putting two police officers in sight. Both

in uniform, armed and looking at him as though he were some kind of caged animal ready to attack. His brain worked to come up with their names, falling short. But he knew them. He recognized their faces. He just couldn't... He pointed at one. "That's a good question, Officer..."

"Ford." Confusion contorted the man's face. Easton's name clicked into place as the former army ranger took a step toward him. "Macie got a request from Detective Dwyer for backup. Said someone was trying to run you off the road. We headed out as soon as we got the call, but it looks like we were too late. You okay, man?"

Ford. Right. He knew that. Recognition supplied the name of the officer at Easton's side. Alma Majors assessed him from head to toe with the darkest brown eyes he'd ever seen, but kept her distance. The Latina archeologist turned reserve officer had been instrumental in taking down Agent Freehan and preventing the rest of Battle Mountain from going up in flames. "Yeah. I must've hit my head. I forgot your name there for a second."

Kendric shook his head. A hulking metal frame demanded attention, and everything inside of him went cold. The flash of high beams, the pickup truck raging at them in the rearview mirror, Campbell's scream as they'd rolled. He forced himself to take a deep breath as the past superimposed over the present.

"Why don't you take a seat, Kendric? You're looking a little out of it." Easton set one hand under Kendric's elbow as Alma took up position on the other side. "The ambulance is two minutes out. Let them give you a once-over before we get your official statement."

"I need to see Campbell," he said. "Where is she?"

"She's not here." Alma pressed her thumb into his forehead to get him to look at her, and a bolt of lightning shot across his vision. And with it another round of pain.

"What do you mean? She was in the passenger seat next to me." He jerked from both of their holds. A good solid foot of snow battled to slow him down, but there wasn't anything that would stop him from getting to Campbell. "Campbell! She's still in the SUV. She might be injured. Help me. Campbell!"

"Kendric, we already searched the vehicle. There's no one inside." Easton's voice softened as Kendric dived for the passenger-side door. "The seat belt is intact. She wasn't thrown free from the wreckage."

Hinges screamed as he nearly ripped the door free from the frame, exposing Campbell's sidearm inside. No. This didn't make sense. Kendric spun toward the open field splayed out for miles. "She was right here. She wouldn't just leave." There was only one explanation. "Something must've happened. The driver of the pickup. The one who ran us off the road, they must've taken her. She must've dragged me out of the wreckage, and they ambushed her."

"Who?" Alma asked.

Pent-up anger, bitterness and resentment he'd denied all these years erupted. Kendric squeezed his eyes closed and pressed his palms on either side of his head. They'd had the license number of the vehicle. Hell, why couldn't he remember? "I don't know, but it has to have something to do with this case. The missing woman. Sabrina Bryon. We were coming back from interviewing the husband. He's the only surviving witness. Maybe someone didn't want us to bring back information.

Maybe Sabrina Bryon isn't who we thought she was. It doesn't matter. I have to find Campbell."

He bolted for the police cruiser. Only when he'd moved to climb behind the wheel, Easton Ford clamped a hand on the driver's-side door.

"Think about this, Hudson. You have no idea where the detective is, if she was taken, who took her or if she's still alive." The war vet refused to budge. "You could be wasting time trying to guess where she was taken, or worse, you could be running straight into a trap. You need to think this through. Come up with a plan before you go off half-cocked."

Kendric didn't have time for this. Neither did Campbell. "Is that what you did for Genevieve when the Contractor had her?" He knew better than to mention Ford's partner. The Alamosa district attorney had barely walked away with her life by the time a serial killer had drilled two screws into each of her knees and left her in a wheelchair. He shifted his attention to the town's rookie officer. "Is that what Cree did for you, Alma? Waited until the time was right? Until he had a plan? Like Agent Freehan was just sitting there waiting for him to come rescue you."

Neither of his fellow officers voiced an answer, and in that silence, he had his own. "That's what I thought." He ripped the door free from Easton's grip and started the cruiser. Fishtailing away from the wreckage, Kendric kept his eyes forward. Not just on the road but the future. Because no matter how many times he'd tried to tell himself otherwise, Campbell was part of his life. They'd become inextricably linked the moment she'd discovered she was pregnant with their daughter, and faced with the possibility of losing her now, he wasn't ready to give up that connection. "Tell me where you are, Campbell."

He scanned the road, looking for signs of a turn-off, tire tracks—anything that would lead him to her. Campbell was a detective. She was trained to take care of herself, and she knew him inside and out. She'd leave something behind for him to follow. She'd know he'd come for her once he realized she'd been taken. Didn't she?

A wave of dizziness distorted his vision, and the cruiser drifted into the oncoming lane. A horn blared from the other side of the road, and Kendric jerked the wheel back. He had to keep going. He had to find her. He wasn't going to let someone take her from Penny. He wasn't going to lose her again. Squeezing his hands against the steering wheel, he leaned forward to get a better angle of a small disturbance in the snow up ahead. A turnoff? Private property? Hard to tell. The incoming storm would do whatever it took to bury evidence. Whatever it was, he had to take the chance.

Water kicked up alongside the car as he took the turn off the interstate. He hadn't come this far out of town before. There'd been no need while Battle Mountain fought to get back on its feet. Crime, for the most part, had taken a vacation while townspeople tried to recover from the devastation of a forest fire and losing their historic Main Street. Unfamiliar territory stared back at him as he maneuvered the vehicle to a crawl along the unpaved road.

Alma Majors's question echoed on an endless loop. On top of that, why take Campbell at all? Why not him? They'd both been involved in the investigation into Sabrina Bryon's disappearance from the beginning. If the goal had been information, it would've been easier to get access to Battle Mountain's reports through him. Had she been injured to the point the abductor had disregarded her as a threat or just a smaller target, easier to handle? Did that mean Campbell was hurt and needed medical assistance?

He didn't have answers. Right now, they didn't matter. Getting to Campbell. That was all he could focus on. The hood of the cruiser dipped and revolted with the rise and fall of the terrain.

A single structure took shape up ahead, and his pulse rocketed into his throat. A barn that had seen better days and lighter storms stood stark against the backdrop of white-sheet mountains and the colorless expanse of property. He wasn't sure where he was or who this place belonged to. Somewhere between the edge of town and a quarter of the way to Grand Junction. Out of the way. Isolated. Private. The perfect place to bring a hostage.

Kendric shoved the cruiser into Park, careful to keep his distance in case he spooked anyone inside. The best chance he had of making sure Campbell made it out alive was utilizing the element of surprise. He wouldn't fail her. Not again.

Unholstering his sidearm, he released the magazine, counted the number of rounds inside and shoved it back into place. There was no telling what lay beyond the double-wide barn doors, but he wouldn't stop now. Couldn't. For the sake of Campbell's life and for their daughter's.

He shouldered out of the cruiser. His ankles disappeared into a foot of snow. He could already see a fresh set of tire tracks leading up to the barn ahead. He couldn't approach directly. He'd have to come in from the trees. Heavy flakes threatened to hold him back as he hit the tree line and jogged around the back of the barn. Branches scratched at the skin of his face and neck and caught on his jacket. Numbness had already taken hold in his toes and fingers. Every minute he spent out here was another minute he risked hypothermia. Or worse.

Campbell was worth it.

She was worth everything.

His teeth chattered as he pulled up short of a single weathered door at the back of the structure. Pressing his ear to the splintered panel, he listened for movement—anything that could tell him what waited on the other side. Nothing but silence. "I'm coming, Bell."

Kendric stepped back, raised one leg and targeted the space next to the old lock with his heel. The door burst open wide. He didn't wait for an answering attack and rushed through a thick layer of dust and falling snow. "Campbell!"

He scanned the bare space for signs of life.

The barn was empty.

"Time to wake up, Detective," an unfamiliar voice said.

Water splashed against Campbell's face, shocking her out of a dream she couldn't quite hold on to. Her lungs spasmed for air, and she tipped her head back as her body caught up with her circumstances. She felt heavy, out of it. Dizzy. The back of her neck burned, but the zip ties securing her hands behind her kept her from reaching up and feeling for the source of the pain. "Where am I?"

"Somewhere no one will hear your calls for help." The voice from behind warbled. Not male. Not female.

Going from one octave to the next seamlessly as though not quite real. Part of her dream? The distinct sound of a gun slide reached her ears. "I tried to warn you off from searching for Sabrina Bryon with that note and snow globe on your car, but it seems you're as determined as I used to be as an investigator."

"You're... You're a cop." Campbell took in the wood-slatted floor beneath the chair she'd been strapped to, her ankles bound to the chair legs. No give in the zip ties. Nothing to leverage against the plastic to escape. The muscles in her neck failed to hold her head upright, and her chin dropped forward. The drug. Whatever she'd been dosed with hadn't yet worn off, limiting her ability to fight back. "That's how you knew to burn Sabrina's vehicle. How you were able to shoot Elliot Bryon in such a close grouping."

A laugh tendrilled through what looked like an abandoned ranger station. "Not quite. Although it would make sense, wouldn't it? I was put through a vigorous training similar to law enforcement. I just wasn't ever in the business of carrying a badge."

What the hell did that mean? Campbell caught movement through the thick coat of dust of a window just below the roofline of the small structure. A tree? Kendric? Her heart squeezed in her chest. She'd gotten him out of the wreckage after her abductor had run them off the road, but had he survived? "And the woman we found near the Bryon home? Who was she?"

"An unfortunate case of collateral damage." Footsteps registered, and Campbell struggled to bring her head up in time to catch a glimpse of her captor. In vain. "Someone whose life Elliot was willing to risk to get what he wanted, but that's not what I want to talk about right now, Detective Dwyer."

Another pinch at the base of her neck shot searing pain up through her spinal cord and along the synapses in her brain. Her scream echoed off the exposed rafters overhead and shook down through her hands clenched around the chair's arms. She tried to stomp her feet to counter the sensation, but it was no use. The fire burning through her veins refused to let up, hiking her heart rate into overdrive.

"Now, I'm sure you're familiar with sodium thiopental and its effects on slowing down the messages between your brain and your spinal cord. Crime and forensic dramas love to claim it as some kind of truth serum, but we both know reality doesn't always live up to our hopes." An outline maneuvered in front of her, dragging an identical chair to Campbell's closer. Her abductor took a seat, but trying to get her brain to narrow down specific details triggered another round of dizziness. "I like to use it to get people to focus. See, the best thing about this kind of drug is its ability to keep your brain from straying off topic."

"What do you want?" The question barely escaped her mouth.

"After your visit to Chelsea Ingar's home earlier today, I thought I should get to know you, Detective. The way you think, the way you carry out your investigations. The more I know about you, the better chance I have of making sure you never find Sabrina." The kidnapper's voice dipped another octave, words fusing together and breaking apart over and over until they became clear. "I've read your file. You have a very impressive case history, but none of it tells me why the

Colorado Bureau of Investigations sent you to Battle Mountain to search for Sabrina Bryon. She's a nobody. Not even a blip on your radar. So, what are you really doing here?"

She couldn't. Campbell shook her head as she battled against the drug's effects. Her vision wavered as she tried to memorize the pattern on her abductor's shirt. Red, blue and green plaid, but not flannel. Sweat built in her hairline the harder she tried to keep her story straight. "Tell me what happened to Kendric."

"Not until I get what I want," her kidnapper said.

A lie. Campbell had been through enough interrogations to see the carrot at the end of the stick. Interrogators promised the world for a grain of truth, but she was stronger than this. She wouldn't break. She couldn't. "I…was the most qualified."

"Tsk. Tsk. Tsk." Her abductor leaned forward. Sharp pain exploded at the back of Campbell's head as the kidnapper fisted a handful of hair. Black fabric swam in and out of focus. A ski mask. "I don't want half-truths, Detective. I want the whole story. Why did the CBI send you to Battle Mountain?"

"No." Strain tightened the tendons on either side of her neck. Her fingers tingled from the zip ties cutting off her circulation. She was hot and cold at the same time and wanted nothing more than… "Hot shower, bed. Penny. Kendric."

Had she said that out loud? Campbell squeezed her eyes shut, willing time to rewind, but as her abductor had said, that wasn't how reality worked. Her teeth chattered as the drug took a stronger hold on her nervous system.

The outline in front of her released their hold on her

hair, and Campbell fell back against her chair. "Kendric Hudson. Your partner. I didn't realize the two of you were so close. Who's Penny?"

She had to fight. She had to be strong. "My daughter."

Anger festered at the back of her mind. Every word she thought escaped her mouth, a risk she couldn't afford. Keep her mouth shut. That was all she had to do, and she couldn't even do that. "No."

"I see. You're trying to protect her." Her abductor's voice softened. "Is that why you haven't told Battle Mountain PD and your partner that you're with Internal Affairs? I can't imagine they'd want anything to do with you if they knew the truth."

Her gaze snapped to her captor's and triggered a whole new round of dizziness the likes of which she'd never experienced. The world tilted on its axis as her body dragged to one side of the chair. But still she didn't fall. "You don't know what you're…talking about."

"It's obvious now. CBI sent you under the guise of recovering Sabrina Bryon, but your real assignment is to investigate the very people trying to find her. Clever, really. You already had your way into the department's good graces." Her abductor stood, rounding the chair in front of Campbell. "But you're afraid that if the people you've investigated will retaliate, they'll come after your daughter in revenge."

Campbell's darkest fear took control. Her fingernails cut into the base of her palms as the repercussions of her career played out in front of her eyes like they had so many times before. There was an undeniable oath law enforcement officers took upon themselves once they joined the force. Watch each other's backs. Stand together, no matter the cost. Once you were part of it, you were family. That was the deal. But for some, that oath corrupted those looking to put themselves above the law. Convinced them their brothers and sisters in blue would never turn on them or expose them for what they really were. Gave them a sense of immunity.

The men and women she investigated were law enforcement. They had the skills, training and drive to tear her world apart if they discovered the truth. They wouldn't just hurt her for betraying that created family. They'd hurt everyone she ever loved if given the inclination. Her parents. They'd take Penny just to watch Campbell suffer. "Please…she's just a child. Please."

"Don't worry, Detective Dwyer, I'm not here to out you. I have no interest in seeing an innocent child hurt because of the choices of those who are supposed to love them made." The black ski mask was suddenly a few inches from her face. Piercing dark eyes—green at one angle, brown at another—zeroed in on her. A calloused hand squeezed Campbell's chin. "Focus, Detective. This is important. All I want is information about your investigation. You visited Chelsea Ingar's home. You talked to her. What did she say about Sabrina?"

Every inch of her skin tingled. Her exhalations crystallized in front of her mouth. It was so cold. She could hardly curl her fingers. She'd lost the ability to feel her toes. "N-nothing. She claimed she didn't know Sabrina, but the phone records—"

"That's good. What else have you uncovered during your investigation? What is your next move?" the outline asked.

"Move?" The edge of the chair seat bit into the backs of her legs. She blinked to clear the last of the dizziness.

The gut-wrenching cry of an infant twisted her head to one side. Had she really heard it? Sodium thiopental wasn't supposed to induce hallucinations but mimic the state of being half-awake and half-asleep. This... this didn't feel right. Something was wrong. "The baby. Where is the baby?"

Her abductor dropped their hand from her face. "What baby?"

"I hear the baby. It's crying. Don't you hear it?" The same way Penny's cries tightened the muscles in her midsection, hearing another child cry initiated a temporary panic that urged her to help. Campbell searched the space, but there was no sign of an infant or that this place was anything more than a cell to be used at her interrogator's whimsy. She wasn't losing her mind. Her voice turned to a whisper. "Don't you hear it?"

"You're reacting to the drug, Detective. There is no baby. There's no one here but you and me." A hard grip on her arm kept her grounded. "Now, tell me what else you know about Sabrina Bryon's disappearance."

Campbell forced her attention from the brown-laced boots she'd memorized at the crash site to the woman standing in front of her. "I know you're her."

Chapter Eight

His gut instinct had led him wrong.

Kendric had searched every damn inch of the abandoned barn. No sign of the truck. No sign of the abductor. No sign of Campbell. He was back at square one and out of time. "Where are you, woman?"

His breath solidified in front of his mouth. The sun had started dipping behind the mountains. While Elliot Bryon's statement didn't sit well, the evidence did. The man who'd claimed his wife had gone off the deep end was stuck in a hospital bed with two bullet wounds in his chest. He hadn't taken Campbell from the wreckage, but could an eight-months-pregnant woman? Despite dropping temperatures, sweat built at his hairline and threatened to throw his body into hypothermia. He had to slow down. He had to think.

Whoever had shot Elliot Bryon—whether Sabrina Bryon or not—was familiar with the area. They'd have to be to stay off BMPD's radar, which meant they wouldn't have chosen a random location to bring a hostage. They'd have done their homework, made sure there was no connection back to the Bryon family. Kendric unpocketed his phone and scrolled to Macie Barclay's number.

The line rang once. Twice. The dispatcher didn't indulge in any pleasantries. "Kendric, I've been trying to get through to you for the past thirty minutes. Easton and Alma said you just took off from the crash site. Do you have any idea—"

"Macie, listen to me." He scanned the barn again, catching sight of a satellite structure through one of the windows. One he hadn't noticed on his drive in. He crouched to get a better view. "Campbell—Detective Dwyer—has been taken, and I need your help."

"Tell me what you've got." The sarcastic, bohemian redhead Kendric found difficult to talk to turned all business.

"Campbell and I visited a woman named Chelsea Ingar earlier this morning. She claimed she doesn't have any connection to Sabrina Bryon, but phone records tell a different story."

"I know Chelsea. Married into one of Battle Mountain's oldest families. Doesn't socialize a whole lot, but I've talked to her a few times at the Baptist church annual picnic. She's always been nice to me, if a little rabbity." Macie lowered her voice as though afraid to get caught up in gossip. "Wait, you think she might be involved in what's going on?"

"I don't know, but it's all I have. I need you to run a property search on the Ingars. Anything out by the interstate." He needed something—anything—to get him closer to Campbell. Kendric backtracked through the door he'd busted past and hiked in thick snow toward the garage-looking structure he'd spotted from the barn. "Anything?"

"Hold your britches, Hudson. It takes a few minutes to break the chief's protocols and run property searches behind his back. But you and I both know I'm going to have to fill him in once he's finished with his midday crash on his keyboard." Distinct taps filtered through the line. "Here we go. Looks like there's a good four acres of land registered to Budd Ingar, Chelsea's husband, not far from your current location."

Kendric pulled up short of the garage and studied the dense line of trees closing in. "How do you know where I'm at?"

"It's not because I put a tracker in your bootheel when you weren't looking," she said. "I'd never do that."

He kicked up his back heel. It was a joke. The dispatcher never would've had access to his boots. Except those first couple of weeks he'd stayed at Whispering Pines Ranch/temporary Battle Mountain PD station while the old station was brought back to life. No. She wouldn't have. He would've noticed. "Where's the property?"

"Keep heading west. You're practically on the border. Kendric, in all seriousness, be careful. The Ingars aren't known for hospitality—" The phone cut out.

Kendric closed in on the dilapidated structure ahead. Tire tracks disappeared under the beaten and weathered garage door. Fresh. Not more than an hour old if he had to guess. The edges of the imprints were still razor-thin. No hint of erosion. He crouched, wrenching the heavy door above his head. And exposed a pickup with a dented fender parked inside. An echo of Campbell's voice raced through his head. *ADL 211*. This was the truck. The one that had run them off the road. He set his hand over the hood. Still warm. "You couldn't have gotten that far."

Unholstering his weapon, he rounded to the driver's

side of the vehicle and pried open the door. Warm air escaped the cabin as he studied the interior. A hint of bleach tickled the back of his throat. Hell. The entire inside had been wiped down. Steering wheel, dashboard, even the leather seats. No chance for prints or DNA, but considering how far Sabrina Bryon had gone to cover her tracks, he shouldn't have expected any less. Pulling himself inside, Kendric went for the glove box and tugged the vehicle's registration free. "Ingar."

Made sense. The truck was being stored on land registered to the same owners, but were they aware of what someone had done in their name?

"You're going to want to get of out my husband's truck real slow." The feminine voice barely registered over the cocking of a shotgun held in the hands of a woman too small to shoulder it correctly. One pull of that trigger and Chelsea Ingar would find herself in a world of pain. "Now."

Guess that answered his question. Kendric raised his hands in surrender, the truck registration still in one hand, as he slid from the driver's seat. His weapon stared back at him from the leather seat, but he only had attention for the five-foot woman who'd caught him with his hands in the cookie jar. "Chelsea, good to see you again."

"This is private property. Battle Mountain PD has no right to step foot on this land without my permission, and I sure as hell don't remember giving you permission when you came to my house this morning." Chelsea Ingar's nervous gaze darted from Kendric to the truck and back. This wasn't the spitfire mother of three he'd met this morning. No. This was a woman on the edge. Afraid he'd found something inside?

Kendric stayed within arm's reach of his sidearm. Although, he hoped to hell and back he wouldn't have to use it. "Oh, good. You do remember me. Then you'll also remember the woman I was with. Detective Dwyer. She's gone missing."

"What does that have to do with me?" Chelsea adjusted her grip on the shotgun.

"Maybe nothing," he said. "Maybe everything. You lied to us this morning when you said you didn't know Sabrina Bryon. You've been in contact with her. You've been helping her. Now, I'm not sure how much she's told you about what happened with her husband and his mistress, but I can guarantee you're helping her with faulty information. Someone used this truck to run me and my partner off the interstate about an hour ago, and now my partner is missing."

"It wasn't supposed to be like this," she said.

"I can understand you're a woman lodged between a rock and a hard place. You want to do what's best for your friend. You're trying to help, but Sabrina Bryon isn't who you think she is, Chelsea." Kendric angled himself behind the driver's-side door. "Do yourself a favor. Put down the gun. Think about those kids you've got back home. Think about Budd. What shooting me will do to your family."

A humorless laugh escaped the woman's throat, and suddenly the woman's nerves weren't what Kendric was most worried about. "You want me to think about Budd? No, Officer Hudson. You don't want me to think about my husband with his shotgun in my hands. Not unless you won't miss your organs." Chelsea Ingar shifted her weight between both feet. "You want to know how Sabrina and I met? In the clinic in town. She was there to get a checkup on the baby while I was there to see if the one I had was still alive after my husband was finished with me. She was nice. She listened to me. She held me while I cried right there in the middle of the damn waiting room. No one had ever done that for me. My family doesn't believe me when I tell them what a monster he's been since he lost his job in the mines, and his family only reminded me that's the cost of marrying an Ingar. Sabrina was the only one who cared, the only one who was just as angry as I was. Do you really think I was going to turn my back on her when she needed my help?"

"So you lent her Budd's pickup, told her about the property out here to give her a place to hide until she could get out of town," he said. "If anyone came asking, you were to deny you knew each other. Did she tell you what happened with her husband?"

"She didn't have to tell me." The weight of the shotgun exhausted Chelsea's arms, and the barrel dipped lower. "I could see it on her face when she showed up on my doorstep after Budd had left for the liquor store. I could see the blood on her clothes. I didn't ask questions. I just handed her the keys to the truck and this address."

Kendric slipped his hand along the driver's-side door, closer to his sidearm. "You wanted to help her same as she helped you. I can appreciate that. Truth is, I'm in the same kind of position with my partner. You see these scars?" He motioned to the right side of his face. "I spent eight weeks in the hospital burn unit recovering after a bomb blew up in my face. Every time I woke up, no matter what time of day, she was there. When I look back, I realize she's the reason I pulled through, of why I'm standing here today. Now, all I want to do is help her, but I can't do that without you, Chelsea. I need you to tell me where Sabrina is keeping her."

"I don't know." Chelsea shook her head. "I haven't heard from her since yesterday morning. I waited until Budd passed out, dropped the kids off with my neighbor and came up to check on her."

"All right, then. I believe you. So, what are you going to do now?" His heart rate kicked into overdrive as his gaze lowered to the end of her shotgun staring right at him. "Are you going to kill an unarmed man, a Battle Mountain police officer, for Sabrina? Are you going to let her kill my partner? She has a daughter, too. A four-year-old. Are you going to leave her little girl without a mother?"

Her eyes watered with unshed tears as Chelsea positioned her index finger over the trigger. "You weren't supposed to be here. Neither of you were."

He wasn't getting through to her.

"Chelsea, listen, I can help you. I can make sure you and your kids walk away from this. I can make sure you get away from Budd. We can forget it ever happened." Kendric slipped his hand around his weapon, heart in his throat, as the seconds ticked by. "But you need to hand me the shotgun."

"I'm sorry, Officer Hudson." Chelsea took aim. "I can't do that."

A gunshot exploded through the garage.

A GUNSHOT.

Campbell heard it clear as day. It had been close. Within at least a quarter of a mile. Someone was out there. Someone was coming. Kendric? Her chest tightened as she considered the danger he'd walk into by coming after her, countered by the hope he had.

The watery outline of her captor in front of her twisted toward a single window on the opposite wall of the ranger station.

The drug was still messing with her senses, but they were getting clearer every second. She just had to focus. Campbell swung her left elbow out wide to twist the zip tie securing her to the chair. "You have no idea what you've done, do you? What kind of hell you're bringing down on yourself? Save yourself the trouble and let me go. You don't want to face what's on the other side of that door."

"You're trying to scare me, to get me to react irrationally, but I promise, Detective Dwyer, I'm thinking clearer than I have in years." A femininity tinted her abductor's words, then faded, verifying Campbell's theory. Sabrina Bryon had run them off the road. She'd drugged Campbell, brought her here to interrogate her about the investigation, but the woman's shape wasn't that of an expecting mother. Not entirely.

Campbell caught herself in the middle of the thought. That didn't make sense. Were the drugs still altering her perception, or had Sabrina Bryon been lying about the pregnancy all along? She recalled the pregnancy pillow discovered with Jane Doe—now Rachel Stephenson— in the woods near the primary crime scene.

Sabrina withdrew a weapon Campbell hadn't noted from the small of her back and turned to face her hostage. "No one is coming for you. Not until I get what I want."

"I've answered all of your questions. You made sure of that." Closing her eyes, Campbell fought to regain control of her own body, but the drug, coupled with dropping temperatures, had stolen every last ounce of her defenses. "I don't have anything else to say to you."

"Sure, you do." Sabrina Bryon slipped the ski mask from her face. A tumble of curly auburn hair staticked against the fabric. Wide brown eyes targeted Campbell as her abductor took her seat again, but the woman smiling out from the photos in the Bryon home didn't compare to the real version. Smooth skin unmarked by scars or age, straight white teeth. "While I have the training and skills to carry out an investigation of my own, you can appreciate how limited I am considering the police have posted officers guarding my husband's hospital room."

Campbell couldn't hold back her disbelief, and a scoff escaped her fraying control. "So that's what this is about. Your husband. Why lie about the baby?"

Surprise countered the hard set of Sabrina's mouth. "Who said I was lying?"

"We found a pregnancy pillow at the scene, and you're obviously not eight months pregnant." Campbell's gaze drifted down the length of her abductor's body without her consent, her attention locking on a darker stain near the woman's breast. "Why convince your husband and everyone in town you're expecting? To what end?"

Sabrina sat back in her chair, the gun laid across her lap. "You really have no idea who or what you're investigating, do you, Detective? I wasn't lying. I was pregnant."

"But you're not anymore." Her gut clenched. She'd thought she'd imagined it. The cry of an infant nearby. Campbell took in the bareness of the ranger station, the dust, the growth of weeds long dead through the floor slats. "You had the baby."

Her abductor leaned forward. "Let me guess. Elliot told you I was the one who shot him. That I'm the one who went off the deep end when I found out I was pregnant. Do you believe him?"

Campbell didn't know what to say, what to think. Sabrina Bryon had been forced to give birth in this place, without support, without a medical team to make sure nothing went wrong. How? How had she done it? Why did it matter? There'd been a gunshot not far from here. If Kendric had been on the receiving end, he was running out of time. She had to get out of here. She had to get to him. Campbell lowered her voice and dropped her head, succumbing to the drug entirely. "It doesn't matter what I believe. I follow the evidence."

"And what is the evidence telling you, Detective?" Sabrina got even closer, burying the gun in her lap.

"That you're out of time." Campbell brought her head up fast. The back of her skull connected with Sabrina's chin. The zip tie around her left wrist snapped with added effort, and she shoved her abductor away.

Sabrina and her chair tipped backward.

The gun fell from her abductor's grip and slid across the floor as Campbell pulled her right wrist free. Only she wasn't fast enough. A hard right hook slammed into her face as Sabrina got her footing. The floor rose to meet her as she collapsed from her ankles still tied to the chair's legs. Her fingers brushed the grip of the gun a split second before a bootheel slammed down on the back of her hand. Bones crunched beneath the weight, and Campbell's scream filled the station.

Another round of crying pierced her ears as Sabrina collected the weapon from the floor and took aim. "Hasn't anyone ever told you not to wake a sleeping baby?"

Campbell twisted onto her back as much as she could with her ankles still attached to the chair. "You don't want to do this."

"I thought you and I could be friends, Detective." Sabrina pulled the slide of the weapon back and loaded a bullet into the chamber. "But you're just like him, aren't you? A fraud."

The door of the station slammed back against the wall. A distinct outline filled the frame. "Put down the gun. Now." Kendric stood there with his weapon aimed, every ounce the police officer she'd imagined him to be. Justified. Strong. Rational. Everything she'd needed right then. "Sabrina Bryon, you are wanted for questioning in the shooting of Elliot Bryon and Rachel Stephenson, as well as vehicular assault and the abduction of a law enforcement officer."

"Officer Hudson, glad you could join us, and bullet-free and healthy, from what I can see." Sabrina kept cold eyes on Campbell. Full lips flattened, and for a moment, Campbell could've sworn there was real regret in those dark eyes. "I take it Chelsea is dead?"

"No, but she's not going to be using her right arm anytime soon." Kendric crossed the threshold. "Drop the weapon, get on your knees and put your hands over your head. Refuse and you and Chelsea Ingar can have side-by-side hospital beds, complete with your own set of matching cuffs."

"Kendric, the baby." Campbell fought to control her breathing as her memories of her own child flashed at the back of her mind. Penny. The dark stain on Sabrina's shirt had doubled in size. Breast milk. The woman had gone on the run eight months pregnant and become a mother in less than twenty-four hours. "Her baby is here. She delivered a month early. We need an ambulance."

"She's not going anywhere with you." Sabrina arced her weapon up, taking aim at Kendric. "And neither am I."

"No!" Campbell lunged off the floor.

The gun discharged before she managed to wrap both arms around Sabrina's legs. Her abductor fell back, another shot exploding close to Campbell's head. The sound had punctured her ears—too close in such a small space—but it was the heavy drop of a body that forced ice through her veins. They hit the floor as one in a tangle of limbs and survival. Her damn ankles were still bound to the chair, but she had enough movement in her upper body to wrestle the gun away and pin Sabrina Bryon to the floor. Until Campbell caught sight of her partner.

"Kendric." His name tore from her lips. Panic infused along her muscles as the world came to a crashing halt. She'd come to Battle Mountain on her own agenda. A few days ago, all Campbell had wanted was to find the source of the problems in the small sleepy mining town on the verge of collapse. Now all she could think about was what she'd lose if she left. "What did you do?"

A hard strike rocketed white lightning across her vision. "What I had to."

Campbell fell back, and she hit the floor a second

time. The bite of hardwood didn't take the sting out of her face or the grief charging up her throat as she studied Kendric's still frame.

Sabrina Bryon shot to her feet.

Reverberations of footsteps rumbled beneath her as Campbell shoved herself off the floor. Twisting one ankle at a time, she broke the zip ties securing her to the chair just as her abductor leveled her weapon at Campbell's chest.

"I gave you a chance, Detective, but if you're not with me, you're against me, and I will do whatever it takes to win." The new mother clutched a still, blanket-wrapped package to her shoulder from a closet on the other side of the room. The baby. It wasn't crying anymore, and Campbell's heart hurt at the possibility dropping temperatures had triggered the infant's body to start shutting down. "If you want to make it back to your daughter, do yourself a favor. Don't follow me."

Sabrina Bryon disappeared out the opposite entrance to the ranger station. Every cell in her body wanted to chase after the woman responsible for the shooting of three people, but she couldn't leave Kendric to bleed out.

"Kendric." Campbell raced to his side. Blood spread from a shoulder wound—too much blood—and she set both palms over the hole to contain the flow. She wasn't a field medic. She didn't know a damn thing about patching bullet wounds. "Don't you dare give up now. You hear me? Hang on."

Keeping pressure on the wound with one hand, she searched his person. She needed a radio or a cell phone. Some way to contact his department. For the second time in less than two hours, Kendric's life had been left in her hands.

And she wasn't going to let him go.

Chapter Nine

He'd come to Battle Mountain to escape the pain. Not make it his best friend.

A groan worked up Kendric's throat as he tried to roll off the arm that had fallen asleep. Another explosion of pain ricocheted across his back and down his arm. Not asleep. Oh, hell.

"You're awake." That voice. Her voice. It charged along his nerve endings and released the tension building down his spine. Campbell. He wasn't sure he'd ever hear that sweet sound again. "Take it easy. The EMT just got the bullet out."

Bullet? The past rushed to meet the present and filled in the missing holes in his memory. The crash. His race to find Campbell alive. Sabrina Bryon pulling the trigger. Warmth radiated from his right side, beading sweat at his temple. The last thing he remembered was a never-ending coldness dripping through him like an IV. Kendric rotated his wrist, flaring another round of pain. Wait. That was an IV, but this didn't feel like a hospital. Too warm. Too quiet. Dryness caked the inside of his mouth as he pried his eyelids open. Dark wood lined the ceiling and highlighted exposed rafters. The heat trying to sweat him dry was coming from a fireplace nearby. Flannel pillows, animal skins, the head of a deer mounted on the opposite wall—he certainly wasn't in Kansas anymore. "Where am I?"

"You're safe." She brushed his hair away from his forehead, staring down at him with those cerulean blue eyes he'd dreamed of so many times. Hair pulled back to expose the length of her neck and full shape of her face, Campbell had changed out of her pantsuit armor and into a white T-shirt and jeans that emphasized the bruises and cuts along one side of her face and down her arms. "You told me how much you hated hospitals. I figured you would recover easier someplace you already know. Your chief brought in an EMT to take care of the wound."

"Just in time, too. Another few minutes, and you might've bled out right there in the middle of the woods." Another outline penetrated his vision. Cold metal from a stethoscope slipped across his chest and stole a hiss from between his teeth. An elfin-thin face and wide brown eyes solidified above him as short brown hair dislodged from behind the woman's ear. Isla Vach—one of Battle Mountain fire and rescue's EMTs—stretched her mouth into a thin, compassionate line. "Sorry. I always forget to warm these things up. Vitals are stable. Should be good as new in a few weeks. Just try to take it easy until then. Got it?"

"Thank you." Campbell stood to shake the tech's hand across his bed. "For everything."

A wrap of white bandaging encircled the hand at her side. Coupled with the butterfly closure across her forehead, she obviously hadn't gotten out of this as unscathed as he'd hoped.

"Always happy to help." The EMT flashed another

weak smile as she packed her supplies and hauled her duffel bag over one shoulder. "Now, if you don't mind, a certain six-year-old is waiting for me to come home and read her a book for the thousandth time today. Glad you're okay, Hudson. Not sure we could afford to lose you with all this excitement going on." Isla didn't wait for them to answer, heading for the cabin's door.

Recognition permeated through the haze threatening to pull him back into unconsciousness. He'd visited Whispering Pines Ranch enough times to place the cozy cabin decor usually reserved for big city tourists looking for a bit of ranch life. The proprietor and owner, Karie Ford, had taken over running the place since her husband had been murdered by a serial killer going after Battle Mountain's very own coroner, Dr. Chloe Pascale. It was on this land her son Easton Ford had built his veteran rehabilitation center after his fiancée had lost the use of both legs. Recently, though, it had served as a police headquarters while the engineers tried to piece the original station back together.

"How long was I out?" Sandpaper lodged in his throat.

"Two days." Campbell trailed her thumb along the back of his hand while his two lives intersected. One after a bomb had tried to rip him apart and one where he'd believed he could actually make a difference in a small town on the brink of destruction. Funny how Campbell had been such a big part of both. "The bullet nicked your brachial artery. Isla didn't want to risk you tearing your sutures, so she gave you something to sleep to get over the first hurdle of recovery."

"And Sabrina?" he asked.

"Gone. I didn't… I didn't want to leave you to chase

after her." A hint of regret cast her gaze down where she'd interlaced her fingers with his. She'd wanted to catch Sabrina, to be the one to solve this case, and he'd just been dead weight. An obligation. Same as before. "Your officers—Easton and Alma—found Chelsea Ingar in cuffs in the cruiser. They took her into custody, got the graze on her arm patched up and have filed charges with a condition that if she gives up Sabrina Bryon, they'll drop them. So far she hasn't said anything."

"She won't talk." Unwinding his fingers from hers, Kendric struggled to sit up, forgetting all about the hole in his shoulder. Another groan tore from his throat, and Campbell moved in to help.

"You shouldn't try to move," she said. "You could start bleeding again."

"I'm fine." The words left his mouth harsher than he'd intended, but it was nothing compared to the resentment bubbling to the surface. Who had he been kidding? How the hell did he expect his new life to be any different than the old one? People didn't change. He didn't change, and he wouldn't be the reason this case failed. Kendric inched his weight to the edge of the bed and sat up, one hand slapped over the thick pads of gauze on his wound. "I know you'd rather be out there looking for Sabrina Bryon. Go. I can take care of myself."

"Chief Ford and Gregson are combing through the scene to get a lead on where Sabrina might've gone. Officer Majors is with Chelsea Ingar. Given their shared... history, I thought it best for her to take point during the interrogation." She lowered her voice, carrying far more respect for Battle Mountain PD's newest recruit than he expected. While Alma Majors's history with domestic abuse wasn't public knowledge, Campbell had made a good call. "Sabrina can't get far. She has an infant with her now. She has to think about them both, which will slow her down. The only thing I'm concerned about right now is you."

"Like I said, I can take care of myself." He needed a shower, a clean set of clothes and anything Karie Ford had lying around the kitchen. Kendric moved to stand, but his body had yet to catch up with the order. He tipped forward. He automatically commanded his wounded arm to catch his fall, and a gut-wrenching pain lanced down his back.

Campbell caught him before he face-planted in front of her. Hauling him against her hip, she angled him back down onto the edge of the mattress. "Right, and may I say, you're doing a fantastic job."

Damn it. Whatever sedative Isla had given him had wreaked havoc on his nervous system. He wasn't going anywhere anytime soon. Settled back onto the bed, Kendric forced himself to not look at her. He didn't want to see the pity there. He couldn't do this again. "Just like old times."

"Except this time, we're not separated by a hyperbaric chamber." She swiped her uninjured palm down her jean-clad thigh. "And you've still got your good looks."

Kendric's control slipped, and he raised his gaze to hers. Only there wasn't pity in her expression as he'd judged. It was something else. Something along the lines of…admiration. How was that possible? He hadn't done anything back at that ranger station but make the situation more complicated, and here she was looking back at him as though he'd saved the day. "How do you do it? How can you sit there pretending I don't look like this? Like I'm still the man you knew all those years ago?"

"Because you are the same man to me." Campbell shrugged as though she hadn't just rocked his entire world. As though her answer was the most obvious thing in the world. "No amount of circumstance or scars is going to change that. You tore through those woods looking for me the same way you tore through that building looking for civilians. I'm able to sit here without a bullet of my own because you charged into that room no matter what was waiting on the other side, same as you charged into that conference before the bomb went off. I can go back to our daughter in one piece after this case is closed, and I will always be grateful for that."

She raised her hand to his face, slowly, cautiously. "You keep telling me the man I loved all those years ago doesn't exist, but I still see him in your eyes. I felt him when you kissed me."

He braced himself for the fear and contempt that always followed physical contact, but she felt so good. Grounding and exhilarating at the same time. Warm and reliable. Perfect. "Campbell…"

"I see the idealistic, passionate, protective man I asked out for a date in the middle of that crime scene." She scanned his face from forehead to chin, and in that moment, he'd never felt more exposed. Or more trusting. "Nothing has changed for me."

Her words drilled past his defenses and tore down the self-hatred he'd been thriving on for years. She couldn't have meant what had come to mind. Not after all this time. Not after everything he'd done. "Nothing?"

"Nothing." Her wide smile flashed bright, and Campbell kissed him.

Soft lips glided against his. The action rocked him straight to his core. Every cell in his body ignited with each stroke of her tongue, and there wasn't a single part of him that could fight it. He'd convinced himself kissing her in his kitchen a few days ago had been a fluke, something that couldn't be replicated. In a way, he was right. This was nothing like that first kiss between them. In that moment, he'd never experienced anything more intense, more satisfying, and hell, it turned him inside out faster than before.

Kendric pulled her against him, immediately regretting the strain on his arm. He ended the kiss, but he was far from finished tasting her. Coming out of his wince, he opened one eye in a flood of embarrassment. "I forgot about the arm."

"It might take some getting used to," she said. "For both of us."

"Worth it." He crushed his mouth to hers.

CAMPBELL MANEUVERED OUT from under Kendric's arm and slid free from the bed.

He'd fallen asleep mere minutes after kissing her, and she couldn't blame him. The bullet had nearly killed him. Beating death once from that bombing—let alone twice—was a process. One he couldn't push through or skip steps.

The fire had died to low embers, and she set another log from the pile off to one side on top to get the heat back up. Whispering Pines Ranch was unlike anything she'd experienced before. The owner, Karie, had fed her and the entire Battle Mountain PD uncomplainingly, with warming, filling foods Campbell hadn't indulged in since she'd been a kid. Fluffy waffles, handmade hash browns, perfect eggs, sugary syrup. And that had just been for breakfast. Her parents had always ensured she hadn't gone hungry when she was growing up, but Karie Ford had no trouble making sure Campbell couldn't squeeze in another bite. And then some.

She studied the man unconscious on the bed as the new log caught fire.

This place… It felt different than Denver. Different than the CBI. Like there was a warmth she couldn't quite define. She'd listened to Easton and Weston Ford bicker and banter since the moment she'd stepped foot on the land. During the large mealtimes around the old hand-carved table for twelve. During chores around the main cabin and on the property. Even while the brothers worked to protect the town they obviously loved. Only it wasn't just them but Cree Gregson, too, a man she'd known from her former days in the sheriff's department. All of them took cheap shots with wide smiles, and when it came to the women in their lives—their mother, their partner, their fiancée, their dispatcher and the mother of their child—the connection carried through. The men and women serving this town had a bond unlike anything she'd seen in Denver, even when she'd been in the midst of it. And for the first time since she'd taken this case, she saw what Kendric saw here. A family.

These people had obviously welcomed him as one of their own. They cared. They worried and hovered like overprotective siblings. They had his back, which was more than she could say in her current position in Internal Affairs. For the officers who knew where her loyalties lay, she'd become a pariah. Someone to avoid, to fear. Every word had to be calculated, every question answered just so, so as not to raise her suspicions. She'd become an outsider in her own department when what she'd really wanted, what she'd needed, was…this. A family of her own.

But every family had secrets.

And what she and Penny had was perfect. They were happy. They were enough.

Campbell donned the pair of boots Genevieve Alexander—Easton Ford's fiancée and the district attorney of Alamosa, CO—had lent her to replace her mud-caked heels after the showdown with Sabrina Bryon. With a final glimpse to make sure Kendric was still asleep, she gathered her coat from the hook on the wall and escaped out into the night, closing the door softly behind her.

Six satellite cabins surrounded the main house. Chief Ford and Dr. Pascale in one, Cree Gregson and his partner, Alma, in another, Kendric and Campbell in the third and Easton and Genevieve in a fourth. The fifth cabin had been left empty for any tourists wanting to brave the desolate Colorado winters here in the mountains, and the sixth held the answers she needed.

Snow twinkled and crunched under her feet as she cut along the main cabin. The drift of laughter reached her ears across the barren landscape, and Campbell slowed. Lights from inside the nearest satellite cabin highlighted Cree Gregson and Alma Majors locked in an awkward dance around a small kitchen table. Both still wore their uniforms with wide smiles plastered on their faces, and before she had a chance to realize what she'd done, she'd stepped closer to get a better view.

They looked happy. In love. The way Cree stared down at his partner lodged in her mind until Kendric's face superimposed over the scene. They'd had that once upon a time. That kind of…bliss. It had been short and fleeting considering the time they'd been together, but that hadn't made it any less real or monumental. Would he ever look at her that way again? Could he after everything he'd been through? It didn't matter. Even if he'd managed to overcome his own self-loathing, she'd lied to him since the moment she'd stepped onto that crime scene four days ago. While they'd had a full and rich relationship—one that had resulted in the most beautiful little girl—they weren't compatible now. Not as long as she led the investigation into his department. Not as long as she couldn't be honest with him.

"You're out late, Detective." Chief Weston Ford left the shadows of the main house. He tossed a toothpick into the bushes lining his mother's cabin and swept his jacket back away from his weapon for another in his pocket. "Can't sleep?"

Campbell swiped at her face, only then realizing how close she'd come to blowing her cover. Had he been watching her the entire time? "Something like that. I didn't realize anyone else was still awake. Hope I didn't bother you." From the look of him fully dressed and armed, she hadn't.

"You'd think I'd sleep like a rock with the baby being up every couple of hours, but once I'm up, I'm up. Chloe, though, I don't think a marching band could disturb her," he said.

She didn't miss those days. "Wait until he can scream

your name. That'll really get your blood pumping in the middle of the night."

"I didn't realize you had children." Chief Ford bit down on the second toothpick. "Actually, I don't really know anything about you other than what Kendric has told us. You both worked for the Loveland sheriff's department before you made your way to CBI in Denver. Got a pretty good case history in missing persons under your belt. More cases closed than any of your peers. Your file doesn't say a whole lot more than that. Although, I've gotta say, it's impressive."

He'd looked into her. Of course he had. Anyone in his position would've done the same, but what was the point in telling her now? "I'm sorry I haven't had much opportunity to debrief you myself. It wasn't my intention to leave you out of my assignment. In missing persons cases, the faster I can get my feet on the ground, the better."

"Hey, I understand. When CBI sends their best investigator to help recover a missing young mother in my town, I'm not going to fight it. Anything we can do to bring her home." The chief closed in on her, completely at home with the dropping temperatures and surroundings. "What I don't understand is why you're still here."

Her instincts prickled warning. "What do you mean?"

"I mean this isn't a missing persons case anymore. This is a manhunt. We've got testimony from a witness point-blank accusing Sabrina Bryon of shooting him. Kendric gave a statement she's responsible for running the both of you off the interstate, and you were abducted by the woman for information. When we catch her, and we will, she'll be arrested for murder, attempted murder and anything else I can charge her with." Weston Ford tipped his ten-gallon hat back, exposing deep lines across his forehead. "So that leaves me wondering, why are you still here?"

Her mind instantly went to the sixth satellite cabin, but Campbell held his gaze so as not to give away anything that might compromise her assignment. Battle Mountain had gone forty years without a single homicide, but within months of Weston Ford taking the helm, there'd been two serial killers, a spree killer and a rogue ATF agent ripping through this town. She should be the last concern on his mind. "Kendric was shot. I wasn't just going to leave him."

He stared at her as though trying to see into her mind, but Campbell had perfected the art of compartmentalizing a long time ago. It was a skill that had saved her life more than once in the line of duty. His gaze flickered toward the cabin she'd targeted, before getting caught up in the couple through the window, then back to her. "You should get some rest, Detective Dwyer. If this case leads where I think it will, you and Kendric are going to need it."

He maneuvered past her, putting at least another two feet between them as he headed for the sixth cabin housing Battle Mountain PD's temporary headquarters.

She spun to meet him. "You're not taking him off the case?"

"Couldn't even if I wanted to." Chief Ford kept walking. "The man is more stubborn than he knows what's good for him. Good night, Detective."

"Good night." She watched the chief unlock the satellite cabin door and disappear into the darkness on the other side. A moment later, light filled the cracks around the covered windows. She buried her hands in her coat and retraced her steps. So much for making headway tonight. Shoving through the door to her and Kendric's cabin, she peeled out of her boots and jacket as quietly as she could, so as to not wake him.

"You're back." Gravel laced his voice and triggered a wave of goose bumps down her arms. "Good to see you haven't changed your mind."

"Just went for a walk. Ran into your chief along the way." Despite the warmth of the fire and being in such close quarters, the chill in her bones refused to abate. Had Chief Ford suspected why she'd been out tonight? Would he tell Kendric the first chance he got? Campbell slid onto the edge of the mattress, right where she needed to be. "He told me he wasn't in the business of taking his officers off their cases, even with fresh bullet wounds."

"He knows I won't back down. Not until we find Sabrina Bryon." He ran his uninjured hand along her forearm. "You're freezing."

"Not sure you know this, but it's snowing outside. That usually only happens around the freezing point." She couldn't fight the smile on her lips as she studied him. It was easy to imagine him swinging her around the kitchen, just as she'd seen Cree Gregson and Alma Majors dancing in their cabin, unaware of her attention. Easy to imagine them cozying on a couch for family movie night, his hand laid over the back of hers across the couch as Penny sat between them. Of him taking her to bed each night and waking with satisfaction every morning, of vacations and runs to the grocery store. Of being in love. All the things a family was supposed to be. Her smile faded. Those fantasies were of another life, one in which Kendric wanted to be a father and a partner and where she wasn't lying to him every second she kept a part of herself hidden. Fantasies wouldn't do either of them a bit of good.

For now, they just had to accept reality and make every moment count before they moved on with their lives. She back in Denver with Penny. He here, serving and protecting the people of this town. Her heart pinched in her chest as grief flared hot over her skin. She'd lose him again. Only this time, she wouldn't be alone.

Kendric dragged her beneath the covers, fully clothed, until she pressed against him from shoulder to toes. His heart beat steady under her hand, strong. He kissed her temple, then cuddled closer. "I think I can help warm you up."

That was what she was afraid of.

Chapter Ten

The constant reminder of something he couldn't ever have was painful.

Kendric peeled his cheek from the crown of Campbell's head. The haze of sleep had taken them both harder and faster than he'd expected. His shoulder screamed for relief as the muscles around the bullet wound stretched and relaxed at his instruction, but he wouldn't wake her. Not yet.

She turned her face up to his, still asleep in his arms. The stress lines around her mouth and eyes had faded through the night. Blond hair caught along her bottom lip, and Kendric brushed it back to get a better view. Absolutely beautiful. Intense, secretive even, but beautiful. She was right before. About Penny. The four-year-old had Campbell's eyes and blond hair, but the rest came from him, and the possibility of having both beauties in his life thawed his icy rejection of the idea he'd able to have a normal life. A family. That he deserved to be happy.

He could be happy with them.

The thought took him by surprise. The past four days had turned his entire life on its head. He'd run from Loveland, from the ATF in Denver, from the people who'd cared about him, from a daughter he hadn't known existed, and he'd ended up nearly right back where he'd started. With Campbell. Faced with the same choice all those years ago after the bombing, Kendric knew what he wanted to do this time.

Blue eyes blinked up at him, followed by a wide, close-lipped smile. Her fingers grazed the skin above his T-shirt collar, light and electric. "How long have you been staring at me without my knowing?"

"Not long." And he still couldn't look away.

"I get the feeling that's a generous estimate of time." Staring down the length of their bodies intertwined, Campbell stretched as much as the small twin bed would allow before looking back up at him. "How's the arm?"

His initial response would've compared this wound to the ones he'd sustained after the bombing, but for the first time—ever—he held back. A single event had changed the course of his entire life, but was there any point in living the rest of it in fear and bitterness when there was so much more he hadn't experienced? Warm skin slid against him as he considered all his resentment had granted him. Isolation. A hefty weight of anger. Hollowness. Loneliness. How long before it consumed him completely? Where did that path end? "Sore, but better."

"Good." She peeled herself from his side, and he immediately missed her extra warmth. She'd always run colder than him. It was why they'd never been able to share blankets in the same bed. He'd preferred to sleep with a sheet while she'd taken possession of every comforter she could buy on a good Black Friday sale. She'd lost her jeans in the middle of the night, leaving her legs bare and flawless aside from the wool socks climbing her shins. The T-shirt she'd borrowed from Dr. Pascale brushed the tops of her thighs, giving him the perfect view of lean muscle as she bent to collect her jeans. She straightened and closed her eyes.

"You okay?" Kendric moved to sit up, but his shoulder took the fight right out of him. He collapsed back. Hell. How was he supposed to bring Sabrina Bryon in when he couldn't even get himself out of bed?

Campbell finished dressing. "I can already smell bacon. I swear Karie Ford is going to single-handedly be responsible for me failing my next physical fitness test."

"Yeah. She's good at that." He rubbed at the bruises darkening across his chest. "I once tried to tell her I would only have a grapefruit for breakfast after a late night. From the look she gave me, I thought she might not let me come back."

"Is it always like this?" She stared out the small cabin window over the kitchen sink, morning light brightening the shadows under her eyes. "The big family meals, letting perfect strangers borrow clothes and jackets and boots. The teasing and jokes and laughter. It's November, and there's already a Christmas tree set up in the main house like we're in some holiday mystery movie. I mean, come on. This can't be real. It can't last with the way things are going for this town. You have to know that."

Kendric considered her question. Not the words, but her tone, the way she talked with her broken and scraped-up hands. A surge of energy helped him from the bed, and he rounded to stand in front of her. A desperation took hold in her eyes as though she needed him to tell her the truth about this place, but there wasn't anything he could say that she didn't already know for herself. "It bothers you, what we have here."

"Yes." Campbell shook her head. "No. I don't know. It's just not like any department I've come across. You guys act like you're part of this family, and I'm…" She laughed. "I don't know what I'm saying, and it doesn't really matter. I'll bring you back something to eat."

She maneuvered around him, but Kendric caught her arm, turning her into his chest. Right where he needed her. Close. Part of him. He threaded his uninjured hand through her hair as her fear solidified in her expression. "You feel it, too."

"Feel what?" she asked.

"That Battle Mountain is special." He didn't know how else to explain it. "This place… It's not just somewhere I accidentally came across as part of my investigation into Agent Freehan. It's become part of me as much as it's part of the Fords and the Ingars and anyone else who grew up in this town." The truth resonated deeper than he thought it would. "For the first time since I left Loveland, I feel at home. Like I belong, and I'm not ready to give that up. You and Penny… Your lives are in Denver. I don't want to take that away from you. Your parents and the rest of your support system are there, but…"

He wasn't sure he had the courage to reveal the need clawing at him from the inside.

"But, what?" Campbell tugged free of his hand, standing up to him in her own right. So close. Reachable. Yet still guarded.

"But after everything that happened with Sabrina Bryon, after she took you…" He could still feel the tension down his spine, echoes of the panic, of the desperation to get to Campbell. He never wanted to feel that way again. Losing her once had been hard enough. Part of him had always had hope for reconciliation, but if her abductor had followed through, that would've been the end of it. He wouldn't have had anything left but a daughter who didn't know his face, and a lifetime of regret and guilt. "I realized I wasn't ready to let go of you again. Either of you."

"What are you saying?" Her eyes glittered with hope. Campbell stepped into him, notching her chin higher.

"I'm saying my time here in Battle Mountain might be coming to an end." His gut clenched. While he'd set out to find a new normal after the bombing had stolen half the feeling in his face and then to make up for the sins of the ATF, Kendric couldn't give up the opportunity to be part of Penny's life. Or start each day waking up next to the striking missing persons investigator he'd never forgotten. He couldn't give up the chance for happiness. "Once this investigation is concluded, I want to come home. For good."

A wide smile brightened her face, and Campbell crushed her mouth to his, careful of his arm in a sling. She intertwined her fingers with his and pulled him toward the door. "Then we better see about wrapping up this investigation."

After donning their boots and coats, they stepped out into the blistering cold and crossed to the main house hand in hand. As natural a feeling as he'd ever known, her connected to him like this. It had snowed more than a few inches overnight, and the flakes were still coming down. Campbell kept a watch out for compacted ice for both of them, catching him once as they neared the steps leading up to the front porch. The door hissed open before Campbell had a chance to knock, and a wall of warmth invited them inside.

Karie Ford ushered them in with hurried motions as they kicked snow from their boots to keep from tracking sludge inside. A knowing light glimmered in the Ford matron's eyes. "It's about time you two finally got out of bed. Come on now. Everyone's waiting."

Kendric rounded into the main room, complete with bearskin rugs, mounted animal heads and hand-carved bear statues. Old tile that had seen better days spread through the two-story living room, dining room and kitchen, but it wasn't the age of the house that had him considering turning around. It was the six sets of worried eyes on him and Campbell that clenched his insides. "What?"

"Here, dear." Karie Ford handed him a fresh mug of coffee. "You look like you need this more than I do."

He took the coffee, letting the heat chase back the dread solidified at the base of his spine.

Chief Ford's gaze slipped to Campbell and back, her shoulders slightly straighter than a moment before. The youngest Ford brother anchored his arm over Dr. Chloe Pascale and their newborn son in her arms at the far end of the massive oak dining table. "You good?"

"Never better." Kendric took a seat he'd claimed as his the past few times he'd been inside the main cabin, the weight of his department's study pressurizing between his shoulder blades. He leaned back in his chair as Karie Ford set a steaming plate of biscuits and gravy in front of him and poured him a fresh glass of orange juice. She definitely knew a way to a man's heart. "You going to stare at me all during breakfast, or are you going to tell me what's on your mind?"

Campbell slid into the seat beside his, her own mug in hand. "Something happened."

"We just got word." Alma Majors folded her arms across her chest, leaning into her partner on her right side. She glanced at Cree before turning her attention back to Kendric and Campbell. "Elliot Bryon just checked himself out of St. Mary's Medical Center."

"How is that possible? He was shot point-blank twice in the chest four days ago." Kendric rolled his shoulder forward, and instant pain contorted his expression. "I can barely stay on my own two feet from a single bullet wound in my shoulder."

Campbell slid her fingers down his uninjured arm, interlocking her fingers along the backs of his.

"We're not sure." Chief Ford looked to each one of them, and in that instant she saw a man who'd shouldered the well-being of this town for years on his own. A man who liked to test the truth for himself, who would do anything to defend Battle Mountain and the people he cared about against threats. Including an internal investigation into his department. In that way, they were alike. They each believed in procedure, protocols and the law. The way Weston Ford glanced out the window every minute or so said he always kept himself on alert and reminded Campbell of herself. They were realistic, always asking questions and trying to learn as much as they could about any given subject that would help their agenda. But living like that was exhausting. She would know. "The two officers Grand Junction PD posted on his room didn't even see him leave. They're checking with hospital security and going over surveillance as we speak. My guess, Elliot Bryon waited until a shift change and took advantage of the distraction."

Her instincts flared. She'd always been good at reading people. It was what made her one of CBI's top Internal Affairs investigators, and, considering she and Chief Ford followed a similar line of thinking, she had no doubt where this conversation would lead. Campbell fit her hands around her mug. "You think Sabrina Bryon had something to do with it."

"You tell us. You're the only one here who's had a face-to-face with her before the bullets started flying." Easton Ford, in all his muscular glory and sour attitude, locked his gaze with hers as he raised a heaping spoonful of oatmeal to his mouth. The former ranger had a way of foreseeing problems before they occurred, a skill Campbell wished she'd acquired. But one that hadn't saved his fiancée's ability to walk after surviving a serial killer's attack. "Did she say anything to give you an idea she'd try to finish what she started with her husband and the woman he was sleeping with?"

"Not that I can remember. She had me drugged. Sodium thiopental. Like I said in my statement. There's not a whole lot I remember from our conversation." All eyes settled on her as though she commanded the floor, and a hint of nervousness pooled at the base of her spine. "But I can tell you, she's scared. She's on the run, a new mother without any support. She'll be sore and have very limited energy considering she had to deliver her daughter with no recovery time. She knows we're watching her phone activity and financials. She has no access to funds, and we haven't been able to determine any living family she can go to for help. Even with her training and background, she's out of her element."

"What background is that?" Cree Gregson narrowed his gaze on her. "Based on what we've put together so far, we can't even be sure if Sabrina Bryon is her real name."

"I'm not sure yet. I'm waiting for my sources at CBI to get back to me, but I can tell you she's trained in our protocols. She's familiar with the law enforcement playbook, and she knows her way around this town. She can elude police for a long time," Campbell said. "What is the crime lab saying?"

"The blood you collected from the Bryon home belongs to Elliot Bryon, which isn't a surprise considering he took two bullets and nearly bled out in his own bedroom. Jane Doe has officially been identified as Rachel Stephenson, a parts manager for the auto parts store Elliot Bryon owns. Chloe was able to compare dentals from Dr. Corsey a few hours ago." Chief Ford nodded to his new wife and mother of the son currently asleep in the coroner's arms. "For now, there's nothing in her background to suggest she was anything more than a casualty of an affair gone wrong, but we're still looking into other possibilities. The sample Isla Vach took of your blood, Detective, is identical to a batch of sodium thiopental that went missing from Sabrina Bryon's ob-gyn's office. As for Sabrina Bryon's baby, her ob-gyn verified Elliot Bryon is the father. Perfect DNA match."

"What doesn't match are the bullets recovered from Elliot Bryon during surgery to the one Isla Vach took from your shoulder, Kendric." Alma Majors set one elbow on the table and her chin in her palm. The Latina archeologist turned cop glanced at each of her fellow officers in turn. "Ballistics from Unified Forensic is still trying to ascertain if either weapon was used in any other crimes."

"Based off what Campbell has said about our suspect, Sabrina Bryon would've ditched the gun used to shoot her husband as soon as possible. She's too smart to let something like that lead us back to her, but without either gun, we have nothing solid to tie her to the death of Rachel Stephenson and Elliot Bryon's shooting." Kendric turned his attention on Campbell and squeezed her hand beneath the table, out of sight from the rest of his department. "One thing I know for sure, Elliot Bryon lied to us when we questioned him about the events in that house. He was too calm, almost calculated. He claimed he can't remember what happened. Either way, we need to find him."

Genevieve Alexander leaned forward. "You said Sabrina Bryon knows police protocols and has knowledge of forensics, but she's not a cop. We've already checked. Her fingerprints aren't registered in the database, but in Colorado, private investigators aren't required to register their prints. I can pull licenses when I get back to the office, if that will help."

A private investigator. It made sense. While most PIs tended to specialize in legal investigations and computer forensics, there were several who went the homicide investigation route. Had Sabrina Bryon been one of them? Possibly under a different name? There was only one way to find out, and it wasn't by pulling expired rosters of private investigators from Colorado's Department of Regulatory Agencies. "Thank you. That would be really helpful." Campbell released her hold on Kendric. "If you'll excuse me, I need to check in with my CO."

She didn't wait for an answer, heading for the front

door, her phone in hand. Campbell raised it to her ear just before stepping outside in case anyone at the table decided to follow. "It's me," she said to herself. From the position of the dining room—staring out at the first three satellite cabins—she hadn't been able to get eyes on the sixth cabin. And neither had anyone else.

Her CO had no interest in Sabrina Bryon's whereabouts, in the death of a mistress or a witness on the run. In fact, she'd been instructed to sever contact until she had something concrete to bring home. And she would bring this home. Something was going on in Battle Mountain, and her entire career—Penny's future—depended on her proving it. Campbell ducked beneath the dining room window as she followed the perimeter of the main cabin, just as she had the night before. Only this time Chief Ford was more occupied with his department than her. Stuffing her phone in her coat pocket, she pulled a lock picking set she'd acquired when she'd first agreed to sign on with Internal Affairs.

Agreed was a strong word. *Forced* had a more truthful ring to it. Straightening, she climbed the small set of stairs leading up to the sixth cabin and inserted the torque wench low into the keyhole with the slightest pressure. Sliding the rake along the top of the hole, she pushed it as far into the lock as it would go. Blinding sunlight reflected off glistening snow as she searched for any signs of interruption. No one had followed her from the main house, but she still had to move quickly. Within a few seconds, she'd set all the pins in the lock and twisted the torque wrench as though she were simply unlocking the door with a key.

Hinges protested against her intrusion, but there was no hint of an alarm. Silent or otherwise. No sensors on the doors or windows. Campbell closed the door behind her. This cabin had been meant to serve as a temporary location for Battle Mountain PD. Not Fort Knox. With the department's dispatcher able to work from home, there was no need for on-site personnel, either. A strain of guilt fired through her as she gazed back at the main cabin. She and Battle Mountain PD were on the same side. If corruption had taken hold of the small department and this town, she had to believe Kendric would want to know. She slipped her tools back into her coat pocket and faced the small living space covered by three equal-size workstations. The one with the most paperwork drew her closer. Chief Ford's. "Okay. Show me what you got."

Campbell took her seat in the slightly too tall office chair and tapped the keyboard. A log-in screen brightened on the monitor. "Password. Password. Password." Her mind panicked to supply the answer when a neon green sticky note came into focus. She ripped the note free from the bottom of the monitor and typed in the intricate and complicated password. She had to hold in a laugh. Thank goodness for sleep-deprived chiefs of police. "DontStealMyPassword."

She was in.

Hesitation gripped the back of her neck as she located digital case files uploaded in the past year. It didn't take long to verify the information she'd already collected on three prior homicide cases here in Battle Mountain against the original reports filed by Chief Ford himself. Next, she skimmed through the department's finances, then background checks for each officer and BMPD's dispatcher, Macie Barclay. No payoffs. No bribes. In fact, it looked as though Chief Ford sacrificed his own

salary to ensure his officers were paid first and foremost for their service. At least on the surface. "Come
on. There's gotta be something."

Her fingers ached as she forced them across the
keyboard. She pulled call history for the chief and his
brother, Easton. Then Cree Gregson and Alma Majors.
Nothing out of the ordinary. She reviewed personal finances for each officer in turn, the uneasy feeling in
her gut taking hold.

It wasn't possible. No department she'd investigated
had ever been this clean.

According to all available records, the men and
women of this department had nothing to hide. No connection to any of the suspects arrested and sentenced
over the course of the past year. No evidence of corruption or favors. No pension fund to embezzle from or
speeding tickets to pursue. Nothing. After all this—her
taking jurisdiction for the Sabrina Bryon case, facing
the man who left her, surviving an abduction and breaking into BMPD's files—she had nothing.

Drowned Deep

Chapter Eleven

He couldn't make up for the past.

Kendric passed off the last dish from breakfast in the main house to Campbell, his fingers coming into contact with hers. Such a simple action but one that threatened to rip the world straight out from under him. Despite the bullet wound in his shoulder, he hadn't slept as well as he had the night before in years. Because of her. Her heat, her determination to protect the people she cared about, her drive to prove she could handle any task without an emotional break. She was reliable and beautiful and a challenging handful he wanted to take on. He always had.

"Missed a spot." She pointed out some crumbs on the bottom of the plate he'd handed her. "I know you think you can only clean the top of the plate because that's where the food goes, but that's not how Karie is going to see it when she pulls these out from the cabinet again."

"Hey, give me a break. I'm doing this one-handed." And he was paying the price for that much. The hole in his shoulder had started roaring the moment he'd been left without her touch at breakfast, but he couldn't hold her back from doing her job. "Anything new from CBI?"

"What?" She swiped the drying rag around the perimeter of the plate, her expression distant as though her mind was somewhere else entirely. "Oh, no. Not yet. One of my colleagues is looking back through name change records, but he hasn't found anything we can use. In my experience, most people who file to change their names don't vary from their originals. Makes it easier to remember. So I have him looking into *S* names changed in the past ten years. Could take a while."

Kendric finished cleaning the contentious plate a second time and passed it along to be dried, but something wasn't right. Not just the distance. He could count on that anytime Campbell found herself in the middle of an investigation. There'd been days when they'd been together when nothing he said got through. She'd lose herself completely in any given case. Staying up all night, reviewing files and notes all day. Especially the ones that involved crimes against children. For those, he'd just had to leave her to work, knowing any interruption would only increase her pressure to solve the case on her own. "You okay? If you're still hurting after the car accident, I can—"

"No. I'm okay. Thanks." She didn't look at him, consumed with her duty to clean and put away Karie Ford's serving dishes. One by one.

He turned off the water and tossed the dish brush into the sink. "I can see the wheels in your head spinning, Bell. I know when something is bothering you."

Campbell blinked up at him, a mere inch of space between them. He'd sure as hell gotten her attention. "What did you call me?"

He thought back, not exactly sure of her point. Then it hit.

"I called you... Bell." Kendric's weight nearly buckled, and he leveraged one arm against the counter to keep himself upright. He hadn't done that in a long time. His nickname for her had come to life on their second date all those years ago. She'd been skating in the middle of the ice rink, a physical glow emanating around her with her high-volt smile. It was then he'd known. He'd wanted to spend the rest of his life with her. They'd made love for the first time that night. In the frenzy of passion and mind-blowing sensation, he'd lost his mind and screamed the last half of her name. No one had ever called her Bell before. In that moment, he'd turned what they'd agreed would be a casual experiment into something special, and she hadn't allowed anyone else to use the nickname as long as they were together. Had that changed? "I'm sorry. It just slipped out."

"No, it's okay." She shook her head, fisting the drying towel on the counter. "I just had this flash of ice-skating and roasted almonds and going back to your place that night. It surprised me is all."

"You didn't answer my question." Kendric moved into her, forcing her to either stare at his feet or look up into his eyes. "What's bothering you?"

She chose to direct her attention over his shoulder, but the difference in height between them only meant she was choosing the ceiling over meeting his gaze head-on, and a sick feeling set up residence in his gut. "I'm not sure I want you to move back to Denver."

"That's…not what I was expecting." Kendric stepped back. If her words had carried physical weight, he would've landed on his ass and not been able to get back up. Confusion ripped through him as he reviewed every hour they'd been forced to work this case together. No. Not forced. It had felt that way at the beginning, but now he couldn't imagine solving this case without her. Without her insight, her single-mindedness, her passion for saving lives, they wouldn't have gotten past the primary crime scene. "I don't understand. You're the one who urged me to reconsider staying here. You said you wanted me to come home, to have a relationship with Penny, that you still feel something for me. What changed? If I've done something wrong or offended you—"

"No. You didn't. You didn't do anything wrong. And I know I'm the one who proposed that you leave Battle Mountain and that you should come home and meet your daughter, and I still want that. I do." Campbell gripped his uninjured arm, then ran her thumb along his bicep. "It's just…"

"It's what, Campbell?" he asked.

Her gaze met his, and she lowered her voice as footsteps and movement increased in the cabin's main living space. "You're thriving here. I've met and talked with the people you work with, and I can hear how much they care about you in their voices. I see how much this town needs you. I didn't want to acknowledge it at first. I thought you coming here was your way of detaching from the world and hiding to punish yourself for all the things you couldn't fix, but it has nothing to do with the past at all. You're happy here. You made a life here. You genuinely believe you can make a difference to the people of this town, and I don't want to be the one to take that away from you."

He wasn't sure what he was supposed to say to that, what he was supposed to think. His instincts reminded him he'd once suspected an ulterior motive for her involvement on this case, but he'd ignored that drive in favor of bringing a missing young mother home. The stakes had changed since that first visit to the crime scene. They'd uncovered the truth. At least, what they understood of the truth, and now Campbell wanted him to stay in Battle Mountain in the name of his happiness. "And if I said I'd be happy in Denver with you and Penny?"

Her mouth parted, but Campbell didn't let any emotion escape her gaze. Because she was a professional. He had to remember that. "Then I wouldn't be able to stop you, would I?"

Hurried steps and shouts penetrated the small kitchen they'd sequestered themselves inside. Kendric rounded the corner to get a full view of the living room, Campbell at his side.

"What's going on?" she asked.

"I don't know." He headed for the front door just as Karie Ford maneuvered Genevieve's wheelchair down the hallway leading to the back of the house. Dr. Pascale carried her and Weston's son after them. No sight of the chief, Cree, Alma or Easton, but the box the Ford matron had dedicated to holding firearms just inside the front door had been emptied of everything but his and Campbell's weapons. "Come on."

Campbell retrieved her gun, released the magazine and slammed it back into place. Angling to get a better view through the windows on either side of the front door, she waited for him to arm himself. "Looks like your chief and the other members of your department are waiting for something. They've taken positions behind the satellite cabins."

She glanced back at him.

He motioned for her to get behind him as he

wrenched open the front door. They stepped over the threshold one at a time. Crisp November air burned down his throat as he took in his fellow officers' positions. Campbell was right. Something had spooked them. He didn't wait for the surprise, heading straight for Chief Ford at the head of the pack.

"Chief, what's going on?" he asked.

"Spotted a pickup truck coming up the mountain. Same description as the one you detailed that ran you off the road two days ago. See for yourself." The chief handed off a pair of binoculars, then turned his back to the cabin, staying low. "Nail strips took out the tires just beyond the gate. Whoever it is, they're coming in on foot."

Kendric pinpointed the truck's location down the mountain. The driver's-side door had been left open, but the tree line prevented him from picking up any other signs of movement. Both front tires were flat against the combination of dirt and snow. Whispering Pines Ranch might've become Colorado's ultimate mountain getaway over the past year, but the Ford brothers had gone to great lengths to keep the uninvited off their property. He handed off the binoculars to Campbell to get a look for herself. "How long do we have?"

"Your guess is as good as mine," the chief said. "Could be minutes, could be hours. All depends on why they're here and what the hell they want."

"The truck belongs to Budd Ingar. Chelsea Ingar loaned it to Sabrina, and she used it to run us off the road, leading to Chelsea's arrest." Campbell lowered the binoculars between her crouched thighs. "Could be he wants reparations. For his truck and his wife."

"We're about to find out." Kendric caught movement

in the tree line east of their position and unholstered his weapon. The rest of his department followed his example, taking aim at the same spot.

And waited. Two seconds. Three.

"Don't shoot! I'm coming out unarmed!" Sabrina Bryon stepped free from the cover of trees, a soft bundle clutched to her chest. Dark brown eyes took in the officers ready to take her down. Then locked on Campbell. Obvious relief pushed tears into the woman's eyes. "Detective Dwyer, I need your help."

"My REAL NAME is Samantha Horsley." Sabrina Bryon stared down at the baby girl nestled against her chest with a love Campbell felt down to her core. "I moved to Battle Mountain from Las Vegas to find a man named Dean Pratt."

"Why?" Kendric asked.

"I'm a private investigator. Although I guess you could say my license has lapsed. I was hired to find Dean by a woman he assaulted and raped six years ago, but the closer I got, the more dangerous it became for my client." The woman on the trigger end of the bullet in Kendric's shoulder rocked back and forth in the recliner in the Ford's living room as though she belonged. "She started getting death threats in the middle of the night. At one point she called me to tell me she was being followed by a man she recognized worked for Dean. I had to back off or risk him tying up any loose ends."

"I know everyone in this town. There's no Dean Pratt around here," Weston Ford said.

"There wouldn't be. Not unless you saw a photo of Dean." Sabrina rolled her lips between her teeth. "It took me months and a lot of favors to find where he'd disappeared to, but I finally caught up to him five years ago."

"And you married him." Campbell's gut clenched. She raised her gaze to Kendric, knowing the danger Sabrina had put herself and her baby into by divulging this information. "Elliot Bryon is Dean Pratt."

"Yes." Another line of tears welled in Sabrina's eyes as she clutched her infant to her chest. "I didn't have anything to prove he'd assaulted my client. I had to get close to him. I had to do something. After a while it was easy to forget why I was here. He was charming. He had a drive to conquer me as strong as my drive to conquer him, and it turned into a game. He'd pursue, I'd resist. I'd pursue, he'd resist. Until we finally got what we both wanted."

"That sounds like it's more than just a job." Easton rubbed his fingers into thick eyebrows, upsetting the delicate pattern. "Chasing after a suspected rapist across state borders without a license to investigate in Colorado, getting close enough to the guy to not only sleep with him but marry him, have a child with him. How much farther were you willing to go to prove he hurt someone?"

Campbell inhaled sharply. She felt both sympathy and revulsion. This woman had married a criminal, one who'd victimized her own sister, knowing what he'd done.

"As far as I had to," Sabrina said.

Campbell softened her voice as she considered everything that had happened in the past few days. A private investigator wouldn't put her life—her child's life—on the line so easily. There had to be a deeper reason. "The client who hired you. She wasn't just any client, was it?"

"She was my sister." Sabrina traced her infant's cracked lips with the tips of her fingers.

"Was?" Kendric asked.

"Dean." That single name brought visions of bitterness, anger, resentment and grief all in one tone. Sabrina seemed to hold her baby tighter at the inherent evil crossing her mind. "She only lasted a week after he'd assaulted her. Internal bleeding in her uterus. The emergency room doctors never caught it and released her not knowing they were signing her death warrant. She dropped dead right in front of me, and I knew right then what I had to do."

Silence closed in around the new mother.

"So you came looking for him, hoping to catch him on something he could be charged with." Awareness of Kendric flittered down her spine, and Campbell wanted nothing more right then than to forget this investigation, to forget her assignment in Battle Mountain, to tell him the truth. That same bitterness Sabrina held for her sister's attacker had taken up too much of Kendric's life. And she was making it worse. Lies were dangerous. They spread like wildfires and could become just as irreversible. They'd already been through so much. She wanted him to be part of her and Penny's lives, but fear of the truth, of how he'd take her involvement with IA, had her second-guessing every decision she'd made since she'd stepped foot into that crime scene. What she wouldn't give to make it all go away, to give them a real chance. "Sabrina, tell us what happened with Elliot and Rachel Stephenson four days ago."

"Isn't it obvious? Dean—Elliot—found out the

truth." Real fear widened Sabrina's eyes. "I don't know how. Maybe he found something connected to my past, or I said something he thought was off. It doesn't matter. All I know is I came home to find that woman and my husband waiting for me. They each had a gun. She was holding my pregnancy pillow, I assume to muffle any gunshots if she had to pull the trigger. He said he knew everything and that I couldn't prove anything if I was dead. I tried to reason with him. I tried to get him to consider his daughter's life. He didn't care. He just wanted to make me disappear."

"His mistress had the gun?" Kendric asked.

A humorless laugh escaped Sabrina's well-curated control. "Rachel Stephenson wasn't his mistress. She's just one of many who handle the jobs he doesn't want to do himself. As far as I was able to tell, she's on Elliot's payroll, but she doesn't report to him. Her bosses are using the auto shop to smuggle all kinds of things." Sabrina bounced the baby against her chest. "She was just there to make sure nothing went wrong."

"And when Elliot found out why you'd really come to Battle Mountain, you were a problem that needed to be dealt with." Kendric's voice dipped into dangerous territory.

"I wasn't going to let him kill me and our daughter. I went for Rachel's gun. There was a struggle, but I somehow got control of it. I ran out the back door." Sabrina closed her eyes. "I remember two shots. Elliot was shooting at me. I heard a groan, and I turned around to see Rachel collapse, but I couldn't stop. He shot her. I circled around through the trees, staying out of sight, and got in the car. I drove out of there as fast as I could, and I didn't look back."

Campbell could see it all play out as though she were the terrified mother on the run.

"Where is the gun you took from the house now?" Chief Ford asked.

Sabrina drove her hand into the pile of ratted blankets against her chest and pulled the weapon free. Every officer in the room tensed in case she turned the gun on them, but Kendric stepped forward to collect it with an evidence bag. "I'm sorry about your shoulder. I just couldn't let you take her from me."

"How do we know any of this is true?" Cree Gregson asked. "You could've made it all up on the way here, for all we know."

"I wouldn't have come here if I didn't need your help. I know what I'm risking by turning myself in, but I didn't have any other choice. My baby... She's... Something's wrong." Sabrina turned dark eyes to Campbell. "Detective, you're a mother. You would do anything you had to, to protect Penny. Please, I don't know what to do. My milk supply is gone. I can't feed her, and she won't wake up to eat."

"It's the stress. For both of you." Campbell moved to take a seat beside the woman who'd abducted and interrogated her. She stretched out her arms. "May I?"

"Campbell." Kendric's warning tone hardened the muscles down her spine. "Can I talk to you in private?"

Her gut said it was a waste of time answering questions he wouldn't understand the answers to, but as partners, they had a responsibility to one another. A respect. She wouldn't break that. Not until she had to. "I'll be right back."

Kendric pulled her back into the kitchen, clear of his department and Sabrina Bryon. "What are you doing?

That woman ran us off the road. She kidnapped and drugged you. Not to mention shot me. Now you want to help her?"

"Yes." She shrugged her shoulders in an attempt to soften the blow.

"Why?" he asked. "This woman married her sister's rapist. Doesn't that strike you as a little bit off? What makes you think she won't turn on you as soon as she gets the chance?"

"Because she's scared for her daughter's life, and I know exactly what that feels like." Those bleary-eyed, desperate memories of Penny's birth threatened to tear through her, but Campbell held strong. Her voice broke as she willed Kendric to feel what she'd felt. "I know the physical pain that comes with the thought of losing a piece of you. The fear. There isn't anything you wouldn't do to make it go away."

The anger he'd resurrected in her defense drained. Setting his uninjured hand on her hip, Kendric pulled her against his chest. "I'm sorry. I wasn't thinking."

Campbell held on to him as her legs threatened to give out. She was so tired. Of the distance between them, of keeping four years of their daughter's life to herself, of shouldering it alone. She stepped back but couldn't force herself to let go. "I know it doesn't make sense, and I don't expect you to understand, but I believe her. I believe she's telling the truth. In which case, you were right. Elliot Bryon—Dean Pratt—whoever the hell he is, lied to us. He tried to kill his pregnant wife and then called 911 before hiding Rachel Stephenson's body in that tree and shooting himself twice in the chest to make it look like Sabrina had snapped. It was a risky move that could have ended badly for him, but this man obviously has a huge ego and some skill."

His strong exhalation brushed against the underside of her chin. "As much as I don't want to admit it, the evidence supports her statement over his. So what do you want to do now?"

"The stress is draining Sabrina's milk supply. We need to take her into protective custody and have Isla Vach come back to the ranch to examine the baby." She studied their original suspect, felt the gut-wrenching anxiety emanating from Sabrina Bryon's every pore as BMPD waited for her to make one wrong move. "Based on what Sabrina said, I don't think Elliot Bryon will stop coming after her. He'll be checking hospitals and—"

Campbell's phone trilled, and she unpocketed the device from her coat. Unknown number. Swiping her finger across the screen, she brought the phone to her ear. "Dwyer."

"Detective, I'm glad you picked up," Elliot Bryon said.

She locked her gaze on Kendric and hit the speakerphone option on the screen. The hardness was back in his expression in an instant as he snapped for the other members in his department to get their attentions.

Chief Ford was instantly on the phone, most likely to his dispatcher, Macie, to run a trace, but considering how careful Elliot Bryon had been to this point, she knew it would be useless.

"Mr. Bryon, we just got word you checked yourself out of the hospital." Campbell infused a false sense of care into her words. "Is everything okay? Where are you?"

"You can drop the pretenses, Detective." Elliot's voice deadpanned. Nothing like that performance he'd given in the hospital. "I know Sabrina is with you. Or should I call her Samantha? It's hard to keep all the lies straight these days."

"What do you want?" Campbell asked.

"You have something I want," he said. "Funnily enough, I have something you want, too."

The line staticked a split second before a second voice pierced through the speaker. "Mommy?"

Cold shot through Campbell's veins. Gravity increased its hold on her body until she wasn't sure she would be able to keep standing. She clutched the counter to stay upright. "Penny?"

"Mommy, I want to go home," her daughter said.

"And you will get to go home." Elliot Bryon had taken control of the phone again. "Just as soon as your mommy gives me what I want. Bring me Sabrina and Penny gets to go home. You have two hours, Detective. Make them count."

The line went dead.

Chapter Twelve

He was already moving.

"Macie didn't have enough time to get the trace." Chief Ford's voice registered as some distant dream. Real but faded. "Detective Dwyer, with your permission, I'd like to—"

"Kendric?" Campbell called after him, but the waver in his name wasn't enough to slow him down.

Kendric closed the distance between him and Sabrina Bryon and her infant. "Where is he? Elliot. Where would he go?"

"I don't know." Sabrina shook her head.

"You're lying." The rage, the resentment, the bitterness—everything he'd tried to let go of these past few days—reared its ugly head. Fire back-drafted through his chest until all he saw was red. Desperation unlike anything he'd felt before exploded through him. "Where did he take my daughter!"

Silence infiltrated as the weight of his department's attention centered on him.

Sabrina's infant wailed, but nobody moved.

"Kendric." A warm hand slid over his forearm and turned him to face the blonde beauty he couldn't imagine disappearing from his life again. Campbell framed his face, forcing him to look her dead in the eyes. Those same hands that held him shook as though she were ready to break apart at any moment. "We are going to find her. We are going to bring her home, but we have to hold it together. For Penny. Do you understand me?"

"He took her." Three simple words had the power to destroy him.

"And we are going to get her back," she said. "Please, help me get her back."

"I've put together a list of properties Elliot owns over the past few years. It's not much, but it's a place to start. I'll send you the addresses." Sabrina got to her feet in his peripheral vision. "I'm sorry. I never meant this to happen. I just wanted justice for my sister, and I made a mess of it... I'm sorry."

"Chloe." Campbell released her hold but never detached her attention from him. "Sabrina's milk supply isn't enough for the baby right now. Could you please help them?"

"Of course. I have some formula in the diaper bag." The coroner ushered Sabrina toward the hallway and presumably into one of the back rooms, out of sight.

Kendric couldn't take his eyes off Campbell. Off her strength, her determination to keep them from shattering right here in the middle of the damn living room when their world was under attack, her ability to compartmentalize, even in the face of loss.

"The rest of you, could you please give us a minute?" she asked.

The other officers filed from the living room without questioning her motives or argument, and it was then Kendric saw the power she held over everyone she came into contact with. The power she held over him.

They were left alone, but the disquiet in his blood had reached an all-time high.

"Tell me what to do." A fraction of the fear Campbell described during Penny's birth singed his nerve endings. He couldn't think straight. He could barely keep himself breathing. Every cell in his body urged him to charge out that front door and rip the world apart to look for his daughter. He wanted to do something—anything—to stop the echo of thoughts running through his head. What if he never got the chance to meet Penny? What if he was too late? What would her loss do to Campbell? To him? What would losing their daughter do to them? "Tell me how to get her back."

"You can't." Campbell slipped her hand into her coat and pulled her phone free. She scrolled to a contact he couldn't read and tapped the screen. "But I know someone who can."

Confusion threatened to tip him over the edge. "What do you mean?"

"This is Officer Campbell Dwyer." She listed off her badge number. "I need a unit sent to my parents' address on file to make sure they're okay. My daughter has been kidnapped and is being held by a suspect considered armed and dangerous. Send an EMT." She gave them Elliot Bryon's details. "Have units search my home as well. Victim is four years old. Her name is Penny Dwyer. I'm sending a photo to you now."

"Officer?" Kendric didn't understand. She was a detective in the missing persons bureau of CBI. Not an officer. "Campbell, what's going on?"

"Yes, please transfer me." Campbell didn't move, didn't even seem to breathe. "Sir, I need a trace on a call that just came to my cell phone. Six minutes ago. Source is a man named Dean Pratt, operating under the alias of Elliot Bryon. He's holding my daughter hostage in exchange for his wife and infant." She shook her head. "Sir, we don't have time—"

A muffled voice intensified on the other side of the line.

"No, I understand you wanted no contact, but I—" Campbell raised her gaze to his, the color washing from her face. "No, sir. I have not uncovered any evidence of corruption or misconduct in Battle Mountain. As far as I can tell, BMPD has no influence over the violent events that have occurred here in the past year."

Misconduct. Corruption. Connection. The words tornadoed through his head until they became a single syllable he couldn't pick apart. Heat flared through his gut, and Kendric stepped back.

"Thank you, sir. I'll be waiting for your call." Campbell disconnected, her phone still in hand. "Kendric—"

"You're Internal Affairs." The words clawed free from the box he hadn't been willing to look inside since she came back into his life. A part of him had known. Not the specifics, but that there was something else at play here. Something he couldn't let go of. Now he knew. His instincts had been right. "All this time, you made me think you were here to recover Sabrina Bryon, that you were a missing persons agent here to help, but you had your own agenda. You were sent here to spy on my department. On me."

"Yes." Such a simple answer but one that held influence to obliterate entire lives. "CBI sent me to assess BMPD. I didn't choose it, Kendric. I was told to join IAB or lose my career. I did what I had to, to provide for our daughter. I never intended any of this to happen, but that's not what's important right now. Penny is out there with a psychopath who will hurt her if we don't do something to stop him."

"Don't give me that." He couldn't contain the spiral pulling him beneath the surface. A low ringing pierced his ears as the future they'd built together these past few days faded. "You and I both know there's not a damn thing in this world that can force you to do something against your will. You had a choice. You chose wrong."

Campbell let her mouth part. "Do you think I don't worry about that every day I'm on the job? That I don't lie awake at night wondering if the men and women I investigate will try to get revenge on me or Penny or my parents? I didn't want this, Kendric, but I did what I had to, to survive being a single parent."

"Is Penny even mine?" He hadn't meant to ask, but it was too late to take it back. "Or was that a lie, too? A play to pull me in, to get me to fall for your lies and trust you?"

Her voice barely reached across the few feet between them. "You really think so little of me I'd lie about our daughter?"

"I don't know what to think of you, Campbell," he said. "I don't know you. Maybe I never have." Kendric headed for the front door. His phone chirped with an incoming message. The list of Elliot Bryon's properties Sabrina had offered to supply. Whether Penny was his or not, a four-year-old girl was out there. Alone. Scared. She wanted nothing more than to go home to her family, and Kendric had the duty to make that happen. He'd search every address on the list if he had to. No matter how long it took. He collected his weapon from the storage by the front door and holstered it at his side.

"Where are you going?" she asked.

He thought the answer was obvious. "To find your daughter."

"You don't even know where Elliot Bryon is keeping her. You could be wasting time, and that's not something I'm willing to risk. My CO will call back with a location after the computer squad finishes the trace. Look at me." Campbell squeezed her hand around his arm. "It's not solely up to you to bring her home. We have to work together. Penny needs us."

"Us? There is no us." His skin burned with her touch, and Kendric pried his arm from her grip. "The day I partner with the rat squad is the day I stop being a cop. You're not police. You're a glorified hall monitor hell-bent on ending careers. You want to know why I came to Battle Mountain, why I signed up to help this town? Because of the men and woman in that other room. They protect each other. They're honest with one another. They're a family, and they would never turn on each other for a paycheck. Ever. And you… You're nothing like them. Penny deserves better, and so do I."

He regretted the words the moment they'd left his mouth.

Campbell stepped back, that iron control slipping. Just for a moment, he recognized the woman he'd started falling for all over again. A momentary glimpse of her heart and all the reasons he'd wanted her to be part of his life. "You don't get it, do you? Why I'm here instead of another IAB officer."

"It doesn't matter." He stripped free of his arm sling and tossed it on the back of the worn leather couch stretching in front of the fireplace where so many holidays, birthdays and family dinners had been spent. He'd bought his cabin after visiting Whispering Pines Ranch one time. That single visit had been enough for him to want his own place to create the warmth and safe haven this place provided, maybe even start a family to fill it with. He'd already envisioned Campbell and Penny on Christmas mornings, eating breakfasts at the table, cozying up on the couch in front of the fire at night. But that was all it was. A fantasy. "As soon as Penny is safe and the bastard who took her is behind bars, I want you gone. Forever."

"Don't do this again, Kendric." Tears welled in Campbell's eyes, but they wouldn't have a hold on him this time. "You don't understand."

"No, that's the problem, Campbell. I understand everything. You lied to me. You got close to me, and you used me to investigate my department, and I fell for it. I should've seen the truth. I should've known you were more interested in closing your case than being with me. Because who would want to be with someone like this?" His scars burned as though aware of his accusations. "You made a choice when you came here, and it sure as hell wasn't us."

"You're right." Her face voided of expression. She'd already detached from him. As though she'd simply switched off a light. So easy. It was like Elliot Bryon had said. What was the point of keeping up pretenses when the truth had come into the open? "Why would I want to be with someone as angry and bitter and distrusting as you?"

He stepped out into the freezing day. Elliot Bryon

had taken his daughter. And Kendric was going to get her back. With or without Campbell's help.

HE WAS GONE.

Again.

Campbell stared after a pair of blurry brake lights out the cabin's front door as Kendric made his way down the mountain. All the things he'd said, the accusations—her heart gripped in her chest and refused to let up. *Penny deserves better, and so do I.*

Footsteps reverberated up through her from the old hardwood floors. Chief Ford and his Battle Mountain officers had heard every word between her and Kendric. She closed her eyes, willing this moment to stretch as far as possible to avoid what came next. But reality didn't always work the way she wanted.

"The night I ran into you outside. You weren't enjoying the fresh air, were you?" Chief Ford's voice warned her answer would decide her fate in this small town she'd come to love. "You were running your own investigation."

"It sounds like you already have your answer, Chief." Campbell pried herself away from the window, slid her hands into her coat pocket and unpocketed her credentials. She tossed them his way.

He caught them against a broad chest, never once taking his gaze off her. None of them did. Easton Ford and his fiancée, Genevieve. Cree Gregson and Alma Majors. Even Dr. Pascale. This…family that had supported Kendric the past few months, who'd fed her, clothed her, talked to her like a human rather than a rat. They deserved answers. Answers she couldn't give. "Officer Campbell Dwyer. Internal Affairs Bureau of

CBI." He threw her badge and credentials back. "So, Officer. Did you get what you came for?"

Such a simple question. But one she didn't have an answer for. She'd come to this sleepy mining town for an assignment, but she'd uncovered so much more along the way. A department of men and women who treated each other more like siblings than colleagues. A town that felt more like home than Denver ever had. A man she'd imagined spending the rest of her life with, who accepted her and protected her. A sense of purpose she hadn't ever experienced in her position with CBI or any other job. All of it had been within reach, just for a moment. And it was slipping through her fingers. "I won't be pursuing my internal investigation into BMPD, if that's what you mean."

"Then the Sabrina Bryon case is no longer under CBI jurisdiction." Easton Ford stepped to the front like a true alpha male protecting his pack. "It looks like you're done here, Detective."

But she wasn't. Not yet. And running with her tail tucked between her legs had never been part of her personality. "Listen, I understand none of you may respect what I do. You may not even like me, but you don't know my reasons for doing what I did, and you don't know me. My daughter is everything to me. She is the only thing that motivates me to do my work, and she's out there right now being held by a man from your town. Whether you like it or not, that makes him both of our problems, and I'm not leaving Battle Mountain without her. So you can either help me find Penny, or you can stay out of my way."

"We're Battle Mountain police, Officer Dwyer. We swore to protect this town and everyone in it, including you. We'll do whatever it takes to bring your daughter home." Chief Ford maneuvered past her toward the front door, his officers filing behind him. "As for what went down between you and Kendric, you're on your own." He turned to his wife. "Alma will stay with you and Sabrina Bryon until Isla can check her and the baby out. I'll be on the radio in case you lose cell service and need to get a hold of me." He kissed her, then his son before slipping out the door.

Easton Ford crouched beside Genevieve's wheelchair, saying nothing. It was as though they could read each other's minds when he pressed his forehead to hers. The district attorney held on to his hand as long as possible before she was forced to let go, and Campbell's heart pinched.

Even Gregson seemed to have a hard time letting go of his partner.

That kind of love only came around once in a lifetime. And she'd ruined her chances of earning it for herself. Campbell reached for her weapon from the storage bin just inside the main house's front door as BMPD dispersed to their vehicles. Stepping out into the frigid night, she braced herself against the cold working through her. Not from the dropping temperatures or the flakes falling from the sky. From the emptiness she couldn't seem to shake.

At missing Penny. Fearing for her.

At knowing Kendric would never look at her the same again.

At losing the future she'd started to imagine. Just the three of them.

She cut through deepening snow as Kendric's department pulled their vehicles down the long driveway to head back to town. Kendric had brought her to Whispering Pines Ranch. Her rental had probably started collecting parking tickets on Battle Mountain's Main Street where she'd left it four days ago, and getting lost down the mountain as a storm closed in wasn't going to help Penny in the least. She needed a vehicle.

The growl of an engine cut through the silence pressurizing the air in her lungs. Headlights illuminated glistening snow as a pickup seemingly built for war curved into the driveway. Campbell shielded her eyes as the spotlights centered on her. The driver's-side door opened. "You know there's a truck with two flat tires down the road? I nearly ran into a tree trying to avoid it on the way up here."

Isla Vach, the EMT Chief Ford had called to tend to Kendric's wound, hopped down from the oversize monster that didn't fit her personality at all. Followed by a smaller version of the brunette a moment later. "You've got another patient for me, Detective Dwyer? Wait. Did Kendric tear his stitches? I warned—"

"No. He's fine, and thanks again for helping him. The chief wanted you to take a look at someone else. Sabrina Bryon and her baby are inside. Officer Majors can give you all the details." Campbell studied the resemblance between the EMT and the girl who'd climbed down from the passenger seat. "Is this your daughter?"

"Yeah. Mazi, this is Detective Dwyer. She's helping the police with an investigation." Isla pulled her girl closer, back to front, with obvious pride in her smile.

"Wow! Do you solve crimes like my daddy?" Mazi asked.

"Um, yeah. I do, but not the kind you're thinking of." Campbell's own smile stretched across her mouth as she compared Penny's four-year-old attitude against the girl in front of her. Her daughter hadn't bothered to ask what Campbell did to keep a roof over their heads. Penny's entire world was currently dictated by her next snack. It was the most frustrating thing to keep having to go to and from the pantry dozens of times throughout the day, on top of cooking meals, but Campbell wouldn't give it up for the world. Tears burned as her determination to hold it together cracked. She had to be strong. For Penny. It was the only way to get her back. "What does your daddy do?"

Instant regret stabbed Campbell in the gut as smiles fell from Mazi's and Isla's faces. "I'm sorry. I didn't mean to pry."

"No. It's okay. We lost my husband on his last tour to Morocco a few months ago." The EMT scrubbed her hands up and down Mazi's arms. "A government-sanctioned weapons deal that went bad. I don't really know all the details."

A tear escaped Campbell's control, and her heart threatened to beat straight out of her chest. "I'm sorry for your loss."

"Us, too. Anyway, it looks like the entire department was headed someplace. We won't hold you up. Have a good night, Detective." Isla maneuvered her daughter toward the main cabin.

"Isla, wait." Campbell turned after them. "Is there any way I could borrow your truck for a few hours? I wouldn't normally ask a complete stranger, but it's an emergency." Her gaze dropped to Mazi. "I have a daughter, too, and right now, she needs me more than ever."

Isla tossed the keys. "We're not strangers. Us moms have to stick together."

"I'll take good care of it. Thank you." She didn't wait for a response, pumping her legs as hard as two feet of snow would allow. Climbing into the massive truck, Campbell got behind the wheel and headed down the mountain. She didn't know where she was going. Didn't know if her CO would ever get back to her with Elliot Bryon's location, but she couldn't sit around and wait. She had to do something.

Her phone chimed from her coat pocket. An incoming message.

She hit the brakes and pulled off the side of the slushed-out road leading to the highway that would take her back in to Battle Mountain. The screen illuminated the inside of the cabin. Her CO had come through. The bastard who'd taken her daughter had called from a property on the outskirts of town. Not too far. She went to send the information to BMPD but didn't have any of their contact information. Dialing 911, Campbell relayed the location to Macie Barclay and prayed the dispatcher would get it to them in time. She hung up. "Got you."

Campbell tossed her phone into the passenger seat and pushed back onto the road. If she lost Penny... No. She was going to make it. There was no other option. "Keep it together, Dwyer. Just a little while longer."

The miles passed in a blur, but the closer she came to her destination, the tighter she held the steering wheel. Elliot Bryon had assaulted, raped and ultimately killed one woman before trying to murder another. She couldn't risk a direct approach and force the psychopath to cut his losses. She needed another plan.

Campbell brought the truck to a stop a quarter mile

from her final destination and switched off the head-lights. Night had already consumed any outline she might've been able to see at this distance during the day, but her gut said there was something worth inves-tigating up ahead. There was no sign of Battle Mountain PD. She couldn't wait. "I'm coming, baby."

She hit the icy pavement and closed the driver's-side door as softly as possible. Elliot Bryon was smart. He'd evaded authorities this long. He wasn't going to take any chances of letting someone just walk onto his prop-erty, and neither was she. The terrain flattened once it dipped off the road and spread out into never-ending fields on either side. Not a whole lot of places to take cover, but she didn't have any other option.

Staying low, Campbell jogged a few yards off the main road. Snow and ice worked into her boots. Numb-ness had already started in her fingers, but she kept her index finger over the trigger of her sidearm. Within a few minutes, she'd gotten close enough to the prop-erty to make out the dark shape of a structure ahead. A long outline with a pitched roof. Striations cleared as her vision adjusted to the dark. Not a residence or a warehouse. But old. Something original to the area. She cut across the landscape to a small growth of trees ahead and took cover.

Lights glimmered from vertical windows across the front. Patches of dark soil or volcanic rock peeked through the snow leading to the front door. Recently used. Penny was here. She could feel it. Tightening her grip around her weapon, Campbell took a step closer.

Her boot caught on something, and she tipped for-ward. She slammed into a tumbleweed, cutting her palm on the same kind of volcanic rock leading up to the structure. Pain ignited through her broken hand. What the hell?

Swallowing a groan, she tugged the line free of her bootlaces. Fishing line. Why… Warning exploded in her gut, and Campbell shoved her heels into the ground to propel her forward.

She slapped her hand over her weapon.

A split second before a man's boot pressed down to stop her. "Hello, Detective. Penny's been waiting for you."

Chapter Thirteen

He'd already gone through four addresses from Sabrina Bryon's list of her husband's holdings. Every single one of them empty.

There were at least twenty locations left. He couldn't do this all night. Not when Penny's life was at stake. Damn it. He should've waited for a location from Campbell's CO. He'd just been so angry, betrayed. Now he was out in the middle of nowhere hoping to stumble upon his daughter and bring her home.

"Hell." Kendric put the SUV in Park and stared out across white-covered farmland through the windshield. Campbell's parting words had drilled into his brain and wouldn't let up. *Why would I want to be with someone as angry and bitter and distrusting as you?* That had been it, hadn't it? All this time, since the moment she'd interfered in his case, he'd wanted to prove he was more than the defective former ordinance tech, the failed ATF instructor, the has-been. That he could be someone she would respect and love. Someone she'd be proud of, someone worthy of her fire and commitment. He scrubbed a hand down his face to clear the bleariness and exhaustion from his eyes. "You screwed that up."

No. She was the one who'd lied. She'd kept him in the

dark about her real agenda for coming to Battle Mountain, made him feel balanced, good. Like she cared about him. It had all been a lie. He knew that now, but knowing one thing and accepting it were two completely different things. Still, a part of him had longed for it to be true. There'd been countless minutes he'd watched her while she'd slept next to him in that too small cabin at the ranch, imagining the three of them together. Him, Campbell and Penny. They'd get their own place. Not his here in Battle Mountain or hers in Denver. Someplace new that they could grow into and make their very own. A fresh start.

Wasn't going to happen now, though.

Their lives were headed in two different directions. His as a reserve officer and hers doing everything in her power to sabotage the very departments she was supposed to support. He didn't really believe that. He'd said it—to her and to himself—at least a dozen times, but the truth was, he knew why she'd joined Internal Affairs. And it hadn't been to put a roof over their daughter's head. He just hadn't wanted to admit it to her or anyone else. But the investigation into what happened the day the bomb had taken almost half of his face and injured a dozen other techs hadn't given her any excuse to lie to him.

He shifted the SUV into Drive and maneuvered back onto the main road. Something heavy slid under the passenger seat. Glass shattered, and Kendric braked on the isolated road. "What the hell?"

He shifted across the center console and felt around for whatever it was, the floor sopping wet. The hole in his shoulder screamed as it pressed against the steering wheel. Then his hand. He pulled back, watching a line of blood trail down the side of his middle finger. Angling over the passenger-side seat, he grabbed for the glove box and pulled a fresh tissue from inside. Along with his flashlight. Dark upholstery peppered with glass brightened under the beam, and Kendric realized what had broken beneath the seat. Slowly slipping his hand between the adjustment bars, he tugged the base of Campbell's snow globe free. The one Sabrina Bryon had taken from her luggage at the motel and mounted to the hood of her rental with a note.

Fake snowflakes clung to the sides and stuck to his fingertips. The glass had been destroyed thanks to his driving skills, but the insides looked all right. He checked out the gingerbread house decorated with icing and gumdrops, and the small gingerbread couple too large to fit inside their house. Peppermint candies lined the rooftop and the pathway leading to the front door, and Kendric had the slap of déjà vu. Of him picking it out just for her in the overpriced boutique Campbell had talked about visiting during Christmas one year. He'd gone without her, hoping to surprise her. And he'd succeeded that first holiday they'd been together. She'd loved it.

Hell. She'd kept it. No. She hadn't just kept it but had brought it with her on an assignment to Battle Mountain. And he'd been an idiot. "Son of a bitch."

She'd been telling the truth. Not about her assignment from Internal Affairs but everything else. She'd had no intention of using him to investigate his fellow officers. She'd wanted him to come home.

He set the remnants of the globe on the passenger seat and pulled his phone. Dialing Chief Ford, he stared at the perfect gingerbread world around shards of glass lined with his blood. The line rang once. Twice. He didn't wait for the chief's greeting as the call connected. "I need to talk to Campbell."

"Then you've got the wrong number, buddy," Chief Ford said.

"I don't have her number." Which was probably up there in the stupidest decisions he'd made over the past few days. "Just give her the phone…sir."

"That would be a great trick. After you left, Officer Dwyer asked us to help find her daughter. Last I heard, Isla Vach handed over the keys to her truck. Said Campbell had a daughter who needed her and took off. Cell service is getting weak with the incoming storm. Can't even get ahold of Macie."

Damn it. "How long ago?"

"Ten minutes, maybe less." Voices filtered from the other side of the line. Both feminine and male. "Listen, Hudson, I'll be honest. We weren't exactly thrilled she'd been sent to investigate the department. Words were exchanged, and I get the feeling Detective—Officer—Dwyer won't be back anytime soon. I've got Easton and Gregson out clearing roads, but I'm still doing a sweep of some of those properties Sabrina Bryon sent you. If we come across her, I'll let you know."

The snow was coming down harder now, and a chill went through him. Denver saw snow, but it wasn't anything compared to this. Battle Mountain didn't have the personnel or the funds to maintain a fleet of snowplows. It was BMPD's responsibility to salt and clear the roads. One wrong move and Campbell could find herself hurt or worse. He had to find her. "You said Isla Vach lent Campbell her truck. Is there a GPS on that monstrosity?"

The pickup had belonged to her late husband, a military man, who'd put everything he had toward keeping his family safe and supplied. A prepper in every sense of the word. That truck had doubled as a bunker, from what Kendric had heard. Fully stocked with supplies, ammunition, a weapon, blankets and extra fuel. A lot of money had gone into it. The man would've made sure he knew where it was at all times, even while on deployment.

"Isla's at the ranch with Majors, Chloe and Sabrina Bryon and the baby. Hold on. I'll check." The line cut out. Seconds ticked by across the screen, every moment more tense than the last. The chief came back on the line. "You were right. The truck is equipped with GPS. I'll send you the coordinates and redirect there. Until then, I want you to be careful."

"Thanks, Chief." He disconnected, more on edge than the second preceding an explosive tearing across his face. Campbell had gone after Penny. Without backup. The snow globe rocked gently in the passenger seat as he accelerated back onto the road. The storm had arrived. It was only a matter of time before it would white out everything in sight.

His phone pinged. A message from the chief. With an address containing the last known location of Isla Vach's truck. Recognition flared as he recalled the list Sabrina Bryon had sent him. It was the same address as one of the listings toward the bottom, one he might not have gotten to in time without the chief's help. Campbell had to be there. Kendric floored the accelerator, risking going off the road, but time was already running out. If she'd found Penny, there was no telling what Elliot Bryon would do when he realized she hadn't held up her end of the deal in handing over Sabrina and his daughter. The man was dominating, angry and relied on a survival instinct more volatile than any offender Kendric had come across. Campbell didn't have a chance.

He wasn't going to lose her again.

He loved her, damn it.

Despite the fact that Campbell had kept the truth from him, he loved her. He didn't want to see her or Penny hurt. He'd gone five years without Campbell in his life, and there wasn't a single part of him that wanted to risk another five. Her job had nothing to do with her ability to care for their daughter, her determination to bring Sabrina Bryon home safely or to stop a madman from getting away with murder. Campbell stood as a testament to everything he wanted in his life and everything he'd been missing since he left her all those years ago. And he was going to bring her and Penny home. For good.

Falling snow stuck to his windshield and smeared with the aid of the wipers. According to another message from the chief, the GPS on Isla Vach's truck hadn't moved. He took the next turn too sharp, the back tires fishtailing out of alignment. The muscles in his jaw ached under the pressure of his back teeth. The coordinates landed outside of town, approximately a mile from the city center. Another area he hadn't taken the time to familiarize himself with the past few months. Didn't matter. He'd been trained in rescue and recovery. Only this time, there were two victims Kendric intended on walking away with tonight.

The engine of his SUV coughed as the readout on the dashboard dropped below ten degrees. All Battle Mountain PD vehicles were equipped with emergency

supplies. Fuel, blankets, Kevlar vests, shovels and cal-
orie bricks. Nothing that would keep the engine warm.
The vehicle jerked forward without instruction. "Come
on. Don't do this. Not now."

Too late. The engine sputtered twice more, then died.
He tried to wrestle the wheel as the power steering gave
out, and tapped the brakes. Within a few hundred feet,
he was stalled. Headlights expanded out in front of him.
Nothing but deep snow and dead trees in the distance.
Every second he wasted was another second Campbell
and Penny didn't have. Grabbing for his phone, he tried
to pick up a signal. "A dead spot. Great. You wanted to
be on your own all this time, you got it."

He didn't have any other choice. He couldn't leave
Campbell to deal with Elliot Bryon alone. Not when
their daughter's life hung in the balance. Kendric shouldered out of the warmth of the SUV and stepped out
into the cold. Zipping his jacket, he rounded toward the
bumper and unhitched the cargo door. The fuel wouldn't
do him a damn bit of good. Even anti-freeze had its limits in temperatures this low. The blankets would protect
him from the thrashing winds, but it wouldn't be enough
to keep his body temperature from dropping. That left
the Kevlar vest. It was heavy. Not exactly something
he wanted to pack around for the next two miles, but
it was all he had.

Kendric strapped in, tightening the Velcro over the
wound in his shoulder. He locked up the vehicle and
headed straight into the wind, a blanket wrapped around
his middle and face. "Hang on, Bell. This isn't over."

JERKING MOVEMENTS BROUGHT her around.

The pain in her hand flared as Campbell forced her

eyes open. Cold whipped at the exposed skin of her face and neck. She was still outdoors. A thick blanket of white eased down from the wide-open, velvety sky. Blistering winds dried her lips until the smallest movement pulled the split along the bottom apart. She tried to reach for a passing bush, but her fingers wouldn't obey her command. The boots Genevieve Alexander had lent her caught in a mixture of compacted snow and black rock. The building with the pitched roof, Elliot Bryon, the fishing line acting as a security system—it was all coming back now. "Penny."

"Don't worry, Detective. You'll see her soon enough." Elliot Bryon pulled her coat tight against her neck with each tug. He was dragging her.

Wood stairs cut into her spine as he hauled her into the structure, and Campbell hit the floor facedown. Warmth burned along her nerve endings against the cement floor, dust kicking up with each exhalation off the surface. She notched her chin higher to get a view of her attacker as he strode to the other side of the open room containing two massive firepits. Each had been lit and allowed to rage, and an instant sweat built at the back of her neck. "Where is my daughter?"

"Safe. For now." Elliot shouldered a rifle while stoking the fire closest to her.

She could turn around right now. She could run for the door. Get help. Storm this place with backup and save Penny. But there was no telling what Elliot Bryon would do to her daughter in the meantime, if he'd even still be here when she returned. She couldn't risk it. No. This was it. It was now or never. For her and her child.

"I wouldn't do that if I were you." A broad smile pooled dread at the base of her spine. Dark eyes glittered as bright as the embers fleeing the flames a few feet from him. "I might not look like much, especially with two fresh wounds in my chest, but I can still hit a moving target at three thousand yards."

Campbell rose to her feet, slower than she wanted to get a lay of the building he'd brought her to. No interior walls. Fire highlighting every corner and the full wall of what looked to be antique blacksmith tools. "What the hell do you want?"

"I told you what I wanted. You were to bring me Sabrina in exchange for your daughter's life. I thought I made that clear." He wagged his finger at her, no evidence of pain in his expression. "Although, I will give you credit for sticking to the two-hour time frame. In these situations, most people would have gone to the police and tried to bust in here, guns blazing. But you... You surprised me. You came alone." Elliot slid a strand of her hair behind her ear. Too close. Too intimate. "You must really love Penny."

She jerked away. "Touch me or Penny and those two holes in your chest won't be your only problem."

His laugh drilled through her confidence and filled every inch of the single room. "I like you. It's a shame you can't follow simple instructions, though. I didn't want to have to hurt Penny. She's sweet. Just like I envision my own daughter to be one day, but I did warn you what would happen if you failed to come through."

Elliot started walking away from her.

"You wouldn't." Campbell had to believe that. Despite the cases she'd investigated and the studies she'd reviewed, she had to believe that kind of evil couldn't touch her daughter. "She's just a child. This is my fault. This is my responsibility. She has nothing to do with this."

He turned to face her, one arm sweeping outward as though he'd taken center stage. "She has everything to do with this, Detective. Don't you see that? Without her, I don't have you, and without you, I don't have Sabrina. Without Sabrina, the people I answer to aren't going to be very happy." His expression hardened as he pulled the iron he'd used to stoke the fire free from its perch. Closing the distance between them, he positioned the hot metal in front of her face. "Now, you can either tell me where my wife is, or you can lose your little girl. The choice really is quite simple."

Heat licked along her neck and cheek. He wanted her to choose between her daughter and the woman and infant he'd tried to kill? She fisted her hands against the urge to lash out at him, to punish him for giving her such an impossible task. She'd joined the sheriff's department all those years ago to save lives. Even inside IA, she protected the public and police departments against corruption and misconduct. She couldn't just hand over Sabrina and her baby. Not when she'd experienced this man's anger firsthand. "I can't."

"Shame. In that case, I'm afraid we don't have anything more to talk about." Elliot Bryon headed for a door she hadn't noticed until now, perfectly level and painted the same color as these old walls.

"No. You can't do this." Her head spun, from the violent change in temperature, the pain in her hand or losing Kendric all over again—she didn't care. He'd taken her gun, but she wasn't going to let him get away with this. Campbell ran for the wall organized with tools she'd never seen outside of television and movies set in medieval times.

A bullet whizzed past her arm and embedded in a small section of grating holding the tools in place a split second before she reached for one. "Now, come, Detective. You don't want this to get messier than it already has."

"I don't mind getting my hands dirty." Campbell ripped a hammer from the immaculately preserved collection. It was no match against the rifle in Elliot Bryon's hands, but her gut said she had to act fast enough to keep him away from Penny, wherever she was. "Do you?"

An amused smile flittered across his weathered and strong expression. He pressed his tongue against the inside of his bottom lip with a nod. "I knew there was something I liked about you." He didn't wait to give an official start and rushed her.

Campbell swung the hammer high, but her attacker caught her wrist. She knocked the rifle from his grip. It skidded across the floor, out of reach. A hard kick to her stomach shoved her back against the wall stocked with tools. They fell around her, bouncing off her shoulder, as air locked in her chest.

Elliot Bryon reached for the closest weapon, a metal poker stoking the fire to his right.

"Come on, Detective. You're better than this." Swinging the red-hot metal above her, he pried the hammer from her hand. He tossed it out of reach.

She couldn't lose. For Penny's sake. For hers. Campbell backed away from the burning rod and widened her stance. She'd trained in close quarters defense. She could do this. Forcing her lungs to work overtime, she lunged. She faked a head-on strike, then pivoted and rammed her fist into Elliot's gut. She heard the air crush from his lungs, but it didn't slow him down.

Pain ignited as the stoker connected with her arm. She jerked back. The momentum threw her off balance, and she hit the floor. A gut-wrenching kick to her ribs caught her off guard. Campbell rolled into the same wall to protect her organs. But it wasn't enough. She wasn't enough against him. She wasn't strong enough for Penny, for this town. For Kendric.

White pulses of light lined the edges of her vision. Tears burned in her eyes, but she wouldn't let them fall.

"You know, I'm actually quite disappointed, Detective. You hear about all these mothers desperate to save their children. So desperate they can lift cars or chase down the people responsible for hurting their kids." Heat flared and ebbed as Elliot Bryon prowled in front of her between her and the flames. Back and forth. Back and forth. "You… You're just like everyone else I've had to deal with. Weak. Penny deserves better, don't you think?"

Penny deserves better, and so do I. Kendric's words took her out of the moment. She'd come to Battle Mountain as an assignment and to find closure, but she didn't want closure. She wanted the man who'd tied himself to her through their daughter, who'd come for her when Sabrina Bryon had abducted and drugged her for information. The rational part of herself warned pursuing a future with Kendric would be a lost cause, but love wasn't rational.

Love.

She'd fallen back in love with him. Through all the hurt, the loneliness, the secrets, he'd given her permission to just be…her. Intense, defensive, high-strung. She'd always been an outsider within her own department, with her friends, but none of that had stopped him from working his way back into her heart. He'd supported her despite his bitterness toward the world because maybe she'd left an impression on him, too. And that was worth living for.

Campbell fisted her uninjured hand. Proving her worth had nothing to do with her career as she'd convinced herself all these years. Yes, focusing on her job had been a way to put a roof over her daughter's head and to ensure Campbell never got hurt the way Kendric had hurt her again, but that wasn't all there was in life. She wanted more, and she wasn't going to stop until she had it. No matter the cost. "You're wrong."

Sweat dripped into her eyes, but she didn't have to see Elliot Bryon in order to take him down. Campbell rocketed her foot into the back of his knee. He went down, swinging the stoker wide. Campbell wrestled the handle from his grip. The heavy metal connected with his elbow, and an ear-piercing scream filled the open space.

Campbell shoved to her feet and ran for the door on the other side of the room. "Penny!"

"Mommy!" a familiar voice cried.

She brushed the doorknob with her uninjured hand a split second before searing pain enveloped her scalp. Elliot Bryon fisted her hair, wrenching her away from the door. Clawing at his hand, Campbell stabbed the poker backward with everything she had left. In vain.

He slammed her face into the nearest wall and the steel fell from her grip. Bone-deep aches spread along her neck and skull as Elliot spun her to face him and wrapped a grip around her throat. "Guess you can't handle getting your hands dirty, after all, Detective."

Her heart pumped too loud in her ears. A low ringing filled her head. The air in her lungs pressurized until she was sure her organs would burst. She couldn't breathe, couldn't think. She tried to pry his hand from her throat, but he was too strong. Campbell kicked at him as hard as she could. Her vision wavered. She was going to pass out.

Penny. She had to fight for Penny.

A cold burst of air exploded across her skin.

Elliot Bryon's head shot around, confusion dragging his eyebrows together.

A familiar voice stripped her nerve endings bare. "Get your damn hands off my partner."

Chapter Fourteen

"Officer Hudson, what a pleasant surprise." Elliot Bryon raised his hands in surrender, but Kendric knew better than to look a gift horse in the mouth.

Campbell slid to the floor, coughing as she tried to catch her breath.

"Mr. Bryon." Kendric took aim with his sidearm, finger over the trigger. "You're looking better than I expected for a man with two holes in his chest."

"Ah, well. Turns out my wounds weren't as severe as my surgeons thought." A hint of exhaustion and pain contorted Elliot Bryon's mouth. "Helps when you know exactly where to shoot yourself."

Campbell rolled to her side. His gut clenched as he took in the sweat, dirt and blood caked across her beautiful face. She'd fought nearly to the death for their daughter. Why the hell had it taken him so long to realize they were meant to be together? That he'd walked away from the best thing this life could ever provide?

"You okay, Bell?" he asked. "Can you walk?"

Campbell nodded, rubbing her throat as she climbed to unstable balance.

"Good. Find Penny. Get her back to the truck." Kendric raised his gaze to Elliot Bryon. "I've got this."

He didn't have to ask her twice. Campbell shuffled toward a door at the back of the building. The work of two fires chased back the numbness taking hold in his hands and feet as he kept his attention on the bastard who'd tried to destroy his world and that of Sabrina Bryon and her infant daughter. "It's over, Elliot. Sabrina told us everything."

"Are you sure about that?" Elliot asked.

Campbell almost fell through the opening she'd created at the back. The door hit the wall behind it, but she didn't go in. "Penny?"

Instinct and Elliot Bryon's casual demeanor triggered warning in Kendric's gut. "What's wrong?"

"She's not…" Campbell stumbled back, shaking her head. "She's not here. I heard her. She was calling for me. I heard her!"

"Did I forget to mention that?" Elliot Bryon cocked his head to one side and lowered his hands.

Kendric closed the distance between him and the son of a bitch responsible for all of this. He fisted Elliot's jacket in one hand, pressing the barrel of his weapon into the man's side. Pain exploded through his shoulder, but he wasn't going to let it stop him from getting to Penny. "Where is she!"

"Tsk, tsk, tsk. That's not how you want to treat the man who holds her daughter's life in his hands, is it?" A wide smile deepened lines around the perpetrator's eyes and mouth. Then drained. "Tell you what. I'll offer you the same deal I gave to your partner there. Arrest me, and you'll never see that little girl again. Tell me where my wife is, and you have my word I'll send you Penny's location as soon as I'm clear of this backward town. I just hope you're not already too late."

"You son of a bitch. You'd let an innocent child die just to get your revenge? So you don't have to face what you've done?" Nausea churned in Kendric's gut as the answer surfaced.

Elliot shrugged as best he could. "We all have motives for making the choices we do, Officer Hudson. Mine is survival, and Sabrina is standing in my way."

"You won't get away with this, even if you do get to Sabrina," Kendric said.

"Judging from the fact you're bleeding through your shirt, I already have." Elliot nodded toward Kendric's shoulder.

Campbell moved faster than he expected. Grabbing a rifle set against one wall, she swung the butt of the weapon against Elliot Bryon's head. The man dropped harder than a sack of rocks at Kendric's feet. "That's for kidnapping my daughter."

"Well, that didn't go as expected." Admiration flooded through him. Her strength would save their daughter. He just wished he'd trusted her sooner.

"Cuff him. If Penny's not here, he wouldn't risk being out of touch to make sure she can't escape wherever he's holding her." She crouched at Elliot Bryon's side and started patting him down. Pulling a phone from the bastard's pocket, she set the device in front of the kidnapper's face to unlock the screen. "She has to be close."

Kendric collected the man's wrists behind his back and cuffed him. "There's spotty cell service out here. Even if we access it, we might not have a location."

"Then we look for her." Campbell shot to her feet, heading for the door. Muted bruises were already swelling across her face. She'd held off the suspect responsible for taking her daughter alone. Was there anything this woman couldn't do?

Kendric turned to stop her. "Campbell, you can't march out there in the middle of a blizzard to search for her. Hypothermia isn't a joke out here."

"I'm not just going to let her die, Kendric. She's my daughter," she said. "She's out there, alone and scared. All she wants is to go home, and I'll do whatever it takes to make that happen. You ran to escape the world and everyone in it. But isn't there just one person in your life you'd be willing to die for to ensure they'd live? Or are you really so angry and resentful that no one has a shot to earn your love anymore?"

His throat dried. "We have to stick together. It's the only way—"

Campbell's gaze slipped over his shoulder a split second before she swung him around. Putting her between him and the rifle in Elliot Bryon's cuffed hands.

"No!" The gunshot ripped through her back and exited her front, barely missing him. She fell forward into Kendric's chest. Her fingers fisted in his jacket but released just as quickly as she collapsed. The hard *thunk* of her knees hitting cement reverberated through him.

Elliot Bryon ran for the door and out into the storm. Gone.

Kendric's hands shook as he laid Campbell across the floor. Blood seeped between his fingers. He added pressure to the wound, but it had gone through and through. He couldn't stop the bleeding alone. "Shhh. I've got you. It's going to be okay. Just keep breathing. Okay. Try not to move."

"He's getting away." Her voice wavered as tears slipped down her cheeks. Campbell pressed her chin to her chest to get a better visual of the wound and slipped her hand over his.

"Don't worry about that. I need you to focus on staying conscious. You got me? Stay with me." After everything they'd been through, it couldn't end like this. Damn it. He needed to get her out of here. "Hang on to me. I can get you to the truck. The radios should still be working."

"You need to go," she said. "Without me. I'll just slow you down."

Not an option. Kendric fit his injured arm beneath her knees and hauled her to his chest. His strength buckled as the tendons in his shoulder threatened to dislocate. A groan clawed up his throat as he got to his feet. "You're out of your damn mind if you think I'm leaving you."

"Penny." Campbell raised her bloodied hand to his face, following the pattern of scars on the right side. His internal shame for the physical evidence of his failure wanted him to pull away, but he couldn't. Not from her. Over the course of the past few days, she'd inexplicably become part of him. He could extricate her from his life as easily as one of his organs. He wasn't leaving her. "I thought I could protect her, but she needs you. Go. Please."

"She needs you, too. You're all she's ever known." He smoothed her hair away from her face to avoid the truth. She was right. Campbell was in no condition to brave the dropping temperatures, and any movement on her part could increase blood flow. She had to stay here. And he had to go. Kendric set her down as gently as possible. A moan escaped her control and gripped his heart in a vise. He pressed his forehead against hers.

"I'll be back as soon as I can with help. Stay here. I'm not finished with you."

"I'm not finished with you, either." A weak smile exaggerated the paleness of her skin. "Bring our daughter home."

"I give you my word." Kendric slipped out the same door Elliot Bryon had escaped, leaving his heart behind. His skin contracted along the back of his neck and scalp as the storm did its job to sweep across the landscape. One arm raised to protect his face, he struggled through shin-deep snow in search of some other structure nearby, somewhere the bastard would've stashed a four-year-old. Winds whipped through the tree line that surrounded the back of the property. He hadn't spotted it on approach. Divots pockmarked pristine snow leading from the door toward those trees. If Elliot Bryon had wanted a clean escape, he'd get out of sight as quickly as possible.

Kendric jogged to catch up. There was a chance he was walking straight into a trap, but the reward at the end of this was far worth the risk. His family was all that mattered. His throat burned against freezing temperatures. He ducked into the tree line, immediately finding himself in a whole new world of muffled silence and stillness. The tracks veered northeast. No sight of Elliot Bryon or an ambush, but he couldn't discount the possibility. Tension bled down his spine as he took each step with care. The weight of being watched settled between his shoulder blades, and Kendric turned a split second before the crack of a gunshot.

The bullet whizzed by his right ear and clipped the shell of cartilage. He pumped his legs hard, struggling through snow to get to cover. Another round ripped through the tree bark at his left.

"It's over, Officer Hudson. There's nowhere for you to go." Snow crunched beneath heavy footsteps, growing louder second by second. "That little girl is going to freeze to death because of you, and if she doesn't, she'll starve. And to think, you could've stopped any of this from happening. All you had to do was tell me where you're keeping Sabrina. You sure you can live with that choice the rest of your short life?"

Kendric pressed his skull against the tree at his back. His time had come. He could either choose to stay disconnected from the world he'd left behind—to hide from his circumstances—or he could fight his way back into it. Back to Campbell and Penny. He checked the rounds in his magazine and loaded a bullet into the chamber.

His decision was already made.

"The question isn't whether or not I can live with it, Elliot. What you should be worried about is what I'll do to find her." He brought his weapon up and took aim at the man on the other side of a small clearing.

Kendric pulled the trigger at the same time another bullet jerked Elliot Bryon's head back.

THE GUNSHOT ECHOED through the building. Louder than it should've been. Close.

For a moment, it paralyzed her lungs before only the sound of crackling flames broke through the haze. Campbell pressed her hand into the bullet wound in her side. The pain threatened to tear through her, but she'd survived heartbreak and loss and the physical pain of

Penny's birth to get to this point. She wasn't going to just roll over and die. "Kendric."

The muscles in her jaw protested under the pressure of her back teeth. Another groan vibrated as she forced herself to stand. Kendric was out there against a mountain of threats. Including the damn elements themselves. If Elliot Bryon had gotten to him…

Campbell took a step forward. Then another. Her strength escaped as quickly as blood seeped from her wound, but she had to know if he'd made it. She had to know her daughter was safe. Dizziness thrust her into the doorjamb. The storm had intensified, but she'd do anything to see Penny again. To see Kendric. To sit in front of the fireplace at Whispering Pines Ranch and sleep away the day with the two of them snuggled up next to her. It wasn't a fantasy. It was as real as the cold seeping past her coat, and she wasn't going to let it slip through her fingers. "I'm coming."

Her heel caught on the stairs, and she pitched forward. Her broken hand screamed in agony as she hit the ground. Campbell rolled onto her back. Snow melted against her face as the world threatened darkness and hollowness and cold. She had to get up. Gravity tried to convince her this was where she needed to be. Right here in the open, beneath a cloud-covered sky with the trees and mountains to protect her, but her heart warned otherwise. It infused her with an energy she hadn't known existed and allowed her to get off the ground.

The wind burned against her skin and whipped her hair into her face. Pinpricks of numbness climbed up her fingers as she pushed toward the trees. The blood leaking from the bullet wound had slowed with the frigid temperatures. Or her body had already started shutting down. She wasn't sure which one she preferred. Either way, she wasn't going to stop until she found Penny and Kendric. Her throat tightened as she hummed the lullaby she sang to her daughter every night before bed. "Twinkle, twinkle, I love you."

Silence descended all around her as the storm failed to batter against the surrounding trees. Two sets of tracks led northeast of her position, but every cell in her body had her following a different path. She shuffled through heavy snow, her jaw no longer quivering to keep her warm. She'd stopped shivering altogether. "Ooh, my baby, this is true."

"When you snuggle next to me," a small voice said. "I'm as happy as can be."

Campbell froze. She'd already lost too much blood, but she hadn't imagined it. Spinning in circles, she searched the whitewashed wilderness for signs of life. She caught sight of a small shed tucked back, camouflaged in snow and wood. She took a step forward. This was it. It had to be. Because if she was hallucinating… Her stomach revolted against the idea. "Penny?"

"Mommy!" The solid wood door of the shed—brand-new from the look of it—jerked against an equally solid padlock with a combination dial.

"Penny! Hold on. I'm coming, baby." The snow was deeper here. It fell into the tops of her boots and soaked her jeans straight through. Campbell pulled on the padlock with everything she had, but it wouldn't budge. Elliot Bryon had taken her gun, she'd left the hammer in the abandoned smithing building and there was no chance in hell she'd guess the combination to the lock. She swept bloody hands down the door. "I'm going to get you out of there. I promise."

"Mommy, I want you. I want to go home," Penny said. "The man took me from Grandma and Papa. I tried to scream, but he wouldn't let me. He said I had to be quiet or he'd hurt them. I'm sorry, Mommy. I just want to go home."

"I know. I know. It's not your fault. We're going to go home. Okay? I'm right here. I just need to find something to break the lock." Pain flared into her side, and Campbell doubled over. Catching herself on a fallen tree, she forced herself to catch her breath.

"Don't leave me! Mommy!" Anxiety punctuated the girl's kicks against the shed door.

"I'm…right here, baby." Her vision distorted as she pulled her hand free of her wound. The faster her heart beat, the faster she'd bleed out. The trees tilted on their axis despite the added leverage of her hand on one of the wood's fallen soldiers. It was harder to breathe now. Heavier on her chest. "I'm not going anywhere."

Campbell pulled at the branch in her hand. Desperation flooded through her as she tried again and again. But it wouldn't break.

"Mommy!" Penny's cries pierced through the low ringing in her ears. "I want out of here!"

"I'm here. I'm not leaving you, Penny. I'm…" The world ripped out from under her. Ice infiltrated the collar of her coat as she tried to find that legendary strength she'd always relied on. Why couldn't she use it when she needed it the most? Being run off the road, surviving a rollover, resisting a drug and an interrogation, getting through heartbreak and isolation and loneliness not once but twice, the trauma of Penny's birth and hearing the love of her life had been caught in a deadly explosion—none of that had broken her.

This wouldn't, either.

Campbell hauled her hand up, and she latched onto the same branch she'd tried to dislocate to get back on her feet. Wood groaned in her hand until it gave way, and she stumbled back. A small sense of victory charged through her, but this was only the beginning. She still had to break the lock. The oversize branch dragged behind her as she trod through another pass of snow. "Get back, baby. I don't want you to get hurt."

Bringing her makeshift bat over her shoulder, she bit back the scream of pain and put everything she had into swinging it as hard as she could. The padlock bounced, then settled back into place. She swung again, angling down to separate the lock from the mechanism. Twice. Three times.

The padlock busted along one side. Relief softened the tension in her legs, and she fell forward against the door. Wrenching it open, she reached for the four-year-old lunging at her from the dark. Mangled, matted hair caught in her fingers as she clutched Penny to her chest. "It's okay now. I'm here. You're safe."

A glimmer of light in one corner of the shed stared down at them. The light from a small camera. The bastard had been surveilling Penny the entire time. Had most likely put a similar camera in the smithy building. That was how she'd been able to hear Penny's cries. Elliot Bryon had set out to not only physically punish her but emotionally and mentally destroy her. But it hadn't worked. Campbell framed her daughter's small face between both hands and kissed her cheek. "Let's get out of here. Okay?"

Penny nodded, her tear-streaked face coated with dirt.

Campbell picked up her daughter and retraced her

steps through the trees. Managing the added weight kicked up her heart rate. She just had to get Penny to the truck. From there they could call for backup if Kendric hadn't already.

They left the safety of the trees, every sense she owned on alert for something off. The crush of wind and snow stole her breath. She tucked her coat around Penny and held on tight. Her exhalations weren't fogging in front of her mouth anymore. Her body temperature had dropped too far.

They weren't going to make it.

Tears froze on her cheeks as snow caught in her lashes. Mere minutes would separate them from life and death out here. Campbell smoothed her daughter's hair against her head and tucked deeper against Penny's cold ear. Her side had soaked through with blood. "I love you. You know that, right? You know I'll always protect you. No matter what. You were the best thing that ever happened in my life. Do you understand? I don't regret a single moment we had together. I love you so much."

"I love you, too, Mommy." Penny pressed her pink face into Campbell's neck, squishing her arms between them.

Her strength gave out. Campbell's knees buckled, and she wrapped her arms around Penny's back to soften the coming blow. They fell in a tangle of limbs into a cushion of snow, her daughter trapped beneath her. She couldn't force her body to respond.

"Mommy, get up! You have to get up. I'm stuck." Penny's scream pierced through the dizziness determined to pull her under. "Mommy, a man!"

"It's okay, Penny. I'm a friend of your mom's. I'm not going to hurt you. I'm here to help. Okay? Your mom's going to be okay. I promise. I'll get you some-place warm." A dark outline took shape beside them. So familiar. Safe. Warmth encased her back as the shape pressed a large hand between her shoulder blades. "Damn it, woman. I told you to stay put."

Her desperation to keep Penny close fired as he pulled her daughter free. Campbell reached to hang on to her even as recognition soothed her fight-or-flight instincts. "No."

"I've got her, Bell." Kendric soothed Penny's back as the four-year-old's sobs intensified. "Over here!" He turned back to her, his hand still in place. "Stay with us, Campbell. Don't you dare give up. We need you. Penny and I need you."

A myriad of voices filtered in and out as lethargy and cold and pain took hold. She didn't know if she could do as he asked. Going to sleep felt like a much better solution.

"Here, I'll hold Penny. You and Isla take care of Campbell," a male voice said. The chief?

Another rush of movement penetrated her vision. Although she couldn't pick out one distinct shape from another, she had the feeling she was being moved. She wasn't cold anymore. Campbell gave in to the weight of her eyelids as exhaustion sucked her down.

"Vitals are slowing." Another voice weaved through the darkness. "I'm losing her!"

Chapter Fifteen

"Open your eyes, Campbell." Kendric squeezed her hand again, but it was no use. The surgeon who'd stitched up her insides from Elliot Bryon's bullet had advised him her recovery would take time. Days. Maybe weeks. Not good enough. He needed her to look at him, to ensure him everything was going to be okay.

Was this how she'd felt at the side of his hospital bed after that bomb had torn his life apart? The impatience. The worry. The second-guessing. How had she survived?

Monitors chimed consistent rhythms from the other side of the bed. Bruising and lacerations flawed the creamy skin of her arms and face, but she'd regained more color since her surgery two days ago. Kendric sandwiched her hand between both of his and kissed her torn knuckles. She'd fought like hell to get Penny back, putting her life in danger not once but twice. He'd never forget her strength, her love and commitment.

"Any change?" Isla Vach slipped into the room as quiet as a ghost, almost ambushing him. Or had his defenses worn out since leaving those woods?

"Nothing yet." He counted off the pulse at the base of Campbell's neck.

The EMT rounded into his peripheral vision. "She's been through a lot. Lost a lot of blood. Not to mention exposure to freezing temperatures. It might take some—"

"Time. Yeah. So I've been told." Pressing his cheek to Campbell's hand, he fought the exhaustion slithering through his veins. The past forty-eight hours had undermined every choice he'd made since leaving Denver, but he knew exactly where he wanted to be from now on. Right here. With Campbell. Forever. "How's Penny doing?"

"Good. She and Mazi are having a blast together at the ranch. I think Chief Ford is going to try to help them build snow forts this afternoon. She asks about her mom when she slows down enough to think, which isn't often, I'll admit, but she's getting through it. Especially with Karie Ford's baked goods." Isla took an empty seat on the opposite side of the bed. "How are you?"

"I'm fine." He wasn't sure how many "I'm fines" that made. He'd lost count within the first couple of hours of waiting for Campbell to come out of surgery, but he appreciated the concern. From Isla. From Easton Ford and Genevieve. Even Gregson and Alma had made it a point to check in on him. "Any news I might've missed?"

"Chief Ford closed the case against Sabrina Bryon. From what that district attorney said, she'll most likely get time served because of her circumstances with a new baby. She did abduct and kidnap a law enforcement officer, so she doesn't get off scot-free, but your chief thought it better to let her move on with her life. Unfortunately, we'll never know what kind of life that'll be. Seems she took off after your department got your and Campbell's location. Nobody has seen her or the baby since." Isla got to her feet, studying the monitors recording Campbell's vitals.

His gut said they wouldn't. "What happened with the Jane Doe we found? Rachel Stephenson."

"Now, that's an interesting story. Turns out Sabrina wrestled Rachel's gun away during the struggle at the cabin. It's the gun she used to shoot you." Isla backed away from the monitors. "The crime lab connected the bullet in your shoulder to six other unsolved murder investigations along the West Coast. Seems Rachel Stephenson was exactly who Sabrina Bryon claimed. A hired killer working at her husband's beck and call as long as he was connected to her bosses down south. Now that the investigation is closed, I imagine her body will be returned to her family, if she has any. In my experience, people in her line of work don't have many personal connections. They can't afford to."

"What experience is that?" he asked.

A weak smile thinned the EMT's mouth as she took her seat again. "Have you figured out who shot Elliot Bryon yet?"

"No." Kendric still couldn't get the image of the man's head snapping back with the bullet between his eyes. A shot like that wasn't easy, but nobody in BMPD had come forward to take credit. Dr. Chloe Pascale had sent the bullet to the crime lab in Denver, but it would be weeks before they heard anything. "I keep replaying what happened, but nothing jumps out. Whoever took the shot is one hell of a marksman. They managed to stay out of sight, hit their target and get out of there without being seen."

Almost like Sabrina Bryon had from the primary crime scene.

"I'm sure you and your fellow boys in blue will find the shooter. Which reminds me, they've recovered Elliot Bryon's handgun, the one he used to shoot himself. I don't know how he pulled it off, but he hid it in a secret compartment under his side of his and Sabrina's bed. Right where EMTs found him after the 911 call. His prints were the only ones left behind. Same goes for the boots that went with him to the hospital. A nurse found him trying to toss them in one of the hazardous waste bins. Guess he knew you and Detective Dwyer were closing in," she said. "Listen, Hudson, I know I'm just an EMT and not exactly part of your department, but I can take a shift to sit with her if you want to get some sleep or head down to the cafeteria."

"I'd prefer to stay with her. Thanks, though. For everything." He turned back to Campbell. "If it weren't for you, she might not have made it."

"Anytime." Isla pushed to her feet, heading for the door. "You've got my number in case you need to get a hold of me. I'm happy to watch Penny as long as you need."

The door closed behind her as though she'd never visited.

"You should've let her stay. You look like hell." Campbell's hand twitched in his, and he caught the barest glimpse of her cerulean eyes beneath heavy lids staring across the bed at him.

Kendric sat forward in his seat, his heart shooting straight into his throat. Relief unlike anything he'd felt before produced a burn in his eyes, and he clutched her hand against his chest. "Hey. Welcome back to the land of the living, Detective. How do you feel?"

"Like you should remember I'm not a detective."

Her lips curled at one corner of her mouth. She took in the room around her, the IV feeding into her vein, him. "Where's Penny?"

"At the ranch. Chief Ford and Chloe are watching her until you're recovered enough. I wasn't sure having her here was the best idea." He soothed pressure into the space between her thumb and index finger. "She's been asking for you. She wants to make sure you're okay."

"And my parents?" she asked.

"They're here, and they're fine," he said. "Elliot Bryon didn't hurt them. They've been apologizing and agonizing since the moment they got to town, but they're happy Penny and you are safe."

"Good. The last thing I remember is getting her out of that shed." Campbell moved to lift one arm, stopped by the IV in her arm. She tugged her hand free of his and set it against the wound in her side. "What happened out there?"

"Not much. I followed Elliot Bryon's tracks into the woods, hoping he'd gone for wherever he was keeping Penny. It was an ambush. He fired a couple rounds, but in the end, he was the one to take a bullet." Kendric fit a strand of her matted hair away from her face. "You and Penny don't have to worry about him anymore."

"That's good news." She settled back against the pillows, her expression softening. "You came for me. Even after we said all those things to each other."

"Yeah. Not my proudest moment." He collected the shattered snow globe from where he'd set it on the table beside her bed and handed it over. "I found this in the SUV. I'm sorry to say it didn't survive my driving skills, but I recognized it from the first Christmas we were together. I didn't realize you'd kept it all this time."

"This is why you risked your life for me and Penny?" she asked.

"As much as I wanted to keep living in my misery, I knew if I was wrong about you, it wouldn't matter if I made it out of there alive." Regret and a million other emotions collected at the base of his skull. "I'm sorry, Bell. For leaving you all those years ago. For not being there to help raise Penny. For thinking you were using me to investigate my department. I have no excuse. I was wrong, and angry and feeling like a failure in every aspect of my life. That's why I ran to the ATF, why I resigned after Agent Freehan tried to destroy this town. I thought if I could fix what was broken, I could be someone worthy of you and your love. That I would finally be good enough for you again. And when I failed at even that, I took it out on you and your job with Internal Affairs, but you're the one who deserves better than someone like me. I want to do better. I want to prove I can be the man you and Penny believe I am."

She turned the broken snow globe in her hand before offering it back. "I kinda like the you you've become."

"Just kind of?" A smile pulled at his mouth. "Is that all?"

"Well, I mean, there's room for improvement. For both of us. But yeah." She nodded. "I remember lying facedown in the snow, and I heard your voice. You kept telling me to hang on while you were holding Penny."

The image crystallized so clearly in his mind, forcing him to relive the worst moment of his life all over again. His throat dried, and he wanted nothing more than to hold her, to make sure this was real.

"You were trying to calm her down while you kept one hand on my back." She motioned over her shoulder with her free hand before returning her gaze to his. "That's what I want, Kendric. I watched you detach from your family and friends, your coworkers, me. I saw how the bombing stripped more than a few layers of skin from your face, and there was nothing I could do to hold on to you. But seeing you with Penny, trying to comfort her despite the fact I was losing consciousness—it showed me how much we've been missing. There isn't a single thing you have to prove to me or anyone else. You can be angry, you can change jobs or move to another town if you have to, you can run. Move to Denver or don't. It doesn't matter. We just need you to love us. Do you think you can manage that, Officer Hudson?"

Kendric traced his thumb along the back of her hand, memorizing the pattern of veins beneath the thin skin. He'd imagined this moment so many times, the invitation to come home and be part of Campbell's life again, the weight of his isolation and anger a distant memory. He'd scripted answers a thousand times, but right now, none of them came to mind. Because this wasn't a fantasy. She was real. Penny was real, and he wasn't going to take a single moment of his future with them for granted. He kissed her hand, aggravating his own wound in his shoulder. Just proof this wasn't all in his head. "Yeah, Detective Dwyer. I think I can manage that."

"DON'T PUT THAT in your mouth!" Kendric lunged across the kitchen. "No, that doesn't mean you can lick it off the floor, either. There's no five-second rule for juice and places we put our feet."

A high-pitched laugh trilled through the living room

as Penny ran down the hallway into her new bedroom. Campbell couldn't help but laugh at the absurdity of their life at the moment. The move from Denver hadn't been easy as she was still recovering from the wound in her side, but Kendric had ordered the movers around like no one's business. The renovated farmhouse they'd found just outside Battle Mountain was perfect. High ceilings, tall enough for the massive fir tree Weston and Easton Ford had dragged inside, lit up with the addition of white Christmas lights and silvery ornaments. The four-foot-deep island in the kitchen allowed all three of them to bake cookies as many times as they wanted with plenty of room left over. And the enlarged soaker tub in the main bathroom had held its own more than enough times since they'd moved in. Absolutely perfect. But none of it meant a damn without the two most important people in the world.

The sectional cushions dipped as Kendric collapsed beside her, winded. Tugging her legs onto his lap, he fanned heated hands across her shins. "I don't understand it. We kicked the soccer ball around for an hour. I took her to the park. She hasn't had any sugar today other than the juice she just tried to lick off the floor. It's like she runs on never-ending batteries. Does she ever get tired?"

"No, but she sleeps through everything." Campbell set the book she'd been reading aside, pulled his head closer and planted a kiss at his temple. The past few weeks had been everything she'd dreamed. Her CO had accepted her resignation with understanding, albeit disappointment. Officers willing to dive into the Internal Affairs world came along few and far between, but they'd manage without her. She'd miss it. Investigating.

Helping people, but until the bullet wound in her side had healed completely, she was out of the game. Not a total loss. Watching Kendric try to parent a stubborn and energetic four-year-old girl had its perks.

"Everything, huh? I like the sound of that." He scratched at his ear, refusing to look at her, but she knew him well enough to follow his line of thought. "What did the doctor say at your three-week follow-up?"

She nudged him with the spine of her book. "Looks good. Minimal scarring considering Isla's fine work to stitch me back together. The woman does good work."

"Anything else?" His voice notched a bit higher as though his nerves had gotten the better of him. "Extracurricular activities you've been cleared for?"

"Such as?" She liked this game. Forcing him to talk about what he wanted—sometimes what he needed—instead of bottling it up to explode later. It was a habit they both had to explore, but the trust was there now. Something they hadn't really had before the explosion all those years ago. Not like this. With Penny to care for, they didn't have any other choice, and Campbell liked it that way. No more secrets. No more half-truths or distance. They were in this together. Partners. Forever.

"Oh, I don't know. Making out and stuff. Just off the top of my head," he said.

"We do that now." She couldn't keep her smile to herself. Their makeup sessions had been fun the past few weeks. Nothing like two bullet wounds to make a woman appreciate the sensuality she'd been missing since nearly losing the father of her child to a madman.

Offense contorted his expression. "We don't do stuff."

"Oh, it's the stuff you're interested in. I see. I misunderstood." Campbell leaned forward, slower than she wanted to go, and pressed her mouth to his ear. "Here I thought you were complaining about my kissing skills."

A scoff escaped his control. The perfect compliment to the red flaring in his cheeks. A shiver chased across his shoulders as she nibbled on the shell of his ear. "No complaints here."

"That's what I thought." She settled back against the arm of the couch and cracked the spine of her book.

"You're not going to tell me, are you?" Kendric set his head back against the sofa. The too-tense, isolated and disconnected reserve officer she'd met at that primary crime scene didn't exist anymore. Not with her, at least. In his place sat the very human, inspiring and hopeful man she'd fallen in love with all over again. A man she wanted to raise her daughter with, one she envisioned growing old with her here in Battle Mountain. This place was home now. Because of him.

"Tell you what?" She dropped her book slightly, enough to give her a view of the desperation in his gaze. "Oh, we're still talking about this? For your information, the doctor did have something to say about stuff at my appointment today. He said he will get back to me."

"You're killing me," he said.

"I'm teasing. He said we're all clear, and I can't wait to show you exactly what you walked away from five years ago." She lifted her eyebrows suggestively.

"A mistake I regret every single day." A low moan strained in his throat. "You're going to drive me insane."

"Just wait. It gets better. Just as soon as Penny goes to bed for the night." Campbell delighted in her ability to set him off with a single look, a single touch. The man beneath her resembled a ticking time bomb. One wrong move, and she'd find herself in his control. "I'm telling you. Nothing wakes that girl once she's asleep. Then you can have me all to yourself."

"Okay. That's great news. We just have to wait until then." Kendric tapped his fingers in an even rhythm against her shin. "Until then you can tell me the truth about why you joined Internal Affairs."

"It doesn't really matter, does it?" she asked. "I turned in my resignation."

He poked her shoulder. "While I was in the hospital for burn treatment, two officers in suits came in to ask me about what happened. They wouldn't tell me who they were or which precinct they were from, so I didn't give them anything. Told them to read my statement." He didn't wait for her response. "They came to you, didn't they? They threatened to open an investigation into me unless you cooperated, and when I left you to raise a baby on your own, they leveraged your career against you. Got you to work for them."

"I wasn't going to let them ruin your reputation or charge you for something that wasn't your fault." She closed her book. "Not after everything you'd been through."

"Why didn't you tell me sooner?" he asked.

"Would you have believed me? Would you have listened to me after the words *Internal Affairs*?" The answer was already in his expression, but none of that mattered now. "Like I said, it doesn't matter now. I'm happy right where I am. With you and Penny, here." She pressed her mouth to his. "Any sign of Sabrina Bryon?"

"Not yet. She's good at disappearing, and now that she's got justice for her sister's death, I don't think we'll see her anytime soon," he said.

"You still think she's the one who shot Elliot Bryon in those woods—Dean Pratt—whoever he was?" she asked.

"Makes the most sense. He tried to kill her and their unborn baby. Stands to reason she'd want to make sure he couldn't come after her again. Although, we'll never have the proof, and it was in defense of a Battle Mountain reserve officer. No prosecutor will come within ten feet of bringing charges." Kendric wedged his uninjured hand against his head, that forest green gaze warming in an instant. "What time does Penny go to bed again?"

"Four more hours." She got back to pretending to read her book, pretending as though his insinuations didn't have an effect on her at all. Between figuring out their new relationship, caring for two bullet wounds, moving in together, resigning from her job and ensuring Penny could accept the new addition to their family, their physical relationship had been limited to a G rating. But with him staring at her as though she were the only woman in the world… She couldn't think of anything else but testing that rating. "Nothing you can't handle, right?"

The crash of something significant and heavy ripped them from the bubble they'd created around themselves. Kendric hauled her legs off him long enough to escape and get to his feet. "I had more luck with the bomb that blew off the right side of my face."

"And yet, you're still as handsome as ever." She watched him disappear down the hallway.

"Holy—" Silence descended for a series of breaths. "Penny Elana Dwyer, you were gone for two minutes. How on earth did you manage… You know what? No. I give up." Heavy footsteps registered. "Bell, she's going to need a bath. And so is the rest of her room. Do you think the fire department would let us borrow one of their hoses?"

The joys of parenthood. Campbell plugged her nose as she identified the problem without moving from her spot on the couch. And the smells. Vapor rub. An entire room smeared with vapor rub. "No. They stopped answering our calls when you called the paramedics after she scraped her knee outside."

"That thing took forever to stop bleeding. I thought she was potassium deficient." Kendric opened the front door, then the back and all the windows in the main living area.

"I'll get her in the bath. You clean up whatever she used to paint her room." Campbell had enough experience to know exactly how long it would take to clean vapor rub off the walls and her daughter's toys. Some of them still had a film from last year. Her side twinged as she got to her feet, but she wasn't going to let this wound stop her from living her life. Or enjoying having Kendric back.

Suspicion narrowed his gaze as he turned on her. "How do you know she painted her room? Has she done this before? Is it going to happen again?"

"Welcome to parenting, honey." She kissed him lightly on the lips, throwing a parody of his first words to her after she'd come to Battle Mountain back at him. "You're going to love it."

Campbell headed down the hallway, grateful this wasn't a job she had to do on her own anymore, and that Penny would be able to breathe clearly for the next few days.

He called after her. "You never answered my question. Is this going to keep happening?"

Campbell started the tub. "I think you already know the answer to that."

Epilogue

Isla Vach stripped gloves from her hands and tossed them into the garbage.

Her twelve-hour shift was officially over. Everyone was saved. She could finally pick up Mazi from Whispering Pines Ranch for their annual Christmas movie marathon tonight.

Collecting her purse from her locker, she smiled at the sound of jokes and laughter of the firefighters upstairs at dinner. Battle Mountain Fire and Rescue had run off volunteers for years, but after the forest fire a few months back, the state had provided funds to hire a full EMT staff and pay the men and women who'd run headfirst into the flames. Just her luck, too. Going back to work hadn't ever been part of her and Clint's plan after they'd had Mazi.

But things had changed on his last deployment.

Now it was up to her to be there for their daughter. Flaws and all.

"Movie marathon night, right?" one of the firefighters asked.

"Yeah. Just leaving." She pulled her keys from her purse. "It's going to be a rager until about eight o'clock when Mazi passes out."

"Have a great night, Isla." He moved toward the stairs, most likely angling to get his share of dinner before it was gone. "Say hello to Mazi for me, will you?"

"Will do. Good night." Crisp December air closed around her as she walked through the engine bay toward her car across the street. It had been a mostly quiet night. Two calls. Nothing she and her partner hadn't been able to handle. Nothing like the terror she'd faced trying to stitch up Kendric and Campbell a few weeks ago. She could live without that kind of anxiety again.

Isla lined her key between her index and middle finger and approached her car. Her reflection warbled in the frosted glass. She used the sleeve of her coat to dislodge some of it, catching sight of movement behind her.

A hard wall of muscle slammed her into the ground a split second before a gunshot ripped through her.

* * * * *

HIS CHRISTMAS
GUARDIAN

CINDY DEES

Chapter One

Nicholas Kane straightened the bow tie at his neck. It wasn't often he wore a tuxedo in his line of work, James Bond movies notwithstanding. The fact of the matter was that being a black operative for a shadowy, government intelligence agency had very little to do with glamour and a whole lot to do with, well, shadows.

Tonight, the man he was following, code-named Gray, was supposed to visit an expensive auction house in New York City and a private preview of the paintings and other objets d'art coming up for sale in several days' time. Hence, Nick's monkey suit.

His quarry, tall, burly and mostly bald, was not hard to spot stepping out of a black limousine and heading for the front door. Nick watched the man's second bodyguard scan up and down the street and move inside behind the main bodyguard and the principal.

He supposed it was odd that the only name he knew the man by was Gray, in spite of Nick having worked for the spymaster for the past four years. He figured Gray had gone by so many aliases over time that the guy had just gotten lazy about coming up with new names for himself.

The limousine pulled away from the curb. Its driver

would be the third member of Gray's personal security team.

Now. This was his window to slip into the auction house unspotted. While the driver parked, nobody on Gray's team would be watching the street. In two minutes or so, the driver would come back on foot and take up an unobtrusive position somewhere down the block and report on anyone suspicious who went inside the building.

Nick knew the protocol. He'd been Gray's driver more times than he could count.

He slipped out of the alley and crossed the street quickly, jaywalking to take advantage of a break in the steady stream of yellow cabs that were the lifeblood flowing through the asphalt veins of New York City.

He slowed as he approached the converted warehouse that had been turned into one of the city's most exclusive art galleries and auction venues. The brick box of a building was ugly, but the worst of its ugliness was hidden behind festive holiday lights and a huge garland of pine boughs around the front door. He knew from casing the joint earlier today that this place was, at its core, a large and very-well-secured vault. Even a guy like him would have a hard time breaking into it, let alone getting out with any of the art consignments inside it.

"Invitation?" a bored bouncer-type murmured as he reached the glass front door. Only by looking closely could Nick spot the spiderweb of steel wire embedded in the glass itself.

He reached inside his tuxedo jacket to pull out the engraved invitation, which he handed to the security guard.

"Have a good evening, Mr. Clark."

Nick had no idea where the Medusas had obtained the invitation for him, nor who the real Mr. Clark was. He was just glad the women special operators had been willing and able to help him out on short notice. They'd obviously pulled strings or called in a favor. That was how it worked in his world. It was all about who you knew. Who owed you. Who would help you out in a pinch.

Just inside the front door loomed a Christmas tree at least twelve feet tall, twinkling with lights. It was lavishly decorated in gold, silver and a creamy champagne color, all very stylish and very elegant. Two large, dim, glass-walled galleries opened off to the left and right. They were crowded with men in black tuxes and women in long gowns, all of them dripping with wealth.

Bare branches, painted white, wrapped in strands of white Christmas lights and hung with tiny red glass balls, were artfully placed all around the room. Somewhere, a harpist was plucking stripped-down versions of Christmas carols, and the air smelled of sugar cookies and... Was that the scent of hot cocoa? For just a second, Nick flashed back to his grandmother's kitchen at Christmas, helping her decorate cookies with colored sugar and sprinkles.

This place was far too chic to succumb to an actual festive air, but he appreciated the nod to the holidays. He didn't often get to celebrate them in his line of work. Sadly, evil stopped for no date on any calendar.

Downward-pointing spotlights hung on tracks across the ceilings of the galleries, creating isolated pools of brilliant radiance in the darkness. Each column of light illuminated its own treasure, some bit of color and shine created by an old master, a painting or sculpture, a piece of exquisite porcelain or jewelry.

Nick wandered into the left-hand room, keeping an eye out for Gray.

He snagged a flute of champagne off a waiter's tray and paused in front of a small painting. It was plain and mostly brown, a scene of a Dutch kitchen dominated by a fireplace and a huge iron kettle. A discreet, typed card beside the painting described it as a seventeenth century work in the style of Vermeer. It went on to say that it was possibly an unsigned study by Maria Vermeer.

Nick rolled his eyes. He was no great art expert, but even he knew that no paintings had ever been proven to be the work of Vermeer's eldest daughter. Rumors had long persisted that several surviving paintings attributed to her father were actually her work, but none had ever been proven to be hers. Obviously, the auction house was trying to drive up the price of the ugly little painting by invoking Vermeer's name. He wished them luck with their endeavor.

There.

He caught a glimpse of Gray in the gallery across the hall. Nick cast his gaze down at the Limoges porcelain vase on a stand in front of him but in no other way moved. Gray's bodyguards would be men fully as trained and observant as he himself was. No sense whipping around to stare at his subject or turning his back abruptly on the man and tipping off his security team.

After a moment more of staring at the pale gold vase with its delicate, hand-painted spray of wildflowers, he moved to his left to study a painting. The painting itself didn't interest him. But, if he unfocused his eyes, he was able to watch Gray peripherally while appearing to stare directly at the blurry colors of the art.

Gray was leaving the other display room. He was in

conversation with a man who Nick recognized as one of the owners of the gallery, and the two of them headed up the welded steel staircase rising from the middle of the ground floor.

Nick swore under his breath. Should he follow Gray upstairs and not lose sight of him, or should he hold his position down here and not risk exposing himself to Gray's men?

He compromised and headed back toward what would be a staging area for employees. Nick would lay odds there were more stairs back there, somewhere. He went through a set of swinging doors marked Employees Only and found himself in a commercial kitchen.

The place was busy, bustling with waiters coming and going, returning trays of empty glasses, picking up new trays of champagne and lifting platters of canapés. Nick blended in with the flow of waiters, moving with them through the kitchen, only peeling off to the side when he spotted the treads of stairs tucked in the corner.

He jogged up them quickly and silently. His dress shoes had custom-made soles that looked like regular shoe leather but were softer, quieter rubber.

The entire second floor of the warehouse was a single, open gallery. Paintings hung all around the space, and display stands in the middle held all manner of art objects.

The crowd was much thinner up here. As Nick slipped into the room and browsed a half dozen paintings, he noted immediately that the expected sale-price ranges on the works up here were significantly higher than those of the pieces downstairs. This was where the heavy hitters in art collection would be shopping.

Nick spent several minutes cruising the entire floor

but never spotted Gray or his companion. Swearing under his breath, he headed for the back stairs once more.

Up or down? If he chose wrong, he stood to lose the elusive Gray altogether. It had taken him a week to find out the man was doing some sort of business with this gallery, and it had been more luck than skill that he'd gotten the tip. How long would it take him to pick up the trail again, especially if the guy left New York?

Maybe never. The man hadn't been a spymaster for decades without being killed for nothing. Gray was paranoid bordering on obsessive about his personal security.

Nick made a decision and jogged up the stairs.

The third floor was also a single, spacious gallery. However, this one had a half dozen security guards posted around the space. They all stood stoically still, hands crossed in front of their belt buckles, statue-like. But he wasn't fooled for a second. Their gazes roved constantly, taking in everyone and everything in the room.

If the second floor was for exclusive collectors, the third floor held offerings for only the most serious and wealthy of them. Nick turned to stare sightlessly at the first painting he came to, a modern thing that was mostly geometric shapes. Expected price: one to three million dollars. *Well, okay, then.*

He turned to study a square white-and-blue vase that the typed card beside it identified as a Ming Dynasty piece. Expected price: two million.

Of more interest to him: the glass case protecting the Ming vase made for a decent impromptu mirror. By moving slightly to one side, Nick could scan the whole gallery in the reflection on the glass.

No more than twenty customers strolled around in

here, and it only took him a few seconds to spot Gray and the gallery owner standing beside an exhibit in the middle of the room, just at the top of the main staircase. A gold statue of some kind was displayed in the case the two men were studying. In fact, most of the people in the room were clustered around the same piece.

As Nick moved to another display case, this one holding a pair of gaudy earrings, he watched the reflections of Gray and the gallery owner as they headed for the stairs and disappeared from sight.

Nick debated racing down the back stairs to follow them, but given how observant the gallery guards were, he dared not be so obvious. Instead, he drifted toward the front of the room to take a look at the gold piece everyone seemed so interested in.

It was about a foot tall, a statue of a man on a horse. The horse half reared, its mane and tail flowing artfully around its body. The rider wore billowing Middle Eastern–style robes and a turban on his head, and brandished a curved sword. The man's eyes were emeralds, his clothing and saddle studded with rubies and tiny pearls. The craftsmanship of the statue itself was spectacular. The stallion's mane blew in an invisible wind, his nostrils flared, and tension quivered in his muscular haunches.

Interested, Nick read the accompanying card. The statue dated to roughly the time of the Third Crusade—1189–1192. Weight—nearly three pounds. Made of gold and assorted precious gems. *Origin: Persian. Provenance: unknown.* Possibly a piece from a nativity scene, possibly one of the Three Wise Men. *Estimated sale price: six to ten million dollars.*

Ho. Lee. Cow. For a dude on a horse?

Of course, if the piece was solid gold… He did the

math fast. At current prices, that was nearly four million dollars' worth, just in the meltdown value of the gold itself.

With a mental lurch, he realized he'd gotten distracted. Gray was getting away from him. This time he used the main stairs to leave the gallery. He descended swiftly but was careful to keep his whole demeanor relaxed. Casual. Nothing that would draw attention.

Why was Gray interested in a ten-million-dollar gold statue? Surely the man didn't have that kind of money lying around. Gray was a spy, not a billionaire, after all.

Sure, most people in covert operations squirreled away money over the years. They weren't home to spend their paychecks, which tended to stack up in checking accounts, and it was ops normal to skim a bit here and there from operational cash that passed through their hands to various informants and dealers in stolen goods and information. But ten million bucks? No spy could steal that much over the course of one career and not get caught. Not unless they had a very, very profitable side gig going.

Which was, of course, the entire reason he was trailing Gray in the first place.

As he rounded the turn in the steel staircase to head for the ground floor, he spied Gray, flanked by his two dangerous-looking bodyguards, heading out the front door.

Swearing, Nick hustled the rest of the way down the stairs. He had no choice but to race outside right now or risk losing Gray.

A limousine was parked out front, its passenger door open, and his quarry was just climbing inside.

Nick jammed his hand into his coat pocket, and he palmed the device inside. Moving fast, he went down the steps, across the sidewalk, and toward the back of the limo. The security guard standing beside the limo stiffened.

But without even looking in the guard's direction, Nick hustled past the vehicle, sliding between it and an SUV that had just pulled up to the front of the gallery. As he did so, he touched the limo's taillight briefly, as if bracing himself against the vehicle to keep his tux from rubbing on it.

Then he darted out into traffic and ran across the street. He made it to the far sidewalk without being hit by a taxi, and he strode off in the opposite direction from the limo. Without looking back, he turned the corner.

Stopping now would be an amateur move. He'd planted a tracker inside the rim of the taillight, and he knew to let the device do its job. He walked for another block, doubled back briefly, reversed directions and dodged around another corner, and doubled back again.

Nope. He wasn't being followed.

Finally, he let out a sigh of relief. He paused in the darkened alcove of a closed store and pulled out his cell. The tracker app on his phone popped up, and a red dot was superimposed on a street map of Upper Manhattan. Bingo. The tracker was live and on the move—

The black shape of a man came at him swiftly and silently.

Nick dropped his phone and threw up his hands just in time to block what would have been a lethal blow to the side of his head. Trained hand-to-hand fighter that he was, he stepped forward, closer to the attacker, to cut off the guy's range. While short punches were still painful, they were less dangerous than full-on roundhouses, where a man could really put weight and momentum behind his fist. That and moving in close took kicks out of the equation.

Of course, moving in close meant he couldn't kick or punch effectively, either. Which was why he lowered his head and charged the assailant with the intent to wrap his arms around the guy and immobilize him that way.

Except at the last instant, the attacker sidestepped with blinding speed, stuck out a foot and gave Nick a mighty shove.

He had superb balance, however, and knew not to overextend his weight too far forward when jumping at someone. Hence, Nick was able to catch his balance and right himself without face-planting on the sidewalk. But it was a close thing.

He whipped around to face his attacker, who had settled into a fighting stance.

Nick did the same. He studied his opponent. The guy was close in height to him. Maybe not quite as muscular. But he already knew the guy was wicked fast. And the man's stance shouted of being a skilled fighter.

He wasn't gonna lie. If this fight weren't probably to the death or at least serious injury, he would relish getting to spar with a guy like this, who seemed evenly matched with him.

Without warning, the attacker lunged, feinting left and coming in on the right. Nick matched the move, dodging a blindingly fast, low hook kick at the last second, before the man knocked his foot out from under him. Dang, that guy was fast.

Nick jumped back, eyeing his opponent cautiously. He needed to go on the offensive, and fast, or he was going to be in real trouble against this guy. He charged forward, and instead of trying anything tricky, actually barreled straight ahead into him.

His attacker had already sussed out that he, too, was no amateur in unarmed combat, and had expected him to do something fancy at the end of the straight-on lunge. Instead of bracing for impact, the assailant had remained balanced on the balls of his feet, ready to jump to one side or the other.

Which meant Nick's extra twenty pounds on the other man had its desired effect. The attacker staggered back, barely managing to stay on his feet as Nick delivered a flurry of fast punches that forced the guy to parry frantically.

Nick pressed his advantage, keeping up a barrage of fast slaps, jabs and low kicks. The assailant fell back, retreating down the dark sidewalk.

He seriously wanted to know who this guy was. Nick hadn't spotted him interacting with the other members of Gray's security team. He must've been some sort of overwatch guy, posted to stand off at a distance and observe Gray's movements going into and coming out of the gallery.

That was a new operational procedure for Gray, and Nick wanted to question his attacker about what other changes Gray had made recently. Given that Nick and the Medusas had recently taken an entire team of Gray's operatives into custody, it made sense that the spymaster, in the interest of paranoia and self-preservation, had changed things up.

Nick stalked after the man. Any second now, the guy was going to turn and run. If he didn't miss his guess, he would have about six strides to catch up to his would-be assailant and tackle him before the other man's superior speed took over and he darted out of range.

The guy jumped.

But not away from Nick. *Toward him.*

Nick threw up his hands to ward off a pair of lightning-quick jabs to his face that would've broken his nose if either connected. Dang, this guy was fast. Like… *fast*.

The man jumped again, sliding past Nick's left shoulder with such speed he barely saw the move. He started to spin to face the attacker, but too slowly.

An arm went around his neck from behind. The man's chest plastered against his back, and one of the guy's legs went between Nick's knees.

Not good. *Not good.*

That stance was the first part of bracing oneself to yank a target's head sharply to one side, the goal being to break the target's neck.

Frantically, Nick did the only thing he could. He threw his left hand backward over his shoulder as far as it would go and grabbed a handful of the attacker's hair at the back of the man's head. He hoped he had a solid enough grip on the guy's hair to give a violent yank of his own.

At the same time, Nick tensed all the muscles in his neck and shoulders as hard as he could in what was surely a futile effort to protect his spine from breaking when this guy tried to kill him.

Contrary to television depictions, it took a hell of a lot of strength to snap a person's neck, particularly a fit, strong adult male's. But, if a person knew the right technique and knew how much force to apply, it worked about as fast and effectively as it did on TV. It was a nearly instant kill.

He felt the guy's entire body tense against his back.

Here it came.

He was going to die.

Chapter Two

Alexander Creed was stunned when his opponent whipped a hand backward and grabbed a big fistful of his hair like that. He felt the power in the guy's arm. This dude could undoubtedly yank hard enough to wrench his head around awkwardly to the side. Maybe the guy would only sprain his neck something fierce. But maybe the guy would kill him.

They were at an impasse. They each had a lethal hold on the other. One wrong twitch by either of them, and their opponent would make a good-faith effort to snap their neck.

He didn't want to kill this guy. He wanted to talk to him. Find out why he'd been following Harlan Gray.

Alex grunted in the big man's ear, "I'll let go if you'll let go."

"Why should I?" the man choked out from under Alex's forearm across his throat.

"Because the alternative is for me to break your neck," he snapped. Surely, this man knew that. The guy had shown himself to be a hard-core fighter with serious training in the past sixty seconds.

"I'll break yours first."

"Maybe. But I've got you in a better hold. I will definitely break yours. You *might* manage to break mine. I'm willing to take that chance."

The man plastered against the front of his body was perfectly still for a moment more. Alex could actually feel the wheels turning in the dude's brain, calculating the odds.

The man's painful grip on his hair released.

Alex breathed a sigh of relief. He let go with his left arm, keeping his right arm across the guy's throat for an extra moment. Long enough to jam his left hand in his coat pocket and grab the metal objects inside.

He let go of his target's neck, and the man—predictably—spun around to face him. As he did so, Alex reached out fast and slapped a handcuff down on the top of the guy's left wrist. Then, as the guy jolted, Alex slammed his own right wrist into the other bracelet.

"What the hell is that for?" the man growled, staring down at their handcuffed wrists.

He shrugged. "I don't feel like chasing you across half of Manhattan. And now you're not getting away from me until we have a conversation."

"Indeed," his prisoner said darkly. "I'm looking forward to speaking with you, as well."

"Shall we take this conversation off the street?" Alex asked rather more politely than he was feeling toward this walking, talking, pain in the ass.

"Oh, yeah," the prisoner agreed with way too much enthusiasm. The guy thought that once they were alone they were going to have round two of their previous matchup, did he?

Not if he could help it. The prisoner had been ridiculously strong and nearly as fast as he was. It was the closest he'd come to losing a hand-to-hand fight in years. And he didn't like the sensation one bit. He was

used to being in total control of everything and everyone around him, thank you very much.

Alex murmured, "I have a place not far from here.
Truce until we get there?"

The guy looked grumpy about it but nodded once,
tersely. There was a jerk on his wrist as the prisoner
bent down to scoop up his cell phone off the sidewalk.

"This way." Alex took off, moving briskly in the
same direction his target had been traveling before
they'd fought.

They walked in silence for several minutes, winding along small side streets that were mostly deserted
at this time of night. Here and there, window frames
were lit with Christmas lights. As they reached a major
thoroughfare, some business was broadcasting holiday carols through a tinny speaker, and huge lit snowflakes hung from the streetlamps. As they waited at a
traffic light to cross the intersection, a fat snowflake
drifted down to the ground in front of them. Several
more wafted past, floating gently.

His prisoner shook their joined wrists a little and
asked lightly, "Do you always walk around Manhattan
handcuffed to other men? Doesn't that draw a wee bit
of negative attention?"

Alex shrugged. "I haven't seen anyone tonight ap-
pear to notice, let alone care."

The other guy huffed. "Sometimes, I hate this city."

"Just because folks here aren't freaked out by a little
kink doesn't make it a bad place."

The prisoner shot him a sharp look. "You're into
handcuffs and bondage, are you?"

Alex snorted. "Not me. I'm not paid to have such
preferences. I'm paid to be a straight-arrow type." This
guy had no idea how straight an arrow. He had no choice

in the matter. In his line of work, even the slightest deviation from complete and utter self-discipline was intolerable to his employers.

Alex muttered, "If you're worried about what other people will think, we can always hold hands. That'll hide the bracelets."

His prisoner's eyes lit with...something. Interest? Amusement? Challenge?

"Fine." The guy grabbed his hand firmly as the light changed, shocking Alex to his toes. The man's was hard and callused. But then, so was his. They made a good pair. Holding hands firmly, they walked quickly across the multiple lanes of traffic.

They strode away from the brightly lit avenue behind them and into residential side streets. They stopped in front of an aged brick building, and Alex used a key to let them into the lobby, dominated by a fluffy Christmas tree hung with a motley assortment of ornaments. The tenants in the building apparently each brought down an ornament to put on the tree, and the result was an eclectic and colorful collection of decorations.

A pair of elevators took up the wall opposite the tree and mailboxes. Alex pushed the up button between the elevators, and miracle of miracles, one of them was already down there. The doors slid open with that alarming hitch in their action that they always had.

"Looks pretty rickety," the prisoner said skeptically. "I'm okay with walking up. I'm in reasonably good shape."

He snorted. The man was in significantly better than "reasonable" shape. When he'd had his arm around the guy's neck, it had felt as if he was hugging a lion, one made of pure, honed steel.

"Scared of elevators, are you?" Alex asked lightly.

"Very little in this world scares me," the guy responded quietly. There was no braggadocio in the man's comment, just a simple statement of fact.

As he'd thought. This guy was totally one of Gray's operatives. Aloud, he commented, "It would be a long climb. We're heading for one of the top floors."

They stepped into the elevator and the doors closed partway, stuck a little, then shut the rest of the way. The lift lurched into motion with the faint sound of a gear grinding somewhere nearby.

He pushed the button for the twentieth floor and then looked over at his prisoner in the decent light of the elevator. Strong features were partially obscured by shaggy dark brown hair in need of a trim. The man's face was clean-shaven, but his jaw looked pink and vaguely irritated as if he'd recently taken off a beard.

His earlier assessment had not been wrong. The guy was muscular from head to toe. Not the flashy bulk of a weight lifter, but the hard, functional muscle of a man whose life depended on his strength. He would expect no less of one of Gray's hirelings, of course. But still. The man was an impressive physical specimen. Enough so that a frisson of interest—personal interest—skittered down his spine.

No. This was work. He had a job to do, and no matter how hot the guy handcuffed to his wrist might be, nothing was going to get in the way of his focus.

Still, a little voice whispered in the back of his mind, *this one was hard not to notice in* that *way.*

His employer didn't care in the least if he was gay, but his employer would care very much if he ever let a personal attraction to anyone get in the way of his job.

The elevator dinged, and the doors slid open. He stepped to the front of the conveyance, along with his prisoner, and noted that they simultaneously paused just inside it and looked up and down the hallway before exiting.

No doubt about it. This guy was an operator like him. Maybe not exactly like him—he was, after all, the one who got sent out to fix problems caused by other operators—but definitely similar in skills and abilities.

They reached the door of his crash pad, and he unlocked it to let them inside.

A tiny bathroom on the left and a walk-in closet on the right formed a short hallway. Beyond that was a single, sparsely furnished room, with a kitchenette backing up to the bathroom, a sofa on the left wall, a TV on the right wall and a mattress on the floor under the window. A banged-up table and two chairs took up the corner beside the closet.

But the dingy space also had a state-of-the-art security system with motion sensors, pressure pads under the stained carpet, infrared sensors and a silent alarm, currently linked to his phone, which—on cue—was vibrating in his pocket to warn him of an intruder.

"I have to reach into my pants pocket," he informed his prisoner.

The man nodded and let his left arm go loose so Alex could reach into his pocket with his right hand and pull out his phone. Thank goodness the guy didn't make any snarky comment about asking if he needed help reaching into his pants. If there was one thing he couldn't abide in this world, it was people with no sense of taste or decorum.

The man was cooperative and followed Alex's hand with his own so Alex could type the security code into the phone to disable the alarm system.

"We good?" the guy asked.

"We're good," Alex replied. "No machine gun will pop out of the wall now and mow us down."

"Gee. I rather prefer laser beams that cut intruders in half," his prisoner said dryly.

"You a James Bond fan?" Alex asked.

"Aren't you?"

The answer to that was obvious. Every spy, ever, was a fan. Even if they wouldn't admit it to another living soul. The cool gadgets alone were envy-worthy.

The prisoner's unshackled hand snaked out fast, reaching for their joined wrists. Before Alex could brace himself to fight, the guy had jammed a small handcuff key into the lock and popped the bracelets open.

Alex stared, shocked, at the empty bracelet now dangling from the bracelet still on his wrist. The bastard had a master cuff key on his key ring. He could've unlocked the handcuffs at any moment during the entire time they'd walked across the city to this place. The *entire* time. But instead, the prisoner had dared him to hold hands. What could it mean?

He looked up at his former prisoner, one eyebrow arched in silent question.

The guy shrugged, replying as if he thought Alex was silently asking why he hadn't unlocked himself sooner, "I wanted to see where you would take me."

"Why did you care where I was taking you?" Alex blurted.

"Because I do, in fact, have questions for you. Several of them."

This was new. Usually, he was the interrogator while the other guy fidgeted nervously, awaiting his judgment with fear and trepidation. His attention perked up considerably as he regarded the man standing before him.

Alex's brows slammed together. "I'm the one in charge here. You're my prisoner, not the other way around."

The man held up his naked left wrist. "Was your prisoner. Past tense."

Alex scowled as he unlooped the bracelet from around his wrist and stowed the handcuffs in his back pocket. If nothing else, this unpredictable guy was certainly proving to be interesting. "Nonetheless, I'm questioning you."

"Nope. I'm questioning you," the other man shot back.

Alex glared. "I won the fight."

"You did not! I also had you in a head grip that would've broken your neck. We fought to a stalemate."

"Did not."

"Wanna go again?" the other guy asked aggressively.

"Not particularly," Alex answered honestly. "You're not half bad at handling yourself."

"I could say the same of you," the man admitted grudgingly.

Coming from this accomplished fighter, he would take that as a high compliment indeed.

"We seem to be at an impasse," Alex said grimly. "Again."

At least the guy hadn't bolted out of here already or tried to kill him the moment they stepped inside the crash pad. Maybe they could find a civilized way out of this…whatever this was.

There was a thought. Having one of his jobs actually be civilized. He got so tired of tracking down and killing people, one after another in an endless stream of death. Every single person he tracked always turned out to be corrupt. Why couldn't just one of them turn out to be a good guy? Before he'd gotten into this business, he'd had no idea that finding just one honest man would be such an impossible task.

He stared at his guest, and his guest stared back in what appeared to be frustration. The man's eyes were dark in the relatively dim lighting of the apartment, and Alex guessed they were brown. Either that or the guy was wearing contact lenses. He would need better light to know for sure.

"Tell you what," the man said. "How about I ask you a question, and then you ask me a question?"

Alex considered the suggestion briefly. If nothing else, he might be able to figure out who this guy was based on what he wanted to know. "Fine. But I'll go first."

The man shrugged.

"Who are you?" Alex demanded.

"I'm just a guy. Who are you?"

"That wasn't what I meant. What's your name?" Alex clarified.

"Bob. Call me Bob."

"Right. And I'm Santa Claus," Alex replied dryly.

If the guy wasn't going to cooperate, he had other tools at his disposal to identify him. To that end, he pulled out his cell phone and pretended to read a message on it. As soon as he had his camera app opened, though, he whipped the phone up, pointed it at the guy and snapped a fast picture.

As *Bob* lunged toward him, Alex hit the send button.

"Too late," Alex announced, snatching the phone away from the man's grasping fingers.

"Who did you send that to?" the guy ground out.

"To my employer."

The fellow swore under his breath. "Do you work for Gray?"

"That's two questions," Alex objected. "I only agreed to you asking one question."

The guy visibly vibrated with tension. "*Do you work for Gray?*"

Alex was startled. "You should know, since you work for him."

He watched as the guy's dark eyebrows slammed together, and he blurted, "Not anymore, I don't."

Okay, that was not the response he'd expected. "Explain."

"How do you know who Gray is?" *Bob* asked.

"Nope. Not gonna answer that."

"Then, I'm not saying another word to you."

Alex sighed. This was the problem in dealing with covert operators. None of them trusted anybody. "Fine. Why don't you take a seat? The facial recognition request I sent will be back in a few minutes, and then I'll know who you are anyway."

"Not bloody likely," *Bob* muttered.

Fascinating. The guy didn't think his face was in facial-recognition databases, did he? Too bad he didn't know Alex had access to the classified database the government kept of *everyone*'s faces—the *really* classified database.

His guest lounged on the sofa, taking up way more than half of it as he threw a muscular arm across the back of the cushions and propped one ankle on top of the other knee.

Manspreading much? Alex rolled his eyes at the subtle posturing. Whatever. He was neither awed nor intimidated by such tactics. He took out men like this one every day.

Rather than compete for real estate on the couch,

Alex pulled out one of the kitchen chairs and sat down on it. He studied "Bob," who studied him back intently.

The guy really was good-looking, in spite of that awful haircut that hid half his face and the hint of a dark five-o'clock shadow that hid the rest. Although that was probably the point. The man had rugged features, a square jaw and a nose that either had a slight hawk bump to it or had been broken before. It was a masculine face and sexier than ought to be legal. In fact, the whole man oozed sex appeal.

Not that he was looking, of course.

If the guy didn't work so hard to hide it from view, it would be a highly memorable face. Which in their line of work was a bad thing. Spies needed to be able to slide in and slide out of places without being noticed.

Take himself, for example. He'd completely mastered the art of being blandly unremarkable. He kept his light brown hair in a boring haircut, he made sure never to get too pale or too darkly tanned, his eyes were an indeterminate color somewhere between green and blue, and he always wore exactly the kind of clothes a middle-aged dad would wear in whatever place he was working in. He even knew how to stoop just enough to look tired all the time and how to move to disguise how fit and athletic he actually was.

Silence stretched out between them until it, too, became a competition. Privately, Alex was amused. He could and did go days at a time without speaking to another human being. This guy was going to lose in a battle of who could be quiet the longest.

As he watched his guest, though, he did note the steady, observant way the man's dark eyes took in everything around him, never staying still, flicking from one point of interest to another. And any time Alex even shifted his weight the slightest bit, that penetrating gaze snapped back to him, alert and wary.

He might look relaxed sprawled across the sofa, but Alex didn't miss the way "Bob's" body was coiled, poised to spring at any moment. Definitely a lion in human clothing. A hungry, restless one, on the hunt.

Alex's cell phone buzzed silently, and he picked it up off the table. A message scrolled across the screen. His identification request was complete. He tapped the button to download the file associated with this man's face, and it opened on his screen.

He read aloud, "'Name—Nicholas Kane. Current location—unknown. Current status—inactive, on personal leave of absence. Last assignment—Sunny Creek, Montana. Employer—'" A pause. "Ah. Interesting." Alex looked up. "What on earth is in Sunny Creek, Montana, that would be of interest to a CIA Special Operations Group guy like you?"

Chapter Three

Shock rolled through Nick as the man across the room from him started reading out classified information about him. Accurate, *highly* classified information that in the hands of the wrong person could get him killed in a New York minute. Which was not amusing, given that he was actually in New York at the moment.

He surged up off the sofa and across the room. His would-be captor made it to his feet before Nick was on him, but Nick had jumped behind him and had him by the throat before the man could do much but gurgle.

It wasn't so much fun now that the shoe was on the other foot, was it? He tightened his grip hard enough to cut off most of his oxygen. He didn't sever so much air that the fellow passed out or died but enough that he didn't have enough fuel for his muscles to launch a counterattack.

"Who. Are. You?" he gritted out into the guy's ear.

"Let me go…and I'll…tell you," his target rasped.

This time he was pressed up against the guy from back of the neck to knees. He felt his lithe strength and got a brief impression of an otter—strong, fast and slippery. Nearly impossible to restrain.

Except he was having no trouble holding him in his grasp.

Suspicion that his captive was intentionally not fighting him rolled through him. Nick frowned. Should he reciprocate with a modicum of trust?

Maybe some cautious mistrust…as opposed to outright hostility…was called for. Slowly, carefully, he loosened his arm from around his target's neck. He let go altogether, and the man stepped away from him equally carefully, making no sudden moves.

A vague impression of missing the feel of the man's torso pressed back against his shocked him into momentary stillness.

He stared at his host. The medium brown hair in a neat cut, medium eyes somewhere between blue and green, medium height, medium build—everything about the man screamed, *Don't look at me. Nothing to see here. Move along.*

Although that was the point, he supposed. This man was clearly some sort of black ops guy, himself, and they were all trained to be inconspicuous and fade into the woodwork in any environment. They were all chameleons.

The guy held out both hands, well away from his sides, in plain sight and said soberly, "I think maybe you and I do need to talk, for real."

Nick leaned a hip against the kitchen counter behind him, his casual stance belying his readiness to attack or defend himself again, if need be. "You go first."

"You and me, Nicholas. We work for more or less the same people."

"How much more and how much less?" he snapped. "And call me Nick. Nobody calls me by my real name."

"Okay, Nick. We work for the same company. Different department."

Nick highly doubted that. As a training officer, he

knew pretty much everyone in the Special Operations Group, and he'd never seen this guy, let alone worked with him. And nobody else in the agency would have the skill and experience to go toe-to-toe with him except another SOG guy. There were government covert operatives, and then there were the guys like him, the best of the best, the ones assigned to do the tasks nobody else would even think about trying.

The guy continued, "I'm investigating a colleague of yours."

"Who? Why?" Nick exclaimed.

"We received intel that someone you work with might have absconded with something they shouldn't have on a job."

Nick didn't, by the slightest bat of an eyelash or flinch of a muscle, give away his shock at those words. Indeed, the team he usually ran with *had* stolen something a while back while running a covert operation in a tiny near-Asian nation called Zagastan.

He hadn't gone on the mission. Instead, he'd been sent on a solo job that turned out to be a wild-goose chase. At the time, he'd been damned suspicious of why he'd been diverted to a bust operation at the last minute, too. It had smelled to him as if his teammates had gotten rid of him because they knew he would never go along with whatever they'd planned to do on that mission.

As it turned out, they had not been wrong. He would never condone theft nor the murder of US military members totally uninvolved in their operation. And his teammates had done both.

"Who exactly are you investigating?" Nick asked cautiously. It dawned on him with a jolt that this man could be investigating *him*. After all, he'd been a member of the same team that had committed the crimes.

Plus, this guy probably didn't know the rest of his team was quietly in custody already, captured by him and the Medusas, and being held at a black ops site that didn't exist on any map, anywhere.

The man stared at him hard. Nick stared back. He didn't care if they got into another pissing contest to see who could be silent the longest. In his military career, he'd been a sniper, and he could lie perfectly still and silent in a hide for days on end.

The other guy surprised him by actually answering, "I'm investigating Harlan Gray."

"Harlan? Is that the rest of his name?" Nick blurted.

The man in front of him shrugged. "It's as good as any other name."

Nick was staggered. This guy knew that the name, Harlan Gray, was an alias? Only a handful of people on the planet even knew Gray was alive, let alone knew what handle the bastard was operating under at the current time.

Nick figured his ex-boss went through a whole new identity every few years. Gray undoubtedly scrubbed every trace of his previous persona before assuming the next one. In fact, Nick was terrified that, after his larcenous teammates' recent disappearance, Gray would erase this version of himself and disappear, *again*, never to be found.

Nick had been lying on a beach once when Gray had walked up to him, and in the bright sunlight, looking up from that odd angle, he'd seen the thin white lines of plastic surgery scars under the man's chin. He suspected every time Gray changed his name, he also changed his appearance.

"What did Harlan steal?" Nick had been dying to know that ever since he'd heard about the theft.

A real-time-photo intel analyst had been observing a SEAL operation raiding a terrorist's compound in Zagastan. She'd been using drone cameras hovering above the compound to provide intel to the SEAL team on the ground, and she'd spotted his teammates exiting the rear of the clustered buildings, carrying a large wooden crate among the four of them. She'd described it as looking very heavy.

The way Nick figured it, his teammates had used the SEAL raid to distract the bad guys, slipped in the back way when nobody was looking and moved in to steal whatever had been in that crate. Then, while the SEALs were still mopping up, they slipped out the way they'd come.

The photo intel analyst had also described a man *exactly* matching Gray's description breaking into the remote surveillance facility she'd been working at that night. Allegedly, he'd held her at gunpoint and had stolen the entire computer tower at her workstation. It would've held the only video images downloaded from the drone she'd been using to observe the operation. By taking that CPU, Gray had successfully stolen all evidence of his operatives' theft. So it was only the woman's word against Gray's to say that anything had gone down at all.

Thing was, she had no reason to lie. And her description of the man who'd stolen the computer and video of the theft was so spot-on Gray that he'd never doubted her story for a second. Not to mention, after that night, Gray and his teammates had been hell-bent on finding and killing the woman.

That alone would've convinced him she was telling the truth.

Of course, Gray and company hadn't counted on the

woman being more than a simple photo intel analyst. It had turned out she was also a fully trained special operator in her own right.

Gray had ordered him, along with his teammates to search for her. Nick had made an excuse to leave his team to conduct his own hunt for the woman. Interestingly, his colleagues hadn't objected—at all—when he'd proposed going off by himself to track down a few obscure leads on the woman they were hunting.

He'd done it because he wanted to hear firsthand why his teammates had cut him out of that mission and what she'd seen that had the lot of them so hot and bothered to kill her and silence her for good. His fellow operatives had agreed to the plan because they wanted to get rid of him.

He'd found the woman…and found out the hard way that she belonged to an all-female team of Special Forces soldiers who called themselves the Medusas. An apt name. They were as dangerous as any snake-haired goddess.

The Medusas had set a trap for him and captured him. It had taken a while to establish that they were working toward the same objective, but eventually, he'd told them why he'd been tracking her, and they had asked him to help them set up an ambush for his teammates.

It had pained him to help take down a group of men he'd run with for almost four years and thought of as closer than brothers. But they'd crossed the line with the theft and subsequent murder of three marines. They had to be taken out. Better by him than by some total stranger, he supposed. A stranger like the man standing in front of him now.

There was a code of honor among operators. You

didn't throw your buddies under the bus, but you also didn't ask them to cover up crimes for you. His teammates had broken that code. In every way they could've betrayed his trust, they had. It still stung. A lot.

At least the Medusas had agreed to his request that his part in capturing his buddies not be revealed to them. Indeed, his former team had been led to believe that he'd escaped the trap in which the rest of them had been captured. For their benefit—and for Gray's—the Medusas were continuing to keep up a ruse of hunting him.

He had no idea if his ex-teammates bought the story or not. One thing he did know for sure: he wasn't interested in finding out if Gray bought the tale or not.

"My turn to ask a few questions," the man in front of him said.

Nick noted that the guy had pointedly not answered the burning question of what, exactly, his teammates had stolen. Maybe he didn't know. Or maybe he just wasn't telling.

"What were you doing for Harlan Gray earlier tonight?" the man asked abruptly.

"Nothing," Nick said. "I was following him."

"Why?"

"No comment."

The man sighed. "Look. I get it. You're an operator. I'm an operator. We don't trust our own mothers. But if you don't start giving me some real answers, and soon, I'm going to have to take you into custody. And then things will go sideways for you very fast."

"Why's that?"

"Because I have permission from my superiors to take whatever action I deem necessary to do my job. *Whatever* action I deem necessary."

"Who are your superiors?" Nick snapped.

"The same as yours. Only I report to someone significantly higher up the food chain than you do. Which means you'll get no protection from your bosses regarding what I do to you."

Nick frowned. The guy hadn't said that as a brag. If anything, the answer had been given with a reluctance that rang of truth. "Why would you take me into custody? I wasn't involved in the theft. I didn't know anything about it."

"You know about it now," the man accused. "For all I know, you were the front man stateside who arranged for the stolen item to slip into the United States undetected."

"You think whatever they took is here?" Nick blurted, alarmed. Privately, he was panicked that Gray and his teammates had gotten their hands on a small nuclear device. It would explain the weight of that crate and why they were willing to kill to protect the secret of its existence.

What he couldn't for the life of him figure out was why Gray and the others would want something like that. In the four years he'd worked as one of Gray's personal bodyguards, the man had never once hinted at having any beef with the United States government or the American people.

Gray struck him as more the greedy type. The man liked his creature comforts and was accustomed to a luxurious lifestyle. And, Gray wasn't getting any younger. It was hard to tell his age, but Nick though he had to be approaching sixty. Which was ancient in the world of covert operations.

"I'm certain whatever they stole is here," the man in front of him said grimly. "In New York."

Aww, hell. If they did have a nuke, did that mean it was in the city? Not good.

The prospect concerned Nick enough that he was willing to take a chance and actually answer the worried-looking man in front of him. "I was following Gray because I'm trying to figure out what he and my former teammates stole and to understand why they all turned on me. Why did they cut me out of their mission to steal whatever they stole? And why did they conceal the theft from me?"

"So you're mad you didn't get to participate in the theft?" the other man asked ominously.

What was the deal with him? All of a sudden, the man's entire body had dropped into readiness for violence, relaxed but coiled to erupt into hostility at a moment's notice.

Alarm exploded in Nick's gut. He didn't know who this guy was, but no doubt about it, he was extremely dangerous. Lethal. The guy had gone from calm to cobra in the blink of an eye. Frankly, it was damned disconcerting.

Very carefully, Nick said, "I would never steal anything my superiors didn't specifically order me to take. In answer to your question, no, I'm not mad I didn't get to help steal whatever they stole. I'm angry that they stole anything, apparently off the books, and that they did it behind my back. I'm furious that they betrayed me. I'm here in New York in an effort to clean up whatever mess they've made and right the wrong they've done."

The man studied him intently for several long seconds. His body uncoiled slightly, and Nick slowly released the breath he realized he'd been holding.

"How do you know your teammates cut you out of a theft and are concealing it from you?" the man asked.

Nick shrugged. "Given your presence, I'm gonna go ahead and say it's obvious that whatever Gray and my team stole was *not* a sanctioned theft by the government. As for how I figured that out in the first place, call it intuition.

"First, I got sent on a bogus mission by myself, which made me conveniently not available to go on the op where they stole whatever they stole. Second, they abruptly started excluding me from conversations. Went silent when I walked into rooms with them. Third, they started sending me out on solo ops way below my pay grade to handle, as if they were trying to get rid of me while they dealt with something else. Fourth, Gray abruptly ordered us to hunt and kill some photo intel analyst in *the US military.* I find it damned weird to be ordered to hunt one of our own. And fifth, the guys on my team started acting…jumpy…around me."

"If you are telling the truth, it does sound as if they were hiding something from you," the man replied soberly.

Nick responded, "If you and I are, indeed, in the same line of work, then you know what I'm talking about. Guys like us, we get feelings about people. My gut is yelling at me that my teammates have done something really bad behind my back."

"Yes, but why should *I* trust your gut?" the other man asked.

Nick shrugged. "It's no secret I'm gay. I expect it was in that dossier on me you showed off by pulling up just now."

The man shrugged back. "It was in there. What of it?"

"I grew up in a family where to come out would have

been a death sentence. My father was a violent man with a violent temper, a houseful of weapons and very specific ideas about what my sexual orientation should be. I learned very young to read other people and their intentions. My life depended on it. Which is to say, I'm not wrong about my team. They did something illegal, and they're hiding it from me."

"Any guess as to what they stole?"

"None. That's why I'm following Gray. I'm trying to figure out what they grabbed and do whatever I can to mitigate any damage they've caused."

"What makes you so sure he's in on it?"

"He broke into a military communications facility and stole the only evidence of the theft at gunpoint. Sounds to me as if he's in on it, wouldn't you say?"

"You know about that incident? How?" The guy sounded genuinely surprised.

"Gray sent me and the rest of the team across the country to track down the intel analyst he took the equipment from. He didn't tell me why he wanted her found and eliminated, of course. I had to learn that directly from her once I found her."

"Gray specifically told you to kill her?" the man asked with interest.

Nick sighed. "Gray rarely gives a direct kill order. He knows better than to legally expose himself like that. He specifically told us to call the rest of the team if one of us found her. Then we were to converge on her and do whatever was necessary to silence her about what she saw. The implication was clear that we would take her down—kill her—together."

"Interesting. He wanted you to have blood on your hands, too?"

Nick jolted. He hadn't thought of it like that before.

He'd been too wrapped up in the guilt of leading his team into the Medusa's ambush to clock that Gray had been trying to get him to commit a crime, too, one that would force him to remain silent about his teammates' crimes.

Nick said heavily, "I found the intel analyst in Montana. In answer to your earlier question, that's what was in Sunny Creek. Or rather, who was in Sunny Creek." He added bitterly, "The other guys always did call me too much of a Boy Scout to work with them. They knew I wouldn't murder an innocent American soldier who was just doing her job any more than I would've gone along with stealing something off the books."

The man pursed his lips, as if he agreed with their assessment of him being too much of a Boy Scout for his line of work.

"Hey. I serve my country. I follow any legal orders I'm given, and I've killed more than a few bad guys in my day. But I'm not a random criminal."

"That's good," the other man said seriously. "Because I'm the guy who takes out the random criminals in our ranks."

"Come again?" Nick asked sharply.

"I'm a fixer. And I've been assigned to fix the problem of Gray and his rogue team. You can call me Alex, by the way."

"You got a last name, Alex?"

"Creed. I'm Alexander Creed."

Holy shit. He'd heard that name before. Whispered in tones of respect and fear. Creed was a legendary assassin within the special operations community. His nickname in the Middle East, where he'd spent years working for Uncle Sam, was *Almawt*. It meant very simply *Death*.

In the American intelligence world, he had an even more ominous name. *The Judge.*

"You're the Judge?"

Alex rolled his eyes. "I hate that name."

"But you're him? You're the guy who's sent out to judge other spies and then execute the sentence you impose upon them?"

"I don't impose anything. I investigate allegations against operators. And, when I'm certain of the facts of the situation, I take appropriate action to contain the situation—and contain the operator."

"The way I hear it, you kill them." Nick stated it as a fact, rather than a question.

"I don't always kill the people I investigate. Only the most heinous of criminals are sanctioned to death."

Nick snorted. "Yes, but you're only sent after the most heinous of criminals, aren't you?"

Alex shrugged. "The people I investigate shouldn't have gone rogue. They made their choice, and I make my judgment."

He couldn't argue with that. Especially since it was exactly the same reason he was in New York now. His teammates and his boss had gone rogue. He wanted to know what they'd done, and when he found out, he planned to take action to rectify the situation. Maybe not action as extreme as the Judge might take, but he needed to fix the problem. It had happened on his watch, and he bore some responsibility for not stopping his team from doing whatever they'd done.

A shocking thought made him blurt, "Are you investigating me?"

"I wouldn't be talking with you like this if I was."

Not reassuring.

Nick studied Alex intently. He didn't for a second

believe that Creed was the guy's actual name. Men like them didn't really even have names. They drifted from one legend to the next, never using any details from their real lives. After a while, they'd dealt in lies for so long that they had no real lives left to hide anymore. They were ghosts, wandering through the world without ever leaving any trace of anything substantial about themselves behind.

He found the man fascinating. How could he not? Alex was not only handsome but smart and fully as skilled as anyone he'd ever worked with—but definitely not trustworthy.

He didn't believe for a second that Alex was telling him the truth, the whole truth and nothing but the truth. If Creed was the Judge, he would totally be investigating Nick. It might not be the formal investigation he'd been sent out to do, but the man would watch every operative he came across for signs of corruption.

Heck, this guy might not even be the real Judge. It was entirely possible Alex worked for Gray, and that this entire encounter was an elaborate ruse to get him to reveal how much he knew about the spymaster's involvement in the theft. This could just as easily be a test of loyalty by his ex-boss to find out if Nick was willing to turn him in to the few authorities who had jurisdiction over Gray and his team.

Nope. He didn't trust Alexander Creed as far as he could throw him.

Chapter Four

Alex studied Nick's body language with a certain wry amusement. He didn't expect the man to take him at face value, and from the way Nick's expression was shuttered and blank, it was clear Nick didn't believe his story of being a fixer for Uncle Sam.

The ironic bit was that it was the God's honest truth. However, the act of telling the truth had apparently made Nick utterly doubt it. Not that it was any skin off his nose if the guy believed him or not. He still had a job to do, and at the end of the day, he would get it done with or without Nick's help. And God protect the man if he got in the way of the job.

"How did you spot me tonight, *Alex*?"

His lips pursed a little at the special emphasis on his name. Yes, he was fully aware that Nick didn't trust it to be his name. But then, he doubted Nicholas Kane was on this guy's birth certificate, either.

And they were back to square one, neither of them believing a blessed thing the other one said. For example, he had no reason whatsoever to credit the whole story about Nick being a Boy Scout and Gray and his teammates not trusting him.

It was much more likely that Gray had assigned Nick to pretend to leave the team, to follow Gray from afar and then pick off anyone who attempted to follow him. It was the sort of game within a game Harlan Gray was known for.

"Earth to Alex. Come in, please."

"Excuse me?"

"You zoned out on me there for a sec. So, tell me. How did you spot me tonight?"

"Oh, that. You planted something on the taillight of Gray's limousine. That was what caught my attention. It made me curious. I assume it was a tracking device of some kind?"

Nick shrugged. But that wasn't a denial.

"Perhaps you should check in with your tracking device? See where Gray went? I'd love to know where he's staying," Alex said pleasantly.

"Won't matter," Nick replied. "He never stays in the same place twice. Wherever he goes tonight, he won't go back there again."

That fit with what he knew of Gray. Men like him had more enemies than they could count, and the only way they stayed alive was by taking caution to absurd extremes. Of course, he was the exact same way. Minus the new digs every night. Doing that was more expensive than his personal resources would allow for.

But it did beg the question of how Gray was affording such a lavish spymaster lifestyle. He wasn't doing it on his government salary alone. That was for sure. And the man's dossier said nothing about inheriting family wealth or holding investments that would account for the money his life took.

Sure, it was a known thing that most spies put away emergency cash over the years. They skimmed a little here and there, took side jobs or the occasional bribe for themselves. He wouldn't blink twice at an operative doing that, and he certainly wouldn't kill an operative for building a nest egg for their retirement. After all, the vast majority of them were emphatically not pure as the driven snow, ethically. They couldn't be and continue to do their jobs for long. Espionage was a dirty business no matter how one sliced it.

The men and women he killed were the ones who went fully off the rails, who committed violent criminal acts without permission from the government. Those who killed innocents, caused national security threats and who betrayed their country to its enemies. Assuming the thing Gray and his men had stolen turned out not to be a security threat to the US, he was less concerned about the theft than he was about them murdering three American marines. For that alone, he was prepared to kill Gray and his team without prejudice.

It was Alex's turn to ask a question. "Any idea what Gray was doing in that art gallery this evening?"

Nick surprised him by answering, "Yes, actually. He met up with one of the owners of the place and they went up to the third floor. They took a long look at a small gold statue. Then Gray left."

"Any idea what the statue was?"

Nick frowned. "The card beside it said it might be a piece from a nativity scene."

"Nativity? As in Baby Jesus in a manger?"

"I guess. The card said it might depict one of the Three Wise Men."

"What did it look like?" Alex asked, curious.

"It was pretty. About yea tall." Nick held his hands vertically about a foot apart. "Whole thing was made of gold. It was a statue of a guy sitting on a horse that was half-rearing. It had a bunch of jewels and little pearls on it, too. The card said the sale price is estimated at six to ten million bucks."

Alex whistled low. "Did Gray look at any other pieces while he was in the gallery?"

"Not that I saw. I wasn't doing a tight tail on him, mind you. So I didn't have him in sight every minute. But he wasn't there long enough to browse much."

He murmured, "I wouldn't want to try a tight tail on him. Not with his bodyguards."

"Gee. Thanks. I used to be one of those guys, and I trained most of his current protection team, so I'm gonna take that as a compliment."

Alex rolled his eyes, and Nick grinned. His teeth were white and straight, and impudent dimples flashed in his cheeks. The man had *dimples*. Dammit. He was a sucker for dimples.

Particularly when their owner was a smart operator and hot. So hot.

"How did you pick up Gray's trail, anyway?" Alex asked belatedly.

"The last time I talked with the guys on my team before they were…apprehended…one of them commented out of the blue that he'd never been to the Big Apple at Christmas and he'd heard it was pretty."

Alex frowned. "It could've just been a random comment."

"Nah. Burt's a stone-cold killer. Definitely not the kind of guy who's into holiday cheer. Also, one of the other guys glanced over at me and back at Burt significantly as if to signal him to shut up and not say anything more in front of me."

"Fair enough." Then something else hit him. "What do you mean by 'apprehended'?"

"The four guys who stole the crate? I lured them into

an ambush. With the help of a military team, we captured three of them and killed the fourth guy."

Alex blinked, startled. This man had already done 80 percent of his job for him? Cool. All that was left now, then, was for him to finish investigating Gray and kill him.

Nick was speaking. "…got to New York City, I got lucky. I texted a guy who was brought in for some training with me about a year back. He was being groomed to take a spot on the personal security team. At any rate, he didn't answer my text, but his phone pinged as being in Manhattan. I tracked it to a restaurant and spotted Gray having supper there. I've been on his tail ever since. At least, until you knocked me off him."

"In other words," Alex said, "we need to hightail it over to wherever Gray is bunking down tonight and pick him up before he leaves in the morning."

"If we were working together, it would go something like that," Nick said cautiously.

"Seems to me we're both working toward the same goal. We both want to know what Gray stole. Why not cooperate?" Alex added in his own mind, *And it would have the added benefit of me keeping an eye on you until I figure out just what your role in all of this is.*

Nick nodded readily enough and said a shade too enthusiastically, "That's not a half-bad idea."

Alex snorted to himself. Nick had obviously had the exact same thought—that by running around together, he could keep an eye on Alex, too.

If Nick had, in fact, been pulling a one-man surveillance op for the past week, he had to be dead tired. With nobody to trade off shifts with him, he'd undoubtedly been operating on only short catnaps and practically no sleep for seven days. Which made the fight he'd put up when they met that much more impressive. He made a mental note never to tangle with this man in a dark alley when he was fully rested.

Playing on Nick's fatigue, Alex said easily, "You know as well as I do that two of us teaming up will make the job exponentially easier. We'll both get some rest, we can put up a more effective perimeter around the target and we can run handoff tails. If one of us gets spotted, the other one can take over. It's a win-win for both of us."

Nick huffed. But Alex had seen the man's eyes flicker when he mentioned getting some rest. Nick was running on empty. A frisson of worry for his companion startled him. Exhausted operators made mistakes. Sometimes fatal ones. The idea of Nick dying made him feel faintly nauseated. No doubt about it. Nick needed a partner, and soon.

A partner like him. Someone who could pull his weight, keep up with a top-flight operator and not get in his way. The kind of partner he would want if he ever worked with other agents.

Alex waited him out, not pressuring him to accept the plan. If Nick was anything like him, the harder someone pushed him, the harder he would push back.

"Fine," Nick said abruptly. "We work together to find out what Gray stole and what he's up to now."

That went beyond the scope of Alex's mandate to investigate only the theft, but he was okay with the notion of finding out what Gray was doing in New York. One thing he did know from his mission in-brief, the US government had not sent Gray here. Whatever he was doing in town, he was doing it for himself. Which made Alex fairly certain this junket was somehow related to last spring's theft.

Aloud, Alex said, "Let me grab some gear, and then we can head out and pick up Gray's trail again."

"Sure."

He headed to the safe house's well-stocked closet for the spy in need and pulled out a rucksack that was already stuffed with all the supplies and tools he required to set up a moving surveillance operation. "Do you have a kit?" he asked Nick over his shoulder.

"Not really. I've been having to do everything on the fly."

Impressive. And exhausting. Sure, guys like them could improvise everything from disguises to weapons to surveillance gear anywhere they found themselves, but that didn't mean it was easy. And doing it while also maintaining contact with a wily and suspicious target? Suffice it to say, Nick must be better than most spies at his job.

Alex pulled another backpack out of the closet. "This isn't specifically a surveillance kit, but it's got stuff in it you'll find useful." He started to unzip the pack, saying, "Let me just remove the firearm—"

"Leave it. If we accidentally tangle with Gray's guys, we'll need all the firepower we can get."

He looked up at Nick and studied him long and hard. Did he dare arm a man he didn't trust at all?

It was totally a test. Nick knew they didn't trust each other. He was pushing to see what reaction he would provoke. Thing was, the guy undoubtedly was armed already. One more pistol wouldn't make a difference.

Alex's gaze narrowed, but he said easily, "Sure. No problem."

He rezipped the second backpack and then tossed it to Nick. Surreptitiously, he slid the box of ammo he'd just palmed from Nick's supplies and tucked it into his own bag, which he slung over his shoulder.

"Let's go hunting, shall we?" Alex said lightly.

Nick nodded and flashed another one of those dimpled, killer grins of his. "Lead on."

"You're the guy with the tracking device. You lead the way."

They headed downstairs, and Alex wasn't surprised when Nick headed for a major street. It was what he would do. Sure enough, Nick hailed a cab and didn't have too much trouble getting one at this late hour on a big thoroughfare. It was drunk o'clock for cabbies and a lucrative time of night.

Yet again, he was startled by how similarly they seemed to operate. They thought alike. They *were* alike. Which was exceedingly weird. For most of his life, he'd felt completely alone. Different. Yet here was another person with so much in common with him.

They headed toward SoHo and were let out on a street corner bracketed by trendy bars. A small crowd of patrons stood outside, waiting for cabs and rideshares. Their cab was snatched up the second they climbed out of it.

Alex noted that Nick immediately pasted on a smile and matched his physical movements to those of the people around him, casual, loose, a little drunk. But then, he was doing the same.

A very wasted woman startled Alex by stepping in front of him and draping her arms around his shoulders. She mumbled something about wondering why such a hot guy was going home alone. Usually, women didn't take much notice of him. Must be the booze talking.

He stiffened reflexively, relieved he hadn't snapped her neck reflexively, too.

Nick stunned him, however, by moving over to the woman and gently untangling her arms from around his neck. "Sorry, honey. The pretty guy is taken."

The clear implication was that Nick was the significant other.

He didn't stiffen when Nick casually looped his arm across Alex's shoulders and used his free arm to move the drunk woman aside. If anything, he found himself leaning in against his handsome partner. They continued on through the crowd.

Alex put his arm around Nick's waist, registering that it was hard and lean, slabbed in muscle. The heat of Nick's body permeated his clothing until his entire left side tingled. As they walked, the outsides of their thighs brushed together lightly.

With each step, Alex's breath came a little shorter and a little faster. He was surrounded by the masculine smell of Nick's aftershave, the feel of his powerful body. The man's sex appeal washed over him like a hot sauna, leaving him panting and starting to sweat.

They passed through the crowd and came out of it onto a relatively deserted stretch of sidewalk. Nick's arm lifted off his shoulder, and he turned Nick's waist loose. The night air felt cold against his skin where Nick's heat had just been.

"The signal is stationary. About two blocks that way and one block over," Nick said low, showing him a map view of the nearby area with a red dot parked a few blocks in front of them. Quickly, Alex memorized the layout of the streets and the location of that ping.

"Split up and look for a vantage point?" Alex murmured.

"You'll need my cell number."

Alex pulled out his phone and they traded each other's contact information. It was weirdly intimate touching their display faces to each other in mimicry of a kiss.

Nick cleared his throat gruffly. "Okay, then. Call me when you find a good spot, and I'll do the same."

Alex peeled off at the next corner, turning left, and Nick turned to the right. Whether or not he would ever see Nick again was the main question. He gave it about even odds that the guy would bolt and flee New York at the first opportunity. Which was too bad. The spy was hot.

Work, my man. Work. You're here to nail Harlan Gray, not Nick. He smirked at his own double entendre until the lust from walking past the bar swept over him once more. Okay, so he wouldn't be averse to nailing Nick. After they'd apprehended and dealt with Gray.

He walked fast until he reached the narrow street Gray's hidey-hole was on. He crossed the road, being careful not to even glance in the direction of the safe house Gray was inside. Once out of sight of it, he doubled back, working his way down a fetid alley, made marginally less gross by the thin layer of snow.

Ah, Christmas in the city.

He eased his way to the end of the alley and snaked a tiny camera around the corner on a flexible handle. He scanned the street—bland, residential, lined with beige apartment blocks, mostly in the five-to-ten-story-tall range. He counted rows of windows on Gray's building. Eight stories tall. One of Gray's men would undoubtedly be out there, but Alex doubted he could spot the guy if he was half as good as Nick.

Alex scanned the rooftops around him, looking for one across the street and taller than the building Gray's ping had come from. Two structures down on his left was a ten-story affair that looked to have a brick wall around its flat roof. It would be a cold, wet night up there, but it should be a good spot to watch Gray from.

He backed down the alley a ways and texted Nick.

I've got a place to watch the front from.

Nick texted back.

There's nothing behind the building that'll work for a hide, and I've got one of Gray's guys moving around back here anyway, patrolling.

He's probably trying to stay warm.

He's successfully blocking me from setting up any kind of surveillance back here.

Alex simply texted back.

Join me. I'll text you my location.

He waited for several agonizingly long seconds and then Nick replied.

Coming.

Really? Joy and shock flooded Alex's belly in equal measure.

What was up with that? This was a freaking job. He had no time for a personal life. Even if Nick had made a point of telling him he was gay. Which (a) he hadn't had to do, which made the fact that he'd done it very interesting, and (b) had been in his dossier, anyway.

Alex backed all the way down the alley to the far end and quickly texted Nick his location. It didn't take long for a dark shadow to loom beside him. Dang. He hadn't seen Nick coming, let alone heard him.

Silently, they moved to the rear of the tall building Alex had picked out. He gestured for Nick to open the door and watched with interest as Nick methodically checked for alarms, disabled the standard fire-exit alarm on the rear alley door and picked the lock.

Nick cracked the door open, and when nothing happened, swept it aside and bowed ironically, gesturing for Alex to go first.

He rolled his eyes and headed inside. They were in a stairwell, and Alex headed up it, counting floors as he went. He moved steadily but quickly, certain that Nick would not only keep up but also not be winded by the fast climb.

They moved in perfect sync, kind of like they seemed to do everything. His steps were silent; Nick's steps were silent. His breath was deep and regular: Nick's breath was deep and regular. He paused at each stairwell to make sure the fire door was closed; Nick did the same. If they'd been dancing together, they couldn't have moved in any more perfect harmony.

They reached the top of the stairs, and this time, Nick gestured for Alex to go through the exercise of disarming the door alarm. Amused at how they continued to test each other, he unlocked it quickly and swept the door open for Nick, as well.

Nick slid left, his back against the wall beside the stairwell, so Alex slid right. The roof was flat, with only waist-high heating and cooling units and a rain-water collector on tall steel legs. They made their way across the roof, clearing behind each piece of equipment they came to, crouching as they approached the front edge.

They were alone up here. He was vaguely surprised that Gray hadn't posted a man on this roof to provide overwatch on the building Gray was sleeping in. Huh. So there were limits to the man's resources after all. Good to know.

Whoever had designed this structure had, most obligingly for him and Nick, built narrow drainage cracks into the brick wall skirting the roof. It made the job of running his little camera on its flexible handle through a slit and pointing it down at Gray's building a piece of cake.

Nick dug around in his pack and came up with a second miniature surveillance camera. He ran his through the drainage about three feet over from the one Alex was using.

They observed the building and the surrounding street for several minutes. Finally, Alex spotted the tiniest shift of movement about fifty feet from the front door of the target building. He breathed, "Got him. Gray's guy is under that tree behind the white delivery van."

Nick shifted his weight, tilting his camera that way. He watched for nearly a minute before breathing back, "Good catch. He's well hidden down there."

It started to snow again, and a flake hit Alex wetly on the face. This was going to get real uncomfortable real fast unless they protected themselves from the elements. To that end, he murmured, "There are Mylar blankets in our packs. How about we spread one to lie on and cover ourselves with the other one?"

"Sounds good," Nick replied, already hunting for the palm-sized bundle of thin, heat-reflective polymer.

Alex helped Nick spread out the first blanket, trying to minimize the crinkling sound it made as they unfolded it. The waterproof material reflected their body heat back at them as they stretched out on it, lying on their stomachs. Nick pulled the second Mylar sheet over himself and passed Alex the corner of it.

When they had it positioned over them both, black side up and reflective silver side down, facing them, they tucked the edges under their outside feet and hips. They left the top loose so they could move their arms and shift position to scan up and down the street.

In a matter of seconds, Alex felt Nick's body heat seeping through his warm clothing. As if that wasn't distraction enough, the guy really did smell good. The expensive cologne scent from their embrace while passing by that bar wafted to him once more. Man. That stuff was lethal.

Before they'd left the apartment, Nick had stripped out of his tuxedo shirt and jacket and had borrowed a black thermal turtleneck from him. But the scent of the cologne still clung to him.

Alex wasn't the kind of guy who typically found perfume intoxicating, but the alchemy of cologne and Nick's body chemistry did make his head spin a little.

Nick shifted to look left, and his shoulder rubbed up against Alex's. The bulge of heavy muscle against Alex's own shoulder was distinct, even through the arctic hiking coats with their layers of high-tech insulation, borrowed from the supply closet.

"Clear," Nick breathed.

Alex leaned in against Nick to point his camera in the other direction, vividly aware of how his whole left side pressed up against Nick's. Again.

And again, it made his breath hitch and his concentration scatter. The man was all muscle and bone, and none of it was soft. *Brawn, thy name is Nicholas Kane.*

That man was far too distracting. Alex shook his head. He had a job to do up here, and he didn't need to be thinking about how sexy Nick was, for crying out loud.

He had to force himself to focus on the quiet street below. He divided it into one-building-wide chunks and cleared the sections of street one by one. Finally, he was able to say with confidence, "Clear."

He felt Nick's nod and noted with some shock that Nick made no move to pull away from him and put even an inch or two of distance between them. Well, then. Personally, he was in no rush to move away from the hunky warmth of Nick, either.

He whispered, "I got a full night's sleep last night. Why don't you catch a nap, and I'll keep an eye on things?"

Nick exhaled in relief. "Thanks, man. After a week of this, I'm wiped out. Wake me in about two hours, and I'll be good to go for a while so you can nap. I've gone longer with less sleep before."

Alex would bet he had. They both had.

In the span of perhaps three breaths, Nick's whole body relaxed against his. The guy had passed out, practically before he finished closing his eyes. Yeah. He was exhausted, all right. Apparently, he hadn't been lying about tailing Gray by himself for the past week.

Alex set up a routine of scanning left, scanning right, then scanning Gray's safe house up and down. The ping from Nick's phone told them Gray was in an interior room on this side of the building but not which floor he was on. But they didn't need that info. They would watch the outside man, and when he left his post, they would know Gray was getting ready to move.

In the meantime, he relished the feeling of Nick's body against his left side. Was it creepy to enjoy the feel of the man even though he himself was dead to the world? Maybe, but he enjoyed it anyway. It wasn't as if he ever got any human contact in his line of work.

Idly, he tried to remember the last time he'd gone on vacation. His grandfather's funeral probably didn't count as an actual getaway, but that had been almost three years ago and was his most recent break of any kind. No wonder he'd been getting nasty emails from the Human Resources Department pestering him to take a few days off.

As he lay there, watching the stillness and silence of the street below, a few lazy snowflakes drifted down, creating a magical atmosphere. Was it weird that he was relieved that Nick's story about tracking his ex-boss was starting to look true? Nick hadn't taken off when they'd separated earlier. He could've, and Alex would've never found him again, mostly likely.

Privately, he was starting to root for Nick to be one of the good ones. How long had it been since he'd encountered an honest man? They were few and far between in his line of work. He hadn't realized how cynical he'd become somewhere along the way until just now, when he desperately wished for Nick to be fully the good guy he claimed to be.

He never got emotionally invested in any of the people he investigated. They were just a job to him. A decision to be made. Good or bad. Right or wrong. He really wanted *not* to have to take down this man. And not only because he was skilled enough to be darned hard to eliminate.

To be honest, he was enjoying the human companionship, even if the man could be infuriatingly distrustful. But then, so was he. It was shockingly pleasant to operate on a mission with an equal. He was even enjoying arguing with Nick. He'd known in a distant, intellectual way that he was lonely, but he'd had no idea how alone he'd been until Nick had blasted into his isolation.

He let Nick sleep for closer to four hours than two. At about the three-hour point, Nick entered a REM cycle, his body twitching faintly against Alex's and his eyeballs moving around a lot underneath his closed lids. Alex waited until the dream had completely abated before finally waking Nick. A sure way to feel like crap was to be woken from a deep, intense dream.

Nick's eyes snapped open as Alex laid his hand lightly over his mouth. He nodded once, and Alex jolted as Nick's lips moved against his palm. He lifted his hand away sharply. It burned where Nick's mouth had touched it.

"What time is it?" Nick mumbled.

"A little after four a.m."

"You should've woken me. I said two hours—"

"You were beat, and you hit a REM cycle. Given your recent sleep deprivation, I judged it more important for you to finish the REM cycle than for me to wake you exactly on time. Besides, nothing's happening below. What time of day does Gray usually move?"

"Varies. But he's not an early bird. You still have time to catch a nap."

Alex nodded, startled. He wasn't used to anyone else paying the least bit of attention to his well-being. It was…nice. Weird. But nice. "I think I will. Thanks."

Chapter Five

Nick lay in the dark as snow drifted down gently around them, listening to the quiet sound of Alex breathing beside him. This night had certainly taken a turn he'd never seen coming. He didn't know what to make of Alexander Creed.

The man was definitely very, very good at his job. Nick's own level of good—which was a rather high bar, if he did say so, himself. He was smart, self-contained, and confident in his abilities. And he was laser focused on figuring out what Harlan Gray was up to. At least they had that in common.

Of course, they also had in common the way their breath hitched every time they touched each other. When he'd grabbed Alex's hand hours ago as they walked across town handcuffed together, he'd heard the man's gasp. Which had been a good thing because it had masked the sound of his own gasp.

And then there'd been that arm-in-arm thing at the club. When that woman had rushed Alex, he hadn't even thought twice. He'd just flung himself forward to get her off him. He hadn't exactly claimed possession of the guy in so many words…but that was exactly what he'd done. And Alex hadn't freaked out.

Was it possible? Was Alex gay like him?

Normally, he had great gaydar. But then, his job required him to be expert at reading body language and subliminal signals. Of course, he was good at picking up little clues and hints that a guy was gay. But Alex was so self-controlled, so closed off, so freaking hard to read, that he couldn't tell. At all. Which was frustrating as heck.

They also had in common the fact that they'd both had a moment with their arm around the other one's neck, with every opportunity to break it. *And neither of them had done so.*

He was no murderer, but he got the distinct impression that violence was a routine part of Alex's job. There was a certain detachment, a certain weariness of the soul about the man that spoke of having seen a lot of death and having dealt out a lot of death.

While Nick had eliminated plenty of people in his career, most of them had been in kill-or-be-killed situations that he didn't carry away a large burden of guilt from. Even in his days as a sniper, he'd operated with the sure and certain knowledge that every person he was assigned to take out was a very, *very* bad person.

But if Alex was telling the truth, if he was a fixer for the US government, that meant he was executing sanctions against his own kind. Other spies, soldiers and covert operators who'd gone off the rails in one way or another and had to be stopped. And most of the time, that meant killing them.

Rough job.

He wouldn't want to do it.

Heck, he wasn't sure he *could* do it, even if he was asked to. The only reason he'd been able to stomach betraying his teammates to the Medusas was because the women had promised not to kill anyone they didn't have to. Vince Spinelli had been the lone man from his team to die the night of the Medusa ambush, and only because Vince had put a knife to a guy's throat and tried to kill him.

Alex shifted a little in his sleep, turning slightly toward him and snuggling a little closer. The man's whipcord strength was apparent, even in the total relaxation of sleep, as Nick registered lean, hard muscle everywhere their bodies touched.

Alex was younger than he'd expected. The way he heard it, the Judge had been operating for a number of years. Before his current gig, he'd allegedly worked undercover with some of the baddest dudes on the planet and walked away alive. And with the deep respect, and fear even, of said dudes.

He would've expected Creed to be a big, impressive, charismatic dude who owned every room he walked into. Nick definitely wouldn't have expected this quiet, unassuming, average-looking guy to be one of the most dangerous men on the planet, feared by both bad guys and good guys alike.

But then, he knew better than most not to judge books by their covers. It was why he was still alive. He was cautious and careful and never assumed anything about anybody. In the parts of the world he'd operated in, old men, women, even children, were often his enemies, armed, dangerous and out to kill men like him.

It was warm sandwiched between the Mylar tarps, and were they not watching one of the other most dangerous men on the planet, Nick would really be enjoying lying out here in the snow and silence cuddled up with the man beside him.

It was shocking how much alike he and Alex were. They both were used to working solo, distrusted each other completely but were reluctant to kill each other. And they had this mission in common.

Nick scanned the street below as the first dull gray light of dawn began to creep across the city under the scudding snow clouds. It continued to snow lightly, but a breeze picked up, and the gentle, lazy flakes of last night turned into slanting needles of cold against his skin.

Seven o'clock came and went, and the traffic below picked up considerably. He was just about to wake up Alex to ask for help keeping track of everyone moving below when he suddenly became aware of Alex staring up at him.

Nick pulled his eye off the camera viewfinder to look down at his companion. "G'morning, sleepyhead."

Alex frowned. "You should've woken me earlier."

"I was about to, anyway. It's getting busy on the street, and I can't watch everyone."

Alex rolled away, and something deep and lonely in Nick's gut protested at the loss of that warm, relaxed presence against his right side. Slipping out from under the Mylar tarp, Alex took up a position a few more drainage slits down the wall to get a better angle on the south end of the street. Nick concentrated on the pedestrians heading north.

A gray-haired woman emerged from Gray's building, and he studied her intently, watching everything about the way she moved. How confident was the set of her shoulders? How controlled was the way she gazed around? Did her clothing and purse match her age? Did she move like an athlete or a slightly creaky middle-aged person?

Nothing about her set off any alarms in his head. Either she was just some lady going out to get breakfast or go to work, or she was a better actress than he was an operator.

A man came out of the building and turned left, and Alex murmured that he had him in sight. Nick scanned his half of the street intently. He had yet to see the guy parked under the tree move from his post. He must have a good disguise going down there, because nobody passing by him was even sparing him a second glance.

If he had to guess, Gray's man was dressed as a homeless person and was probably bundled up to the top of his head, such that nobody could see his face. It was what he would've done in the same situation.

Alex murmured, "Should one of us go around behind the building to spot Gray if he egresses that way?"

Nick was oddly reluctant to leave but nodded. "I'll go. I scouted it last night, so I know the lay of the land back there."

Alex nodded. "Have a bite to eat before you go. I'm betting that if you haven't slept in a week, you probably haven't eaten in a week, either."

He scowled. "You're not wrong, but I don't need a mommy."

"You do need calories," Alex retorted.

Nick grudgingly took the protein bar Alex held out to him. He noticed Alex was holding out his other hand and glanced down at two pills in the guy's palm.

"Stim pills," Alex said.

"Amphetamines?" he asked skeptically.

"Nope. Just caffeine."

"Cool." He'd popped the pills and washed them down with a swig from a water bottle before it dawned on him that he'd casually taken a pair of unidentified pills from a man he didn't trust.

Huh. Maybe he did trust Alex after all. At least a little bit.

"Are there earbuds in these kits?" Nick asked.

"I think so," Alex replied.

They both poked around in their packs and came up with small charger cases holding wireless earbuds.

As Nick linked the earbuds to his phone and poked them in his ears, Alex called his cell. Nick accepted and Alex murmured, "How do you hear me?"

"Five by five. How about me?" Nick responded.

"Loud and clear."

Now that they could talk freely without having to pull out their phones, he nodded to Alex, shouldered his backpack and, crouching low, made his way across the roof to the stairwell.

The rear of the building Gray had spent the night in opened up onto an alley that a bunch of other buildings also backed up to. It was a long, brick-walled canyon with only dumpsters for cover. And he had no doubt that long before Gray stepped out here, every last dumpster up and down the block would be checked in, under and behind by Gray's men.

Pulling the hood of his borrowed coat up over his head, he hiked down the alley briskly, searching as he went for a building whose rear exit had some sort of window in it.

He finally spotted one, farther down than he liked from Gray's building, but beggars couldn't be choosers. He marked which building it was and then turned out of the alley. He walked up the street toward the front of the building he'd chosen.

"Is that you I see coming toward me?" Alex asked in surprise.

"Yes," he replied without moving his lips. He turned

into his target building and was lucky to time jogging up the front steps with someone coming out the front door. He didn't have to stand there and try to get someone to buzz the lock, which would surely have drawn the attention of Gray's "homeless man" down the street.

The resident opened the door, and Nick held it politely for the elderly man.

"Aww, look at you, being all Boy Scout-y," Alex teased.

As Nick headed for the back of the building, he told Alex succinctly what he could do with his comment.

He heard laughter in Alex's voice as he replied, "What was that? You're breaking up."

"Stuff it," he bit out.

"You wish."

Startled, he wasn't sure how to reply. His fellow operators on Gray's team had never flirted with him. Ever. They were aggressively straight as a group, in fact. He'd always wondered how insecure they all were about their masculinity and which ones of the others were secretly gay, too. Statistically, he was not the only gay man among them. But nobody had been willing to talk about it. Ever. It had actually been super annoying to him.

"I'm sorry—" Alex started.

He cut off the apology quickly. "No need to apologize. No offense taken. In fact, I was just thinking about how irritating it was that my old team always tiptoed around saying anything that might be construed as sounding gay. It came off as being ultra-homophobic."

"Well, if it makes you feel better, you and I bat for the same team," Alex said lightly.

But Nick heard the strain in his voice. He wasn't used to being open about being gay, was he? Goodness knew, he'd never caught even a hint of a rumor that the Judge might be gay.

Aloud, Nick commented, "Yeah, I already figured that, but thanks for confirming."

"How did you know?" Alex blurted.

He'd arrived at the back door, and Nick peered out the long, narrow glass insert in the fire exit. The view down the alley was not great. Maybe he could cut away some of the weather stripping at the bottom of the door and slip his minicamera out the hole he made.

Belatedly, he answered Alex's question. "My dude. The way you reacted when I held your hand when we were handcuffed together—hot move, by the way. Most straight men would go board stiff if I grabbed their hand and wouldn't know what to do for a second or two. But you were as relaxed as could be about it."

"I was not relaxed about it!" Alex exclaimed under his breath.

"Okay, fair. You definitely felt the…whatever it was…between us. And it threw you for a loop. But not an 'oh, shit, I'm straight and holding another man's hand' loop. It was more of an 'oh, shit, this guy is hot and I'm not sure I want to kill him anymore' loop that I threw you for."

He pulled out his pocketknife and used its tip to start digging at the black weather stripping at the bottom right-hand corner of the fire exit, where there was already a small gap letting in a prick of light.

Alex said slowly, "You may be more observant than I gave you credit for."

"Gee. Thanks. Do you think maybe someday I might have a future in the intelligence business?"

Alex laughed, a barely audible gust of humor in Nick's ear.

Nick enlarged the hole enough to slip the minicam through it, and he sat down on the floor in front of the fire exit. He could be here awhile, crouching over the tubular end of the camera with its attached viewfinder, so he might as well get comfortable. And, barring a fire in this building, he wasn't likely to be disturbed anytime soon. He pressed his eye to the rubber cup and looked out.

It was disorienting getting a mouse's-eye view of the alley. Or, since this was New York City, maybe a rat's-eye view would be more accurate. He tilted the camera up slightly. There. Now he had a clearer sightline down the alley. If Gray and his men left their hide by the back exit, he would see them.

"So, Alex, when did you figure out you were gay?"

"About the time all the boys started getting interested in girls, I figured out girls didn't do anything for me. It probably took another year or two after that for me to realize that when I woke in the morning super, um, uncomfortable, I usually had been dreaming about a boy and not a girl."

"So that would have made you, what? Twelve or thirteen?"

"Something like that. What about you? When did you know?" Alex asked.

"Later for me. I was told over and over when I was a kid that gay people should all die. So, I fought it pretty hard. I was a junior in high school when I got really drunk at a party and another gay kid in my school pulled me into a closet and made out with me. I swore to him I was just drunk, straight and curious. He laughed in my face and gave me my first blow job."

"You said your dad would've killed you if he found out. Does he know now?"

"Oh yeah. When I finished SEAL training and went live on the teams, I thought I might finally be manly enough to please him and went home for a visit. He got more drunk than usual and called me...things. I told him he was exactly right, I was gay, and furthermore, he could kiss my ass."

Nick felt more than heard Alex's wince before he asked quietly, "How did that go over with him?"

"He tried to kill me. When he attacked, I put him down on the floor in a choke hold in about two seconds and very calmly told him that if he ever touched me again, I would kill him and no one would ever find the body."

"Um, wow. That's too bad."

Nick sighed. "I knew better than to rise to his bait. But he'd said so much hurtful, stupid crap to me over the years about the queer community that I snapped. I'm not proud of it. I was a SEAL, for crying out loud. I knew how to control my emotions. I never let people get to me like that."

"He was your father. That's different."

Nick pulled his eye away from the viewfinder to pinch the bridge of his nose for a moment. "Yeah. I found that out the hard way."

Silence fell between them. He went back to watching the alley.

Nick asked heavily, "Does your family know?"

"Yep. They claim they don't care, love me, are proud of me, and have never been anything but supportive."

"Lucky bastard," Nick murmured. "Wait a minute. They claim they're okay with it? What does that mean?"

"Ah, you are perceptive aren't you, grasshopper?" Alex murmured.

"You gonna dodge my question, or are you gonna answer it?"

Alex sighed. "It means my family said all the right things. But I found out later they weren't as okay with it as they said they were. My parents caught blowback from their church and apparently were rather negative about it to their friends and pastor. Behind my back, of course."

"That sucks," Nick said with feeling. At least his parents had been openly hostile to him and hadn't been two-faced about it. Plus, it didn't take a rocket scientist to notice that Alex was the kind of man who would despise being lied to. He wasn't the Judge for nothing.

"What about your mother?" Alex asked. "What does she think about you being gay?"

"She loved me but feared my dad. She was caught in the middle."

"You say that in the past tense. Has she passed away?"

"Nope. She's alive. But after I attacked my old man, she sided with him. Hasn't spoken to me since. I think I scared her. I mean, they knew I was a SEAL, but they didn't really know what that meant. It had never dawned on them that I was actually capable of killing."

Alex snorted. "Duh." Then, soberly, "I'm sorry. That sucks, too."

Nick sighed. At least Alex knew precisely what it meant to have been a SEAL and what he was capable of. And the guy had still snuggled up against him in his sleep.

Chapter Six

"I've got movement from our homeless guy," Alex said low. "He's going inside the building."

Nick murmured in his ear, "They're getting ready to move. They'll send a couple of guys out to watch the street and maybe put a sniper in a window. Then they'll bring around a vehicle and load up Gray."

"Same limo as last night?" Alex asked.

"No way. New place, new car, every day."

"Bummer. That tracker was handy."

Nick grumbled, "Yeah, and it's exactly why they change cars all the time."

"Okay," Alex reported. "I've got a guy deploying out onto the street. He's heading north. Have you got any movement behind the building?"

"Nega— Crap!" Nick bit out.

"What?"

"A car just raced down the alley." He watched it, reporting tersely, "It has stopped in front of Gray's building. Two men just sped fast out of the building and are getting in the vehicle. And, it's on the move again. Heading north. Dammit, they're turning left. Away from you." The whole stop had taken no more than five seconds.

"Did you see Gray get in the vehicle?" Alex asked tersely.

"I didn't see the faces of the two men who got in the SUV."

"What about their heights and builds? Could one of them have been him?" Alex asked. "Or were they decoys?"

"Possibly. I've never seen the team do anything like that before. Gray always stays in places with covered or underground parking. He moves to vehicles unseen. He doesn't go outside to get into cars."

"New safety protocol?" Alex suggested.

"Well, one thing we know for sure," Nick muttered. "If he's still inside the building, he's down at least three bodyguards. A driver for the vehicle, and the two guys who jumped in the car."

"Did you get a license plate number?"

Nick snorted. "As if. Magically, the plate was completely covered. I couldn't tell you if it was taped over or coated in mud. But either way, it was completely obscured."

"Of course it was. Like magic." A pause, then Alex mused aloud, "How do we tell if Gray's still inside the building or not?"

"How ballsy do you feel like being?" Nick asked.

"What do you have in mind?"

"I can approach the team. The guys know me. I trained most of them. I can ask to speak to Gray. Tell him I need to report in on the ambush that got the rest of my team caught."

"Yes, but won't he ask where you've been the past few months?"

"I'll tell him I had to go to ground. That I couldn't

risk approaching him until I knew for sure I was in the clear."

Alex considered. "What if he doesn't believe you? You'd be walking into a death trap."

"We all have to die sometime."

Alex scowled. Nick was the first person with whom he'd made any kind of personal connection with in years. Literally years. He really didn't want to see the man throw away his life. Not to mention, death wishes were not good things for active operators to run around with. When they got back to the safe house—if they made it back to the safe house—he and Nick were going to have a little conversation about the whole prepared-to-throw-away-his-life thing.

Alex asked, with a sense of desperation that surprised himself, "How would you even figure out which unit Gray stayed in last night? Even if the apartments are huge, the building has to have at least three or four dozen condos."

"Call it intuition. I can feel Gray and his guys."

"What exactly do they feel like?" Alex asked dryly.

"They make the back of my neck crawl. As if a scorpion is walking across my skin, and all I can do is be perfectly still and pray it doesn't sting me."

"Spoken like a man who's done a sniper mission or two in a desert environment."

Nick grunted. "Obviously, you've pulled the same sort of mission."

Obviously.

"Let me come with you," Alex said. "I can at least lay down covering fire for you if you have to beat a hasty retreat."

"That's not how Gray's team works," Nick said grimly. "Nobody gets away from them once they decide to detain or kill a target. There's no sense getting us both killed. If they take me out, at least you'll be able to finish the mission alone."

There was nothing Alex could say to that. He was the exact same way. Once he locked in on a target, that was it. He didn't stop or give up until he succeeded in executing his orders.

"Thanks for the offer to come along, but your presence would only raise red flags," Nick said. "I may be able to get close without freaking them out."

"I don't like this."

"I don't like it, either. But you tell me what better option we have."

Alex sighed. "I've got nothing. How are you going in?"

"I'll enter through the underground parking garage. It exits into this alley."

It sounded as if Nick was moving around as he spoke into his microphone. Alex heard a zipper and then faint scratching sounds. Nick was probably packing up his surveillance gear and disabling the fire alarm on the exit to the alley.

Nick said low, "I'm moving out."

"Update me as you can," Alex replied.

Nick didn't reply.

If waiting up here for the past seven hours had tested his patience, waiting for the next few minutes nearly killed Alex. Which shocked him. He could sit in a surveillance hide for days on end without ever getting twitchy. But two minutes of worrying about his new partner, and he was a hot mess.

What if he'd been spotted? What if he'd been shot? Oh, man. Should he go down there and check on Nick? Stage a rescue—

"I'm in the garage. Limo in sight. Gonna retrieve my tracker," Nick breathed.

Oh, thank goodness. Nick wasn't dead.

Alex tried to picture the scene in the parking garage. A dark, low-ceilinged space of tilting concrete ramps smelling of oil and exhaust fumes. Nick, gliding through the shadows, using pillars and vehicles for cover, making his way toward the limo. A pause to check for Gray's people. Then a low, slow approach to the back end of the limousine—

Nick swore quietly in his ear. "It's not here."

Alex didn't transmit it, but he swore, as well. Gray knew someone was on to him. Which would explain the change in security procedures and abrupt departure. Assuming Gray had actually left in that fast-moving car in the alley.

"Going inside," Nick breathed.

Alex couldn't help himself. He replied, "Be careful."

"Aww. You like having a partner?" Nick teased under his breath. "Or do you just like me?"

He liked having *this* partner. Not that he was about to admit it to Nick. No way was he feeding the guy's ego any more fodder.

Instead, he drawled, "Obviously, I prefer not working solo on a surveillance op. I mean, I get to sit back and watch the show while you stick your neck out. This is great. I'm just kicking back, up here on the roof, my feet propped on a rail, eating a power bar."

Nick laughed quietly. "Asshole."

Alex grinned. "Right back atcha."

Alex heard the distinctive ding of an elevator, and Nick said, "I'll try the third floor. Gray won't use the first or second floors—too easy to access. And he won't use the top two floors. They're too exposed to an aerial attack. Which leaves me four floors to search."

"You're not going to actually search apartments, are you?" Alex asked in quick alarm.

"Relax, Grandma. I'm just gonna walk the halls and wait for a scorpion to walk across my neck."

"I'm the hottest grandma you've ever met," Alex retorted.

"No lie, my friend. No lie."

Welp. That silenced Alex but good. Nick thought he was hot, huh? What was he supposed to do with that? Ignore the attraction simmering between them and just do the job? Take a break from all of this at some point and explore whatever it was crackling and sparking between them?

The elevator dinged again, and Alex pictured Nick checking the hallway, then moving out of the elevator, rolling from heel to toe with each step, making no noise whatsoever as he walked smoothly down the hall.

Alex heard once that SEALs had a saying. Slow is Smooth, and Smooth is Fast. They were not wrong.

A door squeaked in Alex's earbud and he tensed.

"In the stairwell. Moving up to four," Nick murmured.

He was only silent for perhaps ten seconds before he whispered in Alex's ear, "Tallyho."

"Scorpion on your neck?"

"Roger that," Nick breathed.

"Any visual on Gray or his guys?"

"No. But they're in one of two apartments. I'm knocking on the first door now."

Alex's whole body vibrated with tension as he heard Nick's knuckles rap quietly, not so loud as to carry across the hallway into the other apartment.

Silence.

Nick knocked again.

Still nothing.

"Trying the other unit," Nick breathed.

Again, there was no response to his knocks.

Alex knew better than to bug Nick while he was operating in a high-threat environment. The man needed to focus all his awareness on his immediate surroundings and be ready to react instantaneously.

Two minutes or so passed in tense silence. *What was Nick doing down there?*

"Sonofabitch," Nick said in disgust.

"What?" Alex blurted, his nerves near the breaking point.

"So, I let myself into the apartment that felt the most scorpion-like."

"You broke in?" Alex squawked. "What if they were there, waiting for you?"

"They weren't. I cleared the place, and it's empty."

"Then, how do you know you have the right one?"

"My tracker is lying on the kitchen table beside a note that says 'You forgot something.'"

Alex's jaw dropped. "Does he know who you are?"

"No idea. But it's vintage Gray. He wants whoever is following him to know that he knows."

"So, he was in the car you saw take off, then?"

"That would be my guess," Nick replied heavily.

"We've lost him."

"Looks that way."

Alex was tempted to punch the brick wall beside his head. "What do you want to do next?"

"I'm gonna search the apartment across the hall to be safe."

"But—"

"I'm going now," Nick interrupted. He might as well have told Alex to shut up. Both of them knew he needed silence in his earbuds while he broke into and cleared the second unit.

Alex pictured Nick checking for alarms, picking the door lock and easing into the apartment. He would clear the space in a pattern—front to back, clockwise—it would depend on the layout. When he'd opened all the doors, looked in every closet, under every bed and anywhere else a human could conceivably hide, only then would he break radio silence.

"Clear. But his team stayed in this place last night," Nick announced.

"How do you know?"

"It's too neat for any normal person to leave it like this. There's not a fingerprint *anywhere*. Every glass in the cupboard is wiped clean. No normal person wipes down the glassware, and certainly not that thoroughly, when they unload the dishwasher."

"Good point."

Alex noted Gray's man at the north end of the street turning to walk back toward the building. He checked the south-end man, and he, too, was on the move. "Nick, you've got two tangos incoming. The guys on the street are coming toward the building."

"I'll bet they just get in a car and drive away. This place is already sanitized and buttoned-up. They won't come back here. I'm going to head down to the basement and see if I can get a license plate and description of their vehicle."

Alex squeezed his eyes shut. It was exactly what he would do, so he couldn't fault Nick for doing the same thing. But he didn't like it. The risk of being seen was considerable, and a two-on-one fight of any kind rarely went well for the solo guy. It took a ridiculously skilled fighter to hold off a pair of attackers.

He heard Nick breathing hard, which meant he must be charging down the stairwell at top speed. Abruptly, Nick stopped huffing, took two long, deep breaths, and then a door latch clicked. He was heading back into the parking garage.

Alex heard an engine rev briefly.

"Got 'em," Nick said in satisfaction when the car noise had died away. "Pack up, and I'll meet you at the north end of the street."

Alex folded the Mylar tarps and stuffed them in his rucksack. He policed the roof for any wrappers or water bottles, then walked around, scuffing his feet until he had obscured any tracks that might have identified him or Nick in any way. Then he headed for the fire escape.

He spotted Nick standing at a bus stop in front of him, looking bored and annoyed…which meant he blended in perfectly with the other people waiting for the bus.

Alex walked up beside Nick and murmured, "Subway will be faster to get back to my place. We'll have to make two transfers if we take the bus. But there's a direct train to my neighborhood."

"Subway it is," Nick replied low.

They had to walk a block or so to the nearest entrance. But a train was pulling into the station as they reached the platform, and it was only a half dozen stops on this line to the subway station just down the street from his crash pad.

A busker played acoustic guitar and sang holiday songs in their car. As the stations flashed by, advertisements for live Christmas trees, department store holiday sales, and seasonal pop-up stores came into view and disappeared again. It was oddly cheerful, given the grim nature of the job they were in the midst of.

The morning rush hour was mostly past, and the subway riders skewed mostly to retirees and moms with small children. Both groups appeared to be interested mainly in their holiday shopping needs.

Nick and Alex walked to their building in the light layer of new snow, rode the rickety elevator up to the apartment, and while Nick took a shower, claiming a need to wake up, Alex scrambled a pile of eggs for them and made toast in the oven. It felt good, right, to cook breakfast for the two of them like this.

Since when did he like playing house, solo or otherwise? Sure, he fed himself and cleaned the spaces he lived in. But he'd never registered enjoyment of simple tasks like this, let alone enjoyment of doing them for someone else.

With a jolt, he smelled something burning. He lunged for the oven and pulled out the rapidly blackening toast.

He scraped off the blackened part with a knife over the sink, shaking his head at how much Nick distracted him. He popped a pod into a single-serving coffee maker and inhaled gratefully as the scent of the steaming brew rose from the machine.

"Oh man. That smells good," Nick said from behind him.

Alex tensed reflexively. He wasn't used to being around anyone who could sneak up on him like that. It took a very, very quiet human being to get close to him without him hearing or at least sensing them.

He turned to face Nick. *Hoo, baby.* With his hair towel dried and brushed back from his freshly shaven face, the full impact of Nick's good looks was on display. His tanned skin and manly features stole Alex's breath away. He wasn't a pretty man, per se. But he was hard to look away from.

Alex's gaze dropped, taking in the fact that Nick's shirt wasn't buttoned. He'd donned the starched white tuxedo shirt from before, and he'd rolled up the sleeves—he probably didn't want to fuss with cuff links—and he hadn't bothered with the studs that would close the garment, either.

His chest was covered in dark hair that looked fantastic against his darkly tanned skin and bulging pectorals. An urge to crawl inside that shirt and lick the man's chest startled Alex badly. "Where'd you get a tan like that at this time of year?" he blurted.

Nick arched one dark, sexy eyebrow at him and said dryly, "You know better than to ask a guy like me stuff like that."

"Yeah. Right. Sorry," he mumbled, picking up a plate of eggs and toast and shoving it practically into Nick's belly button.

He fetched his own plate and followed Nick to the table with it. "I would've made you coffee, but I thought you might want to sleep some more. You've got some catching up to do after the past week. After that, we can figure out how we want to proceed with picking up Gray's trail."

Nick looked longingly at Alex's mug of black coffee but nodded in acquiescence. "What are you going to do while I snooze?"

"I thought I'd go out and do a little sightseeing. Maybe do a little Christmas shopping."

Nick looked startled. As if he hadn't had anyone to shop for at this time of year for a very long time.

His own family wasn't great—he could do without their hypocrisy—but at least they didn't reject him outright.

To be honest, he was probably as hypocritical as they were, buying Christmas presents and sending birthday cards with cheerful messages as if nothing was wrong between them. As if it didn't feel like a hot knife in his belly every time he thought about the things his family said about him behind his back that they thought he wouldn't find out about.

Maybe Nick had the right of it. Maybe he should just make a break and tell them they could come back into his life when they could fully embrace him as he was, or at least be honest with him about how they felt about him being gay. But it was a big step. And he was already completely alone in the world. Did he have the courage to cut off his only lifeline to family?

Alex asked, "When's the last time you celebrated Christmas with your family?"

Nick very obviously deflected the topic, snapping, "I hate Christmas."

"With a name like Nicholas Kane? As in Saint Nick and candy canes? And you hate Christmas? Say it isn't so!"

"Sorry. I'm a born-again holiday hater."

"Okay. Then, when is the last time you celebrated a holiday with anyone? A birthday, New Year's, Independence Day. Any holiday," Alex asked in surprise.

Nick frowned for a moment and then shrugged. "Can't remember."

"Aww, c'mon. A guy like you has to have a pretty decent memory."

"I have a great memory but a lousy family. I guess my

last Christmas at home would've been before I joined the navy, so maybe…eighteen years ago?" he guessed.

"Dang, you're old," Alex teased.

"How old are you?" Nick demanded.

"Thirty-four. You?"

Nick snorted. "You're a babe in arms. I'll be thirty-eight in January."

"Man, you really are ancient. You're just about ready for the retirement farm."

Nick scowled and made a rude hand gesture to him.

Alex grinned even more broadly. His smile still fading, he said to Nick, "Tell me something your family did together to celebrate the holidays when you were a kid."

"We never did much together. But let's see. Holidays at my house. On Christmas Eve, my dad usually went to a bar to drink. My mom went to her bedroom to drink. My older sister went to parties with her friends to drink, and my younger brother snuck booze out of my mom's hidden stash and drank it."

"I'm sensing a theme with your family," Alex responded.

Nick shrugged. "I remember making Christmas cookies once with my granny. She let me decorate them however I wanted. That was fun. She made popcorn for me and her, and we watched a Christmas movie while we worked on those stupid cookies."

"Do you remember what the movie was?"

Nick shook his head. "No clue. She was babysitting me that night. And she brought over Christmas lights and ornaments for our tree. My dad refused to spend money on frivolous crap like decorations, and my mom was too depressed to fight him on it. In his defense, do you know how many fifths of vodka you can get for the same money it takes to buy a tree?"

The pain in Nick's voice was hard to hear. He couldn't think of anything to say in response, so he put his head down and ate in silence.

"Do you actually like Christmas?" Nick blurted without warning.

He looked up, startled. "Yes. Actually, I do."

"Why?"

"Hope. It's a season of love and peace, family and new beginnings. It gives me hope."

"Hope for what?"

"For me finding a little of all those things one day, I guess."

"Whew. For a second there, I thought you were going to say you wish for world peace."

"Umm, I do. Of all people, you and I know the cost of there not being peace on earth."

Nick exhaled heavily. "Yeah. I guess we do. Maybe that's why I hate the holidays."

Alex blinked, shocked. "Are you saying you're a pessimist at heart? I don't believe it. I may not have known you all that long, but you strike me as the kind of man who always believes things will turn out okay for you."

"Maybe professionally." Nick shrugged. "Can't say the same for my personal life."

"Maybe the right person just hasn't come along for you. Maybe happiness is waiting for you right around the corner."

"Dang. You really are a Pollyanna."

Alex merely shrugged in response. He stood by his declaration of affection for the holidays. It was the one time of year when he felt a tiny bit optimistic about the future.

As they finished eating and Nick pushed his plate

back in satisfaction, Alex said quietly, "Regarding your death wish. We need to have a conversation about that."

"What about it?"

Interesting. He didn't deny having one. "It's not a good trait for an active covert operative."

Nick sighed. "I've always expected to die in the line of duty. Don't you?"

"No!" Alex exclaimed. "I don't. I fully expect to retire safely from my job and settle down to a nice, quiet life. And you should, too."

Urgency to get Nick to give up his crazy notion of dying in the line of duty pulsed through him and through his words. Nick had to live if he was going to get his shot at a family of his own.

Nick shrugged. "I guess I've never pictured myself getting a happily-ever-after."

"Why ever not?"

Nick frowned at him. "You know why not."

"Because you're gay?" Alex asked, startled.

"Well. Yeah."

"It's not a crime to be gay. And it certainly doesn't mean you're not allowed to find happiness in your old age."

"I'm not forty yet. I'm not exactly in my dotage, here."

Alex rolled his eyes. "You know what I mean. You're allowed to find a nice guy, settle down, have some kids if you want. Be happy."

"Happy," Nick murmured reflectively. "Not a word I've ever used to describe myself."

"Well, that's grim."

Nick shrugged.

Alex had no idea why it was suddenly so important to him that Nick get a happily-ever-after in spite of all the bad family and bad luck life had thrown at him. But it was important to him. In fact, a desire to be the person to give love and laughter and family to this grim man surged through him.

Alex leaned forward. "I'm serious. You need to get over this eagerness to die. If nothing else, it makes you bad at your job. I'd hate to have to pull you out of the field because of it."

"You'd pull me out of the field?" Nick exclaimed. "Do you even have that power?"

Alex shot him a withering look. "I have the power to execute you, no questions asked. I most certainly have the power to tell my superiors you need to be brought in and taken out of field operations."

"You wouldn't!" Nick sounded aghast.

"I don't want to. Please don't make me do it."

"So…what? I'm supposed to act as if there's a permanent ray of sunshine up my ass?"

"No. And don't be crude." He drank the last of his coffee and set the mug down on the table. "But do think about pulling your head out of said ass long enough to find a compelling reason to stay alive."

"Has anyone ever told you that you're a bit of a jerk?" Nick grumbled.

Alex grinned. "All the time, my friend. All the time."

Nick just scowled, shoved back his chair and carried his plate over to the sink.

Alex insisted on doing the dishes. He waved Nick over toward the mattress in the corner, and thankfully, Nick didn't fight him on it. Which was an indication of just how beat the guy was.

By the time Alex washed the two plates, skillet and coffee mug, Nick was passed out cold, still fully dressed except for his shoes, which he'd kicked off. Shaking his head, Alex fetched a blanket and pillow out of the front closet. He considered waking Nick to hand him the pillow but settled for laying it gently beside the guy's head. He unfolded the blanket and draped it lightly over Nick from neck to toes. Nick didn't even stir as the blanket settled over him, which was indicative of just how deeply the guy was already asleep.

Alex set the alarms for the apartment and headed out. He had an idea. He didn't know if he could pull it off, but he would give it his best shot.

Chapter Seven

Nick woke slowly, groggily. What was the sun doing coming in the window from that angle? When he'd closed his eyes for a quick nap, the sun had been behind the building in the east. Now it was flooding the tiny studio from the west.

Surely he hadn't slept all day—

As the thought occurred to him, he lurched up to a seated position. Where had that pillow come from? And the blanket? And where was Alex?

He looked around and several other things registered in him all at once. In his absence from consciousness, someone—Alex, no doubt—had decorated the apartment for the holidays. A fake Christmas tree perhaps two feet tall stood on the table. Small, shiny objects hung all over it.

Nick climbed to his feet and noticed the window behind him was surrounded by a string of orange-and-green–chili pepper lights held up with black duct tape. The dude version of Christmas lights amused him. He wandered over to the table and grinned at the tree's decorations. Ammunition in various calibers hung all over it from black thread that look suspiciously like trip wire.

He turned on the television to catch the news, pondering how many times he'd found out where he was about to be deployed over the years by watching twenty-four-hour news channels like this one.

The hallway doorknob rattled, and Nick reacted fast, jumping up and moving swiftly to the corner of the kitchen, out of sight of the short hallway. He waited, poised for violence.

"Hi, Lucy. I'm home," Alex called out.

Nick exhaled and lowered his hands as he stepped out into the middle of the living area. "Hey. I love what you've done with the place, Ricky."

Alex set down a pair of flat cardboard boxes on the table beside the tiny, homicidal tree. "I brought us a holiday-themed meal."

"Pizza?" Nick blurted. "How is that Christmas themed?"

Alex grinned and opened the lid of the top box. "Easy. One is topped with tomatoes and basil, the other has pepperoni and green peppers. Get it? Red and green?"

Nick just shook his head. "Pathetic, man."

"Admit it. This is more Christmas-y than anything you've seen in years." Alex waved a hand to encompass the pizza, tree and window dressing.

"How are chili peppers Christmas-y?" Nick asked, reaching for a slice of pizza.

Alex shrugged. "The store I went to was out of lights, and those were the only ones they had left."

"The duct tape really makes the pepper lights special," Nick commented dryly.

Alex grinned and handed Nick one of the pizza boxes, then picked up the other. "I thought you of all people would appreciate my ingenuity in figuring out how to hang them."

Nick sat down on the sofa and commenced eating pizza straight from the box.

"Speaking of holiday moods," Alex said cheerfully, "I got us a couple Christmas movies to watch, too."

"You really went all out. Beneath all that cool, calm killer, are you really a secret Christmas junkie?"

"Guilty as charged," Alex replied, crouching in front of a DVR player sitting on the floor below the flat-screen TV. The screen went dark for a moment, and then a movie started to play.

Nick watched about ten seconds of it and started to laugh. "Really? *Die Hard* is your idea of a Christmas movie?"

Alex grinned at him. "Hey. I'm totally down for watching *White Christmas* or *It's a Wonderful Life*. But I thought you'd prefer a little shoot-'em-up with your holiday cheer."

"You would not be wrong. Nothing says Peace on Earth and Goodwill to Men like a hostage crisis and a little gratuitous violence."

Alex laughed. "Great. Because I've got *Home Alone* for us to watch, too."

Nick had to shake his head. Truth be told, all of this was really thoughtful. He really hadn't celebrated the season, not once, since he'd left home at eighteen years of age. During his military career, he had always volunteered for Christmas duty so the guys with families could stay home with their loved ones. More times than he could count, he'd ended up deployed in some remote corner of the world anyway, chasing bad guys who didn't care if it was December 25 or not.

"Shouldn't we be trying to track down Gray's guys and the car I saw them leave the garage in?"

Alex scowled. "I already had the plates run. It was

a rental car. Got turned in around noon. We lost Gray and his men."

"Well, hell."

"I don't know about you," Alex commented, "but if I do something innocuous to keep my conscious mind occupied, my subconscious usually figures out what I should do next. Right now, I've got it working on how to pick up Gray's trail again. In the meantime, I'm going to pop some popcorn and watch a movie."

Nick shrugged. The plan worked for him.

As Bruce Willis entered the high-rise tower where his ex-wife worked, Alex surprised him by asking randomly, "If you were actually going to celebrate the holidays, what would you want to do?"

"I have no idea. Maybe go sit on a beach somewhere and listen to country music."

Alex laughed. "My sister calls country music the music of pain."

Nick grinned. "She's not wrong. Maybe that's why I like it."

"Party pooper," Alex retorted.

"Why? What would you do for the holidays if you didn't spend it with your perfect family?"

"My family isn't perfect. Far from it." He paused, letting the wave of sadness that washed over him pass. "In answer to your question, though, I would head somewhere snowy. A small town that goes all out for Christmas. Every house would have lights on it and a tree in the front window. There would be snowmen in the yards and kids sledding. I would bake cookies and wrap presents and spend the holidays with my family, hanging out, catching up on one another's lives and laughing."

Nick tilted his head. "What does your family think you do for a living?"

"They think I do financial audits of government agencies and fix any discrepancies I find."

Nick's mouth twitched with humor. "When I was still speaking with my sister, I told her I was a tropical fish importer. Every time I visited her and her kids, I had to stop at a store and buy them a plastic bag full of fish. Lousy legend. Pain in the ass, having to keep getting all those stupid fish."

"Why don't you speak to your sister anymore?"

"Her husband won't let her contact me. He says that, as a former SEAL, I pose a danger to her and the kids."

"Do you?"

Nick rolled his eyes. "They're family. I'd die to protect them, and I would never, ever harm them. Not that they understand for a second what loyalty to family actually means."

Alex put down a strip of uneaten crust and picked up another piece of pizza. "Mine understands loyalty. But they have a real problem with telling the truth. Not to mention they have no idea what it takes to keep a government the size of ours from going off the rails."

"Is that how you see yourself?" Nick asked. "A guy who keeps Uncle Sam honest?"

"Something like that. I'm not so naive as to think we don't need bad people to do bad things from time to time. But those people can't be allowed to slip off their leashes. That's my job. To keep them from losing control and using the government's resources to do terrible things they weren't ordered to do."

"I've never met a fixer before," Nick reflected. "I mean, I always knew at some peripheral level that guys like you must exist, but nobody ever talks about it."

Alex shrugged. "It's interesting work."

"Don't you get cynical after a while?" Nick asked.

"How so?"

"Don't you get jaded, seeing good guy after good guy making a bad decision or losing control and doing something they shouldn't?"

Alex frowned at him, and Nick gazed back, interested in Alex's answer.

"Honestly, I try not to think about it. It's too depressing. I remind myself that, for every person I have to take out of the field, there are dozens or hundreds of operators who don't step over the line."

"How many people have you actually executed in your career?"

Alex grimaced. "You know the deal. I try not to keep count."

"You try. But you remember every face and every name," Nick said quietly.

Alex met his gaze, and for a second, naked pain and grief shone in his eyes.

Of course, Alex remembered every kill. Most of the SEALs Nick had worked with were the same way. In fact, the guys who didn't remember them, who didn't have nightmares about them, were the ones who worried Nick.

Alex said vaguely, "I'm up around fifty sanctions. Of course, those aren't all American operators, and they didn't all end up in a morgue. When there aren't any domestic bad guys to stop, I occasionally pick up a regular assignment."

Alex might have said the word *assignment*, but Nick heard the unspoken word—*assassination*. "How many of your targets were foreign?"

"A dozen, maybe. And only about half of my American caseload ends up in a kill."

"But still, half are guys like me."

"Not guys like you. Guys who've gone rogue."

Nick shook his head. "Still. You're talking about multiple guys of our own who've crossed over to the dark side. That is depressing. I hoped there might be one guy go bad every decade or so."

"If only," Alex said soberly.

Nick turned back to the movie to watch Alan Rickman's villain character burst into a boardroom and shoot it up.

"Promise me something," Alex blurted suddenly.

Nick looked over at him. "What's that?"

"Swear to me you're one of the good guys. That you're not a plant by Gray to track me and stop me from getting to him."

Nick lurched. "I swear. I want to take down Gray as much as you do. The bastard corrupted my entire team and dragged them into whatever criminal enterprise he's got going."

"Where are your former teammates, anyway?" Alex asked. "You said something about them being apprehended. But, they're not listed in any prisoner database I have access to."

"Black site. In the custody of a group I trust absolutely. Not CIA, though. Military."

"Are they giving up any information?"

Nick rolled his eyes. "What do you think?"

"I think people like us are trained to die before we give our interrogators the time of day."

"You would not be wrong," Nick responded.

Alex shrugged. "In my experience, everyone has a breaking point. With people like us, it just takes a lot longer to reach it. Give your teammates a few years sitting in a hole. They'll talk, eventually."

"And what will that accomplish?" Nick asked bitterly.

"Well, if we manage to take Gray alive, he'll also be sitting in a hole somewhere. And when your guys finally talk, we can prosecute him and put him away—or put him down—for good."

"We won't take Gray alive. That I know for sure. The man always has a cyanide pill or something similar on his person. He'll kill himself long before he lets himself be arrested."

"Oh, I don't arrest my targets. Capture them, yes. But I don't do anything so mundane or formal as arresting anyone. That would leave a paperwork trail."

Nick studied Alex intently. "Who fixes the fixers? What if one of you goes off the rails?"

Alex let out a whoosh of air as if Nick has punched him in the gut. "That would be bad. Real bad. I imagine we would join together to go after the rogue fixer."

"Do you know how many of you there are?" Nick asked.

"I have no idea. And if I did, I surely couldn't tell you."

"Aww, c'mon. I've got *all* the security clearances," Nick protested.

Alex shrugged. "I'm afraid there are a few clearances you don't have. There are some whose names are even classified."

Nick never had felt a need to one-up other operators. He was comfortable in his own skin and at peace with the idea that there would always be others who knew a little bit more than him. It was the nature of working in the intelligence community. All information was tightly compartmentalized. He knew everything he needed to know to operate in his own little sandbox. He didn't need to know what was going on in the next-guy-over's sandbox.

Alex said, "Here's where the movie gets funny."

Nick watched, and guffawed, as Bruce Willis ran around barefoot on floors strewn with shattered glass. "What technical advisor let them film anyone barefoot running around on shards like that?"

Alex grinned over at him. "It's the magic of Hollywood."

Nick shrugged. "I mean, sure, he's playing up wincing and limping a little. But he would be debilitated by the pain of running on that much glass. And he would be bleeding everywhere by now."

Willis climbed up into a ventilation duct and commenced crawling through it while Nick shook his head and commented, "How many buildings have you ever been in that had ductwork that easy to access or that went exactly where you needed it to go?"

Alex rolled his eyes. "Or buildings with banks in them that don't have alarms wired directly to police stations?"

Nick grinned, and the nitpicking was on. They surgically dismembered the movie, discussing in detail how they would have gone about freeing the hostages, stopping the bad guys and liberating the building. Alex was a creative and out-of-the-box thinker who challenged even Nick's problem-solving prowess.

They laughed and compared notes—in general terms that didn't violate security protocols, of course—on various missions they'd run, and they discovered their backgrounds were more similar than they expected. They'd found kindred souls in each other.

Except for country music. Alex hated country music.

While Nick had been running around with his SEAL team, Alex had gone the civilian route, working his way up through the ranks of the CIA, picking up training all around the world with various intelligence agencies, like MI6 and the Mossad. He'd run undercover with mobsters and terrorists, and had even embedded with a few private security firms to do mercenary work. The end result was that he was trained much like Nick had been, first in the military and then in the CIA's Special Operations Group.

They both had been all over the world and, sitting here now, expressed fatigue at all the travel. When Alex challenged him to imagine surviving his career, his mind turned to a quiet retirement where he settled down someplace exceedingly dull. To that image, Alex added putting their feet up on the porch railing and watching the world go by for a good, long time.

Yep. That sounded almost good enough to stay alive for.

As the big shootout and explosions at the end of *Die Hard* commenced, Nick asked, "Have you ever thought about having a family of your own?"

Alex winced. "Of course I've thought about it. But it's hard enough to find a partner who won't drive me crazy, let alone one who can put up with a guy like me. I surely don't expect to find someone who can tolerate me *and* who wants a picket fence and kids."

"Why? What's wrong with you? I mean, if you have no hope, surely I have even less chance," Nick said.

Alex shrugged. "It's not as if I can talk like this about my career with anyone else. The first time I casually dissect the best way to kill someone in a movie, any reasonably nice civilian guy will run screaming from me."

"Damn. I hadn't ever thought of it like that," Nick said low. "I mean, I haven't really given serious thought to what comes after my career, because you know, death wish and all."

"You should really give some thought to the idea of building your own family after the one that raised you turned out...badly."

He snorted. "*Badly* is hardly the word I would use. They're a freaking shit show— Sorry. A freaking disaster."

"I'm sorry about that, too. You're a decent guy and deserve better."

"Yeah, well, we don't get to choose our parents." Alex rolled his eyes knowingly.

"What's that all about?" Nick asked. "Why did you roll your eyes when I mentioned your family?"

Alex stared at a spot over Nick's shoulder and didn't look him in the eye. "Let's just say I have a very black-and-white sense of honesty, and they do not."

"Ouch." Nick nodded in understanding. "It sucks being in a business where absolute honesty is required or else people will die. The rest of the world doesn't tend to live that way, do they?"

Alex sighed. "No. They don't. And it worries me for down the road when I rejoin the civilian world. How am I going to compromise my standards and live with someone who can't or won't be totally honest with me at all times?"

It dawned on Nick that he was going to have the exact same problem. Particularly after his team had lied to him and betrayed him the way they had. It had been more devastating to him than he would've anticipated. "Who the hell knew that finding one truthful man to love would turn out to be such a hard thing? If you'd told me back when I was seventeen that honesty would be the one issue that was my deal breaker for relationships, I'd have laughed my head off."

"Why's that?"

"Because being gay and not out of the closet is a completely dishonest way to live. Granted, I needed to stay closeted for my own safety. But I became a fantastic liar out of sheer survival necessity."

"At least you'll be a much better dad to your own kids because of what you went through. I'll bet you create a safe space for your children to be totally candid with you and not face repercussions for it."

Nick's gut tightened at the thought of having children of his own one day. It was his fondest wish to have kids, but he knew full well how unlikely he was to attain it. He barely admitted to himself that he would love to have a family of his own, let alone to anyone else.

"...you'll know what not to do as a parent," Alex was saying.

"That's something, I guess." Nick looked over at Alex. "Are you always Mr. Optimism-and-Find-the-Silver-Lining?"

"Me? My family insists I'm the doom-and-gloom guy of our clan. Apparently, I always have a contingency plan for the worst-case scenario."

"Well...yeah. That's how you've stayed alive this long. People like us always have to be prepared for the worst, the unexpected, the shot out of left field."

"I know, right?" Alex exclaimed. "That's what I keep telling them. But then they remind me that financial audits are not the stuff of life and death."

Nick grinned. "Neither is selling tropical fish."

They traded smiles of commiseration. Their families never would understand them. Not as long as they had no idea what kind of work they'd really done in their careers.

Nick asked thoughtfully, "Do you suppose the day

will ever come when you can tell them what you actually did?"

Alex answered quietly, "Would you tell the people you love how many human beings you've killed in your work?"

Nick jolted. "Good grief. I haven't had any contact with anyone I love for so long that I haven't had to consider how they would react to knowing what I do."

"Hah. And you thought I was the Sunshine Guy," Alex said a shade bitterly.

"Point taken."

The movie ended, and Alex fast-forwarded to the end of the credits and started playing *Home Alone*. The ridiculous humor of a boy getting left behind by accident when his family went on Christmas vacation was just what they needed after the heavy conversation about their careers and families.

One thing Nick knew for sure. If he had a kid, he would never leave him or her behind, by accident or otherwise. Ever. He knew all too well the pain of being abandoned and rejected by the people he loved.

Thankfully, the antics of the dumber-than-dirt robbers trying to break into a family's home, foiled at every step by the boy who'd been left behind, were so silly that Nick felt no need to dissect the tactics or strategies employed by the bad guys or the kid.

He and Alex laughed through the film and munched on the popcorn Alex popped on the stove. They sat side by side, their elbows brushing against each other, balancing the big bowl of popcorn between them. They grabbed handfuls of the buttery, crunchy goodness, and for a little while, life was simple. They ate, they laughed, they relaxed. And it was nice. Really nice.

After the movie finished and twilight was falling

across the city outside, Alex sighed. "We probably ought to have another serious conversation."

"About?" Quick alarm buzzed in Nick's gut.

"Gray. We've got to acquire him again, and this time, we've got to figure out what he's up to before he loses us."

Whew. For a second there, he thought Alex was going to tell him he was in trouble, if not for the death wish thing, then for something else. That for some reason, he'd popped up on the fixer network's radar as a criminal. He would've argued stridently against the accusation if that were the case. He really was a Boy Scout at heart.

Relieved, Nick said, "I have a few thoughts about finding Gray. But before I share those, what exactly are you planning to do to him when you discover what he's involved in?"

"If he's doing something criminal, which I have reason to believe is the case, given his paranoid behavior, I have the authority to decide whether what he's done warrants capture or if it warrants more extreme measures."

"So, you really do have the authority to kill anyone who you decide is in need of killing?" Nick blurted. "Isn't Gray a stupidly high-level asset for the US? I mean, surely you need someone's permission to take out someone like him."

"Nobody's above the law, Nick."

He rolled his eyes. "I know that. But…you can kill him if you want to?"

"I never want to kill anyone. But it is my job. If he's done something bad enough, yes, I'll put him down."

As if calling it "putting someone down" made it anything less than what it really was. Cold-blooded murder.

Not that he had any right to cast stones over eliminating people. It was part of his job, too. Except he killed enemy combatants. Not members of his own government and fellow countrymen.

"You are aware that Gray's team murdered three American marines on their way out of the compound where they stole the crate, aren't you?" Nick asked.

"I am."

"Not that I'm trying to tell you how to do your job, but isn't that…well…put-down worthy all by itself?"

"Indeed, it is," Alex answered soberly. "Which is why I'm delighted to hear that team—Gray's team—is off the street and in custody. But I have yet to determine if Gray ordered them to kill those marines. I won't sanction him over the deaths of those marines if he had nothing to do with the decision to take them out."

"Oh, he totally had something to do with the decision," Nick declared.

"How do you know that?" Alex asked quickly.

"I worked for the man for four years. We didn't sneeze without his permission. I'd lay odds he had his own surveillance drone hovering over that compound, and he was directing every bit of the operation to infiltrate the place, steal the crate and get out."

"But you don't know that for certain," Alex said gently. "Would you want me to kill you because someone had a strong gut feeling that you'd done something wrong? Or would you want me to do my due diligence and find actual proof of your wrongdoing before I put a bullet in your brain?"

Nick huffed. "I get your point. Your job is to be impartial and have proof before you act. But I'm still dead sure Gray told them to hijack the Hummer those marines were in by whatever means necessary. Including killing the marines inside it."

"Time will tell. And once I know for sure, only then will I take action."

"And in the meantime, Gray knows someone is following him. He will be insanely dangerous to tail from now on. He even left the tracker from the limo and that note to warn us off."

Alex retorted, "I'm not intimidated because one of his guys spotted a tracker planted in plain sight. Even a routine inspection of the vehicle by a total amateur would've gotten that tracker found."

Nick frowned and said urgently, "Listen to me, Alex. Gray isn't like anybody you've gone after before. There are dangerous people out there, and then there's Gray. He's in a whole other class of nasty."

"I'm not worried—"

Nick cut him off. "Then, you're a damned fool. You should be scared silly of going up against him. He has his own private army, for crying out loud. It may not be that big, but it's *all* men and women like me. Like *you*."

Alex studied him intently for a long time and finally said quietly, "Okay. I hear you, and I believe you. I'll take this guy and his people very seriously."

"You have to do more than that. You have to be careful like you've never been careful before. And you should probably get help. You said there are other fixers. This is the guy you should call in the *whole* cavalry for."

Alex opened his mouth to say something. Given the stubborn set of his jaw, Nick guessed he was about to declare that he didn't need that much help, and he cut off Alex again. "I know you're very, very good at your job. I don't doubt that for a second. In fact, I've heard about you before. You're a bit of a legend in the business."

Alex looked surprised and not superpleased.

Nick continued, "It's probably why you were assigned to deal with Gray in the first place. But please, for the love of God, don't take him on by yourself."

Alex was silent for a long time. Thoughtful. And then his gaze hardened. "Will you help me?"

"Me?" Nick exclaimed. "I'm not a fixer."

"But you know him better than anyone. You worked inside his organization. You know his habits, how he thinks, what he's likely to do in any given situation. Help me investigate him…and, if necessary, take him down."

Nick said grimly. "It'll be necessary to take him down. I feel it in my bones. He's done something very bad. His grand finale on the way out the door, as it were."

"So, you do think he's gone fully rogue?" Alex asked.

"I know it."

Chapter Eight

Alex wasn't sure if he fell for Nick while listening to the outrageous ideas Nick had for how to take over the Nakatomi Tower in *Die Hard*, or if it was when they laughed together at *Home Alone*. Or maybe it was when Nick's whole face softened as he talked about having a family of his own someday. But regardless, Alex had a problem.

He liked Nick. Really liked him.

Now he just had to pray Nick wasn't lying to him. He wanted to believe Nick was telling the truth and not still working for Gray. In fact, he was probably staking his own life on that being true. Nick was not wrong about Gray. The man was exceedingly dangerous. No way would Alex survive both Nick and Gray if they teamed up together to kill him.

Alex looked over at Nick. "Talk to me about how we reacquire Gray."

"The art gallery. Gray was definitely interested in the gold statue there. I think we should go back and stake the place out. See if we can find out why he's so interested in the statue and then wait for him to show up there to buy it. My impression was that the horse-and-rider piece is part of an auction at the gallery in a few days. At least, everything else on display was going up for sale. It makes sense the statue would be auctioned off, too."

"That's a good plan. Is your tuxedo clean enough to wear again after our scuffle, or do we need to get you a decent suit?" Alex asked.

"The tuxedo is destroyed. I ripped out a sleeve in that move to keep you from breaking my neck and killing me."

He couldn't help but smile a little at the memory of being pressed up against Nick's entire backside and having his arm around all that vital energy. "I wasn't planning to kill you, Nick. I just needed you to quit trying to kill me for long enough so I could talk with you."

"Hah! I wasn't trying to kill you, either!" Nick exclaimed. "If I'd been trying to kill you, you'd be dead now." He shot Alex an impudent grin, but there was a hint of seriousness in his dark eyes.

He answered with a hint of his own seriousness, "No, you'd be dead."

They exchanged frank stares, acknowledging their mutual lethality. Alex dipped his chin in a slight nod of respect.

Nick scowled but followed suit, nodding as well. But then he went and ruined it by muttering, "You didn't win. It was a stalemate."

As Alex smirked skeptically enough to visibly irritate him, Nick snapped, "I was not planning to enter high society when I came to New York. I'm equipped to hide in the underbelly of the city. Which means I didn't pack a spare tuxedo."

Personally, he rather liked Nick lounging around like he was right now in a T-shirt and jeans that were both just a smidge too tight on his muscular physique.

Realizing he was staring at said physique in fascination, he jerked his attention off Nick's bulging biceps and nodded briskly. "A new suit it is. I know just the place. Are you feeling up to a shopping trip?"

"Yeah, sure. I feel great after getting eight hours of solid sleep. Thanks for that, by the way."

The rough gratitude in Nick's voice sent a little shiver of delight down his spine. He shrugged and had to clear his throat before he choked out, "Gotta keep my assets sharp."

"Oh, I'm an asset now, am I?" Nick teased.

"You are if that means you understand I'm in charge of this operation."

A snort from Nick. "No way. I'll work *with* you, but I don't take orders from anyone."

Alex couldn't resist poking. "That sounded like a challenge, Mr. Kane. Do you want to place a small wager on who'll take orders from who when things heat up?"

Nick's gaze snapped sharply to his. He'd been talking about things heating up as in the heat of combat. Danger. Like a gunfight. But it was clear Nick thought he'd meant when things heated up in the bedroom.

He reluctantly met Nick's gaze and was startled to see the guy's dark eyes blazing with something that looked a whole lot like interest. Romantic interest... not gunfight interest.

Well, okay, then.

Nick unfolded his tall body off the couch and strolled toward where he leaned a hip against the kitchen counter. It was all Alex could do to hold his position and not flinch away—or fling himself at Nick—as the man sauntered toward him.

At the very last second before Nick would have run

right into him, he veered away and moved around Alex to head for the closet.

Alex let out a shockingly wobbly breath.

Jerk. Hot, *hot* jerk.

HE TOOK NICK to a menswear store that specialized in odd sizes off-the-rack. It was less of a big-and-tall-men's store and more of a bodybuilder's-physique or bulge-under-the-left-armpit kind of place.

The owner knew Alex and greeted him warmly when they came in. It was supper time, and the place was deserted, which suited Alex's purposes just fine.

"Hi, Tony. This is my colleague, Bob, and he needs a suit."

The tailor eyed Nick critically and then asked Nick, "Are you right-handed or left-handed?"

Nick frowned. "Right-handed. Why?"

"Then, you'll need the extra allowance for a holster under your left arm."

Nick glanced over at Alex, his eyebrows up around his hairline.

Alex said dryly, "I've done business here for a long time. Tony used to work for the Mafia but went straight some years back when I took down the family he was having to pay protection money to. One of my first jobs."

"Saved me a fortune, young Alex did," Tony said warmly. "I put both my kids through college on the money he saved me. I've got a nice retirement nest egg now, too. You're a good boy, Alex."

He smiled at the elderly man. "Any chance we could have something off-the-rack for my friend this evening? We're pressed for time and need to go someplace nice."

"No problem. I've got a charcoal gray suit that I

think will work well for him. The trousers will need hemming, but if you can wait fifteen minutes or so, I'll do that myself. These old hands still remember how to sew."

"That would be great."

"You'll be needing a dress shirt, too?" Tony asked,

"From the skin out, I'm afraid. Socks and shoes if you have them, as well."

"I'll keep my own shoes," Nick said quickly. "I like the custom soles."

Alex glanced down, startled. "Are those crepe? They look like leather."

"Yep. They're soft rubber, but the edges are finished to look like shoe leather."

"Nice. Where'd you get them? I could use a pair like that."

"I've got a guy in Istanbul. Hand makes every pair of shoes he sells. Doesn't take many new clients, but he'll make an exception for me because I always bring him good tobacco. I'll hook you up next time you're in Turkey."

Alex nodded his thanks to Nick. They made a weird pair of ducks, all right. He knew where to get suits cut for concealed weapons, and Nick knew where to get silent shoes for stalking targets.

Tony dressed Nick and marked the hemline of the pants, then shooed them out of the shop. He said he worked better without customers hovering over his shoulder, watching him sew.

As they sat in a coffee shop down the block, Nick commented, "Man, I'd love to see that guy's client list. Can you imagine the people he's dressed?"

Alex smiled. "Tony is the soul of discretion. Never names names. It's how he stays in business and alive."

He noted that they both watched everyone who walked past the coffee shop, assessing body language, looking at how people's gazes moved around, how they held themselves. He spotted a few people who looked like martial artists, but nobody that made alarm bells go off in his head.

Still, he did the courtesy of asking Nick, "See anyone of interest out there?"

"Nope. Coast is clear."

They headed back to the clothing store, and Nick dressed in the suit. Tony said he would have a second suit ready for Nick tomorrow by noon and promised to hang on to Nick's other clothes until they could come back to pick them up.

As they stepped out onto the street, Nick—looking darned sharp—said briskly, "To the gallery?"

"Let's do it."

WHEN THEY ARRIVED at the warehouse turned art gallery, it was lit up and crowded with customers. Apparently, the upcoming auction was a big one, and the establishment was stuffed with potential bidders interested in previewing the items that would be coming up for sale.

Alex murmured as they stepped inside, "Do you know anyone we can talk to about the statue?"

"I met one of the owners the other day. Nice guy. Flag-carrying Rainbow Mafia member. So, lean into being gay when we talk to him and be your most charming self."

"You think I'm charming? Aww."

Nick rolled his eyes. "By charming, I mean that you lie better than me."

"Now who's lying? You *do* think I'm charming. You have a crush on me, don't you?"

Nick's scowl was entirely too ferocious for the topic under discussion. Yep. The guy had a crush on him. But Alex also knew the harder he pushed Nick to admit it, the more stubborn Nick would become about not admitting it.

Still scowling, Nick reached out to straighten Alex's tie. It was a small, intimate gesture, the kind of thing one lover might do for another. Alex's heart pitter-pattered frantically under Nick's knuckles.

"There. Perfect," Nick murmured.

Alex got the impression Nick wasn't talking about the tie, but rather about the man wearing it. *Aww.* And there went his heart again.

Alex mumbled, "Um, okay. Are we on a date, then?"

"Sure." Nick grinned at him. "Just don't call me sweetheart."

Alex rolled his eyes. "There's nothing sweet about you, Mr. Grinch."

"There he is," Nick murmured. "C'mon. Oh, and he thinks my name is Stephan Clark. New Yorker. Real estate guy."

Alex always had an emergency legend metaphorically and literally in his hip pocket, and he employed it, now. "Call me Luca. Luca Serrano. Born in Spain, raised in New Jersey. Banker."

"Got it."

The beauty of working with a man of Nick's skill was that Nick really did get it. Both of them were completely adept at assuming cover stories on short notice and rolling with them smoothly. Not many people could do what they were both doing right now, and even fewer people could flow into a new identity quickly and seamlessly with another person.

Alex took his lead from Nick, who made no effort to

hurry toward the gallery co-owner. He took the flute of champagne that Nick handed to him, and they clinked glasses, smiling intimately at each other over the crystal rims before sipping the bubbly. *Hubba hubba.* If Nick kept looking at him like that, this was going to turn into a real date, job to do or not.

He and Nick must have both calculated the path of the gallery owner identically, for they moved as one into the way of the man. It took a couple of minutes, as other patrons stopped their target to chat with him and the man said hello to various guests. But eventually, the middle-aged proprietor walked up to them and said pleasantly, "It's Stephan, right? Stephan Clark?"

Nick said warmly, "That's correct. I'm flattered that you remember me. Otto Katzinger, this is my good friend, Luca. Luca, Otto."

Alex's gut tightened a little at the possessive way Nick leaned into saying the word *friend*. He smiled at Otto, turning on the charm Nick had requested. "Stephan tells me you own this place. I'm so impressed."

Otto waved a heavily ring-clad hand. "Oh, I only own half of it. My husband, Yuri, owns the other half. We decided to go in on it together so we can never divorce each other. No matter how much we drive each other crazy, neither one of us could bear to part with this place."

Alex laughed. "An interesting technique for ensuring longevity in a marriage. And clearly successful." He looked over at Nick. "How do you feel about going halfsies on an art gallery with me?"

Nick grinned. "Maybe halfsies on a martial arts studio or firing range would be more my style, but sure."

"Oooh, dangerous," Otto purred, stroking Nick's bulging biceps through the fine wool of his new suit.

Alex was shocked when an urge to swat away Otto's hand passed through him. Since when was he possessive of anyone, let alone Nick? In the spirit of their cover story of dating, he let a hint of his actual jealousy show on his face. Nick must've caught it, for he grinned widely behind Otto's back. Alex rolled his eyes at Nick, and the infuriating man's smile only widened. If only those dimples of Nick's weren't so killer cute.

"By the way, Otto," Alex said lightly. "Nick was telling me that the last time he was here, he saw a fantastic statue. A man on a horse, done in gold. Can you tell me a little more about it?"

Otto's eyes lit with unholy avarice. "Ah, the crown jewel of our collection. It's going to take the art world by storm when they find out what Yuri and I have got our hot little hands on."

Alex said with real interest, "What's so special about it? Can I see it? Steph said it was stunningly beautiful."

"He doesn't know the half of it. Shall we wait for the elevator, or are you magnificently brawny beasts up for taking the stairs? It's on the third floor."

Alex gestured at Nick and Otto to go first up the hypermodern steel staircase. While Otto continued to pet Nick's arm all the way to the third floor, Alex consoled himself with an outstanding view of Nick's muscular rear end flexing in front of him as Nick climbed each step. Tony really did know how to fit a suit to a man's body. The gray wool clung to Nick's rear end to perfection—tight enough to catch every flex of powerful glut muscles but loose enough to leave just enough to the imagination.

Hubba hubba, indeed.

They reached the third floor, and Alex looked around casually, taking note of the intense security. Not only were armed guards stationed every fifty feet or so around the perimeter, but he spotted pressure plates in the floor, a steel drop-down portcullis overhead that would block off the stairs, motion detectors, cameras and what looked like some sort of infrared-beam system.

Otto led them forward to a white columnar display stand. The gold statue Nick had described stood upon the waist-high column, and the whole thing was covered by a glass tube that extended from the floor to the ceiling. Undoubtedly, that tube and the display stand itself had pressure and motion sensors built into it. If he were in charge of security around here, he might even fill the tube with some sort of knock-out gas. Break the glass and get a lungful of it.

Alex finally took a good look at the statue itself. Nick wasn't kidding. It *was* stunningly beautiful. If he didn't know better, he would say it was a real horse, miniaturized and dipped in gold, so perfectly was it rendered.

"Whoa," he breathed.

Otto said proudly, "Remarkable, no?"

"Yes," Alex said reverently. "It's incredible."

Nick, however, was more prosaic and asked, "Why the steep price tag? I get that the value of the gold alone is in the neighborhood of four million, but ten million? What gives, Otto?"

Otto leaned in close and said under his breath, "We've already got interested parties hinting they'll bid as high as fifty million for it."

Alex's jaw dropped. "Fifty? Million?" He turned to stare at the gallery owner.

"What the hell?" Nick muttered. "Why? What's so special about it?"

Otto said conspiratorially, "You didn't hear this

from me. But we believe it to be a piece from the Magi Crèche. We've sent inquiries out to the right people, and we're hoping to confirm that any minute. If we do get confirmation, the price will rise into the stratosphere. Astronomical."

Alex frowned and said politely, "Forgive me for my ignorance, but what's the significance of this Magi Crèche?"

"My dear boy," Otto said, assuming a lecturer's tone, "the Magi Crèche is legendary. Historians say that the Three Wise Men—the Magi—who visited Jesus in the manger were Persian mystics. Astrologers and sooth-sayers, if you will."

Nick interrupted, "Are you talking about the frank-incense, myrrh and gold guys?"

Otto pursed his lips disapprovingly. "Yes. The frank-incense, myrrh and gold guys."

Alex jumped in to soothe Otto's ruffled feathers. "Please forgive him. He's so pretty to look at and so… athletic in certain departments…that he must be for-given for his blunt way of speaking. Am I right?"

"Indeed," Otto murmured, ogling Nick apprecia-tively. Alex joined him in ogling Nick, who squirmed a little under their scrutiny. If Alex wasn't mistaken, Nick's cheeks were turning a little ruddy, in fact. He wore the color well.

Otto resumed his narrative. "Anyway, legend has it that when the magi returned to Persia, one of them carved a set of statues that depicted the birth scene of Christ."

Alex immediately grasped the significance of that and gasped.

Nick glanced over at him questioningly, and Alex ex-plained, "A nativity scene created by someone who was really there would likely be the closest to an accurate depiction of what the actual stable, the actual manger— heck, even the Baby Jesus and Mother Mary—looked like. It would be the only existing firsthand representation of the nativity anywhere."

Comprehension lit Nick's gaze. "Something like that would be *priceless.*"

Alex nodded. "Every major religious group would want to have it for their own, not to mention wealthy art collectors and museums the world over would lust after it."

"Exactly," Otto piped up. "We've already got interest from the Vatican, from a coalition of Jewish bidders, from various major Protestant churches—even the Louvre is setting up a bidding line with us. If the provenance comes through, most of the wealthiest art collectors in the world are expected to bid on this piece, as well."

"When does it go on sale?" Alex asked.

"We're planning to offer it tomorrow evening, but we'll delay the sale if we don't have the provenance on it by then."

"Where do you get provenance papers on a thing like that?" Alex asked.

Otto shrugged. "It's difficult, of course. Legend has it the Magi Crèche stayed in the possession of an order of Persian mystics for centuries. It's said that sometime around the end of the Seljuk Dynasty of Persia—that would have been in the 1190s—the ruling family took it for themselves. The various rulers of Persia passed it down from generation to generation, from dynasty to dynasty, all the way to the Pahlavi Dynasty that fell in 1979. They kept it a closely guarded secret in their personal collections."

"Fascinating," Alex murmured. "They must have known how great a prize it would have been to Christians the world over."

Otto smiled mischievously. "They were very naughty to keep it for themselves, no? It is said that various sultans and emirs added pieces to the original nativity scene. We believe this is one of those pieces. Supposedly, the pieces got more elaborate and exquisite as the centuries passed, each dynasty adding ever more spectacular pieces to the crèche. Rumor has it the entire crèche consists of fifty or sixty pieces, by now."

When Otto fell silent, Alex prodded gently, "What happened to it after the fall of the last shah of Iran?"

"When Mohammed Reza Pahlavi was deposed, nobody knows what happened to it. There was chaos in Iran and the Revolutionary Guard was allowed to loot national treasures at will. Many of those treasures have turned up on the black market. But this is the first sign of the Magi Crèche having found its way out of Persia at last."

Nick asked, "Where did this piece come from? Who's selling it?"

"Ahh, ahh, ahh," Otto said reprovingly, wagging a finger at Nick. "Our consignors are guaranteed anonymity, if they so choose."

Nick shrugged. "I'm sorry, Otto. I must confess, that was a test. I thought you knew Luca and I work for Harlan Gray. I was part of the team that brought the whole crèche out of Zagastan last spring. Heavy sucker. Big crate. We kept everything wrapped up for safety, of course. I never got to look at it. I'm delighted to get to see at least one of the pieces we rescued. Luca handled details at this end, arranging for us to transport the whole thing in the United States."

Alex was startled that Nick had chosen to play such a dangerous gambit. If he was wrong, and Gray hadn't consigned the statue, they would be thrown out of here on their ears and not allowed back inside. Not to mention, Otto would warn Gray that he and Nick were investigating him.

Hah. And Nick called him the better liar. Nick had just rattled off all that information with such casual ease that he almost believed the story—and he knew it to be false.

"I had no idea," Otto said in a tone of distinctly more respect. "Mr. Gray told me he would have his own security keeping an eye on the statue at all times, of course. But I didn't realize you were his men."

Nick smiled warmly at Otto. "No worries. You passed our little quiz with flying colors. And we're not nearly as…tense…as Mr. Gray can be." Alex smirked as Nick rolled his eyes for good measure. Otto visibly relaxed.

Alex said lightly, "Mr. Gray spoke initially of planning to liquidate the entire crèche in a single sale. Now that I've seen this piece, and assuming the others are as exquisite, I can see why he changed his mind and decided to offer them one at a time. Has he made any mention to you of being willing to sell the whole crèche off market if someone were to bid high enough?"

"I do not know. You would have to ask your employer that. I sincerely hope not, however. Yuri and I have our eyes on a charming little Greek island we plan to buy with our portion of the proceeds of fifty more pieces like this one. Can you even imagine what people will pay when the figures of the Christ Child and Virgin Mary come up for sale? What is the worth of knowing what they looked like? What they were wearing? If the baby really slept in a manger or if that's a myth?"

Alex just shook his head. The mind boggled at the idea of glimpsing a firsthand snapshot of the event. "If there's anything we can do to help you with obtaining the provenance papers, do let us know. Here's my card."

He pulled out his wallet and fished around through various fake IDs and matching business cards until he found the one with the name Luca Serrano on it. God bless the legend-building crew at the CIA for their thorough work.

"...historical source in Iran has been most helpful," Otto was saying. "Apparently, no photograph was ever allowed to be taken of the crèche. But there's an eighteenth century sketch of the piece, and various inventories of the Persian rulers that mention it. The only tricky bit is accounting for the crèche between when it left Iran and when it came into Mr. Gray's possession."

Nick rolled his eyes. "It's not as if my teammates and I can offer affidavits of where we got it. At least we got it out of the hands of warlords and back into the legitimate, elite art world."

"Why, thank you," Otto gushed. "We like to think of ourselves as one of the best houses in the business. Christie's and Sotheby's strut around selling fifty-million-dollar paintings, but we're going to put all the big galleries to shame when the identity of this little gem is revealed to the world."

Alex added warmly, "You and Yuri are going to be the most famous art dealers on the planet."

The man preened some more.

Nick said lightly, "I assume Mr. Gray is still planning to attend the auction in person? He mentioned wanting to be there for the big event."

"Most definitely. Of course we've got a discreet viewing area for consignors such as him who would like to attend the sale without being seen."

"Of course," Nick said quickly. "I believe Luca and I will be assigned to the security detail for this beauty, and other colleagues of ours will see to Mr. Gray."

"I'll look forward to seeing you then," Otto said.

"As will we."

"Mum's the word on what I told you. We wouldn't want rumors leaking out to the press, now, would we?"

Alex matched Nick's smile as he murmured to the art dealer, "We work for Harlan Gray. Discretion is our middle name."

Otto got called away by another guest to answer a question, and Alex looked over at Nick significantly. "Wanna scope out the private viewing area that Gray will be sequestered in the night of the auction?"

Nick nodded. "It's probably on the second floor. I'm told that's where auctions are held. I found a back staircase the last time I was here. I'll bet the private viewing room is near that."

Alex followed Nick downstairs and into the large, open second floor. As they strolled around the perimeter of the room, the hairs on the back of Alex's neck felt itchy. "Um, Nick?"

Nick glanced over at him, frowning.

"Do you feel it, too?"

"Yeah," Nick answered grimly. "We have company."

Alex muttered without moving his lips, "Gray's guys are here. And they've spotted us."

Chapter Nine

Nick sincerely didn't want to fight men he'd personally trained to be lethal hand-to-hand combatants. "Let's take this away from all these civilians, shall we?" he muttered to Alex.

"Agreed. Front door or back?"

"There's a big warehouse and a fenced security yard out back. We'd be trapped."

"Front it is," Alex said calmly.

As they moved swiftly through the crowd toward the exit, surreptitiously slipping in their earbuds, Nick talked low and fast. "They'll use team tactics. Don't underestimate their hand speed. They'll fight dirty. And they'll be carrying knives. If they plan to kill us, those will come out midfight after they've lured us into thinking we're just in a fistfight."

As they reached the front door, Alex turned briefly to face Nick. "Thanks for your concern, but I can handle myself. I beat you, didn't I?"

"It was a stalemate," Nick snapped in irritation.

"Better," Alex murmured as they crossed the street in front of the gallery. "I need you pissed off, not panicked over my safety."

"If they outnumber us, we'll need to fight back-to-back. Have you ever trained like that?"

"Yes, dear. I've trained like that. I've even fought like that for real. Quit being such a worrywart. And stop fussing over me. We've got this."

He rolled his eyes at Alex. Oddly enough, Alex was right. He wasn't worried for himself at all, but he was completely freaked out at the idea of Alex getting hurt or killed. What did it mean?

He didn't have time to contemplate the implications of it because Alex said low, "Should we split up? Rendezvous a few blocks from here?"

It was a good idea. Gray's team wouldn't expect it. They never, ever split the team. It was a fundamental protocol Gray insisted upon. "Let's meet at the spot where you attacked me."

Alex flashed him a quick, sexy grin. "I like the symbolism of it. See you there in five."

While Alex turned left, he turned right, walking as fast as his long legs would go without breaking into a run. The moment he turned the corner, though, he took off running.

No surprise, he heard footsteps slapping the pavement behind him. Sloppy. The guys should be wearing quieter shoes. It was not a mistake he would've let the team make if he were still part of it.

Alex spoke in his ear between deep breaths, "I've got two...on me. Don't worry... I'm faster."

He replied, grunting on exhales, "I've got...two on me...also. Don't know...if I'm faster."

"Be faster, Nick...can't lose you...need you."

And it didn't sound as if Alex was talking about needing him for the mission. Warmth that had nothing to do with the exertion of sprinting spread through Nick's body. He dodged left, down a side street, and stretched out into a maximum sprint, arms pumping, legs churning. He focused, the way he'd been trained, on relaxing his entire body and letting his legs, arms, and lungs do all the work.

He swerved right at the next corner and put on another burst of full-out speed. His plan was to circle wide of the rendezvous spot and come in from the other direction—also a tactic Gray's men might not expect. They tended to be direct when entering combat, choosing to rely on their superior strength and training, rather than tricky tactics. But, with Alex's neck on the line, Nick was prepared to pull out every trick in the book.

"I'm one block out," Alex huffed.

It was good to know he wasn't the only one out of breath. Nick replied, "I'm two blocks out. Coming from…the other direction."

Alex must've stopped abruptly, for Nick heard shoes skidding on concrete. Then a grunt as if someone had just slammed into Alex.

Nonononono…

Nick found another gear he didn't know he had. The one where a man he cared about was under attack alone and going to die if Nick didn't get there ASAP.

He spared just enough oxygen to gasp, "Coming in hot."

He rounded the corner and raced the final twenty yards or so to the fight in front of him. Thankfully, his eyes adjusted fast to darkness. He made out Alex's lean form twisting and spinning as he attempted to fight and dodge two men at the same time.

Nick barreled into the back of the attacker directly in front of him, the one who kept trying to get behind Alex, and he and his target hit the ground. Nick had the advantage of landing on top, which meant the other guy acted as a crash cushion for him. Also, he expected the fall and was able to roll and leap back to his feet in a single motion. The other guy lay flattened on the pavement, his breath knocked out of him by the impact with the sidewalk and a two-hundred-pound-plus man crushing him.

Nick spun to put his back to Alex, backing up until their rear ends touched as they crouched in fighting stances. The two men chasing him caught up, and suddenly, Nick was fighting two on one.

Arms bumped into his back. It felt as if Alex's second attacker had closed to grappling distance and had Alex wrapped in his arms. Nick started to turn, to reach for the attacker, but one of his assailants slid around to the side to help the guy on Alex while the other one threw a flurry of punches at Nick.

Nick warded off the flying fists and jumped to his right to block the other guy from grabbing Alex.

All four of Gray's men backed up momentarily to regroup. For the time being, they were all in front of Nick and Alex. Standing shoulder to shoulder for now, they braced for the rush of the four attackers.

Nick muttered, "The end guys will try to flank us. You hold your position and I'll spin to put my back against yours."

"Got it."

Here they came, prowling in slow and dangerous, like circling wolves.

"Knives," Alex muttered.

Nick hadn't seen any blades—Gray's men probably had them tucked against the sleeves of their coats, hiding them until the last possible second. Good thing Alex had spotted them. He dropped his own down into his right hand out of its wrist sheath, and reached down to his left ankle to pull out the field knife strapped there. With renewed caution, he waited for Gray's men to charge.

Sure enough, the two guys on the end did a wrap-around maneuver, both of them ending up in front of him. Holding his knives low, in front of his body, he waited for them to attack.

The fight was fast and vicious. If any single stab from any one knife plunged into someone, the odds were good the target would be seriously injured and definitely knocked out of the fight. Better to take a few slices across the forearms or face than let the enemy gut him. Hence, it became vital to parry incoming swings of the knives with his own blade or his arm, and to jump back from direct thrusts.

Nick was pushed to the limit of his speed and skill, keeping two flashing knives in sight and staying out of the way of them as Gray's men slashed and stabbed at him.

In a fight like this, Alex truly did have the advantage on everyone, given how unbelievably fast he was. Nick had great reflexes but nothing like Alex's.

Nick took a glancing cut to the jaw that hurt like hell and left him more distracted than he liked. He resorted to lashing out with a hard kick to the guy's belly, driving the heel of his shoe hard into the man's stomach. The attacker staggered back, gasping for air.

Nick wanted to pressed his advantage, to follow the guy as he fell back and deliver a debilitating stab of his own, but that would mean leaving Alex's flank unprotected. He held his ground and let the moment of advantage pass.

When Nick didn't follow him, the guy he'd kicked straightened suddenly, less injured than he'd been feigning. It had been a trick to try to draw Nick away from Alex.

Bastard.

Alex pivoted, putting them shoulder to shoulder again as the guy he was fighting slid around to stand next to the man directly in front of Nick. Alex lunged forward, and Nick went with him, protecting his flank, also concentrating on taking down the assailant in front of him as fast as possible. He lashed out with his foot and the guy's knife went sailing in a high arc, away into the darkness. It skittered metallically on the sidewalk.

Without warning, something clamped around his ankle and gave a hard yank.

Sonofabitch. The guy he'd knocked down initially was coming around and had grabbed his leg. Nick staggered, nearly going down before he caught himself. But, in that moment of unbalance, the guy in front of him punched hard, a big roundhouse blow. Nick ducked and the man's fist impacted just above Nick's ear.

He saw stars, and the world started to spin around him. Not good. If he went down, Alex was screwed.

With that thought foremost in his mind, he fought on grimly, swinging his knives wildly in arcs in front of his body and throwing a flurry of kicks to hold off his attacker until his head cleared.

The guy on the ground must've grabbed Alex's ankle, too, for without warning, Alex fell down, pitching forward. The attacker who'd faked being hurt immediately leaped forward to stab Alex, but apparently forgot Nick was still there or chose to ignore him. A mistake, that.

It exposed Nick to the unarmed attacker, but he turned and chopped down as hard as he could with the butt of his knife on the back of the neck of the guy who'd jumped Alex. That attacker went limp, and Nick half turned, throwing his forearm up at the last instant to prevent a similar blow from landing on his own neck.

Well and truly pissed off that these jerks had nearly taken down Alex, Nick surged upward, driving his head into the gut of the guy who'd just tried to karate chop him. He wrapped his arms around the dude and drove him backward.

He got lucky and stepped on the guy's foot, which caused the attacker to topple over backward. The two of them hit the ground, and the other man's head made a sickening, cracking sound as it hit the concrete sidewalk. He went limp beneath Nick.

No time to gloat. Nick shoved upright and turned in a crouch, all in one frantic movement. The lone remaining attacker was squaring off with Alex.

As Nick straightened and prepared to charge in like a bull to defend his man, Alex parried a slicing knife attack and stepped toward his attacker fast, punching him right on the bridge of the nose. As the attacker doubled over in pain, Alex drew his knee up fast and clocked the guy in the jaw. Hard.

Down he went.

Three of the four attackers were on the ground. Two were groaning in pain. The one who had hit his head was still, and a pool of black liquid was growing under his upper torso in the dark.

The fourth man, ankle grabber, had climbed to his feet, assessed his downed teammates, noted Nick brandishing his knives and advancing to stand beside Alex, and thought better of continuing the fight. He turned and ran.

"Chase him?" Alex panted.

"Nah," Nick panted back. "He's got too much of a

head start. Besides, Gray will be plenty pissed off that we whupped his guys. It might just bring him after us."

"Cool. So instead of chasing the killer, now he'll be chasing us," Alex said dryly.

"Something like that."

"Shall we disarm these yahoos?" Nick suggested.

"Grab their cell phones, too," Alex said as he punched the guy groaning at his feet in the temple. The man went still, and Alex commenced searching him.

Nick did the same to the other moving guy, knocking him unconscious, ideally for another minute or two, then reaching into the man's coat for his cell phone. Nick yanked the man's pistol out of its shoulder holster and picked up the knife lying on the ground beside him. The dude probably had at least one more blade, somewhere. Nick patted him down and found it in a sheath tucked inside the back of his pants' waistband.

Nick spotted something rectangular lying on the ground where the ankle grabber had originally gone down. "Oh, look. Runner guy dropped his phone." He bent down and scooped up the device, pocketing it with the other cell phone he'd retrieved.

"Sloppy of them to lose all their phones," Alex commented dryly as he moved over to the man lying motionless in a pool of blood. "This one's not breathing. Want to try resuscitating him?"

Nick sighed. "We're gonna get blood all over ourselves, but yeah. You do the chest compressions. I'll breathe into his mouth."

As he knelt down to administer CPR, Nick got his first good look at the man. "Hey! I trained this guy a while back! Name's Jed. He's not a bad guy. Decent knife fighter."

"But not as good as you," Alex commented.

"Nor you," he murmured back as he pinched Jed's nostrils shut and tilted his head back to begin breathing into his mouth.

It took them nearly two minutes, and administering CPR was more strenuous than it looked. But they got the guy breathing again. True to his forecast, though, both he and Alex got covered in Jed's blood.

"Shall we call an ambulance for him?" Alex asked as they stood up.

"The other two are coming around. They can take it from here."

Alex nodded. "Then, let's get the hell out of here before the runner arrives with reinforcements."

In the concentration of getting the fourth man breathing again, Nick had forgotten about the one who got away. "Yeah. Let's split."

"Do we need to police the area for fingerprints?" Alex asked doubtfully.

"With all the blood you and I went swimming in, there's no way we'd erase every print. We would need a power washer to spray down the whole vicinity. Besides, Gray's guys won't call the police. There would be too many questions about who they are."

Alex nodded and murmured, "Feel up to running? Your face is bleeding, and you took a couple of nasty hits there at the end."

"I was defending you, thank you very much," he snapped as he took off jogging down the street. He certainly didn't feel like doing any more full-out sprints, but he did set a steady, ground-eating pace away from the scene of the fight. His head throbbed, harbinger of a splitting headache to come. He supposed it was better than being dead.

Alex let him set the pace. They ran all the way to the

apartment building, keeping an eye out for any kind of pursuit. He hoped that the immediate need to get their fallen comrade to a hospital had distracted Gray's security team from pursuing them.

The elevator door opened, and they made their way quickly to the tiny apartment.

The door had barely closed behind them before Nick turned and grabbed Alex, wrapping his arms around him in a tight bear hug. "I don't ever want to be in a fight like that with you again," he muttered.

He was shocked to register that his knees felt weak, so profound was his relief at having made it back here in one piece with Alex. So much for his death wish, apparently. This was the first time in years that he was actually freaking out a little at the idea of himself or his teammate getting killed.

And there went his pulse, galloping off toward panic-land again.

It dawned on Nick that Alex was hugging him back fully as tightly.

"All I could think about was what would I do if something happened to you," Nick admitted raggedly.

"Funny. I was thinking the exact same thing. That, and planning how to kill each one of them slowly and painfully if they did anything bad to you."

Nick smiled a little over Alex's shoulder. He'd brought out the guy's protectively vicious streak, had he? That was so sweet. He felt a shudder pass through Alex. He knew the feeling. They might've won that fight, but things could always go wrong in a violent situation. A slip of the foot, a blink at just the wrong moment, a tiny distraction...and the outcome could've been very different. Nick's arms tightened even more around Alex.

"A little air here," Alex wheezed.

"Sorry." Nick turned him loose and stepped back, chagrined. So much for keeping a professional distance from his partner.

Alex looked a little annoyed with him, so Nick expanded upon his apology. "I shouldn't have up and grabbed you like that. Not with us having to work together and all—"

Alex reached up with those lightning-fast reflexes of his and pressed his hand against Nick's mouth, stopping any more words from coming out. "I was frustrated that you let me go, not that you hugged me in the first place."

Nick stared. In the darkness, Alex's eyes were black. But he could swear he saw a glow in them anyway.

"Oh." It was all Nick could think of to say as his mind went blank.

Alex stepped forward and planted his hand on the back of Nick's neck. As he tugged Nick forward, he muttered, "You're such a jerk."

As their faces drew together, he murmured back, "Yeah, but you like me anyway."

"Shut up." Those were the last words Alex breathed before their lips touched.

An urge to grab Alex and devour him alive nearly overcame Nick, but he held himself completely still and let Alex set the pace. He had no idea how much experience Alex had with love, and at a minimum, he gathered it had been a long time since Alex had let down his guard with anyone, let alone kissed someone.

Alex's mouth was warm and smooth against his, and surprisingly confident. But then, Alex was a direct man. He spoke the truth and apparently acted with truth, as well. He wanted to kiss Nick, so kiss him he did.

It was sexy as hell.

Nick kissed him back, enjoying the slide of their mouths, the way their breath mingled, the way Alex took his time. They traded several light kisses, adjusting angles of chin, tilts of the head and body posture until they fit together perfectly. Then Alex leaned in and really kissed him.

Hello, sailor. Nick was startled by the frank intensity in Alex's kiss. This was not a man who played games. There was no coy flirtation, no advance and retreat, no head games whatsoever. And he kind of lived for it. He slipped his fingers into the short, soft hair at the back of Alex's head and opened his mouth, deepening the kiss.

Alex met him halfway, and as their tongues swirled together in a sexy slide of hot, wet flesh, Nick groaned at the exact same moment Alex did.

Simultaneously startled, apparently, they both pulled back from the kiss at the same instant, their fast, shallow breaths panting in exact rhythm.

"Well, then," Alex said breathlessly, "I think we've established that both of us are alive and well after the fight."

More like alive and horny. Nick's body was reacting in all kinds of ways it shouldn't be. He tried to speak, but his throat was too tight for words, and he ended up making a pained sound as lust pounded relentlessly through his body.

Alex took another step back. Nick was relieved the man was no longer in range to grab and throw down to the floor, but it was also all he could do not to stalk after Alex and kiss his lights out again.

"Go take a shower," Alex said lightly. "You smell like blood. We can pick this up later, when we're both cleaned up and patched up."

"Uh, right," Nick mumbled, feeling about as smart

as a fencepost at the moment. Alex had wanted to kiss some more? Well, color him totally on board for that plan. But where had that kiss come from? Alex had given no hint, prior to grabbing him and laying a big wet one on him, that he was interested in jumping anyone's bones. So closed off that man was.

Usually, he was so much better at reading people—

"Go on." Alex waved him toward the bathroom. "You wash up first. And pass out all your clothes to me when you've stripped down."

"Why?" Nick asked.

"I'm going to scan them for tracking burrs."

"You think Gray's guys managed to plant one on me in the middle of a fight like that?" he blurted.

Alex shrugged. "I think we can't be too careful, given who we're up against."

"Sheesh. And I thought I was paranoid," he muttered under his breath.

"How do you think I stay alive, chasing the kind of people I do?" Alex bit out.

Nick threw up his hands. "I bow to your superior caution. I'll pass my clothes out when I'm naked. But first, are there any painkillers to be had around here?"

"Prescription or nonprescription?" Alex asked dryly, heading for the closet that Nick was beginning to think was magically stocked with everything the spy-on-the-go could need, and more.

"Nonprescription, for now," he answered.

Alex emerged a moment later, carrying four white tablets. "This should knock out what ails you. Or at least knock it back significantly."

"Bless you," Nick murmured, swallowing the pills dry.

Alex groused over his shoulder, from the kitchenette, "Hasn't anyone ever warned you that pills can get stuck in your throat if you take them dry like that?" He filled a glass of water and thrust it at Nick.

"Really? We're attacked by four commandos with knives and you don't bat an eyelash, but you're worried I'm going to choke on an aspirin and die?"

Alex scowled. "Drink the water."

"Fine." Nick tossed down the contents of the glass, amused at how Alex was fussing over him. He handed the glass back to Alex, saying, "I didn't peg you as the Nervous Nellie type."

"Me? Nervous?" Alex exclaimed. "I have nerves of frozen stainless steel."

Nick merely arched an eyebrow at him.

"I do!" Alex exclaimed.

Then, how did Alex explain his sudden and excessive worry about their safety? Bemused, Nick headed for the bathroom. He turned the hot water on full blast and stripped down to his skin. He wadded up his underwear and shirt, socks, shoes, tie, and the remnants of the ruined suit and cracked open the bathroom door. Alex's eyes went a smoky shade of blue green, and his gaze dipped downward as Nick leaned around the door frame, flashing a lot of brawny chest and a muscular, dark-haired leg.

The heat in Alex's gaze scorched him, and Nick jerked back, startled. He closed the door, breathing hard. He was just winded from all the exertion before. Yeah. That was it. He was out of air from running all the way back here.

Except he'd fully caught his breath in the elevator. Nope, this puffing like a broken-down racehorse was all about that smoking-hot look Alex had thrown him. And that kiss. Good grief, that kiss. He couldn't wait to do that again. And to take his sweet time about it next time—

Whoa, whoa, whoa. What was happening here? He was a bundle of…*emotions*. He wasn't an emotional guy. And he certainly didn't come off dangerous missions all rattled and discombobulated like this.

Except Alex could have died.

And that scared the hell out of him. Now what was he supposed to do about that?

Kiss him again, apparently.

Parts of his body that he really wished would behave themselves suddenly were totally ignoring him and developing a mind of their own.

Just as suddenly, he was thinking about taking a cold shower instead of a hot one to ease his body's aches.

Well, hell.

Chapter Ten

Alex looked up as Nick emerged from the bathroom with a towel slung low around his hips. It took him a moment to realize he was staring, literally transfixed, at all those acres of muscle. He cleared his throat as he dragged his gaze away. "Uh…nice tan lines," he managed to mumble. Which was to say, *no* tan lines.

"My clothes have any trackers?" Nick asked rather more gruffly than usual.

"Nope. Clean. I'll just, um, jump in the shower, too. I've checked my clothes already, and they're clean. Well, not clean. I mean, they're ruined from that guy's blood. But there aren't any tracking devices on them," he babbled.

Cripes. He never babbled. But Nick's chest was so… bulgy…and in need of crawling all over…and…

"You okay, there, Al?" Nick murmured, smirking faintly.

Do not jump on your partner. Do not yank off that towel. Do not even think about touching Nick. No way could you stop once you started with him—

Alex gave his head a hard shake and stood up. He'd stripped to his underwear to check his clothes for trackers and to get out of the blood-soaked garments. All he wore now were stretchy, athletic trunks that extended several inches down his thighs. They did little to hide the interested bulge in his crotch that was rapidly growing in response to Nick's décolletage.

Vividly aware of Nick checking him out—checking *all* of him out—and of the revealing nature of what little clothing he wore, Alex strode across the tiny living space fast and all but dove into the bathroom. He closed the door quickly and leaned against it, breathing hard.

Work. This was work. Yes, Nick was too sexy for anyone's own good. Hard-to-look-away-from sexy. Hard-to-keep-his-hands-off sexy, apparently.

What the heck had he been thinking to kiss Nick like that? Nick had let him go from that hug. Had stepped back. And then he had to go and grab the guy and try to give him a tonsillectomy with his tongue.

But, it had felt right. They…fit.

And it felt so very, very good to touch another human being intimately. To have another human being touch him back. He'd had no idea how much he was missing and craving human contact until he kissed Nick.

But what to do about that, now? He couldn't un-know how much he wanted to kiss Nick again and have Nick kiss him back. He wanted to crawl into bed and just cuddle with the man for about a week.

Okay, he wanted to do more than just cuddle.

But they didn't have a week to disengage from hunting Gray. For that matter, Gray might very well be hunting them now. And that changed everything. Their lives were on the line. And both of them needed to be as sharp and alert as they were both capable of being. There was no telling when or how Gray's men might come after them.

With a sigh, he turned on the water and stepped into the shower.

As the hot spray pounded his muscles into delicious mush, he thought about their embrace again. It had felt so good to have Nick's arms wrapped around him, as if he wanted to use his entire body to shield Alex and keep him safe forever. He felt the exact same way. If he were to be in another fight and able to choose only one man to have at his back, it would be Nick.

Out of the corner of his eye, he'd seen the moment in the fight when Nick's assailant had tried to fake an injury to get Nick to move away from Alex's flank. And Nick hadn't gone. They guy had given Nick a wide-open shot at him, and Nick hadn't taken it. Instead, he'd chosen to ignore the chance to win against his opponent and protected Alex.

It gave him warm fuzzies all over again, just thinking about it. Nick was an aggressive fighter, offense-minded all the way. It had to have killed him not to jump on the opening the other guy had given him. But Alex's safety had been more important to Nick than every instinct in his body to attack.

An urge to barge right back out into the living room and kiss Nick—and more—nearly overcame him. But, he couldn't go there with Nick. Not yet. Not until Harlan Gray was caught and this mission was over. They had to be safe before they could explore whatever was happening between them. It was the right decision, even if it was the incredibly hard and grumpy-making decision.

But *day-umm*, that man could kiss.

Soon. They would take down Gray, and then he would lay that kiss on Nick. And more. Much, much more.

He scrubbed himself from head to toe with soap and a loofah. When he was covered in suds, he stepped under the hot spray, rinsing off the dried blood and watching it swirl down the drain in a wash of rusty brown. He noticed a faint swirl of bright red in the water running past his feet. He must have a cut somewhere that was still bleeding. No surprise. Nicks and cuts were inevitable in knife fights.

Thank goodness Nick had been there beside him. He hadn't had to worry at all about protecting his back in the fight, which was the only reason he'd successfully been able to hold off two attackers in front of him at once.

As the hot water pounded his muscles into relaxation, fatigue set in, making his body feel heavy and lethargic. That fight had demanded every bit of his skill and speed. But no way had he been willing to lose and put Nick in even more danger than he was already in. Funny how having Nick there to fight for had sharpened his focus and intensified his will to win.

Reluctantly, he turned off the water and climbed out of the shower. As he'd expected, various aches and pains made themselves known quickly as his body cooled down to room temperature. He contemplated pulling on his underwear again, but then he got a better idea.

Why not wrap a towel around his hips and torture Nick the same way the guy had tortured him by strolling out of the bathroom more naked than not?

Smirking, he tucked the end of the terry cloth in securely and opened the bathroom door.

Sure enough, Nick looked up as he emerged from the steamy bathroom and did a hard double take.

His skin burning from the blistering heat of Nick's stare taking in every inch of his exposed skin, Alex sauntered over to the closet and went inside to rummage around. The shelves were stocked with a small selection of men's and women's clothing, and he grabbed a pair of dark slacks and a dark mock turtleneck. His courage failing him, he dressed in the cramped confines of the closet.

When he stepped out, Nick said lightly, "Planning on breaking and entering later, are you?"

Alex glanced down at his black-on-black ensemble. "They were clean and my size. There's stuff in the closet that will fit you if you want to put on more than that towel."

Nick shrugged and made no move to stand up.

Alex frowned. It wasn't as if he could ask Nick to go get dressed. Then the guy would know how wildly distracting he found Nick's bare chest and muscular arms. And those powerful calves and deeply cut thighs—he wanted to crawl all over them, to feel them pressed against his body, to feel the weight of the man pressing down upon him, into him, around him—

Work, dammit.

Except telling himself that didn't curb the creeping sense of longing overtaking his gut. When would he have worked enough? Sacrificed enough for his country? When would there be more than his job in his life? A partner? Heck, he would settle for just a temporary man. Especially a man very much like this one.

He sighed and said, "I grabbed the first-aid kit while I was in the closet. You've got a cut on your chin, and I have at least one somewhere that was bleeding in the shower. I'll patch you up if you'll patch me up."

That did induce Nick to stand up. The towel slipped perilously low, and only a last-minute grab by Nick's fist stopped it from falling off completely. Too bad. His curiosity to see what the towel was hiding was almost more than he could stand.

For lack of anything else to do to cover his reaction

to seeing Nick more naked than not, Alex made a production of unpacking medical supplies from the tightly packed first-aid kit.

Carefully, he laid them in a neat row in the order he was likely to use them. Gauze swabs, alcohol, antibiotic cream, medical tape and butterfly bandages. Most knife wounds required more than a simple bandage. They needed something to hold them closed for a day or two until the edges of the wound started to knit together. Of course, puncture wounds were a different story. They required deep cleaning, draining and potentially being held open to heal from the inside out—

"I don't think some little scratch on my jaw requires all of this fussing," Nick said from directly behind him. Alex jumped, startled. He didn't begrudge the man his silence. After all, it kept Nick safe. But it did freak him out a little to get snuck up on like that.

He looked over his shoulder. "Fine. I won't clean it. But when it gets infected and you have to go to a hospital to reopen it, clean it, stitch it closed and get a nasty scar, I get to say I told you so."

"It's not that bad," Nick protested, fingering the three-inch-long line of red just under his chin, following the curvature of his jawbone.

"Can you even see it?" Alex demanded.

"Well, no."

"Look at your fingers."

Nick looked down, and fresh blood stained his fingertips. "I just got out of the shower. Of course it's bleeding. I knocked the scab off of it."

"I took a shower, dried off and got dressed between you getting out of the shower and now. It should've quit bleeding in that time," Alex pointed out. He picked up the bottle of alcohol and a gauze swab, waiting patiently for Nick to get his head out of his ass.

It took a minute, but finally, Nick shrugged. "Fine. Take a look at it and tell me what you see."

Alex pulled out a chair and Nick sat, leaning his head back to rest on the high back of the chair, exposing his chin. Alex stepped close and leaned down to take a look at the slice along his jawline. Nick smelled clean, like shampoo, and it was the sexiest thing he'd ever sniffed. Up close like this, Nick's eyelashes were long and dark resting against his cheeks.

With his hair wet and slicked back from his face, Alex was struck again by just how good-looking a man Nick was.

"Have you always hidden your face the way you do now?" Alex asked before he could bite back the words.

Nick's eyes opened and they stared at each other from a range of about twelve inches. Nick's eyes were a dark, rich brown, but from this close, Alex spied hints of cinnamon and gold in the depths of Nick's irises. He should've known the man's eyes wouldn't be any simpler than the rest of him.

"I may hide my face, but you hide your entire identity," Nick retorted.

"I beg your pardon?"

"You're so locked down—emotionally, psychologically, physically—that you don't let even the slightest hint of who you really are leak out."

Alex frowned. "I'm not locked down."

"Dude. You could hardly walk across this room in your underwear in front of me. I thought you were going to faint before you made it to the bathroom."

Alex felt the heat of a flush rise to his face. What could he say in response to Nick's accusation? The man was not wrong. "A little modesty does not constitute being emotionally locked down."

Nick just stared up at him steadily.

"Fine. I'm locked down. My job demands it of me."

"Agreed," Nick said evenly. "But what about when you're off duty? When do you let down? Relax?"

"When I go home to see my family."

"The family you don't trust and don't approve of? Do you actually relax when you're around them? But even if I'm wrong about that, when was the last time you did go home and take a break?" Nick asked quietly.

"Two…no, three…years ago."

"I rest my case."

Alex sighed. "Look. I'm not accustomed to having a partner when I'm working. I'm sorry if I'm not being sociable enough for you."

"It's not about me needing you to be sociable. It's about you letting go of the reins a little."

"What reins?" he blurted.

"I'm talking about all that control you exert over every aspect of your life. You've got to loosen up from time to time. Before you, I don't know, explode."

"I wouldn't explode. If anything, I would implode."

"Same diff. You'd end up wrecking yourself. If you don't learn to chill out a little more, you'll be broken-into-little-pieces Alex."

Was Nick right? Was he wired too tightly for his own good? Or was Nick not wired tight enough to be a fixer like him? Frustrated, Alex ripped open another paper package holding a sterile gauze pad.

Nick sucked in a sharp breath and flinched as the alcohol on Alex's pad hit the open wound.

"Seriously?" Alex murmured. "You get sliced by a knife in the first place and don't say a thing about it, then you come all the way back here and take a shower without even realizing you're cut open, and now you get all wimpy about a little alcohol in the wound?"

"I was distracted before. In the heat of the fight, I surely wasn't going to register it. And then, on the way back here, I was too worried about you to let the pain in."

"Aww," Alex murmured before he could bite off the sound.

Nick scowled up at him. "Now that my adrenaline has come back down to normal, of course I'm going to notice. We'll see how painful you think it is when I slap rubbing alcohol on your cuts."

"I make no claims of being a superhero about pain," Alex retorted, getting out a fresh gauze pad to replace the bloody one and then continuing to clean off Nick's jaw and neck.

As he leaned in close, all but sitting in Nick's lap, Nick put his hands on his waist. Maybe the intent was to steady him, maybe the intent was to rattle him. Either way, it worked.

He cleared his throat. "That's a nice little gash, you've got there. Hasn't anyone ever told you it's not a good idea to use your face to block sharp blades?"

"I got that memo, thanks," Nick retorted. "How does it look?"

"It's not quite deep enough for stitches. But that's only assuming you don't go running around getting into more knife fights in the next few days."

"I can't promise that won't happen," Nick responded.

Alex leaned in even closer to examine the angry line of red flesh. "Hence, I'm going to close your wound and hold it shut with a few butterflies after I put this antibiotic goop on it to keep it from getting infected."

He spread a thin layer of the gel on the wound, then carefully cut thin strips of surgical tape, pulling the wound closed and securing it with a half dozen tiny lines of white tape across the wound.

"How does it look now?" Nick asked as Alex stepped back to examine his work.

"The dressing makes you look like quite the pirate. But you'll live."

Nick rolled his eyes and stood up. "Your turn. Let's find out where you're bleeding from."

Alex stood still in front of Nick, startled to feel butterflies flitting around in his stomach. Surely, they had more to do with someone, anyone, staring intently at him than with how warmly Nick was looking at him.

Yeah, that was it. He just didn't like people in general to notice him. It had nothing to do with how Nick put a finger under his chin to lift his face slightly. Nick was only an inch or two taller, but significantly bulkier, and a thrill passed through Alex's still fluttering flock of stomach butterflies. He stared at Nick's intent features as the man leaned left and right, examining his face, neck and shoulders.

"The cut must be somewhere you can't see it," Nick murmured. "Behind an arm, or the middle of your back."

"I don't feel anything," Alex replied, frowning.

"Adrenaline. I've seen guys get shot and not know it. They can go an hour or more in the heat of combat without ever realizing they're bleeding from a giant hole."

Alex had seen the same thing a time or two, but he elected not to share that with Nick. The guy would no doubt point out that he should know better than to believe only his body's pain was an indicator of overall health and well-being.

"Your black clothes aren't showing me any bloodstains. Sorry, but you're going to have to strip down again."

Alex blinked up at him, startled for a moment. Right. Get naked in front of his hot partner. Okay, then. He could do this. He reached for the back neck of his shirt and pulled it over his head. As his face popped free, he thought he caught a glimpse of Nick ogling his torso hungrily. But then Nick's eyes went shuttered, their expression closed.

Feeling a little like a stripper, and kind of loving it more than he cared to admit, he unbuttoned his pants, pulled down the zipper, and pushed the black denim down his hips. He bent over to push the trousers down his legs, and when he straightened, he again caught a glimpse of raging interest in Nick's heavy-lidded gaze.

Must. Not. Pant.

But it was a struggle to keep his breathing light and even to pretend a calm he entirely didn't feel.

He chickened out at stripping off his cotton-spandex undershorts. Besides, they were white, and if he was bleeding beneath them, Nick would be able to see a red line of blood.

He'd never been a huge exhibitionist, but he also hadn't been bothered getting naked in front of his colleagues over the years. Of course, he'd been careful to make sure none of them knew he was gay. He didn't want his coworkers worrying about him eyeing them in *that* way nor did he want them eyeing him weirdly, either. But that particular cat was already out of the bag with Nick.

He'd been right for all those years not to let on about his orientation. This was awkward as hell.

Of course, it wouldn't be awkward at all if he weren't so freaking attracted to Nick.

But that cat, too, had long ago departed the bag for parts unknown.

Unsure of what to do with his hands, he let them hang loosely at his sides. He supposed that was better than grabbing Nick by the back of the neck and dragging him in for another hot wet kiss. Right?

As inappropriate thoughts roared through his brain, one after another, he managed to stand perfectly still. Which, frankly, was a minor miracle. Please God, let his trunks be tight enough to contain the growing arousal he felt starting to build in his crotch.

Nick walked around him slowly, checking for wounds. His belly tightened and got wildly jumpy as Nick moved out of sight behind him. Awareness rolled through him that a lethal predator was right there, right behind him, close enough for him to feel the heat of Nick's breath on the nape of his neck. A shiver chattered down his spine.

Nick knelt down, no doubt checking his legs, but the intimacy of it was almost too much to bear as Nick's warm breath drifted across his skin.

"Well, you've got several cuts that could be the bleeder," Nick announced. "There's this one on the back of your thigh—"

Alex about leaped out of his skin as a single warm, firm finger pressed against his right leg just where it turned into the first swell of his rear end.

"You've got another slice, long and thin, running across the middle of your back. Looks as if some-one nicked you as you were turning during the fight. Blade got dragged across your skin. And then, as I suspected, there's a third cut up here, where your arm and back meet."

Another finger touched him lightly, just below his left armpit. He did jump that time. Not only did Nick startle him but he was ticklish, and that finger had come a bit too close to his ribs for comfort.

"Hand me a swab and the alcohol, will you?" Nick murmured.

Alex reached forward to the table for the supplies Nick needed. He was shocked to notice that his hands were trembling ever so slightly.

This was necessary wound care. Not two minutes ago, he'd harassed Nick about the stupidity of not cleaning and covering knife wounds. Metal blades could be dirty things that harbored all kinds of bacteria and dirt.

Nick's hands were gentle and efficient as he cleaned the wounds. When Nick ran a piece of breathable tape from his left shoulder all the way to his waist on his right side in a descending spiral, Alex was shocked. When Nick said the cut was long, he'd had no idea the thing ran all the way across his back. He was lucky he'd had on a lined suit coat, shirt and undershirt to take the brunt of the blade.

Alex said wryly, "Next time I have Tony make me a suit, I think I'll go ahead and take him up on his offer to put a Kevlar layer in between the lining and the outer shell."

"He can do that?" Nick exclaimed.

"Takes him a few days, but yes. He can put full body armor inside a suit coat if you want it."

"Wow. He really is a full-service tailor, isn't he?"

Alex shrugged. "In a town like this, plenty of people have dangerous enemies. Now that Tony has your measurements, you can call him anytime and ask for a suit, and he'll make it and ship it to you."

"Of course he will," Nick muttered, shaking his head. "I think I've got you all patched up, my friend. You're good to fight another day."

Alex was too tense to sit still, so he packed up the first-aid supplies and burned the gauze pads in a bowl before rinsing the ashes down the sink.

Nick commented as the last of the ashes swirled away into the New York sewer system, "You take opsec to a whole new level."

Alex shrugged. "Operational security is a life-and-death matter to guys like me."

"You say that as if it isn't to someone like me."

Alex turned to face him. "Gray relies too heavily on the intimidation factor his bodyguards provide. That, and his high mobility. They've both become weaknesses for him."

"Weaknesses you think we can exploit?" Nick asked, sounding alert.

"Indeed. He also is too quick to go on the offensive."

Nick perched on the edge of the sofa. "Meaning what?"

"Meaning he's too fast to send his guys after a perceived threat with orders to eliminate it. He would be better off moving away from threats and hiding, rather than confronting them so aggressively."

Nick nodded slowly. "Now that you mention it, he has become more inclined to go on the offensive recently."

"How recently?"

"Say, the past year."

Alex frowned. "What has changed in the past year that has made him switch up his long-established, cautious behavior patterns?"

Nick frowned and was silent, appearing to think. "He did say something a while back about being forced to retire. Do you know anything about that?"

It was Alex's turn to frown. "Most field operatives leave the business when they start to slow down. They have a close call with someone younger, faster, smarter, more up on the newest technology. They realize they're getting old and getting left behind. That's when they leave. I assume he has amassed a rather nice retirement nest egg for himself?"

"Ten-million-dollar gold statue notwithstanding?" Nick asked dryly.

"Do you think the theft was his retirement plan?"

Nick nodded. "I do. Of course, I think he and my teammates stole the entire Magi Crèche, not just that one statue."

"Why do you think that?"

"Because to get my guys to steal something, to risk their lives and throw away their careers and reputations—not to mention murdering American marines in cold blood—Gray had to have offered them each a crap-ton of cash."

"No amount of money could make me kill an innocent person—soldier or otherwise," Alex replied fervently.

Nick nodded. "Same. Whatever Gray offered to pay his guys, it was enough to convince them to give up everything they believe in for the payout."

Alex winced. "So, whatever he stole had to be worth enough to fund not only his stylish retirement but the comfortable retirements of at least four of his bodyguards."

Nick nodded. "A crap-ton times five. That's a lot of money. If Otto's right about how much the statue and other pieces will fetch at auction, we're talking several hundred million dollars at a minimum. Maybe closer to a billion before it's all said and done."

No wonder senior government officials had sent him after Gray to investigate and possibly kill. Alex asked, "Didn't you say one of the four thieves died when you and that team of women operators ambushed them?"

"He did," Nick said heavily.

"So Gray is down to splitting the proceeds from selling the crèche with three other guys."

Nick shrugged. "You're assuming the other three will make it out of their—current incarceration—alive."

"You think he'd let his own guys die?" Alex blurted.

Nick stared at him a long time, the look in his eyes deeply troubled. At length, Nick answered heavily, "I think he would go one step further. I think he would kill his own guys if the payoff was high enough. Which it clearly is. At the end of the day, all that matters to Harlan Gray is Harlan Gray."

Alex stared back. "If you're right, then I'll have no choice. I'll have to put him down."

"And by putting him down, you mean you'll kill him?" Nick asked sharply.

"I do."

If the last pause had been long, this one was several times more drawn out. Then, slowly, painfully, Nick said, "I'll help you."

Chapter Eleven

Nick watched warily as Alex moved swiftly to the sofa and sat down beside him. Alex's body was visibly tense, and as he leaned in close to Nick and their knees brushed, Nick felt intensity vibrating through him.

"Are you absolutely sure you can kill your old boss?" Alex asked soberly. "Unlike Gray, loyalty means something to you. When the moment comes and you're looking at him through your gun sight, can you pull the trigger?"

Nick's emotions were turbulent as he considered the questions. It had been devastating to betray his teammates to the Medusas, who had only been planning to capture his brothers-in-arms. That was a far cry from planning to execute the man he'd worked for and been willing to die to protect.

Alex was speaking again. "…won't hold it against you if you can't do it, Nick. But I have to know now whether you can or can't kill him. My life is probably going to depend on you following through if you tell me that you can take the shot."

Nick nodded slowly, once. Twice. "You are correct. But here's the thing. It will take both of us working together to take down Gray. There's no telling which one of us will get the kill shot. But whichever one of us it is, neither of us dares hesitate to pull the trigger. With this man, we'll only get one try at him. After that, he'll kill us both and not think twice about it. To be blunt, you're going to need my help."

Alex laid a hand on Nick's forearm, which tensed beneath the light touch of Alex's palm. "No harm, no foul, Nick. If you don't want to be part of taking down Gray, I can do it alone."

He surged up off the couch, agitated. "No, you can't! That's what I keep trying to tell you! You still don't get how dangerous a man he is, do you?"

Alex gazed up at him steadily, waiting him out. Alex knew him too well. He sensed that Nick was spoiling for a fight and had no intention of giving one to him.

He shoved a hand through his damp hair. "Hell, Alex. *I'm* afraid of him. And you're a damned fool if you're not."

"Just because I'm afraid of someone, that doesn't mean I can't do my job and eliminate them."

He glared at Alex. "Maybe. But you and I both know that being scared of a target bloody well makes it harder to succeed in taking them out."

Alex shrugged. "I'll cross that bridge when I come to it."

"That's not how it works. You'd better get your head straight before you ever tangle directly with Harlan Gray or he'll use your mental weakness against you. He'll chew you up and spit you out."

"You think I'm not tough enough to do this job?" Alex challenged, rising to his feet and standing chest to chest with him.

Nick huffed. "That's not what I said."

"It's what you implied," Alex accused. "I took you in a fair fight, didn't I?"

"It was an *effing* stalemate," he ground out.

"Let's go again. Right now. I'll kick your ass again."

Exasperation exploded in Nick's gut. This wasn't about who was a better fighter. It was about Alex's mindset. If he didn't go into the fight with Gray utterly prepared for anything Harlan could throw at him, Alex would lose. And then he would die.

"Don't you get it?" he ground out. "You *have* to listen to me. You'll die if you don't!"

"I will not—"

Nick's exasperation overcame him, and in an excess of irritation at Alex and worry for him, he stepped forward fast, grabbed Alex by both shoulders and kissed him. Hard.

There was nothing soft or romantic about it. This was a kiss born of sheer frustration. Alex's mouth opened against his, whether in shock, delight or rage, Nick couldn't tell. Sensations slammed through him. The heat of Alex's lean, muscular torso against his. The resilient warmth of Alex's lips. The hunger vibrating through both of them as their lips and teeth and tongues clashed.

And then it hit him. He was *really kissing* Alex. And Alex was kissing him back. Neither one of them was holding back. At all.

And it was freaking wonderful.

Wonderful enough to give up everything and walk away from all of this. To run away with Alex and never look back. To find that quiet town and picket fence and settle down for good. Just the two of them. To start a family. A new life. A new love—

Nick stumbled backward, tearing his mouth away from Alex's and swiping the back of his hand across his mouth. Dammit, the swipe did nothing to erase the minty-toothpaste taste of the man. Nor did it eliminate the citrus and sandalwood smell of Alex's deodorant, or the clean, soapy scent of his skin.

Oh man. It didn't erase the feel of Alex's mouth against his, either. Not the warm, smooth texture of Alex's lips nor the heat of his surprised breath in Nick's mouth nor the way their mouths fit perfectly together, matched in hungry strength and in raging desire.

Nick swore under his breath, long and violently. Then he said raggedly, "I'm sorry. That was out of line."

Alex cleared his throat. "Uh, yeah," he mumbled. "It was. But given that I kissed you the first time, I can't very well hold this kiss against you. Care to tell me what that was all about?"

"I needed you to shut up for a minute and listen to me. Gray is more dangerous than anyone you've ever tangled with. By a mile. He's a lot more dangerous than me, for example."

"You kissed me to shut me up?"

"You're still not listening! I kissed you to get you to engage your brain."

Alex laughed painfully. "You engaged me, all right. Just not my brain."

Nick's gaze dropped involuntarily to Alex's nether regions. That was a definite swell behind the zipper of Alex's jeans. Well, hell. Now he really was tempted to kiss the guy again and then run away with him. Far, far from here and from Harlan Gray.

Alex was speaking, and Nick dragged his attention away from Alex's crotch and back to the man's words. "...do hear you. I swear."

"You can't just hear me. I need you to truly grasp what I'm telling you about Harlan Gray. He's possibly the most dangerous man on the planet."

Alex huffed. "I grasped that the first time you said

it. And trust me. He's personally not any more dangerous than you are. The only things that make him truly
dangerous are his bodyguards and the resources he uses
to move around so much with and hide his tracks with.
That's what I was trying to tell you earlier. Take those
away, and he's just a spy who's gone off the rails. He's
just one man—"

Nick slashed a hand through the narrow space between them. "I heard *you* before, too. And I'm telling you this isn't about Gray's resources. It's about his
mindset. He's willing to do things you and I are not.
He's willing to kill innocent marines who were merely
in the wrong place at the wrong time. He won't hesitate to slaughter civilians who get in his way. He thinks
nothing of taking hostages, killing children, murdering dozens or hundreds of people at a time to protect
himself."

"I get all of that," Alex said carefully. "I believe you.
And that's why I have to stop him. I can do it with your
help or without. But I need to know which it's going to
be. And I have to be able to trust you completely after
you give me your answer."

Nick sighed. "Yeah. Trust. That's a hard one for guys
like you and me, isn't it?"

The fight went out of Alex, and his belligerent stance
relaxed. In fact, he sank back down onto the sofa. Cautiously, Nick sat down beside him, watching the play of
emotions across Alex's smooth-skinned facial features.

For a man who held himself so much in check at all
times, a whole lot of feelings were racing across his
face right now. So many, in fact, that Nick wasn't sure
he could name them all. Frustration, for sure. Worry.
Determination.

He had to admire the guy. Alex didn't seem deterred

by anything Nick had said about how bad and dangerous Gray was. If anything, it seemed to have hardened Alex's resolve. Reluctant admiration coursed through him. Anyone who knew who and what Harlan Gray was and was still willing to take on the man…? Nick had to give Alex mad props for courage, if nothing else.

Alex's blue-green gaze lifted to his. "It's the right thing to do. Someone has to stop Gray. And for better or worse, it appears the job has fallen to me. I'll die if I have to. If that's what it takes to finish him, so be it."

Nick pinched the bridge of his nose with his right hand. Four aspirin weren't turning out to be enough to control the headache Alex was giving him. "I don't want you to die. That's why I'm volunteering to help you take him down. And yes, if push comes to shove, I can pull the trigger when I've got Gray's face in my sight."

"You're dead certain about that?" Alex pressed. "No pun intended."

"Yes. I am."

"Well, then. I guess you and I are going hunting together," Alex said lightly.

A heavy sense of dread filled him, but something else came with it. Relief. Relief that Gray was finally going to be stopped. Relief that he would be the one to take down his former boss—a man he'd admired and emulated for far too long. Relief that, if Alex died trying to take down Gray, he would undoubtedly die beside Alex, protecting him with his own life, the way he'd protected Gray's for so long. Yep. That felt all kinds of right.

He and Alex would survive this thing together, or they would die together.

He reached over and took Alex's hand in his. For an instant, Alex resisted, but then his arm relaxed and he quit fighting the touch. Nick turned over Alex's hand and ran his thumb over the tough shooter's callus at the base of his thumb.

"The only way you and I are both getting out of this job alive is to work together and trust each other and for both of us to be completely committed to killing Gray. There can't be even one second of hesitation when the time comes to pull the trigger. You hear me? If you get the shot, Alex, take it. Period. Promise me you won't overthink it."

Alex blinked at him, looking startled. Whether that was the result of their holding hands or Nick's sincere plea, he couldn't tell. But Alex laid his other hand gently over Nick's, sandwiching it between Alex's warm, battle-toughened palms.

"Nick. This is not my first rodeo when it comes to eliminating fellow American operators. Of course I'll take the shot. It's what I do. I never hesitate."

Nick stared into Alex's unusually colored eyes, losing himself in their sea-colored depths. "We're agreed, then. I promise not to hesitate, either, and I also promise that I will, indeed, kill him if I get the chance."

"Remember, we have to prove he gave the order to take out those marines. *Then* we can kill him."

"The Medusa photo intel analyst *saw* Gray's guys carry that crate out of the compound in Zagastan. She saw them approach the Hummer with the marines in it, and she saw the Hummer drive away, seconds later. What more proof do you need?" Nick demanded.

Alex said soberly, "There was a glitch in the video feed from the camera drone. She didn't actually see Gray's guys pull the trigger. And even if she had witnessed them murder those marines, I would still have to get proof that Gray ordered the hit. I won't dispatch him until I have that."

Nick shoved a frustrated hand through his half-dry hair. What was it going to take to convince Alex not to mess around trying to get proof of Gray's guilt first? Gray was going to kill them both long before Alex ever got his precious proof.

Alex said, "If I had been sent to put you down, wouldn't you want me to do my due diligence and assure myself I had the right guy before I pulled the trigger?"

"Innocent until proven guilty, huh?" Nick grumbled.

Alex shrugged. "Sorry. It's how I roll. Even the baddest bad guy gets the benefit of the doubt from me until I'm sure I've got the right person."

"Regardless of the risk that poses to you?" Nick snapped.

"Regardless of the risk," Alex echoed.

And that was why he was falling for this man. Alex's morals were ironclad, and no power on earth would move him off that moral center of his. Nick admired the hell out of that. Truth be told, he trusted Alex like he trusted few others in this world. He used to trust his teammates, but then Gray had bought them off. Nick wondered idly what their honor had been worth. Ten million dollars apiece? A hundred million? More?

Alex jumped up and paced back and forth a couple of times in the small living space. Nick wondered if it was the kiss, or the hand-holding or something else altogether making him so jumpy.

Either way, Alex turned to face him and said, "Do you think nearly killing one of his guards last night was provocation enough to get Gray to come after us?"

Nick frowned. "Why do you ask?"

"I'm sick and tired of chasing a ghost. I want to provoke him to come for us. In fact, I want him to come after us as hard as he's capable of doing it."

"That's a big ask," Nick responded in alarm. "And no, I doubt he'll care if the guy from last night lives or dies. Either way, with the injuries he sustained, the guy is off Gray's detail for the foreseeable future. He'll cease to exist in Gray's mind."

Alex turned to pace back toward him. "Do you think the injured guy would talk to us?"

"You're assuming he's alive and able to talk. Those are both large assumptions. At a minimum, he fractured his skull when he hit the sidewalk and gave himself a serious concussion. Worst case, he gave himself a brain bleed. For all we know, he's lying in a coma or dead by now."

Alex shrugged. "Have you got a better idea?"

"We could just wait until the auction for the golden statue takes place and pick up Gray's trail there."

Alex argued, "We have no idea when the auction will actually happen, and we have no guarantee Gray will show up for it. Particularly after this evening's fight. Would you expose yourself immediately after your bodyguards got their asses handed to them in a violent confrontation?"

Nick winced. "Fine. You make a good point. He may not show up for the auction, regardless of when it happens."

Alex's gaze narrowed thoughtfully. "Let me make a few phone calls. There's a decent trauma unit in a small private hospital about a half dozen blocks from where we fought Gray's guys. I'll bet that's where they took him."

"The hospital isn't just going to tell you if the guy

lived or died. Particularly if it's a snazzy private hospital," Nick objected.

"Oh, I'm not calling the hospital. You forget—I have the combined resources of the CIA and the rest of the United States intelligence network at my disposal."

Nick snorted. "Gee. Must be nice. We did *everything* with Gray off the books. We used to joke around that we took a—" He broke off and made a fast course correction in what he'd been about to say. "We joked around that we even defecated off the books."

Alex grinned as he pulled out his cell phone. "Observe the power of the American intelligence machine."

It took Alex under two minutes to ascertain that Gray's man, named Jed Turner, had indeed been taken to the private hospital last night and, furthermore, that the guy was in stable but serious condition and expected to live. He was still under observation for potential brain swelling on the fifth floor, in the room directly across from the nurses' station.

As Alex pocketed his phone, Nick said reluctantly, "Okay. I'm impressed. You made getting that intel look easy."

"Wanna go see if he's up for a chat now?" Alex asked jovially, well pleased with himself.

"It's after midnight. Visiting hours were over hours ago."

"Since when do rules apply to you or me?" Alex demanded.

"You really do have the bit between your teeth, now, don't you? We're just gonna barge in there, throw our government IDs and our weight around, and talk to Gray's man, huh?"

"I had a little less barging and a little more finesse in mind, but that's the basic idea," Alex replied.

"I guess I'd better have a look in that magic supply closet of yours, then. I can't very well go out in my skivvies."

"I dunno. The nurses might be willing to tell you anything if you showed up like that and shook your junk at them."

"They're nurses. They see junk all the time. They wouldn't be impressed."

Alex threw him a patently skeptical look.

Fine. He knew that women found him attractive. It was just that he didn't usually care what they thought of him. Did he use his looks to his advantage with women on missions? Of course, he did. All spies worth their salt used every tool at their disposal to get the job done. Did he sleep around with women? No. That was an ethical line he drew in the sand for himself.

Alex looked him up and down boldly before obviously losing his nerve and spinning away to stare out the window. The chili pepper lights Alex had strung up yesterday blinked cheerfully, splashing lime-green-and-orange light across his skin.

Nick dragged his gaze away from Alex's athletic physique and forced himself to step into the closet.

Wow. This thing really was stocked with everything a covert operative could ask for. The only thing missing was an arsenal of firearms. But he spied a dozen different kinds of ammunition, and he suspected there was a false wall or hidden compartment somewhere else in the apartment that did include weapons to go with all that ammo.

He rummaged through the folded stack of men's clothing and came up with a pair of charcoal gray jeans and a dark blue cotton sweater that looked as if they would fit him. He pulled them on and headed back out into the living area. As he laced on his shoes, Alex sat at the table, typing rapidly on a laptop computer.

"Whatchya doin'?" Nick asked with interest. He was intrigued by the total focus Alex brought to his tasks.

"Reading up on the Magi Crèche."

"Learn anything new?"

"Not much beyond what Otto told us at the gallery. There are thought to be around fifty pieces to the entire collection. The original set made by the magi is thought to consist of perhaps six or eight figures, probably carved from wood. It's possible they were encased in a metal, likely gold, at a later date. Given that fabulously wealthy Persian rulers commissioned the pieces, speculation is that they're made of precious materials by master artists. My classified intel sources do make one mention of the set."

"Do tell." Nick perked up with interest.

"About two years ago, the CIA picked up a bit of chatter saying the Magi Crèche had been liberated from the Iranian government and might be on its way out of Iran. The rumor hinted that some sort of arms deal was done in return for the crèche, perhaps missile components."

"As in nuclear-missile components?" Nick blurted.

"The report doesn't say. But that's a logical assumption given how frantically Iran is working at building a fleet of nuclear-capable weaponry."

"Ugh." Nick added, "What are the odds Gray saw the same intel report and decided to steal the crèche for himself?"

"I'd say those odds are pretty high."

Nick frowned. "So, what's the end goal here? Are we only interested in Gray, or are we interested in finding and recovering the crèche?"

Alex shrugged. "Stopping Gray is the primary objective. If we happen to recover the crèche in the process, that'll be frosting on the cake."

Nick nodded. "I'm thinking we ask the guy in the hospital if he knows where the rest of the crèche is stored."

"Would Gray share that information with the whole team?" Alex asked in surprise.

Nick laughed. "Not hardly. The actual question we should ask the guy would be something along the lines of is there any place Gray has gone back to a couple of times in the past year."

Alex nodded, catching on immediately. "You think he has stowed the crèche somewhere obscure and had to go back to it to retrieve the gold statue to bring it here to sell?"

"Exactly. The intel analyst who saw the crèche stolen said the crate was big and very heavy. Gray can't exactly haul it around with him, as he goes to a new safe house every night."

Alex asked, "What makes you think the guy in the hospital will tell us where it is?"

Nick shrugged. "We saved his life. He owes us."

Alex winced. "The way I hear it, there's not a whole lot of loyalty among thieves."

"Only one way to find out. We have to ask him."

Chapter Twelve

Alex tugged at the white lab coat he'd lifted off a hook in a break room two floors down. Nick hunched his shoulders in his jacket beside him. "You remember your name?" Alex asked low as the elevator dinged its arrival on the fifth floor.

"Yeah. I'm Roscoe Turner. Jed's older brother."

"Let me do the talking." Alex added, grinning, "I am, after all, more charming than you."

As the doors slid open, Nick told him under his breath exactly what he could do with his charm. His grin widened even more.

Alex stepped up to the nurses' station. "Hi, I'm Dr. Sylvan from labor and delivery. I was walking through the lobby when this nice man asked me for help finding his brother, a Jed Turner. I'm told he's a patient on this ward?"

The nurse nodded politely. "That's correct. He's right across the hall."

"I know it's breaking the rules, but Mr. Turner has driven all the way from Alabama to see his brother. Maybe he could just peek in for a minute to assure himself that Jed is all right?"

She came around the high desk and said to Nick, "You're his brother?"

"Yes, ma'am." Nick asked anxiously, "Is he okay?"

"Well, he took a pretty bad fall, but he should make a full recovery. If you'd like to see him for a moment, it's time for me to wake him up and check his vitals anyway. Come with me."

"I'll leave you to it, then," Alex said pleasantly, heading for the elevator. "Nice to meet you, Mr. Turner."

"Thanks for your help, Doc," Nick replied in a Southern drawl that made Alex want to laugh.

As soon as the nurse and Nick stepped into the room, Alex reversed direction and ducked fast into the patient room next to the one Gray's man was in. Thankfully, the bed in the room was empty. He heard the nurse's footsteps come back out into the hall, and as he'd hoped, she headed away from the nurses' station, likely doing hourly rounds.

He peeked outside, and watched her enter another patient's room. Quickly, he slipped into the hall and ducked into the room with Nick and Jed.

Nick's former student had a bandage wrapped around his head and looked pale. Bits of brown hair stuck out around the gauze strapping.

Nick was leaning over the bed. He looked up, spied Alex and muttered, "He's sedated. Pretty groggy."

"Perfect."

Nick nodded, and for a bare instant, flashed him a wolflike smile. Then he looked back down at the patient. "Jed, it's Kane. How're you feeling, buddy?"

The man's eyelids fluttered and his blue eyes half-opened. A vague frown crossed his features.

"Nick." A long pause while the guy peered up at him. Then, "Did we fight?"

"I trained you last year in hand-to-hand combat. Remember?"

"Guess so."

"How's your head? The way I hear it, you took a pretty good fall."

Jed's hand lifted weakly off the mattress toward his head and then fell back to the white sheet. "Hurts," he mumbled.

"I'll bet."

Jed seemed to be struggling to retrieve something from his memory, and Alex waited him out along with Nick.

At length, Jed finally mumbled to Nick, "You're gay?"

Alex stared. That was not what he'd expected to come out of the guy's mouth. He glanced up at Nick, who was staring down at the injured man as if Jed had grown a second head.

"What the hell are you talking about?" Nick finally said gruffly.

"Gray said…"

Alex caught Nick's eye roll of genuine frustration and Alex shared the sentiment. Wow. Gray had outed him to his teammates? What a douchebag.

"Not a problem for me," Jed was mumbling. "Do your job. Who cares what you do on your own time?"

Nick smiled gently at Jed, who frowned up at him as if struggling to retrieve some other important tidbit.

Without warning, Jed blurted. "Traitor. He said you were a traitor. Turned in the guys who got arrested in Montana a while back. Did you turn on us, man?"

He traded brief glances with Nick that spoke volumes. Nick was going to be hard to stop from killing Gray if and when they uncovered the man. Alex glanced down at Jed significantly and back up at Nick, who caught the hint. He pasted on a smile and looked down at the groggy man.

"Gray's full of shit." Nick paused to take a deep breath. Then he continued, "I would never betray my own guys. Hell, I trained you myself."

"Then what…tonight…why're you here?"

Nick lied easily, "I was trying to catch up with you and the other guys after you took off out of the art gallery. I came upon you after some kind of fight. You were on the ground and bleeding. You had stopped breathing. I did CPR on you and saved your life. Do you remember that?"

The man's frown deepened as he visibly sorted through blurry snippets of memory, but then his expression eased. "Yeah. Thanks," he sighed.

"Of course. You'd have done the same for me. We're brothers-in-arms." He smiled down at the guy and said smoothly, "I need you to do me a favor. I've gotten separated from the team and need to reconnect with them. After y'all found that tracker on the limo and things heated up the way they have, Gray ordered me to head out and sit on the crate. But before he could text me the location, I lost my damned phone. He's gonna kill me if I don't get to the haul ASAP and make sure it's safe."

Jed nodded faintly and then sucked in a sharp, painful breath after the small head movement. The guy must have the mother of all headaches after hitting the concrete the way he had.

Nick murmured, "I know the town, but I don't know the address of the storage place. Do you have those, buddy?"

"Phone," Jed muttered. "Phone."

"Yeah. My phone was stolen. I've got a replacement on order, but it won't be here until tomorrow, and I was supposed to leave tonight to check on the statues."

At the mention of statues, some of the tension went out of Jed's body. His eyelids drifted shut.

"Don't fall asleep on me, now," Nick said teasingly. "Where am I supposed to go?"

"Phone," Jed sighed with the last of his consciousness.

His eyes shut. Alex reached out to shake his shoulder lightly. The jostling should have made the man cry out in pain, but he merely moaned a little and went still again.

"Did the nurse put something in his IV when you two came in here?" Alex asked low.

Nick swore under his breath. "Yeah. Must be some sort of sedation and painkiller."

"We're not going to get any more out of him for a few hours," Alex said in disgust. "We can come back in the morning, I suppose. He did seem willing to talk with you, at any rate."

"He must not have recognized us as the guys from the fight."

Alex nodded, his sharp hearing detecting a door closing down the hall. "Time to go. That nurse will finish her rounds soon."

Alex went to the hallway door and watched as the nurse stopped in the hallway beside a door to hang up a clipboard. She moved to another room and disappeared inside. Alex waved for Nick to follow, and they raced down the hall quickly and quietly.

The elevator had left, and there was no time to wait for it to come back. They slipped into the stairwell beside it and Nick closed the door softly.

They jogged down the steps in silence. They ducked out onto the second floor, and Alex returned the lab coat to the break room where he'd found it. No sense causing a ruckus that might cause the night nurse to remember Dr. Sylvan bringing an after-hours visitor to a trauma patient.

They headed out, making sure to turn their faces away from each of the security cameras they encountered on their way. They walked back to the apartment building without speaking, and Alex relished the relative quiet of this time of night. Usually the city was so busy, so bustling and noisy, he could barely hear himself think. But tonight, with shiny Christmas decorations hanging on lamp poles, lights twinkling in store windows and a fine layer of snow coating the ground, it was magically serene.

"I do love this town during the holidays," he murmured.

"You're just a Christmas junkie," Nick teased.

"I like how the holidays bring out the kinder side of people. For a minute we forget to be rotten to one another and we come together to make kids smile and connect with our loved ones. Call me sappy at heart and I'll plead guilty as charged."

He smiled and shrugged, and Nick grinned back, if a little reluctantly, and muttered, "I think it's nice."

"What? Have I converted you into thinking the holidays are nice?"

"No. I think your secret optimism about the decency of the human race is nice. And if it takes all of this schlocky holiday crap to bring it out in you, so be it."

"Be careful, Nick, or I'll turn you into a holiday lover, too."

"Nope. Never."

They got back to the apartment and Nick fell onto the sofa in frustration. "I can't believe Gray outed me to the team. What a jerk."

"That's a nice word for him," Alex said dryly.

"What are we supposed to do now? Jed was no help at all."

Alex flopped down at the kitchen table. And then it hit him. "Phone!" he exclaimed. "Of course!"

"What?"

"Before we resuscitated Jed, we disarmed Gray's men and took their cells. Did you happen to grab Jed's?"

Nick blinked, startled. "Yeah. I did. I stuffed it in my pants' pocket before I started CPR." Understanding dawned in Nick's gaze. If they could get into the phones and poke around in them, they might be able to figure out where Gray was staying. Or at least, they might be able to find the man's trail again.

He loved working with a guy as smart as Nick was. It saved so much explanation and argument to convince someone else that his hunches were worth following. But then, the best operators usually relied heavily on their intuitions and gut feels. Thankfully, Nick had gotten that memo somewhere along the way and was immediately on board with his hunch that they should check out the phones.

Alex pulled out the garbage bag full of their bloody clothes and untied it. He dug around in the crusty garments, stiff with dried blood, and found Nick's slacks. He checked the pockets and came up with a phone. He carried it back to the table.

Nick joined him as he pressed the power button.

"It's password encrypted," Alex announced.

Nick swore under his breath. "By the time we unlock the thing, Gray will have sold his statue and be long gone."

Alex shrugged. "I don't know about that. I know a few things about phone decryption. First thing tomorrow morning, I'll head over to an electronics shop and buy a few things. Then maybe I can get us into Jed's."

"The way he kept saying 'phone,' over and over, I'll lay odds the information we need is in there," Nick said eagerly.

"For now, let's get some rest and hit it again in the morning. There's nothing more we can do tonight."

Their gazes snapped to each other. There was plenty more they *could* do tonight. Just nothing that would advance their efforts to locate Gray.

Never, ever, had he felt this instant a connection with another man. While he was delighted to know that this kind of sympatico existed, why did he have to find Nick in the middle of a mission that very well could be the one that killed them both?

Alex dragged his mind back to the problem at hand. First, they had to find Gray. Then he could explore this thing between him and Nick. But they couldn't indulge in their private desires yet. He couldn't think of anything in the world dumber than stopping, dropping and making out in the middle of a life-threatening operation. He was nothing if not a man of intense self-discipline.

But that didn't mean he had to like it.

They decided that Nick would take the mattress and he would take the couch since he was a few inches shorter than Nick. Not that the stupid sofa fit him, either. After about five minutes trying to figure out how to curl up or stretch out and hang his feet off the end of the thing, he gave up, dragged the sofa's seat cushions onto the floor and stretched out more comfortably.

From the darkness, Nick said, "You can share the mattress with me. I don't bite." There was a momentary pause and he added dryly, "Well, I only bite when invited." Another pause. "When there's an established safe word." A third pause. "And my partner likes it a little rough."

Alex popped to full consciousness, his body abruptly aroused and his mind racing. So much for him sleeping anytime soon.

A little rough, huh? Nick bit? What did he bite? How hard? Could he bite back? An urge to nibble his way across all of Nick's body made him toss and turn long after Nick's breathing slowed and deepened into sleep.

A safe word? Heck yeah, he would invite the man to bite a little—

He tossed and turned some more. He threw off the blanket, way too overheated to need it. *Dang it.* He was going to end up having to go into the bathroom, relieve the pressure in his groin by hand and then take the coldest shower the apartment could offer up.

He did end up taking that shower, and he did eventually fall asleep in the wee hours of the night. But Nick could stop making any more comments like that around him at bedtime in the future.

He woke to the smell of something cooking and rolled off the sofa cushion and onto the hard floor before fully waking. He stared up at Nick grinning at him from over by the tiny stove and brandishing a spatula like a sword.

"Whatchya got cookin'?" Alex mumbled.

"Farmer's breakfast, lazy head. It's a thing my German nana used to make. She called it *Bauernfrühstück.* My brother and I called it the everything-but-the-kitchen-sink meal."

Alex sat up, grinding the bases of his palms into his eye sockets.

"Didn't sleep well?" Nick asked cheerfully. "You should've shared the mattress with me."

As if. He wouldn't have gotten a wink of sleep all night if he'd done that. Safe words and biting, indeed.

Sometime in the wee hours of the night, awareness of another feeling crept insidiously into his mind. Fear. It was an unpleasant and unwelcome sensation and he'd spent a long time trying to banish if from his mind.

But the harder he fought it, the more stubbornly the fear lodged itself in his mind. What was he going to do about the problem of Nicholas Kane?

What if Nick and he gave it a go and things didn't work out between them? How was he going to walk away from this man and not look back?

What if Nick walked away from him? How was he supposed to just watch him go?

What if Nick couldn't overcome his hang-ups about dying, or heaven forbid, allowing himself to be a tiny bit happy?

He, of all people, knew better than to expect anyone to change to suit someone else. He couldn't ask it of Nick. It would have to come from inside Nick himself.

Could he stand by and watch this potentially magnificent man self-destruct? Could he let Nick sacrifice himself in the grand gesture Nick seemed to envision as the way he would leave this world?

Alex could see their whole future in his mind's eye, unfolding in snapshots of family and fun and warmth and love. If only Nick could see it, too, and allow himself to reach out and take it all for himself.

Gah. He hated not being in control of this whole situation. He was always in control. And then Nick had blown into his life and turned everything upside down.

He tossed and turned until dawn was starting to creep around the curtains and past the chili pepper lights.

Grouchy, he got up and took yet another shower,

this one hot enough to melt candlewax. He felt vaguely human by the time he emerged. Nick shoved a double mug of coffee into his hand, and he gulped it too quickly, burning his mouth. He didn't care. He took another big swig of the caffeinated goodness.

He finished the coffee just as Nick plated up a concoction of meat, potatoes and chopped vegetables held together by an egg-and-cheese mixture. It was a lot like an omelet but much heartier.

Alex ate quickly, mentally making a shopping list for himself. "Will you be okay here alone while I run out and buy a few things?"

Nick smirked. "I'm just going to do the dishes and watch talk shows all morning. Maybe catch up on my favorite soap opera. Call my girlfriends and talk on the phone."

Alex rolled his eyes and grinned. "Right. Back in about an hour."

It turned out to be more like two hours. The first store didn't have a key component he needed to build a decryption device, and he ended up having to stop by the local FBI field office to requisition the most sensitive part he needed—a motherboard with a high-speed number generator programmed on it. He brought his whole haul back to the apartment and spent the remainder of the morning wiring and soldering. But by noon, he had a crude device ready to try out.

He pulled out one of the other men's phones to test his device on first, in case it fried the content instead of unlocking it. He popped the back off the phone, connected the cell's guts to his crude device and sat back to wait.

"How long will this take?" Nick asked with interest.

"Depends on how long the password is. Anything

over six numbers could take a while. With each digit you add in length, the number of possible combinations goes up exponentially."

"Cool. Wanna watch a game show with me?" Nick asked drolly.

Alex frowned. "I don't remember the last time I watched television."

Nick guffawed. "You're missing out, man. With all the streaming services these days, there are more shows than you can shake a stick at."

Alex shrugged. "My work keeps me pretty busy."

"Don't you ever take time off?" Nick asked, sounding a bit incredulous.

"Why would I? My work is important."

"Not even for Christmas?"

Alex rolled his eyes at him. "That's a low blow. This mission is important or I'd be ice skating in Rockefeller Center right now, wearing a bad Christmas sweater and sucking on a candy cane."

"Don't you ever burn out? Get exhausted? Need to rest up and, I don't know, heal?"

"I don't get hurt," Alex replied indignantly. "I'm good at my job."

"I bandaged you up last night. You do, too, get hurt."

"Only since I started running around with you."

Nick snorted. "You mean ever since you decided to tangle with Harlan Gray."

Alex opened his mouth to retort, but the phone in front of him lit up just then. "We're in."

Nick jumped up and came over to stare down at the unlocked device. Alex held it out to him. "You poke around on this one while I hook up Jed's phone."

It didn't take long to get the decryption device set up and it went to work.

Nick asked, "Do you know how to find out if these phones have GPS tracking on them? I'd love to see where they've been the past few weeks."

"Weeks? They should store location information dating back for months," Alex replied, taking the cell from Nick and typing into it. A screen popped up. "Here we go. This device takes a lat-long location snapshot every few hours. We'll have to enter the latitude and longitude coordinates into a separate map program to find out exactly where it has been, which will be a pain in the butt, but we can definitely track where it has been."

"Sweet," Nick exclaimed.

Alex opened up a simple mapping program and shoved the laptop over to Nick. "You type in the coordinates I give you."

For the next half hour, he read out geographic info while Nick placed virtual pins in an online map. They were just finishing up when Jed's device finally lit up.

"Dang, he had some good encryption on that puppy," Alex commented.

"Wanna map where his phone has been, too, and compare the list of locations to the first one?" Nick suggested.

"Sure. We've got the third guy's locations we can map, as well. Between the three of them, we should get a decent idea of where Gray's been for the past year."

"He'd croak if he knew we could track his movements like this," Nick said in satisfaction.

"Feel free to tell him after we've apprehended him," Alex said, amused.

"Oh, I will. I have a lot to say to him when we catch his sorry ass."

"I'm glad to hear you talking in terms of catching and interrogating him rather than just killing him on sight."

Nick's gaze narrowed. "Forget what I just said. I'm going to go ahead and blow his head off. You can question his corpse all you'd like."

Alex sighed. "I have to do my job first. Then, depending on what we learn, we can kill him."

"I'm amending my earlier statement that whoever gets the shot should take it," Nick said grimly. "I want to be the one to take him out."

"If we have the luxury of choosing, I yield the honor to you," Alex said formally.

Nick's eyebrows sailed up. "Do you mean that?"

"When's the last time I lied to you?" Alex retorted.

"I don't know. When?"

"Never," Alex snapped, offended at the mere idea of lying to Nick.

"Don't get your knickers in a twist. I believe you," Nick said mildly. "You're not a lying kind of guy."

Alex subsided, mollified, and went back to work on decrypting the third cell phone.

It took them several hours, but finally, they had a map on the laptop's screen with sets of red, blue and green pins sprinkled across mainly the East Coast of the United States, one color for each of the three phones they'd plotted.

Alex stared at the dozens of colored dots on the map. "Now we just have to look for a place that makes no sense for Harlan Gray to have visited."

Nick snorted. "As if anything that man does makes sense."

A half hour later, Alex stared down at a hand-written list of nearly sixty cities that all three phones had in common as having visited in the past year. Surely most of them contained overnight safe houses that Gray slept at and then left. There had to be a way to narrow down where he might have stashed a crate full of price-less statues.

"Give me Jed's," Alex said suddenly. "Jed kept re-peating the word *phone*. What if there's other informa-tion in his that we're missing?"

Nick passed it to him, and Alex commenced pok-ing around.

"Hah! Jed keeps copies of documents from the cloud on his phone! Bad, bad operational security. But good for us."

"Can you open the files?" Nick asked eagerly.

"It may take another round of decryption," Alex warned. He typed the command to open the files and put his decryption device to work, trying every pos-sible combination of letters, numbers and symbols to open them.

For a while, he watched the device flickering, cycling through permutations of passwords faster than his eyes could read them. By now, if it was a six-digit combo, the phone would've opened. Which meant they were in for at least several more hours of seven-digit possibilities.

"Guess I'm stuck watching that soap opera with you," Alex sighed.

"It's too late for soaps. We've got talk shows or early news. Unless, of course, you'd like to watch some after-school cartoons."

"News," Alex declared.

Nick changed the channel, and Alex jolted as an image of the gold statue from Otto's gallery flashed across the screen. The reporter was describing how the piece was thought to come from a priceless collection of statues depicting the birth of Christ and created by one of the Three Wise Men, and that it was going to be sold tomorrow night in a highly anticipated auction.

Alex looked over at Nick. "Welp. I guess Otto got his provenance papers."

Nick replied grimly, "And that means we have an auction to attend."

Chapter Thirteen

The gallery was buzzing with activity when they arrived. People milled around on the sidewalk, wearing tuxedos and formal gowns. A red carpet was rolled out all the way to the curb, and the rich and richer of the art world were out in force, tonight.

News trucks were parked up and down the street. All the major news networks were here to cover the auction of the statue from the Magi Crèche. Everyone who was anyone in the art world wanted to be seen here, and it had the feel of a major gala. Security was tight, and people were being scanned with metal detectors before they entered the building.

Nick led Alex away from the chaos out front, however, and they headed around to the back of the property. It was just as chaotic behind the gallery, with catering trucks, security guards and warehouse crew racing around getting ready for the auction to commence. A hundred other works of art were also on sale tonight, and they all had to be numbered, lined up and transported inside on a tight, smooth schedule.

Crouching beside him in an adjacent alley, Alex murmured, "We'll never get inside unseen."

"We don't have to. We just have to piss off Gray so bad he wants to kill us."

"You think this'll work?" Alex replied.

"If one gambit doesn't work, the other will," Nick muttered. "The one thing Gray can't stand is being embarrassed. He's going to go nuts when our guy inside calls the statue a fake."

"Otto's going to have heart failure," Alex added. "This could ruin him."

"The statue is stolen, and he knows it. He deserves to be ruined," Nick bit out.

"Wow. And I thought I was the one with the rigid moral code."

He glanced over at Alex and shrugged. "You and I do bad and illegal things at the behest of our government, and always for a higher cause of right and good. Men like us had better have a rigid moral code so we never lose sight of why we do what we do."

"Exactly." Alex went still as a pair of black SUVs pulled around behind the warehouse. They had darkly tinted windows and came in fast. Three men jumped out, took a quick look around, and then a fourth stepped out.

"And there's our man now," Nick breathed. "That's Gray in the tuxedo."

"We won't have a shot from this angle when they bring him out," Alex whispered.

Nick looked around at the tight confines of the alley. "We're gonna have to go high."

As Gray and his team disappeared inside, the SUVs pulled away and turned the corner. Nick commented, "The only place we'll have a shot that the SUVs won't block is that brick building next door to the gallery."

"It's not very tall. It'll be a shallow angle. Hard shot."

"Better than no shot," Nick replied.

"Let me see who's in that building," Alex murmured

as he typed on his cell phone. "It holds a hodgepodge of small businesses."

"I've seen enough, here. Let's go find ourselves a perch and get ready," Nick murmured.

The rear door of the brick building was a joke to unlock. They slipped inside the dingy, converted factory. They climbed the metal fire stairs to the top floor and turned left, heading for the office on the end. The cardboard sign taped to the inside of the glass door declared it to be a talent agency. For what, Nick had no idea.

The lock was simple, and the dead bolt above it not much harder to pick. Alex got through both in under a minute. They slipped into an office even more depressing than its exterior.

"No wonder this place has no security," Alex murmured. "There's nothing worth stealing."

Alex said low, "You clear this place, and I'll head across the hall. Find us an egress point. Back in a few."

Nick moved quietly across the room to the pair of corner windows, one facing the gallery and the other facing the alley behind it. He checked quickly for any hidden security measures, even though he agreed with Alex that there was nothing here worth protecting.

A half dozen tall filing cabinets lined one wall, and a battered oak desk took up the middle of the space. Broken slat blinds hung askew over the panes. Perfect. He and Alex would be able to point their weapons past the blinds without disturbing them.

Nick laid the long plastic rifle case on the floor beside the window and flipped the lid open. For Alex, he laid one of two short-range precision rifles inside on the sill facing the warehouse, and he picked up the other. He flipped down the bipod stand attached to the barrel and examined the windowsill facing the warehouse.

Alex opened the office door and announced, "Straight across the hall, I've got the door unlocked, the window opened and two rappelling lines anchored and ready to throw down."

"Cool."

Alex moved over to the window beside him and picked up the rifle.

"Lots of dust on the sills," Nick commented. "Either we clean it off or we'll have to hide the marks from the bipods."

Alex snorted. "Anything recently cleaned in this office would be a huge red flag. How about using a few of these files?" He picked up a handful of manila folders holding what looked at a glance to be résumés and headshots, presumably of actors. Based on the clothing and hairstyles, they were decades old—or auditioning for a period piece from the 1980s. "We can lay them on top of the dust. They may make marks, but it's plausible that whoever works here might lay files on these wide sills from time to time."

"Works for me." Nick carefully placed a couple of the folders on the broad sill, while Alex did the same at the other. They slid the windows open just enough to extend the tips of their rifles, and cold air streamed in. It felt good on Nick's face and dispelled a bit of the stale odor that clung to this place.

The auction started, and the activity calmed down behind the warehouse. The food and waiters were all inside, and the art would be rolling through the warehouse like an assembly line.

Nick said reflectively, "This is weird, having a buddy in a shooting nest."

"I know. Right?" Alex added, "What do you usually think about while you're waiting for a target to show up?"

"Truth?"

"Of course."

"I plan the house I'm going to build when I retire. I design the garden, furnish it, the whole thing."

"What does it look like?" Alex asked.

"It's not fancy. Just a farmhouse. Big porch. Comfortable rooms. Furniture you can live on. The kind of kitchen people want to gather in. You know, sit around and talk while someone cooks."

"Was your childhood home like that?"

Nick snorted. "Hardly. I grew up in a piece-of-crap shack a strong wind would've blown over. Only garden my mom grew was a stand of marijuana out back. Until my older brother discovered it. Then my dad burned it down." He added dryly, "Only time I ever got high. My brother and sister and I all ran out back and breathed in as much of that smoke as we could."

Alex chuckled.

"How about you? What do you think about when you're sitting in a hide?" Nick asked.

"Sometimes I think about the family I'd like to have someday."

"Oh yeah? What does that look like?" Nick asked with interest.

"I picture me and my husband. He's a nice guy. Happy. A homebody. Doesn't know anything about my past and doesn't care. Loves kids. Likes to cook."

Nick winced. He was none of those things. "I've never been around kids, so I can't say if I like them or not."

"Do you put a spouse and some kids in your imaginary farmhouse?" Alex asked.

"Sometimes," he admitted reluctantly.

"What's your perfect spouse like?"

Nick frowned. "I don't know. Hot, I guess."

Alex laughed. "That's it? Your only requirement in a life mate is that they be hot?"

Truthfully, he didn't like to think about a person who would never exist. He blurted, "I don't actually see myself living past my career. I figure I'm gonna die in the harness. Why get all worked up over hopes and dreams that are never going to happen?"

"Note to self—Nick is neither nice nor happy. He's not a homebody, hates cooking and is undecided about kids. He knows everything about me and my job…and only cares if a guy is hot." Alex added wryly, "Yep. You and me—we're a match made in heaven."

Nick frowned. "Yes, but you're hot. From my end of this equation, we'd get along just fine."

Alex laughed lightly. "Sorry. My standards extend beyond how much I enjoy looking at you and the fact that we'd be fantastic in the sack together."

"You like looking at me?"

"C'mon. You know you're a good-looking man. You don't need me to tell you so," Alex retorted.

"And you think we'd be fantastic in bed together?" Nick asked before he could stop the question from slipping out.

"I know it," Alex said firmly.

"What makes you so sure?"

"Because I know what I'm doing, and you're a trainable monkey."

Nick snorted with laughter. "Hah! I have a ton more experience with sex than you. I'm the one who'd be showing you a trick or two."

"Care to place a wager on that?"

Nick actually lifted his eye away from his rubber gun sight to glance over his shoulder at Alex. "Sure, but would I want to win that bet or lose it?"

Alex had also looked up from his weapon. "Depends on whether you prefer to give pleasure or receive it, I suppose."

"I like to do both," he answered frankly. "Where's the fun in sex if your partner isn't having as good a time as you are?"

Alex made no comment. Instead, he reached up to his right ear and pulled out a small, wireless earbud. He held it out toward Nick. "Here. Listen. The auction has started."

Nick popped the device in his ear. A man was speaking. "I have sixteen thousand. Do I have seventeen? Sixteen thousand for the Tiffany earrings. Going once. Going twice. Sold. To bidder number 192."

"Is this the actual auction, like in real time?" Nick asked, startled.

"Yes. There's a wireless feed of it for sellers and remote bidders to log into. I hacked the link before we left the apartment."

"Sweet."

Nick listened as a piece of art was being bid on. It was from some painter he'd never heard of. It sold for just over twenty thousand dollars.

"I thought auctioneers talked really fast," Nick remarked.

Alex replied, "Not at fancy auctions like this one. There's no need to. I expect only a hundred or so pieces will be auctioned off tonight, so there's no hurry to get through it all. Plus, bidders like these here won't get swept up in the excitement of it all and pay more than they intend to for anything. It's probably more effective for the auctioneer to speak normally so everyone can understand the dollar amounts getting thrown around."

"I assume the gold statue will sell last?" Nick asked.

"For sure."

One by one, the other works of art sold. As the sale progressed, the prices climbed higher and higher.

And then it was time. Nick recognized Otto's voice, personally announcing, "And now, the piece we've all been waiting for. Yuri and I are proud to offer for sale a gold statue of a Persian warrior riding a horse. I'm pleased to announce we received papers earlier today confirming this statue to belong to the Magi Crèche."

Over his earbud, Nick heard the collective gasp from the crowd.

Another voice became audible, yelling, "This statue is a fake! The Iranian regime had copies made of the crèche and let them be stolen to hide the fact that the original is still in the hands of the government! I'm one of the artists who was paid to make the copies. I escaped Iran before the government could kill me to silence me…"

The last sentence or two got fainter and harder to hear as the shouter was clearly pulled out of the auction room and struggled against Otto's security men.

An audible buzz of consternation rose from the crowd.

"Was it enough?" Nick asked. "Will Otto suspend the sale?"

Alex shrugged. "We'll find out in the next few seconds."

Otto's voice rose over the crowd noise, calling, "We will be happy to let the buyer examine the provenance documents and have his or her own independent investigator verify the authenticity of the statue. Of course, we guarantee the product and will offer a full refund if the buyer is not satisfied at the findings. Settle down. Settle down. Let's get the bidding started. Mr. Abdow? If you'd like to take over and start the auction?"

The auctioneer's smooth voice returned to Nick's ear. "I'll start the bidding at ten million dollars. I have twenty. Thirty. Forty. Do I have fifty million?"

Nick listened in awe as the bidding quickly spun up toward one hundred million dollars. "Dang. Gray sure knew what to steal to pay for a nice retirement."

"No kidding," Alex muttered. Then, "I've got movement at the back of the warehouse."

"Gray?" Nick bit out. He was staring down at the alley and couldn't risk moving his weapon too much to peer over toward the warehouse. He would have only a second or two as it was to make any corrections, take final aim and pull the trigger.

"Unknown—I recognize one of his guards. Two men have come out. They're clearing the alley." A pause. "The vehicle should pull up any second—"

Nick spied two pairs of headlights swing into the far end of the alley. "Got it. Gray will move fast."

"He'll be moving faster once I shoot at him," Alex murmured.

"Don't hit him by accident."

"You do know what I do for a living, right?"

Smiling a little, Nick took a long, slow breath, willing his heart rate to slow. Time to go to work. Another longer, slower breath, with emphasis on drawing out the exhalation. His humor drained away. Only the utterly still, calm presence of Alex beside him registered. And then, even Alex stopped registering. Everything else ceased to exist. It was just him, the cold steel against his cheek, the circular view through his gun sight of the alley and the approaching SUV.

"Target acquired," Alex said quietly. He, too, was already into his shooting sequence, controlling heart rate and breathing to make sure his shot was steady. "Ready. Aim."

Nick braced himself for the sound of Alex's rifle firing beside him. They'd decided not to use sound suppressors since the idea was to scare the crap out of Gray and not actually kill him tonight.

Bang.

Bang.

Bang.

Wow. Alex was fast at lining up shots and taking them.

Nick aimed at the SUV's door window and squeezed his trigger. A spiderweb of cracks exploded across the bullet-resistant glass.

He swung the tip of his rifle slightly to the right and lined up the torso of the bodyguard holding the door. He and Alex had debated whether or not to shoot any of the guards and had ultimately decided to use small caliber rounds and aim for the Kevlar vests all the guards would be wearing. It was always a risk to shoot at a human being. They could move at the last second, turning a safe, nonlethal shot into a deadly one.

He and Alex were outstanding snipers, however, and properly provoking Gray took precedence over a small but calculated risk.

Nick squeezed the trigger and watched the man he'd just shot stagger and right himself.

The alley filled with fast-moving bodies. Gray was shoved into the SUV. One man jumped on top of the spymaster and another slammed the door shut behind them, almost catching Gray's feet in the process.

For good measure, Nick swung his weapon left and put two fast rounds into the bullet-resistant windshield. The first shot left no more than a divot, but the second, placed almost exactly on top of the first, caused a rather satisfying spiderweb to blossom across the whole driver's side of the windshield.

There. Gray's men should feel as if they'd been in a full-on shootout now.

"Pack up," Alex said calmly. "Two hostiles incoming."

Nick noted a pair of Gray's men sprinting away from the SUV, both gripping handguns. They were moving *fast*. He would bet they were mighty pissed off someone was taking potshots at their principal.

As he quickly policed his spent shells and put his rifle in the plastic case beside Alex's, he said urgently, "You hung two ropes, right?"

Alex shot back, "Did you remember to put on your rappelling harness?"

He rolled his eyes as he took Alex's rifle and shoved it in the case. Nick scooped up the rifle case and slung it across his back. Alex headed out to deploy their escape ropes, and he hung back for a second.

Just in case their first two gambits to force Gray to follow them didn't work, he had a third one up his sleeve. One that should point Gray squarely at him and not at Alex.

He shouldn't do this. Alex would kill him if he found out—

Don't overthink it.

He had feelings for Alex and didn't want to see the guy die. That was all this was.

Sure it was. He didn't wake up sweating from erotic dreams of him and Alex in bed together. He didn't find the man endlessly fascinating. He didn't respect Alex's skill at his work more than just about anyone else's. The guy didn't make him laugh. Or think about family, friends and what came after this career of his…

"You coming?" Alex called from across the hall.

Nick propped the envelope he'd prepared earlier on the windowsill Alex had shot out of. The name Harlan Gray was printed on it in large letters. Gray's men couldn't fail to see it sitting there.

He followed Alex across the hall, closing and locking the talent agency's door behind him.

"Footprints," Alex whispered urgently.

Nick looked down and saw he was leaving dusty footprints on the linoleum flooring. He rubbed his shoe back and forth across the floor, obscuring the marks. It was a hasty counter-tracking job, but he doubted Gray's men would stick around to do a full forensic analysis of the scene.

Alex was still, listening, and Nick froze beside him. There. He heard running footsteps on the metal stairs they'd used to come up here. Gray's men were inside the building. Which meant the two of them were clear to head outside.

Nick moved swiftly to Alex's side as he sat on the open windowsill and swung his legs over the ledge to dangle outside.

Nick hooked his rappelling harness on to the second rope and gave the anchor point a hard tug as Alex jumped, disappearing from sight. Nick sat on the same metal window frame, swung his legs out and jumped.

He twisted in midair, contorting his body into a jackknife. His feet impacted the brick wall, and he pushed off with his legs, swinging out and down, letting the rope slide freely through his gloved hands. Three big jumps and one small one, and his feet hit the ground. He yanked on the thin nylon release rope, and both rappelling line and release rope slithered down, hitting him in the head.

There was no time to be fancy. He gathered up the ropes in a messy armful and took off running behind Alex. They reached the end of the alley and ducked around the corner, out of sight of the building.

Alex stopped and methodically started winding rope around his left hand and elbow. Nick did the same, listening hard as he coiled his own. A few small loops around the middle of the larger ones, and the cords were neatly formed into bundles. Nick stuffed his ropes and Alex's into the rucksack Alex wore, and they took off, walking briskly.

They turned the next corner into a darkened industrial area. They ran then, putting some distance between themselves and the alley. They emerged onto a decently lit street with bars and restaurants, where running would attract attention, and they slowed to a walk again. And so it went. They ran when no one was around to see them; they walked when there were other people present.

When they'd satisfied themselves no one had followed them, only then did they head for home.

In the apartment, Nick sat down on the sofa and opened the rifle case at his feet. He passed Alex one weapon and took out the other. Working in silence, they cleaned the firearms.

"So," Alex asked, "did we piss him off enough to come after us?"

If he was ever going to mention the note, now was the

moment. But Nick let it pass. No need to tell Alex that he'd written to Gray, telling his former boss he knew where the team who'd stolen the crate were being held. He'd also intimated that the imprisoned men were being subjected to enhanced interrogation and starting to talk about Gray. He offered to tell him where the men were stashed if Gray would cut him in for a share of the cash proceeds from selling the Magi Crèche.

Gray would lose his mind. Not only would he be desperate to silence Nick's old teammates, there was no way he would be willing to cut Nick in on the fortune. Gray never had been any good at sharing his toys.

Aloud, Nick said, "I would say we've definitely got Gray's full attention. Which means we're no longer hunting. We just became the hunted."

Chapter Fourteen

Alex nodded grimly at Nick's quiet pronouncement. It was one thing to theorize about Harlan Gray wanting them dead—it was another thing altogether to realize that had become a reality. He didn't for one second think this was going to be anything but an all-out fight for their lives going forward. Thank goodness he had Nick at his side—

"Um, Alex. Your decryption thing has a red light flashing on it."

"Good. The last phone is finished. Let's see where the guy who ran away from the fight has traveled over the past few months. Maybe with his info we can narrow down our search area some."

In fact, the fourth man's travel data was significantly different from the other men's. While the others had generally journeyed together, no doubt acting as personal security for Gray, the fourth man had traveled alone. A lot.

Specifically, he'd gone to the same place in Upstate New York three times in the past half year, and each time, he'd stayed there for exactly a month, with exactly a month in between visits. Like a person would if he were pulling alternating shifts keeping watch over something or someone.

Alex commented, "Looks like this guy wasn't part of Harlan's personal cadre until recently."

Nick nodded. "Do you suppose he was guarding the crate of statues?"

"Maybe. Where do his coordinates put him each time he parks for that long?"

Nick typed in his phone for a moment. "Place called Pleasant Falls, New York. It's several hours north of here by car if the roads are clear of snow."

"Good spot to stash a valuable item. Not far from a big city where it can be sold, but not so close that anyone would look for it there," Alex remarked.

"I gather we're heading up that way in the morning?" Nick asked.

"Great minds think alike." Alex searched on the laptop for places to stay near Pleasant Falls. A list of local bed-and-breakfasts in and around the picturesque town popped up. He spotted a sprawling white farmhouse with a big porch called the Pleasant Run Inn. It looked just like the place Nick had described wanting to retire in.

Alex pulled up the availability of rooms at the inn. It only had one room vacant for the next two weeks, but it was the honeymoon suite. It would have a big bed, if nothing else. He booked the room. "I got us a place to stay in Pleasant Falls."

"Cool. I just rented us a car."

Alex asked in alarm, "Did you use a clean alias? One Gray wouldn't know?"

Nick smirked. "I may be hot, but I'm not stupid."

Alex looked around the tiny flat. "I'm gonna miss this place and all its Christmas cheer."

"Should we take the bullets off the Christmas tree?" Nick asked doubtfully.

"Nah. Anyone who comes here will appreciate the décor theme."

"I never did ask. Is this a CIA safe house?"

"Don't ask, and I won't tell," Alex answered cryptically. The people he worked for preferred not to be named, and honestly, he wasn't entirely sure who *they* worked for. He just knew they were the final decision-making authority when it came to sanctioning American assets who needed to be forcibly removed from the field. He didn't ask who they were, and they didn't offer up any information to him. When they gave him an address and told him he could hide there, he took them at their word and asked no questions.

"Are you finally going to agree to share the mattress with me tonight?" Nick asked as he stripped off his shirt and kicked off his shoes.

"If you'll quit undressing any more, I might," Alex retorted. He removed his shoes and set them neatly in front of the sofa, laces loosened and ready to be stepped into fast. He laid out clean jeans, a cotton button-down shirt and clean underwear, as well.

"Are you always that anal-retentive about arranging your clothes?" Nick asked, curious.

"If we have to make a fast getaway, I'm going to do it fully dressed. You're going to end up running down the fire escape in your undershorts because you can't lay your hands on any clothes," Alex replied dryly.

Nick sighed. "I'm usually more careful about such things, but the past few days have been a little nuts."

"You don't say."

Alex was gratified when Nick reached for his shoes and fixed the laces so they'd be easy to don. He even put out his clothes beside Alex's on the sofa. Wow. Was he actually having a positive influence on Nick? Would wonders never cease?

He stretched out beside Nick on the mattress in the dark, unsure of what to expect. They really needed to stay focused on Gray for now.

But that didn't mean he had to like it.

When this thing was over, there was going to be a lot less sleeping going on when the two of them lay side-by-side in a bed like this.

THE NEXT MORNING dawned gray and cold, with snow flurries swirling in the air. Nick left to fetch the rental car and swing by the tailor's to pick up his second suit.

While he was gone, Alex wiped down all the surfaces fingerprints could be lifted from and used a hand-held vacuum to pick up any stray hairs around the place. When Nick texted that he was three minutes out, Alex hoisted their bags and gear, carrying the lot downstairs.

He'd just stepped outside when Nick pulled up and double-parked. Alex loaded everything in the trunk of the car while a cabbie behind them yelled at him in colorful Russian. Amused at hearing Nick called an asshole with ears, he hopped in the passenger side.

Nick pulled away from the curb, grinning.

"You speak Russian?" Alex asked.

"No. Why?"

"I thought you were smiling at the things the cab driver was calling you."

"What did he say?"

"Never mind," Alex said.

Nick continued to smile as he guided the car onto the entrance ramp for a freeway that would take them north out of the city. "What are you so happy about over there?" Alex demanded. "Nobody likes driving in this congestion."

"We're going on our first road trip together."

"With a vicious killer on our tails."

"Details, schmetails," Nick said jovially.

Alex shook his head. "How long before he comes after us, do you think?"

"Oh, he's already after us. The question is, how soon will he find us?"

"What's your guess?"

"Depends on how many favors he calls in. I rented this car under a new alias that only got built for me a few weeks back. Gray won't attach it to me."

"How can you be sure of that?"

"Because the Medusas created it for me, and Gray doesn't have direct access to anyone who works with them. The military keeps the Medusas tightly compartmentalized and hidden away from regular Special Forces' teams."

"Why's that?"

Nick glanced over at him. "The fewer people who know the United States has women special operators, the more effective the Medusas are in the field."

"I can see that. If nobody's looking for women agents, they could move around freely without arousing suspicion."

"Exactly."

"How long have these women been around?" Alex asked, curious.

"No idea. You'd have to ask them."

"I'd love to meet them someday."

"Maybe you will. They're pretty sharp. More physical than you can believe and superbly trained. What they lack in brute strength, they make up for with smarts and teamwork. They're fun to run with."

The snow of the past few days had been cleared off the highway and was piled in black, half-melted piles along the shoulder of the road. It looked more like sludge than snow.

But as they cleared the urban sprawl of New York City and headed upstate, the snow piles became taller and whiter and the amount of snow coating the forests along the highway increased markedly.

The north-south line of mountains in the state of New York was divided roughly in half by the Mohawk River, which ran west to east. South of the Mohawk Valley were the Catskill Mountains, and north of the valley rose the Adirondacks. It was to those they headed.

Pleasant Falls lay roughly midway between Albany and Lake Placid, where the mountains started to get tall, and the snow became a thick blanket of white covering everything from trees to building roofs to parked cars.

It took them just under four hours to spot a sign pointing toward Pleasant Falls and Great Neck. As Nick turned west toward the town, on a two-lane road that wound up into the mountains, Alex looked around in delight. "There must be three feet of snow on the ground!"

"Let's hope the roads are plowed all the way to the place you've booked for us."

Alex grinned. "You're a big, strong guy. You can push the car while I sit inside and steer it."

"Hah! I'll steer and you can push!"

"How about we don't get stuck?" Alex suggested.

The road curved through thick forest. The black, bare-branched deciduous trees gave way to stands of fluffy evergreens wearing thick layers of snow that reminded Alex of extravagantly frosted cupcakes.

They crossed over a mountain pass, and the road began to wind down into a narrow valley with a town tucked into it. As they drove down Main Street, Alex looked around in glee.

"Look at all these Christmas decorations! I love this place!"

Nick said grumpily, "This is how I imagine the North Pole—or wherever Santa lives—must look. It's so cheerful and festive I could puke."

Alex laughed, his excitement undimmed by Nick's sour attitude. "Where's that whole going-on-a-road-trip enthusiasm, now? C'mon. Get into the spirit of the holidays. This place is adorable."

"I don't do adorable."

"You like puppies, don't you? Everyone likes puppies. And they're the most adorable things on earth. Or kittens. Or cute little kids. Also adorable. And then there are hand-knit sweaters. Homemade pies. Christmas cookies—"

"Enough already! If I promise to pretend to enjoy myself, will you stop talking about adorable things?" Nick said in what sounded like real desperation. "You sound like that song in the *Sound of Music* about favorite things."

"I love that song!"

Nick rolled his eyes. "Of course you do."

"I'll stop talking about adorable things if you'll give this place a chance to win you over."

"Oh God. You're going to make me drink hot chocolate with little marshmallows and peppermint sticks in it, aren't you?"

"You bet. And we're going Christmas shopping, and looking at lights, and maybe even going caroling."

"I do *not* sing," Nick said forcefully.

"You don't sing, *yet*."

"You're killing me, here."

"The inn should be just ahead, on the right," Alex said, smiling in spite of himself. They might be different in many ways, but they were alike in all the ways that counted. It was a little crazy how well they fit each other.

The quaint shops gave way to big, old Victorian houses. They were all beautifully restored, colorful and covered in elaborate gingerbread trim.

Alex exclaimed, "This place looks like a postcard!"

"Great. I always did want to die inside a smarmy greeting card," Nick grumbled.

Alex just laughed and didn't try to contain his delight over this town and truth be told, his delight at being here with Nick.

A sign announced that they'd arrived at the Pleasant Run Inn. Nick turned into the driveway, and Alex watched him closely for a reaction as the big white farmhouse with its wraparound porch and welcoming, casual air came into view.

Nick glanced over at him, looking startled. The expression in his eyes went softer than Alex had ever seen it.

"You picked this place for me, didn't you?" Nick murmured.

"I did."

"Fine. I admit it. This is perfect."

Alex shrugged modestly. "I figure if we're gonna die up here, we might as well enjoy ourselves first."

Nick snorted. "And on that optimistic note, the two idiots arrive at their destination."

Alex grinned. "Wait till you see the room I've reserved for us."

They walked inside, and an elderly woman greeted them with big hugs as if they were her long-lost grandkids. "I'm Jeanette Tucker, and you must be Nick and Alex. I'm so delighted you're here. Your room is ready. Goodness. Look at all those bags. We'd better take the elevator."

"This place has an elevator?" Alex asked.

"My great-grandfather was a close friend of Elisha Otis. He's the fellow who introduced elevators to New York City. Elisha and his wife had a summerhouse just down the street. Mr. Otis installed an elevator here when my great-grandmother had a stroke."

"Nice," Alex commented. It wasn't a huge elevator, and the three of them and their pile of bags had to take turns using it. But in a few minutes, they all had been duly deposited on the second floor in a wide, gracious hallway.

"The honeymoon suite is this way," Jeanette said, leading the way toward the back of the house. "It has a lovely view of the pond and the woods behind the house. It's very peaceful."

Nick's eyebrows all but disappeared in his hairline. Alex grinned at him unapologetically.

Jeanette asked, "How long have you two been married? Are you actually on your honeymoon?"

"What makes you think we're a couple?" Alex blurted, surprised.

"I see how you look at each other. And the way you stand close. It's as if there's a gravitational pull between you. Of course you're a couple. The love between you is plain as day to see. My Edgar and I had it, too."

Alex glanced over at Nick, startled. Nick looked about as disconcerted as him. But neither one of them contradicted her.

In minor shock, he carried his luggage and gear bag after the diminutive woman.

"How many rooms does this place have?" Nick asked, curious.

"I have four guest rooms. The house itself has seven bedrooms if you count the old servants' quarters on the fourth floor. But I use both of those rooms for storage nowadays."

"How many bathrooms?" Alex asked.

"Six. My husband added a few more when we converted this place to an inn so every room would have its own."

"This house is great," Nick said with what sounded like genuine admiration.

"It's too much for me to handle anymore. I really ought to sell it, but I can't bring myself to let go of all the memories."

Nick said gently, "Have you considered hiring a manager to run the place for you?"

She smiled sadly. "Young people nowadays don't want to live in a quiet little backwater like Pleasant Falls. I haven't had any luck finding someone who is interested in the slow pace of life around here, let alone in running an old inn for an old lady."

"I don't know," Nick said warmly. "I think this place is pretty wonderful."

"Do you have children? Grandchildren? Anyone you can leave the place to?" Alex asked.

"I have a daughter who lives in England—she married a doctor over there—and my son is a stockbroker. He lives in New York City and has no desire to come back here. They're good to me, but they have no interest in this old house. Both of them just see dollar signs when they look at it."

Alex ran his fingertips across the glossy surface of a beautiful console table. It looked like old mahogany inlaid with a lighter wood. Maybe maple. It was a gorgeous piece of furniture. In fact, everywhere he looked he saw beautiful antiques, lovingly cared for.

Jeanette opened the door at the end of the hall and threw it wide to reveal a large room with a king-size bed tucked off to the left. To the right, a huge riverstone fireplace rose to the ceiling. A sofa and a pair of chairs clustered in front of it.

"The fireplace burns wood," their hostess said. "There's a fire laid, and you can light it whenever you'd like. I only ask that you be sure to check that the screen is closed anytime you leave a fire unattended. There's plenty of wood in the bin there. Spare towels and blankets are in the armoire, and if you don't like the pillows, I have several different kinds in the hall closet. Let me know if there's anything else you need."

Nick said politely, "When is supper, Miss Jeanette?"

The elderly woman preened a little and then laughed warmly. She seemed to like the moniker. "I'll bet strapping young men like you are hungry all the time. The sideboard in the dining room always has snacks on it. Help yourselves anytime. Breakfast is from eight to ten a.m. every morning, and supper is served promptly at six o'clock. Don't be late, though, or there won't be any food left."

"Yes, ma'am," Nick replied, smiling broadly.

Alex also smiled. There was something truly wonderful about having a grandmotherly woman fussing over them like this. It felt like home. Or at least an idealized version of what he imagined a perfect home would feel like.

Now that he thought about it, his had always had a

vague sensed of strained politeness to it. Had that been about him being gay? Had his family really been that tense about it? At least Miss Jeanette didn't seem to be the least bit bothered by the fact.

The woman left and Alex went over to the window. The view of a frozen pond tucked in the trees was as bucolic as the rest of this place.

"The honeymoon suite?" Nick said from behind him.

"It was the only room available. And I figured it would have a big bed we would both fit in."

Nick looked askance at the king-size bed and back at him, his expression dire. "Do you think this is a good idea?"

"I don't think it's a terrible idea," he answered evenly. Although, given how heavily Nick was frowning at the moment, maybe he was wrong about that.

Nick just shook his head.

Alex didn't rise to the bait. They could argue about the sleeping-arrangement issue later. Right now, he wanted to go out and explore.

"I'm going out," Alex announced.

"Let me guess. You spotted some adorable boutique you just have to go check."

Alex answered dryly, "I was thinking more in terms of scoping out places to hide around town, ingress and egress points, good spots for shootouts, and places I don't want to get trapped in. And, of course, establishing our cover. But, sure. If you want to go shopping and check out the local boutiques, I'm up for that, too."

Nick snorted.

"Let me grab my coat," Alex said.

"You might want to grab a sidearm while you're at it," Nick remarked. "From here on out, we need to be ready at all times to get jumped."

"And there went all the joy. Sucked out of the room and replaced with a giant cloud of *bah-humbug*."

"Just keeping it real, man."

"Lighten up. We've got at least a few days to relax and enjoy this place before the boogeyman arrives. Weren't you telling me just last night that I have to learn to let down my hair a little?"

"What hair? You practically have a buzz cut going."

"Says the guy doing his best to imitate a caveman."

"Hah."

"Hah!"

Chapter Fifteen

No way was Nick going to admit to Alex how much he was enjoying walking around Pleasant Falls. The long street through town was lined with dozens of little stores, each one more interesting and adorable than the next. He wasn't much of a shopper, but he got a kick out of watching Alex browse through the eclectic mix of décor, clothes, crafts and tchotchkes being offered for sale.

He was still reeling from Jeanette's declaration that he and Alex loved each other. Did they? Surely not. Except…

Except he felt wildly protective of Alex. And if he stopped to admit it to himself, he felt an underlying panic at the idea of Alex dying at the hands of Gray and his thugs. Was it weird that he didn't much care about dying himself if Alex just made it out of the coming confrontation alive? Was that love?

Or maybe love was the random flashes of the future he and Alex could have together. They could settle down in a place exactly like this. Take over running an inn exactly like Jeanette's. They could have a few kids, fill that big house with laughter, family and friends.

A family of his own. He hardly dared think of it. And certainly not with the threat of Gray hanging over him and Alex. But still. The idea would not get out of his head. Was Jeanette right? Had he found a man he could achieve all his most closely held dreams with? The same dreams whose existence he barely admitted to, even to himself?

The SEALs had always been his family. The guys in his platoon had been like brothers to him, and the married guys' wives had adopted him and the other single guys, inviting them over for home-cooked meals and holiday get-togethers. Sure, it had been fun, but it hadn't been the same as having a family of his own. One with real love, who would be there for him through thick and thin.

Alex found a handmade stuffed toy for his niece, and his whole face lit up at the cute pink lemur. "Natalie's going to love this. She's bonkers for lemurs."

"Aren't lemurs black-and-white?" Nick asked doubtfully.

"This is a magic lemur," Alex said stoutly. He smiled down at the soft toy fondly, and Nick's gut twisted. How nice would it be to have someone look at him like that?

Correction: How nice would it be to have Alex look at him like that?

The thought shocked him. It was just that big old farmhouse playing tricks with his head. It was so identical to the one he pictured retiring in that it was making him think about starting his own family. And Alex just happened to be here with him, staying in the charming inn with him, chattering on about his family, telling stories about funny gifts he and his siblings had gotten for one another over the years.

Still. Jeanette had sounded so sure of herself when she'd declared them to be in love.

It was a Sunday afternoon, and the sidewalks were

crowded. As they approached the middle of town and the big town square, families were gathering there in anticipation of some event.

Alex asked a shopkeeper, "What's going on outside?"

"The annual snowball fight is about to get started. You should go join in. It's great fun."

Alex looked over at him with such excitement and hope in his eyes that Nick couldn't resist. He grumbled, "Okay, fine. I'm in. Let's go."

The shopkeeper said helpfully, "You can leave your shopping bags here if you'd like. I'll keep an eye on them for you."

They deposited Alex's bags with the woman and headed outside.

As they stepped into the large, open space, a man with a bullhorn shouted, "Pick your sides, folks, and start making ammunition. Same rules as always. Snowballs must be made only of snow. Don't throw them hard at children, and for you adult kids, if any child under the age of six hits you with one, you are required to execute your best dramatic death fall. As soon as the kiddo laughs, you are allowed to get back up and rejoin the fight. When you get tired of the fun, back up and move to stand on the sidewalk around the square. People who've removed themselves from the fight are off-limits as targets. Of course, if you're on the sidewalk, it's still up to you to dodge errant snowballs. The contest continues until there's no more snow, or until everyone is on the sidewalk."

"Death falls?" Nick muttered to Alex.

"I can't wait to see yours," Alex said back, grinning. "Personally, I'm planning to clutch my chest, spin around, stagger a little, and then splat face-first in a drift."

Nick grinned. "To see that, I might just nail you with a friendly fire snowball."

"You're not under the age of six," Alex retorted.

"If I act like a five-year-old, will you still die for me?"

Alex rolled his eyes. "That's it. I'm finding some little kid, picking him up and carrying him over to ambush you. Prepare to die, Kane."

"You wish, Creed."

And that was how they ended up on opposite sides of the snowball fight, running around like maniacs, picking up little kids under the armpits and chasing each other around the town square while the kids laughed hysterically and clobbered Nick and Alex with packed snow from a range of about two feet.

The pratfalls were epic, and he and Alex were covered in white by the end of the snowball fight. It stuck to their coats and pants. Their wool gloves were soaking wet and caked in snow, even their hair stuck up in wet spikes thick with the stuff. Alex's scarf looked like a white rope draped over his shoulders, and Nick was pretty sure his boots were both filled with snow.

The fight ended and a mighty cheer went up from all the participants. Nick found Alex, who threw an arm around his waist and dragged him close for a laughing kiss. Their lips were icy cold, but the heat between them changed that fast.

"Thanks for playing with me," Alex murmured against his mouth.

"That was fun."

"I love seeing you laugh," Alex admitted, leaning back to look up at him, his eyes shining.

"Ditto, Creed. Ditto."

"Really? Ditto? That's all you've got? My dude, you need to seriously up your romantic banter game."

"How about this? I can't wait to get you back to that giant bed in our room, get naked and kiss you again."

Alex gulped. He *never* gulped. Last time he could remember gulping, he was about fourteen years old and his first crush had just admitted to having a crush on him, too.

Very belatedly, he mumbled, "Well, okay then. That's better, Kane."

Nick grinned and threw his arm across Alex's shoulder as they headed off the snowball battlefield.

They headed toward the store where they'd stashed Alex's bags, but before they got to it, they encountered a food cart selling hot chocolate and soft pretzels. Nick groaned.

"There's no escaping my holiday cheer," Alex declared. "Deal with it."

They bought steaming cups of hot chocolate and sipped at them as they strolled toward the store. The salty pretzels were the perfect counterpart to the sweetness of the drink. They finished the snack and threw away their cups.

"Admit it. That was tasty," Alex said.

"It was."

"Are you willing to admit that you're having fun getting into the holiday spirit?"

"As long as you don't make me sing, I will so stipulate."

Alex grinned at him and ducked into the store to get his bags. As he came back out onto the sidewalk, Nick asked, "What's next in our holiday tour of Christmas spirit?"

"The shopkeeper told me there's a terrific diner

the table and laid his hand on top of Nick's scarred, callused hand. He said simply, "I'll fight for you, too."

And there it was. Exactly what Jeanette had seen between them. The irresistible pull, like gravity between two suns orbiting each other. Nick felt it all the way down to his bones. This man was the one.

But he had no idea whatsoever what to do about it.

Was he supposed to say something about it to Alex? Wait for Alex to come to the same conclusion and say something about it to him? Was it a mutual thing? What if Alex didn't feel the same way?

And that was what silenced him. He couldn't bear the idea of baring his soul to Alex and having the man say something awkward like "thank you" or "the timing isn't right for me."

Distracted, he let Alex pay for the meal after extracting a promise from him that Nick would get the next one.

Alex picked up the check and slid out of the booth, grinning. "You do realize we're both on expense accounts from the same government agency, right?"

Nick shrugged. "It's the principle of the thing."

"You're going to want your own checking account even when you're married, aren't you?" Alex tossed out.

Nick stared at Alex's back for a moment before lurching into motion to follow him toward the cash register. Him? Married? A joint checking account? That was possibly the most domestic thing he'd ever heard of. But having thought about it, now it sounded like the most wonderful thing on earth. He absolutely wanted a joint checking account.

What the hell had happened to him? One sweet old lady declared him in love, and the solitary man he'd known and lived inside his head with for his entire life had done an abrupt about-face on everything he'd ever believed having to do with love and relationships.

"C'mon. There's a crowd gathered around the tree at the edge of the square," Alex said eagerly.

Nick allowed himself to be dragged along by the hand, enjoying Alex's unbridled excitement indulgently. What would the people around them think if they knew one of the most lethal men on the planet was beside them, grinning like a little kid as the Christmas tree lights flashed on and sparkled like stars captured in a tree's branches?

A group of men, women and children stepped up beside the tree and began singing "We Wish You a Merry Christmas."

People around them joined in, and before long, most of the crowd was belting out holiday classics.

Nick caved when "Silent Night" started up, singing the solemn carol quietly beside Alex. He reached out to take Alex's hand in his, and they stood there, shoulder to shoulder in the crowd, their voices rising in harmony toward the black sky sprinkled with stars that matched the tree before them.

It was a magical moment.

When the song ended, everyone was quiet for a few breathless seconds, absorbing the beauty of it all.

And then the carolers burst into "Jingle Bells," and the spell was broken.

Nick knew he had a problem. His holiday-hater's heart had done the whole redeemed-Grinch thing and grown several sizes inside his chest today. He loved being here with Alex. He loved all the schlocky Christmas stuff around him. And he loved Alex.

He was *so* screwed.

Chapter Sixteen

Alex smiled over at Nick as the crowd around them began to disperse. No doubt about it—he loved everything about this town and all its silly, romantic holiday rituals. Someday. Someday he would live in a place just like this, heck, maybe this place. And he would immerse himself in family, friendship and every ridiculous, wonderful town tradition.

"A dog," he declared suddenly. "I want a dog."

"Right now?" Nick blurted, sounding surprised.

"No. When I retire and move here."

"What kind of dog?"

"A big friendly one."

"Like a golden retriever?" Nick asked.

"Maybe. But with all this snow, maybe a husky?"

"They're pretty high-maintenance."

Alex shrugged. "What else am I going to have to do with my time besides pamper a high-maintenance dog?"

"Maybe pamper your high-maintenance partner?" Nick suggested.

Alex grinned. "I'll have time for both."

Nick said thoughtfully, "I could see you with a dog. You were great with those kids in the snowball fight."

"So were you!" he exclaimed. Truth be told, he was more than a little surprised at how natural Nick had been, scooping up little kids and chasing him around the town square with them. He would never forget the unfettered joy on Nick's face. It had transformed him from someone dark and dangerous to a much younger, lighter version of himself.

He made a mental note to get Nick to laugh much more often.

Nick said low, "How about we return your gifts to the inn and then go out and do a little reconnaissance?"

"What did you have in mind?"

"Maybe finding wherever Gray has the rest of the crèche stored?"

Alex sighed. Today had been a delightful interlude, but real life called. It was time to buckle down and get back to work. "You're right. The faster we find it, the sooner we can set up surveillance on it."

Nick shrugged. "Actually, I was thinking about stealing it."

"I beg your pardon?"

"Can you think of a better way to infuriate Gray and throw him off-balance?"

Alex stared. "It's bold. Are you sure you want him enraged when he comes for us?"

Nick shrugged. "He's brilliant and calculating when he's calm. I figure he can't be any scarier when he's so mad he can't see straight."

"Have you ever seen him mad?" Alex asked, surprised. Men like them tended to be icy-cold operators when the chips were down.

"No. I haven't. That's why I think it might be an interesting gambit to infuriate him."

Alex nodded. "I like it. Let's go find that crèche and liberate it."

They had the latitude and longitude coordinates from

Gray's man's phone, and it turned out to correspond to a fenced lot full of storage units. The trick would be figuring which one the crèche was in.

"What do you say we set up a hide in those trees above and behind the lot?" Alex suggested.

Nick nodded. "Should we take turns pulling shifts around the clock, or should we both stay here?"

"Let's spend a few hours here together and get a feel for the flow of traffic, and then we can decide."

Nick nodded. He pulled his field knife out of its ankle sheath and commenced hacking at low-hanging pine boughs on trees around them. Alex gathered the cut branches and poked their larger ends into the ground at an angle. The needled boughs all leaned inward, tent-like. When they lay down on the evergreens, they would act like springs and help hold them up off the cold ground slightly. When they'd built up a thick layer, they spread a heavy plastic tarp Alex fetched from the trunk of their car on top.

Alex gestured for Nick to crawl under the low, bushy tree where he'd built the hide. He followed Nick into the cave-like space. It took a little wiggling around and moving branches that were poking him, but before long, he'd settled comfortably on his stomach next to Nick under an insulated tarp.

Nick passed him a set of binoculars, and he scanned the storage lot below. The place was still and deserted.

Alex murmured, "Do you suppose Gray's man stops by to check the unit on a regular basis? Or does he just stand off like us and keep watch over it from a distance?"

"Given the value of the crèche, I'm betting Gray's guy is paranoid as hell about losing it. He'll check it at least once a day, if not more often. Gray's not the kind of man to be forgiving if you lose his billion-dollar retirement plan."

Alex murmured, "I'll bet he varies up the times of day he checks, it, too."

"If we're lucky, he'll check the storage unit after hours, when nobody's around to see him come and go."

"It's what I would do."

"Let's hope you're right," Nick said low.

They settled into silence, waiting patiently for their quarry to show himself. Alex noted that vehicle traffic along the road in front of the storage lot was light and getting lighter as the evening aged. This was the kind of place where everyone went home and was tucked into bed at a reasonable hour.

After about an hour, Nick murmured, "You do realize we could be back at the inn, sitting in front of a nice fire and relaxing, instead of sitting out here, freezing our…toes…off."

Alex laughed ruefully under his breath. "Don't remind me. Those are the sorts of thoughts I try not to have when I'm on a job and trying not to think about how cold my…toes…are."

Nick's shoulder nudged his fondly, and he nudged back. It was nice being out here together, sharing the misery. The companionship did make the time pass faster and, if nothing else, kept him a little warmer.

A few minutes after ten o'clock, a pickup truck slowed on the road and turned off its headlights. Alex's attention riveted on the vehicle. It rolled into the drive and approached the security gate of the storage lot. He felt Nick go utterly relaxed beside him as if he would melt into the ground. He, too, went perfectly still, becoming one with his binoculars, which he trained on the truck as it pulled into the lot, its lights still off.

The truck drove between rows of storage units and stopped in front of one in the middle. A man climbed out of the truck and lifted the combination lock securing the unit.

Alex strained to see the numbers the guy dialed in. He thought the first number was a few numbers above zero. The second number was approximately halfway around the dial, and the last was maybe ten digits to the right of the second one. It wasn't a lot to go on, but it was better than nothing by a long shot. And maybe Nick had seen more detail. Not that he was going to break silence to ask him right now.

The man removed the lock from the hasp and pushed the door up. The metallic noise was loud in the crystalline silence of the night. He disappeared inside the unit.

Alex started counting in his head. *One potato. Two potato. Three potato...*

The guy came outside in under a minute. Sloppy. Alex doubted he'd even checked nails, bolts, locks or whatever it was that secured the crate.

The man closed and secured the door and climbed into his truck. He drove through the gate, turned on his lights, steered onto the road and drove off.

"Did you recognize him?" Alex asked quietly.

"No."

"Do you think it was one of Gray's guys?"

"Who else would go into a unit, carry nothing in, take nothing out and leave that fast?"

"Fair point."

"I caught the first number of the combination, but then his arm moved, and I didn't see the rest," Nick said.

"Perfect. I got a good idea of how the latter numbers related to the first number, but didn't see the first one specifically."

"Cool. Wanna go break in and have a look inside that unit?" Nick asked.

Alex's gaze narrowed thoughtfully. "I do. But did you notice how cursory his inspection of the crate was?"

"Well, yeah. He was inside about sixty seconds total. Why?"

Alex asked, "What if we steal the crèche?"

"You're sure you're okay with that? It's one thing to talk about it. It's another thing altogether to commit a felony, Mr. Law-and-Order."

"We could return them to their rightful owners. Then it would be repatriation, not theft."

"To the government of Iran?" Nick asked doubtfully.

"Okay, so maybe we should give them to the Smithsonian instead."

Nick nodded briskly in agreement. "Do you want to let Gray know we've stolen his toys, or do you want to let him think the statues are still in the storage unit?"

"I could go either way on that. If we make the theft obvious, he'll show up here within a few hours of the next check on the statues. Can we be ready to take on Gray and his whole team that quickly?"

Nick scrunched up his face. "We could use some reinforcements before we tangle with Gray's entire team."

"We could wait to steal the statues until we're ready to pull the trigger," Alex said reasonably.

Nick glanced down at the quiet storage units. "Thing is, Gray's gotta be spooked. He knows we tracked his car. We hospitalized one of his guys and demolished three more of them in a fight. We shot at him in the alley. It's possible he'll move the crèche without warning. I say we go in now, take the statues but hide the theft. Then we finish getting ready for a shootout at the OK Corral."

Alex nodded. "It's an aggressive plan. I doubt Gray will see it coming. He's got to be used to everyone being scared stiff of him."

"He is."

"The gear bag in the trunk of the car has wire cutters in it. I'll start snipping through the back fence while you rewire the security system."

Nick pushed to his feet and held a hand down to Alex. He took the proffered hand and rose to his full height in front of Nick, their fists clasped between them.

"In case we die in the next twenty-four hours, I've really enjoyed working with you," Alex murmured. "You're a good man."

Nick stared at him in the thick shadows, but even with his night vision fully adjusted, Alex couldn't make out the expression in his eyes.

"Is that all?" Nick said low, his voice rough.

"Is what all?"

"Is that all you feel for me? Professional respect?"

He stared back at Nick. Was he ready to make a grand declaration of his feelings for this man? In the middle of a mission that was about to go red-hot? It was a terrible idea. They both needed to focus intensely on the fight to come.

"Hell no, that's not all I feel for you," Alex blurted.

"Care to elaborate on that?" Nick said gruffly.

"Not here. Not now, when we've got a job to do."

"Then, when?"

In desperation, Alex answered, "When we get back to the inn."

"I'm holding you to that."

His stomach leaped and twisted nervously. Did he even know how he felt about Nick? Did he have the words to express it, not to mention the courage? What if Nick didn't feel the same way? Would Nick do what Alex's family had done and say all the right things, smile politely and then stab him in the back?

It would kill him if Nick betrayed him. He hadn't felt this way about any man, ever. If he had stripped down naked and rolled around in the snow, he couldn't feel any more exposed. His entire being felt raw. Hypersensitized. Every tiny snowflake that hit his face felt like a needle piercing his skin. Every whiff of breeze felt like a knife slicing through him.

"Well, are you coming or not?" Nick said from a few yards away.

He lurched into motion, following Nick toward where their car was hidden, a hundred feet down the road, behind some bushes. Operating mechanically, he obscured their footprints, being sure that no compressed tracks were left under the layer of snow he swept over their path.

Nick popped open the trunk and unzipped the gear bag. Alex took the handgun Nick passed him, checked the safety, cleared the chamber, popped in a magazine of ammunition and slipped the weapon in the pocket of his coat.

He took the wire cutters as Nick murmured, "I'll meet you at the unit when I'm done disabling the alarm."

Alex pressed the earbud more securely into his ear. "Let me know if you run into any problems."

"Will do."

They headed out to perform their respective tasks.

Alex found a likely spot in the fence, hidden from the front of the lot by a row of storage units. He wished he had a big set of cutters with handles as long as his arm. He would be through this barrier in a matter of seconds.

As it was, he had to use both hands to cut through each wire, and it was a painful and tedious process.

He finally rolled back a three-foot-wide by two-foot-tall section of the hurricane fencing and secured it with a length of trip wire.

He lay down on his belly and eased through the gap, being careful not to catch his clothing on any of the sharp ends of the cut wire. He made his way to the correct row and ran down it on the balls of his feet, being careful to hug the building and move only on the bare concrete under the small overhang.

When he reached the unit, he commenced checking the cheap aluminum garage door for alarms. Gray's man hadn't disabled anything from the outside before entering the space, and he'd been inside such a short time Alex doubted he had fiddled with an interior electronic alarm. But there were still plenty of low-tech ways to trap a space to tell if anyone had been in there.

He checked all around the perimeter of the door for hairs or pieces of tape tucked in an inconspicuous place, near a hinge or down near the ground.

The door was clean.

Surely Gray's men weren't that sloppy.

Although, if the guy had been coming here once or twice a day for months and never had a problem, maybe he really had gotten that complacent. Alex mentally tsked. The spotlights at each end of the row abruptly went dark.

Thank you, Nick.

He pressed his ear to the door to listen for any beeps warning of a power interruption to a security system.

All was quiet.

Had Gray really parked upward of a billion dollars'

worth of art in a storage unit with no additional protections on it whatsoever?

Maybe that was the point. By not placing any security here at all, Gray was relying on the sheer obscurity of this place and the lack of attention being drawn to it to protect the crèche.

He had to give the man credit for being ballsy. Seriously so.

Satisfied the door wasn't trapped, he pulled out a two-inch-long Cyalume stick and bent it sharply to break the tiny glass divider inside. As the chemicals at each end of the tube mixed, it commenced glowing lime green. He popped the stick into his mouth.

Then he lifted the combination lock and opened his mouth just enough to see the numbers on its face. He tried to release it a few times, with no success.

He said low, "What's the first number?"

"Six. I'll be there in two."

That should give him just enough time to get this lock opened. He dialed in a six and then turned the dial about halfway to the number thirty. He did a full revolution and then stopped at the number forty. He gave a tug. No joy.

He tried again. Six. Thirty-six. Forty-six.

Six. Thirty-eight. Forty-eight.

Click.

Chapter Seventeen

Nick closed the electrical box. It had been a trick to bypass the security system without cutting any wires. But when they were finished here tonight, he needed to reactivate the system and leave no one the wiser that he and Alex had broken in.

He slipped outside the office, eyeing the patch of snow between him and the storage units. He mapped a path using existing footprints and tire tracks and carefully picked his way across. When he reached the units, he slipped under the eaves where there was no snow and ran down the row to the dark shadow standing in front of Gray's unit.

"Any security on the garage door?" he asked Alex.

"None. And I have the lock open."

"Nice."

Alex said low, "Egress point is at the end of the next row. Turn left and go about twenty feet. It's at ground level and tied open."

"Roger that. I'll take the right side. You take the left."

Alex nodded in understanding and reached for the door handle down near the ground. "Ready?"

Nick nodded. "Ready."

Alex slid up the door. The sound was deafening, but there was no help for the metal-on-metal screech.

Nick slipped inside fast, shining his flashlight on the wall just inside the door. Nothing but cinder block. He flashed the light around the small space. He saw no sign of any alarm in here. On the off chance that there might be a microphone hidden in here, he hand-signaled an all clear to Alex, who gave back the same gesture.

Alex pulled out a handheld device and methodically swept it up and down over the walls, looking for electronic signals of any kind. An audio bug, a camera, a radio communication—even the slightest electrical current would register on Alex's meter.

Just in case, Nick took up a position in the doorway, weapon drawn, waiting for any response to the sound of the door opening. He scanned up and down the narrow alley. All was still and quiet.

"Clear," Alex said low from behind him.

Nick eased inside the unit and pulled the door down behind him. "Seriously? He's got no security at all around this stuff?"

Alex replied, "I think that's the point. He's relying on the utter lack of protection to protect it."

"Let's have a look at the crate, then."

It was some six feet long and four feet high. It was perhaps three feet deep from front to back. *At last.* He'd finally found the thing that his team had stolen all those months ago. Raging curiosity to look inside tore through him.

Alex had already run his nifty meter all over the crate, but Nick did a visual inspection now, looking for wires, sensor pads, even tiny strips of foil between the lid and sides to indicate that the thing was trapped in any way.

"Do you see anything?" Alex asked from behind the crate.

"Not a darned thing. And that's freaking me out a little," Nick confessed.

"Me, too. Still. We've got to open it sometime."

"Maybe you should go stand by the door, just to be safe," Nick suggested.

"We're in this together. If you go down, I'm going down with you," Alex replied with an intensity that sent little shivers of delight down Nick's spine.

"Here goes." He reached for the hasp on the trunk and pulled it open. He lifted the lid a millimeter and propped the lid there by resting it on the tips of two ballpoint pens. He inspected the narrow opening, using his flashlight to look for anything attached to the inside of the lid or hinges.

"I can't believe I'm saying this, but it's all clear."

Alex nodded. "Then, let's open this sucker all the way."

Together, they lifted the heavy lid. Alex opened his mouth and dim green light illuminated the interior of the crate. Inside were dozens of individual cartons tucked into wooden packing shavings.

The boxes looked mostly made of wood, but as he took a closer look, they were elaborately decorated. Some were inlaid with precious metals. Others were crusted with jewels. Some were blackened with age, while others sparkled in the Cyalume lighting.

"Shall we open one?" Alex asked.

"Sure. You pick."

Alex reached for the nearest box and pulled it out carefully. He set it on the floor in front of the crate, and he and Nick knelt in front of it. The thing was flattish and square, only about a foot tall but twice that wide. Alex lifted the lid, and a magnificent gold statue of a man lay in a satin nest before them. The man had a long beard and carried a tall staff with a shepherd's hook atop it. His robes were covered in jewels that formed an elaborate swirling pattern all over the garment.

"I'm guessing another Wise Man," Alex murmured.

"Do we want to take the whole nine yards or just the statues?" Nick murmured.

Alex glanced up at him. "I'm thinking just the statues. The storage boxes are probably where the bulk of the weight comes from. I tried to lift the corner of the crate when I was checking it out, and I don't think the two of us could carry the whole thing out of here."

Nick nodded. "Besides, if Gray's man opens the crate to look inside, we'll want him to see everything where it belongs. I doubt Gray's guy routinely opens anything to actually check on the statues."

"We're going to have to get their cases back in the places they came from, though," Alex said. To that end, Nick watched him snap several quick photos of the interior of the large crate. Good idea. They'd have pictures to check their replaced storage boxes against.

"Let's do this in an orderly fashion," Nick murmured.

"Right. I'll pass the top layer of cartons out, and we can lay them on the floor exactly as they were packed inside the box. We can do that with each layer of cases until we reach the bottom of the crate."

Working together, it didn't take them long to unload the entire thing. In all, there were forty-two smaller boxes inside the larger crate.

Nick looked over at Alex. "Okay. Are you ready to see what the birth of Christ really looked like?"

Alex's chest rose in a visible deep breath. "Let's do this."

They started with the top layer, opening each box carefully and lifting out the statue inside. Working quickly, Alex passed them to him one at a time and then used a knife to cut out some or all of the padding inside. In most of the cases, silk fabric lined the box, and Nick took both statue and raggedly cut length of silk from Alex. Gently, Nick wrapped each figurine and then tucked it into one of the two large storage sacks he'd brought along.

Nick tried not to gawk at each statue as Alex handed it to him, but it was hard not to. Most of them were fully as exquisite as the golden horse and rider that had been auctioned off.

As they reached the final and bottom layer of boxes, though, the quality of the workmanship became less refined, the materials less gaudy. These must be the very first pieces added to the crèche. They'd probably been made by the mystics of the order that originally owned the crèche, and not by wealthy Persian kings.

Alex reached for the last box. It was larger than all the others and made of blackened, cracked wood. It had simple iron bands around it instead of gold and jewels. "I'll bet this is it," he breathed.

Nick glanced up sharply from stowing the previous statue. "You mean the original pieces? The ones carved by the Magi?"

Alex nodded. "We should open this one together."

Nick moved over to kneel beside him. "I've never been a religious man, but I'm nervous."

"I know. Right?"

The hinges on the box were made of leather nailed into the back of the case and the back of the lid. It had undoubtedly been replaced over the centuries, for it was in reasonably good shape. Still, he and Alex lifted the lid with exceeding care.

The first thing he saw were bits of straw, turned gray

with age and brittle. Very gently, Alex scooped aside the gray straw to reveal rough fabric that looked fully two thousand years old. It, too, was gray with age and looked fragile.

"I think that's linen," Alex said breathlessly.

"That would track with biblical fabrics, wouldn't it?" Nick replied in a hush.

"Uh-huh."

"Go ahead. Unfold it." He watched with rapt attention as Alex very gently lifted a fold of the fabric. Another fold. One final fold.

Nick stared down. There, nested in more ancient straw, was the Nativity. The first and only *original* Nativity.

"Wow," Alex breathed.

Wow, indeed. The Nativity was carved from wood, the individual figures smaller than he'd expected. A sheep was probably three inches tall, a donkey maybe four inches tall. A bearded man of middle age, wearing a plain robe, was no more than six inches tall. But the detail was incredible. His face looked weary. Worried. But also protective.

"Is that Joseph?" Nick asked, reaching out reverently to point at the figure.

"I think so. Will you look at Mary? She almost seems alive."

Nick looked at the figure on the opposite end of the crate, a young woman carved in the same incredible detail as Joseph. He said in awe, "She looks so young."

"And tired. Like a new mother," Alex added in wonder.

At last, Nick let his gaze slide to the baby in the center of the box. Something profound moved within him.

This depiction of Christ had been made by a man who'd actually gazed on the human face of the Baby Jesus.

The figure of the infant was tiny. Wrapped in a bit of frayed, decaying linen and tucked into one end of a long, low box. The rest of the box held what looked like ancient hay. It was mostly crumbled to dust, but bits of the stalks remained and formed a small pile below where the baby lay.

"The manger doesn't have any legs," Alex said. "It's more like a watering trough."

"Weren't mangers used to feed animals? I should think it would look like a feed trough."

Alex shrugged. "My parents' nativity scene had a little cross-legged thing about the size of a bassinet that depicted the manger. Our Baby Jesus fit in it just about right."

"Welp. Future nativities are going to have to change that," Nick said with light humor.

"I'm afraid to touch the figures," Alex said low. "They're too holy for a guy like me to handle."

He knew the feeling. "Maybe we should just take the whole box. It was packed at the very bottom of the crate. If we put all the other boxes back, we should be able to disguise its absence."

Alex nodded and carefully closed the lid. Nick lifted the heavy wooden box, which weighed a good forty pounds, and carried it over to the sacks. He moved all the other statues over to the second bag, clearing the first just to carry this priceless treasure.

"All right," Alex said briskly. "Let's repack this puppy."

They commenced the challenging job of replacing all the storage containers, now empty, back in their original positions. There was a bit of trouble when they realized they would have to put something else in place of the large nativity box to hold up the ones that had been resting upon it. They experimented with various bits from their gear bag until they hit upon standing both of the binocular cases upright in the bottom of the crate and placing a clipboard across them. The improvised platform was just the right height and strong enough to take the weight of the next layer of storage boxes.

After that, the work of repacking the crate went quickly. They closed the container and headed for the door. Alex bent down to lift it and froze, his hand on the handle by the floor.

"What?" Nick asked quickly.

"Powder. There's powder on the floor, and our footprints are all over the place."

Nick looked down in shock. It was an old spy trick and as simple as they came. On one's way out of a room, a spy sprinkled a fine layer of something like baby powder on the floor and then checked later to see if it had been disturbed.

Alex moved quickly to the back of the unit and dropped to his knees, where he commenced using his neck scarf to wipe the floor clean. Nick left the bags of figures by the door and joined him, unwinding his own scarf and wiping down the faint footprints they'd left all over the floor in the baby powder.

When they'd wiped their way over to the garage door, Alex carefully wiped off the bottoms of his boots while Nick rummaged in various coat pockets until he found a small container of white styptic powder. It was a coagulant sprinkled on superficial wounds to stop them from bleeding. It was the closest thing they had to baby powder.

He watched as Alex worked carefully, sprinkling

a fine layer of the stuff across the floor. Because they hadn't noticed it when they came in, they had no way of knowing where or how much baby powder Gray's man had put down before he'd left the unit the last time. They would just have to hope they got it close enough to the same that the guy didn't notice any discrepancies.

As Alex reached him by the door, Nick pulled the metal panel up about halfway, and they slipped underneath it.

"You get out of here. I'll meet you at the car after I reset the office alarm," Nick murmured.

Alex nodded and took off, cradling the bag with the original Magi Crèche against his chest. Nick headed for the office with the other sack.

It didn't take him long to reactivate the alarm system. As soon as the lights blinked on outside, he sprinted down the row of storage units, turned left and ran hard for the fence, searching as he went for a low hole.

There.

He screeched to halt on his knees and pushed the bulky bag through the hole. Dang it. The bag caught on a wire. He fought grimly to untangle the canvas from a protruding wire. *C'mon, c'mon, c'mon.*

He heard a car approaching on the road. Dammit. It was slowing down. He glanced over his shoulder. It was turning into the parking lot, and its lights were off.

Not good.

Reactivating the alarm had sent a signal to someone that there had been a power interruption.

The bag finally popped free. He shoved it the rest of the way through the fence and crawled frantically after it. His hips had barely cleared the hole when he rolled over on his back, yanked his legs clear and untied the section of fencing. He shoved it down, tucking the edge into the snow. Working fast, he used the length of wire Alex had tied it up with to fasten it down. It didn't want to lie flat, but he had no more time to fix it. A man was getting out of his car and walking toward the office.

Please don't find any evidence of my work and warn Gray.

Nick low-crawled away from the fence, into the woods, pulling himself along on his elbows and taking freezing facefuls of snow that went down the collar of his coat and melted on his chest. He stopped periodically to use a tree branch to mess up his tracks in the snow. He couldn't hide that some critter had come through here, but he could hide the fact that it had been a human.

Finally, the storage lot disappeared into the trees behind him. He pushed upright, slung the bag over his shoulder and took off running through the forest, paralleling the road.

He ought to be about to where the car was hidden, now. He swerved down the steep hillside and charged toward the road as he heard a siren wail in the distance. Crap. They had to get clear of here before the police arrived.

He burst out of the trees practically on top of the hood of the car. He rolled around the side of it and threw open the passenger door. He jumped in and Alex pulled onto the road before he even had his door all the way shut. He turned around and lifted the big bag into the back seat, setting it down as gently as he could as the car jerked and righted itself.

"Sit down," Alex bit out. "Here they come."

Nick slammed his butt in the seat and dragged the seatbelt across his chest as Alex rounded a bend in the road. A police cruiser raced past them in the opposite direction.

"Silent alarm?" Alex bit out.

"I think the return of power sent some sort of message to the owner of the storage lot that there'd been a power outage. I'm guessing he and the cop will walk up and down the rows of units, make sure nothing is out of place and go back to bed."

"I hope you're right. Otherwise, this town just became a very bad place for us to be."

Nick looked over at Alex's profile, lit in the dim glow from the dashboard. "I expect Gray to come soon. Very soon."

Chapter Eighteen

It took all of Alex's considerable discipline to keep the car down to the speed limit and drive sedately back to the inn. He parked in front of the rambling house and glanced over at Nick. "We've got to keep up appearances for now. And we have to find a place well away from all these civilians to confront Gray."

Nick nodded, his eyes more worried than Alex had ever seen them. "For now, let's just get back to the room without arousing Jeanette's suspicion. She's a sharp lady."

"Leave the crèche here or take it with us?" Alex bit out.

"Leave it. She would ask what was in the bags."

He nodded and climbed out of the car. He took a hard look around the front yard for anything out of the ordinary. All was quiet.

A small lamp glowed in the foyer, and they moved swiftly up the stairs and down the hall to their room.

Alex opened their door quietly and they slipped inside. Only when it had closed behind Nick did Alex let out his breath. They'd done it. They'd stolen the Magi Crèche from Harlan Gray.

Nick paced a lap around the room and ended up stopping in front of the fireplace to light the fire already laid there. Alex joined him, sinking down on the sofa in front of the hearth.

Nick finished tending the fledgling flames and joined him on the couch.

"Now what?" Alex asked.

"Now we have a lot to do quickly. We need to get more firepower, and I'm telling you, we need to call in reinforcements."

"We also need to find a place away from Pleasant Falls and figure out how to draw Gray to it. I don't want a giant shootout in the middle of this nice little town."

Nick nodded grimly. "I'm thinking a place up in the woods would be good. With lots of cover. Remote. Hard to get to."

"I saw a pair of snowmobiles in Jeanette's garage earlier. If those work, maybe we could borrow them. Scout out a good place," Alex suggested.

Nick pulled out his cell phone and Alex said in quick alarm, "Who are you calling?"

"The Medusas."

"You think they'll give us support?"

"I know they will." When he disconnected the call, Nick said merely, "They're coming."

The fire popped loudly just then, and Alex jumped. Nick grinned. "A little tense, are you? Does that mean you're finally taking the threat of Gray seriously?"

Alex huffed. "I've always taken him seriously. I'm just a little on edge after stealing a priceless holy relic."

"We liberated it and will make sure it gets into the right hands. We didn't steal anything. We have no intention of keeping it for ourselves and no plan to profit off of it."

Alex shrugged, conceding the point.

"Any chance you would consider calling in a few more fixers like yourself to help us out?" Nick asked.

"You really are terrified of Gray, aren't you?"

It was Nick's turn to huff. "Yeah. What of it?"

"Okay. If you're that scared, I'll call for my own backup." Alex took out his cell and dialed a phone number he'd only used a handful of times in his entire career. It was an emergency contact who would immediately relay his requirement for life-or-death assistance to the appropriate people in his chain of command. He said the code phrase to indicate he needed the whole cavalry to come to the rescue, and the woman at the other end dispassionately replied that she had received his message. But despite her apparent disinterest, he knew it would cause a flurry of panicked activity back at headquarters.

"Who will they send to help you?" Nick asked, curious.

"Guys from the Special Operations Group, if I had to guess."

Nick nodded. "That's where Gray pulls his team from. Sharp operators over at SOG."

Alex should hope so. Only the finest of SEALs, Delta operators and similar types were invited to join the CIA Special Operations Group. It was a small unit of arguably the most lethal human beings on the planet.

Nick said, "In the morning, we need to find a gun dealer and stock up."

Alex replied, "I brought a whole bag of weapons from the safe house in New York City. But we could probably use more ammo, and maybe some low-grade explosives."

"I knew there had to be a cache of arms somewhere

in that place!" Nick exclaimed. "There was all that ammo in the closet and no firearms to go with it."

Alex grinned. "I was sure I was going to come back there sometime and find the walls torn open, the weapons' closet emptied and you gone."

"Nah. I would never have run away from a guy as sexy as you."

Alex's belly tightened involuntarily. Cripes, the effect this man had on him. He'd never been around another person who made him react from the core out.

"Speaking of which," Nick said grimly, "you said earlier that you would explain your feelings for me when we got back here. Thoroughly. And in detail. So, start talking."

Alex didn't know where to look. At Nick? At the fire? Out the window? Maybe at a spot over Nick's head?

Well, hell.

"You go first," he tried lamely.

"Nope. You go first this time," Nick said firmly.

Alex's brows came together in a frown. An urge to pick a fight and dodge this whole conversation surged through him, but he shoved it down. That would be childish and unfair to both of them. Nick had asked him an honest question and the man deserved an honest answer.

"Here's the thing," Alex said slowly. "This isn't the right time to have this conversation."

"Agreed," Nick said evenly. A pause. "But we're having it anyway. Continue."

"I've never had a conversation like this. On or off the job," Alex tried.

"Noted. I forgive you in advance for being awkward or for sticking your foot in your mouth."

He scowled at Nick. "Not helpful."

"How about this? I promise to hear you out without comment."

Alex considered that for a moment. "Better."

"Okay. Ground rules laid. Start talking."

Alex huffed. "This isn't an interrogation, for crying out loud."

Nick just looked at him expectantly.

"I think you're a great guy. Furthermore, I think you're a hell of a fine operator. One of the best." Alex searched for more words. These were not his weapons of choice in life. He used his brain and his hands and his training and let them do the talking for him. "I have… feelings…for you. Do I know what they all are? No. Do I want to figure that out? Yes. Can I describe them all to you thoroughly and in detail? No."

"Try."

He stared at Nick, who, to Alex's vast frustration, was giving no hint at all of what he thought of Alex's declaration of feelings.

"I suck at this," Alex grumbled.

Nick merely arched an eyebrow at him in a silent dare to carry on.

Alex opened his mouth. Closed it. The words were right there, hovering on the tip of his tongue. But he hadn't said them to anybody, ever, as an adult, and certainly not as a gay man to another man.

He'd told his parents and sisters he loved them, when he was younger. And they'd said it back to him. Blithely, while betraying his love behind his back. His gut clenched anxiously. What if Nick did the same thing? What if he laid his heart bare and Nick stomped on it—

"Stop," Nick said sharply.

Alex looked up, startled. "Stop what?"

"You just spun up inside your head and went all tight and closed down on me. Stop overthinking everything for once, will you?"

"But you insisted that I tell you what I feel—"

"There are more ways than with words to do that, you beautiful, brilliant moron."

Alex stared at him in total incomprehension. And then it hit him.

"Oh."

Nick stared back intently. "Yeah. Oh."

The ball was firmly in his court. Nick had batted it back to him and was now silently asking him what he planned to do about it.

All his doubts coiled inside him, tying his heart in knots, while nervousness wrapped around him from the outside in thick, paralyzing loops. He felt trapped. Suffocated. Bound into complete immobility.

This was his life. He'd always been snared by his own insecurities. It was why he was good at his work. He had no life of his own. No feelings of his own. No family. No friends. Nothing that gave him cause to break free of these emotional bonds.

Until now.

He lifted his gaze to Nick in anguish. "I don't know how to do this." He took a deep, unsteady breath, and added low, "Help me, Nick."

Nick surged forward, moving across the sofa until their knees banged together. He stood up, dragging Alex to his feet by the shoulders. "You've got to get out of your head, Alex. That's the only place you're imprisoned."

"I don't know how to do that."

Nick's arms went around him and pulled him close

against the hard length of his body. "Good thing for you, I do."

And then Nick was kissing him, his mouth hot and demanding and hungry. Nick kissed his face and throat, his eyes and temples. And his mouth. Oh, how Nick kissed his mouth.

He kissed Nick back feverishly. It was clumsy and fully as awkward as he'd feared it would be, but Nick didn't seem to care.

They stripped off Alex's utility vest and set it aside. Then his turtleneck sweater went over his head and momentarily got stuck on his face. They laughed a little as they finally tugged it free. Nick's hands reached for Alex's belt, and Alex sucked in a sharp breath.

Nick looked up quickly. "You say the word, and I'll stop. No questions asked."

Alex exhaled slowly, his stomach touching the backs of Nick's fingers. "Don't stop."

His belt slithered free of its loops and fell to the floor. He reached for Nick's utility vest and helped Nick shrug out of it. They unzipped their boots and kicked free of them, and then there was a moment of simultaneous, one-footed hopping as they fought to free their clingy, wet, wool socks from their feet.

Wearing just their cargo pants, they came together once more. Nick put his palms on Alex's chest, and Alex shivered as those callused hands eased across his skin, leaving a trail of goose bumps and utter destruction in their wake.

He couldn't resist. He reached out and plunged his fingers into the thick dark hair on Nick's chest. It was silky in contrast to the rock-hard muscles beneath. He trailed his hands lower, tracing the washboard ridges of Nick's stomach that contracted under his touch. Alex slipped his hands around Nick's lean waist as Nick did the same to him.

Nick grabbed his glutes in both hands and tugged him closer until their zippers brushed together suggestively. Alex groaned a little as the metal teeth rubbed against his burgeoning erection.

Nick released him abruptly and stepped back. A protest rose in Alex's throat but never found voice because Nick reached for the offending zipper and tugged it down. He slipped his hands inside the waistband of Alex's pants and pushed the canvas fabric down.

Oh, clever man. Nick had also snagged Alex's underwear, and the spandex trunks peeled down his body, as well. His erection sprang loose all at once, and freed from the constriction of his clothing, filled so hard and fast the sensation all but drove him to his knees.

But Nick beat him to it, sinking down in front of Alex. Before he'd barely registered that, Nick's wet, hot, slippery mouth had taken him in. Nick sucked once, twice, and Alex's legs nearly gave out. He groaned long and low in the back of his throat.

"Gotta stop that if you want me to last more than a few seconds," Alex managed to gasp.

Nick chuckled and rose to his feet, reaching for his own zipper.

"Let me do that," Alex managed to croak. He pushed Nick's hands aside and pulled the zipper down slowly, inch by inch, vividly aware of the bulge behind his knuckles. He could feel Nick's erection jumping and jerking behind his hands, and Alex all but came then and there. Only an act of supreme self-control stopped his own body from exploding, he was so turned on.

He pushed Nick's pants down, and Nick kicked them off his feet. Alex reached for Nick's underwear and drew it down his body, as well, holding his breath as Nick's erection came free and announced itself loud and proud.

Alex wrapped his fist around the heated organ, loving the feel of it throbbing in his hand. He gave a light, experimental tug, and Nick stepped forward, groaning under his breath. Leading him by it, Alex backed toward the bed, where Jeanette had thoughtfully turned down the covers earlier.

As the backs of Alex's thighs bumped into the high mattress, Nick surged forward, knocking him backward onto the bed. Alex had barely hit the sheets before Nick was there, following him down.

One of Nick's thighs landed between his, and Nick's hands landed on either side of his head. He looked up in the flickering firelight as Nick stared down at him, lowering himself slowly, slowly in a reverse push-up.

Their legs tangled together. Then their bellies touched. Then their chests. And finally, Nick's entire body weight eased down onto him.

It felt so good Alex felt an urge to sob with pleasure. And he was not a sobbing kind of guy.

Nick kissed him slowly this time. Leisurely. They got to know each other's mouths and preferences as they kissed lightly, then deeply, with tongue and without, light nips and deep, drugging kisses. And all the while, their erections pressed against each other's groins, promising pleasure, lust and explosive, mind-blowing release.

Nick, resting his weight on an elbow above Alex, shoved his hands through Alex's short hair, pulling his head back and exposing his neck. Alex gave his throat to Nick freely, loving the heat of Nick's mouth on his skin.

"Um, Nick?"

"Mmm-hmm?"

"Don't we need to have a conversation about who's doing what?"

Nick slid his free hand down Alex's front, past his belly button, followed the line of hair downward, and wrapped around Alex's swollen flesh, pumping up and down its length once. Twice.

"I want to do all the things with you. I want to be inside you, and I want you inside me," Nick growled. "I want not to know where I end and you begin. So, you pick which way this is going to go first. But before tomorrow morning, we're doing it all."

Alex's toes literally curled in delight at that prospect. He realized Nick was staring down at him expectantly and that his fist had gone still. He was waiting for an answer.

Words. He had to use his words again. "Uh, I think, uh, I'd like to stay just like this, but with you making love to me first."

"You've got it."

He purely loved Nick's matter-of-fact response. He didn't make a big deal out of it, didn't make Alex feel weird for asking to bottom first. He just nodded, and oh thank goodness, his fist started to move again on Alex's engorged flesh.

Nick's second thigh joined his first one, and he pushed Alex's legs farther apart. Nick leaned over, laying across Alex's left thigh and hip for a moment, opening the drawer in the nightstand and taking something out. He rose to his knees, and Alex heard foil tearing.

"You had a condom already stowed in the bed stand just in case?" he exclaimed.

Nick looked down at him indignantly. "I'm shocked

you didn't think ahead, Mr. Creed. Since when don't you contingency plan for all possibilities?"

His mouth opened and closed. "I admit it. I fell down on the job."

Nick finished rolling a condom onto his own penis and reached out to grasp Alex's. "Nothing feels fallen to me around here."

Alex rolled his eyes.

But then Nick opened a squeeze tube, and his slippery fingers were abruptly moving around Alex's most private parts. It felt so good he thought for a second that he might faint.

Alex reached down to grip Nick's erection, not so much as to give pleasure but simply to stay anchored in reality. Velvet over granite was the impression that flashed through his mind.

And then Nick took over guiding himself to Alex's eager body.

"You ready for me?" Nick asked. "Because my dude, I'm gonna fill you *all* the way."

Alex panted a little as he felt the stretching pressure. It wasn't quite painful, but that was because Nick went very, very slow and gave him all the time he needed to adapt. And then the worst of it was passed, and he nodded. Nick drove forward steadily then, filling him until he could hardly breathe. When Nick was seated to the hilt, their bellies pressed together, Alex's erection trapped deliciously between them, he stared up at Nick in wonder.

"We good?" Nick asked. His voice sounded gratifyingly strained.

"Uh-huh."

"Thank goodness. I don't think I could've stayed still one more second." Nick began to move inside him, slowly at first, but then with gathering force and speed. And with each thrust, Alex rose to meet him. Higher and higher they drove each other, their bodies straining together, desire clawing inside both of them in search of release.

Alex stared up at Nick, who stared back. The raw intimacy of staring into each other's eyes—into each other's souls—was intense and lifted the sex out of the realm of the physical and into the realm of magic.

Making love with Nick stripped away everything he hid behind, all the composure, all the self-control, all the overthinking, the insecurity, the uptightness. And with each layer that fell away, Alex felt more and more exposed, more emotional. More alive.

It was as if he'd been living in a fog bank for so long he'd forgotten what the sun looked like. But as they burned away the last vestiges of the mist, Nick burned as brightly as the sun. They burned together.

Nick drove into him harder and harder, faster and faster, and Alex drove back. Their bodies slapped together, and the friction became a raging wildfire they'd lost all control of.

When Alex thought he couldn't take one more second of it, Nick's hands slipped under him to grab his hips. Alex grabbed Nick, as well, and hung on for dear life. One last, mighty thrust, and Nick's entire body tensed, arched into him at the same time Alex arched up against Nick, and both of their bodies spasmed for long, long seconds. It went on and on until Alex actually did black out a little, overcome by an excess of pleasure so intense he could hardly absorb it all.

He blinked back into his body and began to register sensations. The glorious weight of Nick's body on top of his. Drugging waves of pleasure coursing through him.

Skin on skin. Their legs tangled together. His breath light and fast.

Alex realized the ropes binding him had, indeed, fallen away. He finally had not only the right words but the freedom to say them.

"I love you, Nick."

Chapter Nineteen

Nick's entire being went still from the inside out. He stared down at Alex in the half dark of the firelight. His hair was uncharacteristically chaotic, but there was nothing the slightest bit chaotic about Alex's steady, warm eyes, staring back at him solemnly. Alex loved him? It wasn't just the delirium of great sex talking?

"Really?" he heard himself asking in a hoarse voice he didn't recognize as his own.

"Um, yeah. You don't have to feel the same way or say it back—" Alex started.

Swiftly, Nick leaned down and kissed the man into silence. Then, when Alex had gone still beneath him, he lifted his mouth away from Alex's far enough to say, "I love you, too, you giant goofball."

"I'm not a goofball!"

"Are, too. But you're my goofball," Nick said fondly.

"You're such a jerk."

"But I'm your jerk," Nick replied more seriously. They stared at each other in wonder, as if they both were struggling a little to absorb the enormity of what had just happened between them.

Alex twined his fingers in Nick's hair and tugged. "Yeah," Alex sighed against his lips. "You're my jerk."

Nick rolled to one side, and Alex rolled with him,

their limbs still entwined and Alex's head lying on his shoulder.

A single thought came to Nick. *If I die this second, I will die a happy man.*

Whoa. *Happy* was a word he couldn't remember ever applying to himself. But there it was. Alexander Creed made him happy in ways he'd never imagined possible. He relaxed in the dark and listened to Alex's breathing calm and settle into sleep, and it was one of the nicest things he'd ever heard. As Alex slumbered beside him, relaxed and warm, it soothed and lulled Nick, as well.

He vaguely registered the dark cloud of Harlan Gray on the horizon, but the calm of being with Alex held. Tomorrow would be soon enough to deal with that problem. For tonight, he and Alex had each other. And it was the best moment of his life.

Who knew that making love with a man that he actually loved had made all the difference in the world? He might be an old dog, but it appeared he was capable of learning new tricks after all.

Love. Not a word, not a thing he'd ever expected to find. But here it was, in all its magnificence and glory. And he was fully okay with that.

NICK WOKE SLOWLY, registering with vague displeasure that the sun was shining around the edges of the heavy curtains. Sometime in the night, between bouts of mind-shattering sex, Alex had gotten up and closed the velvet blinds. True to his prediction, they had done all the things in all the combinations, alternately napping and waking through the night to make love again.

Both of them were inordinately fit men with extreme stamina. It had made for a very long night with very little sleep. But there was no doubt about it. They were a perfect match. Not only did they have similar strengths but also similar creativity. Alex had surprised him like no other lover he'd ever had, and he was pretty sure he'd surprised Alex a few times, too.

Nick stretched lazily, loathe to end their tryst. Oh my. A number of muscles expressed protest. Score another point for Alex. Not many of his lovers over the years had worked him out to the point of actual muscle fatigue. He finally forced himself to open his other eye and noted that the bed beside him was empty, the covers thrown back.

The shower went on in the adjoining bathroom, and he grinned to himself. Had he, perchance, made Alex a wee bit sore as well? The good news was the shower was plenty large enough for two adults. In fact, large enough for two adults to make love in…

THE HOUSE EITHER had a large water heater or a continuous water-heating system, for they ran the water for almost a solid hour, first making love under it, and then taking turns letting the hot spray pound their muscles into relaxation.

At last, Nick had to admit it was time to get on with their day. And they had a big one ahead of them. After a large breakfast of tall stacks of pancakes and enough bacon to feed a football team, he and Alex headed out to the shed where the snowmobiles were stored. Jeannette had told them the machines hadn't been ridden in over a year, but that if they could get them running, they were free to take them out.

It took a quick tune-up and an oil change, but in about an hour, the two machines roared to life.

Jeanette had mentioned over breakfast that local skiers had built and maintained small emergency shacks in the nearby mountains. Apparently, they were stocked with firewood, water, canned food and blankets, perfect for the lost or stranded skier. Nick and Alex were hoping to find one in reasonably good repair and stock it for their own purposes.

They loaded gear bags onto the backs of the machines and headed out. The recent snow was blindingly white, and the ride into the back country was beautiful. They found what they thought was an old ski trail, and they followed it slowly, ducking under branches that encroached upon their path.

It ran for perhaps a mile before coming to a ramshackle structure that must have been one of the old ski shacks. Nick turned off his snowmobile and climbed off it to take a closer look.

Alex did the same, commenting, "It's in pretty rough shape."

"It looks as if a lot of the original wood siding is lying around on the ground under the snow, though. If we brought out nails and hammers, we should be able to repair a lot of it. And this siding is inch-thick oak. It would stop a bullet."

"We need to check out possible approaches to this spot," Alex said. "Make sure the general public isn't likely to stumble on to it."

They spent the next hour doing just that and concluded that they had, indeed, found the perfect place to ambush Gray.

"How are we going to draw him up here?" Nick asked.

"Easy." Alex grinned. "We bring the crèche up here. He'll turn over every rock in the Adirondacks looking for it."

"But it's *priceless*. And you want to use it as bait?" Nick squawked.

"Have you got any better ideas?"

"We could use ourselves as bait."

Alex frowned. "If he thinks we don't have the crèche with us, he won't come after us. The moment he figures out we've stolen the crèche, that will become his sole obsession. He'll find that to the exclusion of all else. Once he has it back, and only then, will he turn his attention to hunting us down and killing us slowly and painfully."

Nick sighed. "I agree. But I hate the idea of using the crèche as bait."

"So do I. But we have to stop Gray."

Nick stared at Alex, who stared back grimly. At length, Nick said, "Fine. We use the crèche. We bring it up here."

"We should set up a defensive perimeter around it. Layers of traps and alarm systems. Then we'll need to find a good spot and set up a hide for ourselves."

Nick nodded. "We should build a series of them around the shack that we can retreat to as he and his men try to overrun our position."

Alex frowned. "You think we'll need to retreat?"

"I think we'd be idiots not to plan for it."

It was a game of anticipating what Gray's men would do and then thinking about how to outfox each move they might make. When they'd outlined a network of spots to build sniper hides in, they marked each location on their GPSes and headed back to the inn.

They grabbed a late lunch and loaded up with the supplies they needed to repair the shack and the ammo they needed to stock in each hiding spot. Lastly, they strapped the bags with the crèche statues to the backs of the snowmobiles. They told Jeanette they would be camping tonight and headed out.

They used the last of the daylight to repair the cabin. Thankfully, it didn't have to be pretty. It just had to repel bullets and have enough slits for them to shoot through. They laid planks in the rafters to form a rough ceiling and tucked the bags containing the precious statues on top of that, where they should be clear of gunfire.

Heading out in the rapidly falling twilight, they went to work setting up sniper hides. They used hollow logs and dug holes under rocks to stash ammunition, tarps and even first-aid kits. Finally, they retired to the shack to catch some sleep and take turns standing watch.

As Alex hunkered down in his bedroll and Nick settled in to observe the surrounding forest, Alex asked, "How long do you suppose it'll take for Gray to find us?"

"I expect him here in the next day or so. Catch some sleep, goofball."

"Love you, too, jerk face."

Nick smiled indulgently as Alex closed his eyes and promptly fell asleep. They hadn't had time to talk today about last night, but there wasn't much to say. It had been perfect, and they were meant to be together. At least that was how he felt, and he was pretty darned sure Alex felt the exact same way. He sure *hoped* Alex felt the same.

As stars wheeled slowly overhead and the long hours of the night passed in a majestically slow march, his thoughts turned to the house he mentally constructed when he was bored.

Except tonight, it looked exactly like the Pleasant Run Inn. He was living there with Alex. They'd built little guest quarters out back for Jeanette to retire in, and there were kids in the house. A whole bunch of them. They would run the inn and go to town snowball fights and sing Christmas carols and drink hot chocolate with silly little marshmallows in it—

A movement outside caught his eye, yanking his attention back to the forest around him.

It was nearly 3:00 a.m. Almost time to hand the watch off to Alex and catch some sleep himself.

He stared at the spot where he'd seen a shadow flicker that shouldn't have flickered. Had the movement been down near the ground, he would've written it off as a raccoon or a fox. It had been about five feet off the ground, though. It had been too big for a bird or a squirrel…

He used his foot to kick Alex's boot lightly through his sleeping bag. "Incoming," he breathed.

Too soon! They weren't ready! They hadn't run practice scenarios. Hadn't finalized an order that they would use the hides in. They hadn't even decided who would take the north side of the shack and who would take the south side.

Truth was, neither of them needed to practice a thing. He just wasn't ready to have this idyllic time with Alex come to a violent end.

Alex rolled out of his sleeping bag, gripped an assault rifle across his chest and pulled night optical devices over his eyes. He moved quickly to the opposite wall of the shack and took up a waiting-and-watching position, peering out at the forest through a slit in the wall.

The biggest problem with Gray hitting them now was they had no backup. The Medusas had replied that they would make all due haste to the area and contact Nick when they arrived. Alex hadn't heard anything at all in response to his urgent request for help.

Crap, crap, crap. Gray had outmaneuvered them. He'd somehow correctly anticipated what Nick and Alex would do. Worse, he'd used his superior resources and private army to move faster and get here before he and Alex got help.

"Clear over here," Alex said just loud enough into his throat-mounted microphone to be heard in Nick's military-grade earphones.

"Negative on heat sources over here," Nick replied into his throat mike. "But I definitely saw a hostile due west of us, about fifty feet out."

"They'll know we're in here, then. They'll have picked up our heat signatures," Alex said matter-of-factly.

"Dammit," Nick bit out. "We should've assumed he'd get here tonight and disguised our heat signatures."

"The idea was for them to find us," Alex reminded him quietly.

"I don't want you to die!" he burst out under his breath.

"Bless your heart, darlin', but I don't want to die, either," Alex drawled.

"I'm serious."

"So am I," Alex retorted. "And I don't want you to die."

Nick huffed. "Is there any way I can talk you into jumping on one of the snowmobiles and heading back to town to call in reinforcements?"

"Not on your life," Alex snapped. "If they know only one man is in here, they'd rush you the second I'm gone and overrun your position. We're in this together, Nick. All the way to the end."

Nick closed his eyes in agony. They'd only just found each other. They'd had so little time together. He wasn't ready for this! He needed more time with Alex. They had so much more living and loving to do before the end.

Because the end was going to be just that. The *end*. Death. For both of them. He *had* to find a way to get Alex out of here.

"I appreciate your loyalty, Alex. Really. But maybe I only saw a scout. It's possible he has gone back to join the rest of Gray's team and let them know he's spotted a couple of skiers in a shack they might want to check out in the morning."

"Or," Alex said coolly, "he's moved over the crest of the ridge so we can't see him and is waiting for the rest of Gray's team to join him before they make their move."

"In that case, do you want to get out of here? Head out the back door to the first hide we set up?"

"Given that they haven't already attacked us, I think we should," Alex answered.

Nick nodded. Moving efficiently, he donned his utility vest, which he'd loaded up earlier with all the ammunition he could cram into it. He picked up a spare assault rifle and slung it across his back, checked the handgun in his pocket, the knife in its ankle sheath and tightened his optical device around his head.

Then he rigged the first of their traps. The remote firing devices he'd attached to a pair of assault rifles on tripod stands pointed outward. When Gray's men hit the trip wires attached to them, the weapons would shoot into the woods. He and Alex didn't care if the flying bullets hit any of Gray's men. They just needed Gray and his team to shoot back and give away their positions by their muzzle flashes.

Alex finished tucking a pair of heat packs into the

neck openings of each of their insulated sleeping bags, simulating their faces poking out. Alex moved to the low trapdoor they'd cut into the back wall earlier.

Nick watched him ease outside with quick stealth that Nick took a moment to admire. And then he followed Alex.

The moon had set hours ago, but it was a clear, starry night with just enough ambient lighting to cause a faint glow to rise from the snow. Their white arctic suits blended in with the surroundings, however, and he raced after Alex, crouching low.

He reached the first hide and eased down behind a giant, downed tree trunk. Nick turned up the magnification on his NODs and scanned the woods around them carefully. All clear. But someone else was out here. He could feel it.

Alex hand signaled, "We're not alone. No contact." Meaning, Alex was convinced someone was out here, too, but hadn't yet seen him.

He signaled back, "Affirmative."

The tense standoff lasted for another hour of complete silence and no movement out there. Whoever was watching the shack was probably still in position and unaware that the two of them had slipped outside. But that would change when the heat packs Alex had left in their sleeping bags wore out in another hour or so and began to cool down.

Then, Nick suspected, all hell was going to break loose.

Only one thing was on his mind now. He had to find a way to get Alex out of this confrontation alive. Even if it meant sacrificing his own life.

Chapter Twenty

Alex scanned the trees around their position for the hundredth time. By now, he was familiar with every branch, every mound of snow, every dead leaf still clinging to a branch overhead.

Any minute, Gray's whole team would arrive and charge the ski shack. Certainty of that rippled across Alex's skin, making the fine hairs on his arms stand up.

He had to find a way to get Nick out of this alive. Nick had finally allowed himself to love again. He was finally starting to get past the betrayals of his childhood, starting to think about having a family of his own. He had to get a chance to fill that hole in his heart.

By rote, Alex ran through the litany of people he'd killed over the years. Far too many of them had been Americans, men and women just like him who'd had a moment of weakness. They'd given in to temptation, and he'd come for them. How many of those people could've made restitution, could've learned their lesson if given a second chance, could've returned to the ranks of productive operatives for the US government if he'd given them the chance?

But no. He was the Judge. He'd deemed them guilty, sentenced them to death and executed the sentence. How many families had he destroyed? How many wid-

ows and orphans had been left in his wake? He was
the one who needed to die out here. Not Nick. Nick
was just a soldier doing his job, a guy trying to right a
great wrong perpetrated by his buddies. Nick was one
of the good ones.

But he was not. He'd amassed a ton of lethal karma
debts in his career, and the time had come for him to
pay up.

Alex breathed, "When they realize we're not in the
shack, you drop back to the second hide, and I'll hold
this position as long as I can. I'll join you once you're
set up to cover my retreat."

In theory it was a solid plan. Of course, he had no
intention of joining Nick at all. He had a large enough
block of C-4 in his pocket to make a crater with a fifty-
foot radius around himself and incinerate everything
inside it. Including himself. And the crèche. He did feel
bad about that. But neither one of them could afford to
get weighed down hauling out the heavy bag of statues, and he was willing to destroy any piece of art, no
matter how rare and valuable, to save Nick.

If he could just draw Gray and his team close enough,
he could take them all out at once.

And Nick would live.

Peace settled over Alex. He'd found true love at last.
Nick knew everything about him and thought he was
perfect just the way he was. And that was enough for
him. It was more than he'd ever expected to find in
this lifetime.

"Here they come," Nick breathed.

Alex tensed. He joined Nick in peering over the log.
Up the hill, the shack lay still and silent. And then, without warning, the two booby-trapped weapons Nick had
set up inside the shack began to fire out into the woods.

An answering barrage erupted from the woods on the other side of the shack. At least they'd gotten the direction that Gray and his team would approach from correct. Alex counted fast. Six weapons were firing at the cabin. He marked their positions and sighted in on the one closest to him. Using the heat-painting feature of his optical devices, he tried to spot the human behind the gun, but the guy had complete cover from a tree.

Swearing under his breath, Alex moved on to the next firing position. One by one, he checked each weapon discharging at the shack, and not one shooter had exposed himself to return fire. Alarm skittered through him. These guys were good. Fully as good as Nick has warned him they would be.

Instinct warned him to turn around and scan down the exposed hill behind them, and he was barely in time to spot the man creeping toward them in stealthy silence. Alex swung his weapon up and double-tapped two shots into the chest of the guy, who tumbled backward down the steep slope.

Alex touched Nick's shoulder twice and then scrambled after the hostile to verify the kill. But when he got to where the man had fallen, there was no body. Gray's man must've been wearing body armor. Crap. But then, he and Nick were also sporting the stuff. Military grade, capable of withstanding point-blank assault-weapon fire.

He ran back up the hill to Nick. Under the noise of the barrage Gray's men were still peppering the shack with, he muttered in Nick's ear, "We have to go. This spot is compromised."

Nick nodded and slid back from the log. Alex took off running down the slope a second time, angling across it toward the next hide they'd set up for themselves. Unfortunately, they were going to have to fight uphill, with Gray's men holding the high ground above them.

Alex flopped down behind a huge boulder that was actually an outcropping of the hill itself. Quickly he scanned the forest behind them while Nick set up his weapon on a bipod stand and scanned in front of the rock.

"Clear," Nick breathed.

"Clear."

The gunfire was tailing off above them. Gray's men would be approaching the shack now. They'd mainly be hunting whoever'd shot at them, and he doubted they would find the crèche. He also doubted Gray was out here in person, running around in the woods like a common foot soldier. It was beneath the great spymaster.

Nick had suggested Gray would send in an advance team to keep them busy while Gray's main force assembled. Time to start picking off the foot soldiers.

"I'll be back," Alex murmured. "Going on a hunting expedition."

Nick nodded, his eye never leaving the rubber sight of his weapon.

Alex moved out into the trees silently. This was what he did best. He was a predator. He moved around toward the far side of the cabin, certain there was at least one more roaming hunter out here besides the one he'd shot.

There. He spied a brief, slow movement. Maybe a hand reaching up to adjust a sight on a rifle. It wasn't much. But it was enough. Moving at glacial speed, he lifted his own weapon. *Bingo.* A heat signature lit up on the ground.

Cognizant of the body armor, he aimed for the target's neck. It was a hellishly hard shot, but well within his capability. He exhaled slowly, emptied his mind and became one with his weapon. He squeezed the trigger and watched as the target went limp and still on the ground.

Splash one.

Now to find the man he'd shot before. He figured the guy must've retreated back toward the main force of Gray's troops to assess his injuries and recover his cool, if nothing else. He headed in that direction.

He'd almost given up on finding the guy when he spied a figure creeping slowly across the hillside toward Nick's current position.

Oh no he didn't. That guy didn't get to sneak up on *his* man, thank you very much.

With cold precision, Alex raised his rifle, lined up the neck shot and took it. The man's legs went limp and he dropped like a stone.

Splash two.

Alex eased closer to the cabin, watching where he went through his rifle sight. There. Gray's men had found the trapdoor, and one was coming out it now. He didn't have a shot at the guy that wouldn't hit body armor, but he didn't need to kill him. He just needed to make him run. Gray's other men would follow behind.

Alex aimed at the man's side and put two bullets into the guy's ribs in quick succession. The impacts would hurt like hell, even through body armor.

Sure enough, the man cried out, jumped up and took off running into the woods. Three more foot soldiers piled out fast and took off behind him. For good measure, Alex shot one of them in the back. He staggered and nearly went down but found his balance and scrambled into the trees.

Alex risked transmitting to Nick, "They've got body

armor and helmets. Neck shots work. Two down. Four incoming to you. I'm hunting the last two." He figured that of the six who'd been shooting at the shack, only four had gone inside, which left two more out here. He didn't think the two he'd already killed were part of that original six-man fire team.

Nick clicked his mike to acknowledge the information.

Alex looked side to side. Which way to go? Since the two guys he'd killed had both circled left around the shack, he decided to circle right in search of the other two hunter-killers prowling around out here.

He came upon the first man no more than a hundred yards beyond the shack. He was positioned to take out anybody who returned to the cabin after his guys cleared out of it.

Alex snorted. As if he or Nick would ever be dumb enough to come back to a location that had already been compromised. It took him a while to circle around behind the guy, and he prayed the men headed toward Nick continued straight down the hill into Nick's kill zone.

He'd hoped to have these two hunters taken care of by now so he could head back toward Nick and cover him from any rear attacks. The last guy had to be out here, somewhere. *C'mon, where are you? Show yourselves.*

There. He spotted a shape in front of him. A shot at the back of the neck wasn't as sure a kill as a throat shot, but it was the only shot he had. His weapon was a large enough caliber to bust through vertebrae and kill his target.

Alex lined up his shot and took it. The man slumped forward over his rifle, motionless.

Off to his left, an abrupt barrage of gunfire announced that the team had found Nick, or they had stumbled into his line of fire. Either way, it was *on* over there.

A quick movement no more than fifty yards in front of him startled Alex mightily. A *third* hunter had broken cover to run for the shootout.

Alex took off running after the guy and was horrified when Gray's man unleashed a barrage of automatic weapon fire at Nick.

A mistake, that. Nobody was taking out *his* man.

Alex stopped moving to calculate the guy's path of motion and exhaled, waiting for him to run into his sights. As Gray's man flashed into his viewfinder, Alex pulled the trigger, quickly adjusted left a hair and fired again.

He took off running without waiting to see if he'd taken out the guy. Killing a moving target was exponentially more difficult than killing a stationary one, and he assumed the shooter was still alive. As he charged toward where he'd dropped him, he raised his weapon again, readying it.

The hunter was lying down, but rolled toward him and shot just wide of Alex's face as he crashed out of the brush. Alex actually felt the heat of a bullet passing by his cheek. Ducking, Alex shot fast, putting two rounds into the guy, who went still. Dang. That had been a close call.

Now to get to Nick.

You'd better be alive, you beautiful bastard. You have children to conceive and raise.

Chapter Twenty-One

Nick picked off two of the four people rushing his position before they had any idea he was just below them on the hillside. But the two remaining guys split up and ran from him at right angles. Not good. They were going to circle around behind him and flank him.

He had to fall back. Now. No matter that Alex hadn't rejoined him. If he stayed, Alex would find a corpse when he got here. And before he died, he had to make sure Alex was safe.

Nick grabbed his weapon, the last magazine of ammo, and took off running down the hill at top speed. He hurdled over the log that was their next hide and flopped to the ground with his back against the cold wood.

"At hide three," he breathed into his mouthpiece.

He watched left and right, his gaze swiveling back and forth, waiting for one or both of the remaining hostiles to circle behind this spot to kill him. He might only take out one of them before going down himself, but at least that would leave Alex with even odds.

He spied a single figure at the bottom of the hill, much lower than he would've expected the pair chasing him to have gone. But, hey. Each to their own. If the guy wanted to have to come uphill to approach him, so be it.

He lined the guy up in his sights and then jolted. He knew that quick, graceful way of moving. He jerked his muzzle up and away from Alex.

"I have you in sight," he breathed.

"Well, hell," Alex replied in disgust.

Nick smiled briefly. Didn't like being seen, huh? "Two hunters flanking me."

"I'm sliding east," Alex breathed.

Nick had complete faith that Alex would find his man and take him out, so he turned his attention solely to the western approach to this position. Which was probably why he spotted the most subtle of movement slightly above him on the hill.

Because of the guy's body armor, Nick had to wait for the man to come closer to get a shot. In the meantime, he lay down, minimizing his own body signature as much as possible behind the log.

The hunter stopped and crouched for a long time. Probably was scanning the area around him. Then, as the guy finally stood up and turned toward him, Nick got a shot. He took it, and the hostile dropped.

"West down," he breathed.

Alex didn't even click his mike in response. He must be right on top of his target and not be able to shift or reply at all.

Nick scanned the whole hillside and saw no movement. Holding his breath, he waited for Alex to report in.

Bang. Bang.

"East down," Alex said quietly.

Thank goodness. He exhaled carefully.

"That everyone?" Nick asked.

"I think so." Alex added, "Coming in over your right shoulder."

A shape dropped to the ground beside him, startling him badly. He hadn't heard Alex approach at all. "Holy—" He broke off. "Glad to see you're alive."

"Ditto, Kane."

"Really? Ditto? Is that all you've got?"

"If we get out of this alive," Alex muttered, "I'm crawling back into that huge bed with you and not getting out of it for a week."

"Deal."

"Ready to clear the hill with me?" Alex asked low, but still managing to sound pleased with himself.

He scowled at Alex for a moment. "Let's go."

"Nice shooting, by the way."

"You, too."

Their gazes met, and they exchanged short smiles.

It took them until about an hour after sunrise to assure themselves that no more of Gray's advance team remained on the hillside. They disarmed the corpses, took the radios and phones, and moved off into the woods to wait and see who showed up next.

Nick caught a couple hours of sleep, and Alex even caught a nap in the late morning. They spent the afternoon doing the preparations they'd hoped to do before anyone showed up, and repositioned nearly to the top of the mountain. They would hold the high ground this time.

As the sun dipped into the west and slipped behind the mountains, Nick braced himself for the main attack. By now, Gray knew that none of his advance team had reported back in.

Tonight, Gray would throw everything he had at them.

Chapter Twenty-Two

Alex looked down the hill through a long-range scope. The black, bare skeletons of the trees only partially obscured the view. He could see the ski shack was badly shot up after last night's attack, with hundreds of bullet holes in the wooden walls. They'd patched it up with more lengths of old siding they'd nailed across the worst of the holes today to make it look fortified. It should be where Gray's army started its search.

They hoped.

The crèche was still tucked up high in the rafters of the shack, well above where Gray's men had been firing at the structure last night. Hopefully, it would continue to stay safe in its hiding spot.

They had briefly debated trying to carry it down the hill this morning and put it somewhere safe, but they hadn't had the time to spare, and they couldn't guarantee that Gray's men wouldn't have spotted them coming down off the mountain and attacked on the spot.

As darkness fell gently around them, Alex glanced over at Nick. "You ready for this?"

"As ready as I'll ever be. I've trained my whole life for this moment. You ready?"

Alex smiled. "I hunt guys like Gray for lunch."

"You made tracking them look easy last night," Nick commented.

"I got a good shock when I went to confirm my first kill and the guy was gone," Alex admitted. "And I had a very close call with a guy who leaped out of hiding when you started firing at the kill team coming down the hill. He might've gotten the jump on me had you not distracted him."

Nick winced. "I take no pleasure from men I probably trained nearly killing you."

"I'm glad I've had some time to work with you so I had an idea of the skill level these guys brought to the table. To be honest, I'd have underestimated them if I didn't already know you."

Nick smiled over at him. "Have I told you today that I love you?"

"You have not."

"Well, I do."

Alex savored the warmth spreading outward from his chest. "When this is over, how do you feel about buying the Pleasant Run Inn from Jeanette and running it ourselves?"

"Funny you should ask. I was thinking last night about building her a little guesthouse out back so she could stay where her family was raised. I figure we'll need her help learning the ropes of running an inn."

"Really?" Alex blurted.

"Really. I love the idea. We can have our wedding beside the pond. Or maybe in the drawing room. Whatever you want," Nick said.

Alex stared. "Our wedding? Was that a proposal, Nicholas Kane?"

"That was a pre-proposal. I'll do it right when we get

off this damned hill. With a ring and roses and champagne and the whole sappy nine yards."

Alex stared incredulously until Nick said a little defensively, "What?"

"When did you become a romantic at heart?"

"Guess I always was one. It just took you coming along to reveal it."

Alex leaned over and grabbed Nick's shirt, dragging him close for a kiss. "That was my pre-acceptance of your pre-proposal."

He started to move back to his weapon, but Nick grabbed his shirt this time and dragged him close for a long, sexy kiss that had him thinking about how soon they could get off this mountain and get back to their room at the inn.

"Shouldn't someone be watching the cabin?" he mumbled against Nick's lips.

"Party pooper."

"Let's get this mess cleaned up so we can get on with our lives," Alex said firmly.

"One cleaning job, coming up."

They went back to watching the cabin.

Alex said thoughtfully, "Last night, I was prepared to die to protect you."

Nick snorted. "I spent last night trying to figure out how to die in a way that would get you off this hill alive."

"How about we agree to both get off this mountain alive?" Alex said soberly.

Nick took his eyes off the binoculars to stare at him a long time. "I'll try if you'll try."

Alex met his dark stare. "I will if you will."

"Okay, then. We both stay alive. We fight to the end. No grand sacrifices in the name of saving the other guy. We live together or die firing the last rounds in our weapons at the bastards."

Resolve hardened in Alex's chest. They would find a way to do this. They would defeat Gray and his men somehow. And then they'd go get that inn and that storybook life they both deserved. Well, Nick deserved it. He was just grateful to be the man Nick had chosen to live the fairy tale with.

It was midnight when Gray's army arrived on tracked snow vehicles that roared up the mountain and rolled straight up to the shack. The rear tailgate of one vehicle dropped, and a Gatling gun opened fire on the cabin, literally shredding the walls as he and Nick looked on in horror.

"I only count four men," Alex murmured in confusion.

Without warning, Nick swore violently and rolled onto his back, taking his gun with him. Instinctively, Alex ducked as a drone overhead unleashed a volley of gunfire on their position, exploding the log where his head had just been. He and Nick scrambled under the cover of a tree and then took off running through the forest, zigzagging back and forth.

Alex noted vaguely that Nick wasn't heading for their next designated shooter's nest. Instead, he was veering off to the south, away from the cabin, toward a rock wall they'd found late this morning. What was he doing?

Grimly, Alex followed, his mind raging with questions over what Nick had in mind. But he had no breath to ask, and Nick surely had no breath to answer.

They burst out of the trees and the rock outcropping rose some thirty feet over their heads.

"Find an overhang and get under it," Nick said tersely. "I'm climbing this rock."

"Why?" Alex demanded.

"Gotta take out the drone. And I should be able to get a phone signal on top of it. We need help now. Or we're dead."

"I'm coming with you," Alex declared.

"No—"

"We agreed."

Nick grabbed him and kissed him hard, effectively silencing him. "Fine. Shut up and climb. But you live for me. You hear?"

Alex smiled a little as he grabbed a handhold and pulled himself onto the rock face. They hadn't scoped out this wall, and free-climbing it at night was suicidally dangerous, but they had no choice. He heard the distinctive whine of the drone somewhere nearby. They had to get a clear shot, and soon.

Alex used every bit of his speed and coordination to pull himself on top of the wall in little more than a minute. He rolled onto his back, pointing his rifle toward the sky and scanning fast.

There.

He aimed at the drone, made the corrections for shooting upward and pulled the trigger. A miss. He aimed again. This time, a puff of smoke rose from the attack drone, and it spiraled down out of the sky just as Nick reached the plateau beside him.

"Dang, you're fast," Nick panted.

"Make the call."

Nick pulled out his cell phone. Alex listened in as Nick said urgently, "If you have any resources to blank out satellite coverage of Upstate New York, now's the time to pull in that favor. We're in big trouble up here."

A male voice answered tersely, but Alex couldn't make out the words.

Nick busted out in a big smile and said, "That's the best news I've had in weeks. We'll meet you down there."

He pocketed his phone and Alex said, "Well?"

"The Medusas are here. And apparently, a few of your friends have arrived, as well. They're inbound to the coordinates of the cabin as we speak. They've formed a cordon at the bottom of the hill and will be herding Gray and his men up toward us in the next few minutes."

"We're inside that cordon?" Alex asked.

"Correct."

"How do you feel about heading for hide twelve and giving Gray a personal welcome to the love shack?"

Nick grinned. "I love that plan. Let's go."

Hide twelve was the last one they'd built and directly above the cabin on top of a good-sized rock outcropping. Although it had no cover overhead, it had the perfect vantage point to take out anyone approaching the shack's front door—or at least the remnants of it, hanging askew in the door frame.

He and Nick moved cautiously through the woods as they made their way down the mountain, but the Medusas and their reinforcements were making no effort to move quietly below them as they closed the net around the cabin and Gray's army. If anything, they were being noisy intentionally, beating the bushes to drive Gray's men toward the place.

Alex stretched out on the cold, rough rock, pressing his cheek against his rifle. "How many men do you guess Gray brought with him?" he murmured off-mike to Nick.

"No idea. Up to twenty, maybe."

"Dang. Do you suppose he's in the area?"

"Gunnar Torsten—he's the commander of the Medusas—said a surveillance satellite was appropriated and pointed at Upstate New York about an hour ago. He got it shut down right before I called him. My guess is Gray was sitting offsite somewhere nearby, watching a satellite feed."

"So, Gray's blind," Alex replied, nodding in satisfaction. "Will he come in person to supervise our murder?"

"No. But he'll come in person to retrieve the crèche," Nick answered grimly.

Without warning, a dozen commandos burst into the clearing around the cabin and took up positions. But instead of pointing at the shack, they pointed outward, away from it, defending it.

"What's up with that?" Alex muttered.

"I don't know—" Nick broke off. "Aww, hell. Gray's already inside the cabin."

"He has the crèche!" Alex exclaimed under his breath, lifting his rifle.

"Not yet," Nick bit out. "If we give away our position before the Medusas get here, Gray's men will kill us before we get help."

Alex subsided, unhappy. Nick was right, but Gray had the crèche. His gut rebelled at the precious relic being in such a monster's hands.

They didn't have long to wait, however. Another line of figures lit up in the heat-seeking optical functions of their rifle sights. A male voice called over a megaphone, "You're surrounded, Gray. Come out with your hands behind your head. Tell your men to lay down their weapons and surrender."

Gray's men didn't move a muscle.

The line of Medusas and whoever was with them closed in a little more. They all took up firing stances, behind trees or rocks. Gray's soldiers were completely exposed in the tiny clearing around the cabin. If they didn't surrender, they were all going to die, cut down in cold blood.

"Tell them to surrender!" Alex whispered urgently to Nick. "They might listen to you since they know you."

"How? I don't have a megaphone."

"No, but we have those phones we took off his guys last night. Can you call them?"

"I don't know if they've changed the group-chat phone number or not," Nick said doubtfully.

"Try. I've seen enough death for one lifetime," Alex begged.

Nick nodded grimly at him. "I'll try." He dug around in the thigh pocket of his pants and came up with one of the confiscated cell phones. He dialed a number from memory. Nick laid it on the ground between them with the Speaker function turned on.

A gruff voice said, "Who is this?"

"Nicholas Kane. It's over, Gray. Your men are outnumbered three to one by people as skilled as they are. There's no way out of that cabin alive."

Gray swore colorfully. "You have no idea how good my men are."

"Yeah, Harlan, I do. I trained a lot of them. But I'm out here with military Special Forces operators and a whole bunch of CIA fixers. You know. The guys sent out to kill men like you when they go rogue. And right now, they're poised to take out not only you but every one of your men. You're done."

"You stole it, didn't you?" Gray accused.

"You mean the crèche? We liberated it from you to return it to the people who ought to have it. Unlike you, we're not thieves."

Gray swore in a steady stream then, ranting about how nobody would've ever seen it if not for him. He was a hero for finding it and stealing it. Because of him, the whole world was going to see it.

He failed to mention that he was going to become rich selling off the pieces first.

"You're not listening to me, Harlan," Nick said patiently. "It's over. You don't get to sell any more pieces of the crèche. You're not going to get rich, and you're not going to walk out of that shack alive if you don't surrender."

That finally seemed to break through to Gray. The other end of the call was silent for a long time. Then he said simply, "If I can't have it, then nobody else can have it."

The line went dead.

Oh, no. No no no. Not good. Gray was not the kind of man who made empty threats.

Alex jumped to his feet and shouted frantically down the hill at Gray's men, "Get away from the cabin! Run! He's going to blow it—"

Ka-BOOM!

Alex was knocked backward violently by the explosion and nearly all the way off the rock he and Nick were perched upon.

Alex hit his head hard, and even though he had on a helmet, he was dazed by the blow. He stared up at the sky, unsure of where he was and why he was lying on his back.

"Alex. Alex! Can you hear me? Are you okay, baby? Talk to me."

"Don't call me baby," he mumbled, barely hearing his own voice. Dang, that explosion had been loud.

He stared up at Nick in dismay. "He blew himself up, didn't he? Did they run? Did his men get away?"

"Some of them. About half stayed by the shack. They're gone," Nick said soberly.

"And the crèche? Did he throw it out?"

Nick shook his head.

"Oh man," Alex said softly. He felt as if he'd just been punched in the gut.

Nick said in dismay, "You and I are the last people who ever saw the crèche. I guess we'll have to tell the world what it looked like."

"Or maybe we should just keep that to ourselves and let people imagine it the way they want it to have been," Alex said quietly.

"Maybe. That's a decision for later. Right now, I want to get you to a medic to look at your noggin. You hit it pretty hard, there, when you tried to save Gray's men. What were you thinking, standing up and shouting at them like that? They could've shot you—"

He reached up and pressed his fingers against Nick's lips. "I was doing what you would've done. I was trying to save lives, for once."

"What are you talking about?"

"You've always been in the business of saving lives, and I've always been in the business of taking them. I wanted to be like you."

"You giant goofball. You are exactly like me! You've saved countless lives. We just went about it different ways."

Nick held a hand down to him and Alex reached up and took it. He let Nick drag him to his feet and pull him into a surprisingly gentle kiss.

And that was how a group of a half dozen women in full tactical gear managed to surround them and break out into cheers and catcalls as Nick kissed his lights out. Of course, he kissed Nick back just as passionately.

"Hey, you two," a man geared up like the women called out. "Get a room, will ya?"

Against his mouth, Nick muttered, "That's Gunnar and his Medusas."

"Suppose he'd be your best man at our wedding?" Alex muttered back.

"I'll ask him. Tomorrow. After we've gone back to our room and I've properly proposed to you."

"Maybe I'll propose to you, first," Alex declared.

Simultaneously, they said, "Will you marry me?"

"I said it first," Alex said quickly.

"It was a tie!" Nick exclaimed. "And we fought to a stalemate!"

"Fine. What's your answer?" Alex challenged.

"Yes!" they said again exactly simultaneously.

"I'm okay with a tie," Alex said, gazing up at Nick. "As long as it's a knot tied with you."

"That's the hokiest thing I've ever heard," Nick declared, grinning ear to ear.

"Then, I guess you're marrying a hokey man, aren't you?"

"Guess I am."

And they sealed the deal with another kiss, the first of a lifetime full of them.

* * * * *

COMING SOON!

We really hope you enjoyed reading this book.
If you're looking for more romance, be sure to
head to the shops when new books are
available on

Thursday 10th
November

To see which titles are coming soon, please visit
millsandboon.co.uk/nextmonth

MILLS & BOON

MILLS & BOON

THE HEART OF ROMANCE

A ROMANCE FOR EVERY READER

MODERN

Prepare to be swept off your feet by sophisticated, sexy and seductive heroes, in some of the world's most glamourous and romantic locations, where power and passion collide.

HISTORICAL

Escape with historical heroes from time gone by. Whether your passion is for wicked Regency Rakes, muscled Vikings or rugged Highlanders, awaken the romance of the past.

MEDICAL

Set your pulse racing with dedicated, delectable doctors in the high-pressure world of medicine, where emotions run high and passion, comfort and love are the best medicine.

True Love

Celebrate true love with tender stories of heartfelt romance, from the rush of falling in love to the joy a new baby can bring, and a focus on the emotional heart of a relationship.

Desire

Indulge in secrets and scandal, intense drama and plenty of sizzling hot action with powerful and passionate heroes who have it all: wealth, status, good looks…everything but the right woman.

HEROES

Experience all the excitement of a gripping thriller, with an intense romance at its heart. Resourceful, true-to-life women and strong, fearless men face danger and desire - a killer combination!

To see which titles are coming soon, please visit

millsandboon.co.uk/nextmonth

LET'S TALK
Romance

For exclusive extracts, competitions
and special offers, find us online:

facebook.com/millsandboon

@MillsandBoon

@MillsandBoonUK

Get in touch on 01413 063232

For all the latest titles coming soon, visit
millsandboon.co.uk/nextmonth

MILLS & BOON
A ROMANCE FOR EVERY READER

FREE delivery direct to your door

EXCLUSIVE offers every month

SAVE up to 25% on pre-paid subscriptions

SUBSCRIBE AND SAVE

millsandboon.co.uk/Subscribe

WANT EVEN MORE
ROMANCE?
SUBSCRIBE AND SAVE TODAY!

'Mills & Boon books, the perfect way to escape for an hour or so.'

MISS W. DYER

'Excellent service, promptly delivered and very good subscription choices.'

MISS A. PEARSON

'You get fantastic special offers and the chance to get books before they hit the shops.'

MRS V. HALL

Visit millsandboon.co.uk/Subscribe and save on brand new books.

JOIN THE
MILLS & BOON
BOOKCLUB

* **FREE** delivery direct to your door

* **EXCLUSIVE** offers every month

* **EXCITING** rewards programme

50% OFF
YOUR FIRST
PARCEL

Join today at
Millsandboon.co.uk/Bookclub

JOIN US ON SOCIAL MEDIA!

Stay up to date with our latest releases, author news and gossip, special offers and discounts, and all the behind-the-scenes action from Mills & Boon...

 @millsandboon

 @millsandboonuk

 facebook.com/millsandboon

 @millsandboonuk

It might just be true love...

GET YOUR ROMANCE FIX!

Get the latest romance news,
exclusive author interviews, story
extracts and much more!

MILLS & BOON
Desire

Indulge in secrets and scandal, intense drama
and plenty of sizzling hot action with powerful
and passionate heroes who have it all: wealth,
status, good looks…everything but the right
woman.

Four Desire stories published every month, find them all at:

millsandboon.co.uk

MILLS & BOON

MODERN

Power and Passion

Prepare to be swept off your feet by
sophisticated, sexy and seductive heroes, in
some of the world's most glamourous and
romantic locations, where power and
passion collide.

ght Modern stories published every month, find them all at:

millsandboon.co.uk/Modern

MILLS & BOON
MEDICAL
Pulse-Racing Passion

Set your pulse racing with dedicated, delectable doctors in the high-pressure world of medicine, where emotions run high and passion, comfort and love are the best medicine.

Eight Medical stories published every month, find them all

millsandboon.co.uk

MILLS & BOON
True Love
Romance from the Heart

Celebrate true love with tender stories of heartfelt romance, from the rush of falling in love to the joy a new baby can bring, and a focus on the emotional heart of a relationship.

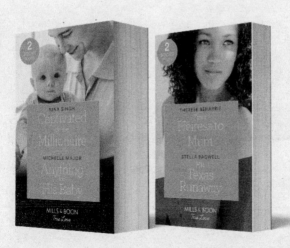

Four True Love stories published every month, find them all at:

millsandboon.co.uk/TrueLove